## THE VOICE IN THE DARKNESS

"Don't you hear it, Daddy?" Beth asked.

*It had been there. She knew it had.*

It was a voice, and it was calling out to her.

Why couldn't her father hear it?

And then, slowly, she realized what the answer was.
He couldn't hear it because he wasn't supposed to.

The voice was calling out only to her.

A chill passed through her, and her skin suddenly felt
as if something were crawling over it. In the darkness,
something had reached out and touched her.

Something in the blackness wanted *her*. Something
that chilled her to the depth of her soul.

Beth had no idea what was in the old mill, and part of
her hoped never to find out. But another part wanted
to go back, wanted to plunge back into the darkness—
and discover what was there. . . .

## HELLFIRE

D0932296

Also by John Saul

BRAINCHILD
NATHANIEL
ALL FALL DOWN

# HELLFIRE
## John Saul

BANTAM BOOKS
TORONTO · NEW YORK · LONDON · SYDNEY · AUCKLAND

HELLFIRE
A BANTAM BOOK 0 553 17255 7

First publication in Great Britain

PRINTING HISTORY
Bantam edition published 1986

Bantam Books are published by Transworld Publishers
Ltd., 61–63 Uxbridge Road, Ealing, London W5 5SA, in
Australia by Transworld Publishers (Aust.) Pty. Ltd.,
15–23 Helles Avenue, Moorebank, NSW 2170, and in New
Zealand by Transworld Publishers (N.Z.) Ltd., Cnr. Moselle
and Waipareira Avenues, Henderson, Auckland.

Printed and bound in Great Britain by
Cox & Wyman Ltd., Reading, Berks.

FOR THE SACK FAMILY—
Burt, Lynn and the boys

# Prologue

The boy turned off the path that wound down from the big house on the hill—his house—and wandered along the riverbank. A hundred yards ahead, he could see the wooden trestle that carried the railroad tracks over the rushing stream. He had always imagined that the stream was a boundary, a visible line that separated him from everyone else in the little town. If the river weren't there, he sometimes thought, then he would be part of the town.

But of course it wasn't just the river; there was far more to it than that.

He came to the trestle, and paused. Partly, he was listening for the sound of a train, for he knew that if he could hear the low rumblings of an engine, it wasn't safe to cross the river.

You had to wait until the train had come and gone, or until the sound had faded away into silence.

Sometimes, though, he was tempted to try the crossing even though he could hear a train coming, just to see if he could make it in time.

But of course he'd never tried it. It was too big a risk.

Not that he didn't like risks. He did. There was nothing he liked more than going off by himself, exploring the woods that covered the hillside, poking along the riverbank, skipping from stone to stone, though sooner or later he would miss his footing and slide into the rushing waters.

But the rushing waters wouldn't kill him.

A train, catching him defenseless in the middle of the trestle, would.

For a moment, he visualized himself, crushed under the weight of the streamliner that roared past the town twice a day, his mutilated body dropping into the river below. . . .

He put the thought out of his mind, and instead—as he often did—pictured himself already dead.

He saw himself in a coffin now, with flowers all around him. His parents, their eyes wet with tears, sat in the front pew of the little Episcopalian church in the middle of the town. Behind them, he could see all the other people of the town, staring at his coffin, wishing they'd been nicer to him, wishing they'd been his friends.

Not that he cared, he assured himself. It was more fun to be by yourself anyway. Besides, he had friends most of the time anyway, and when he came home from school in the summer it was nice to be able to play by himself, without anyone else wanting to do something he might not want to do.

Abandoning the fantasy, he listened carefully. When he heard no sound of an approaching train, he started across the trestle, carefully stepping from tie to tie, then continued along the tracks as they swept around the village in a long and gentle curve.

Suddenly he felt eyes watching him, and glanced off to the left. A quarter of a block down the road two boys stood side by side, staring at him.

He smiled, but as he was about to wave to them they turned away. He could hear them snickering as they whispered to each other.

His face burning with sudden anger, he hurried along the railroad tracks until he was certain he could no longer be seen from the road. Between himself and the other boys, separating him from the village, stood the forbidding brick walls of a building that had fascinated him for as long as he could remember.

The boy hesitated, remembering the stories he'd heard from his father, remembering the legends about what had happened in that building so many years ago. Terrible things that could only be spoken of in whispers.

No one knew if the legends were really true.

As he stared at the building, he began to feel as if the other boys—the village boys—were still watching him, challenging him, laughing at him because they knew he didn't have the courage to go inside.

Always before, when he'd stood here contemplating the old building, he'd eventually lost his nerve, and turned away.

But today would be different.

Ignoring the knot of fear that now burned hot in his belly, he left the railroad tracks and scrambled down the slope of the roadbed.

He started along a weed-choked path that paralleled the side of the building. Halfway along the wall, he came to a small door, covered over with weathered boards that had long since shrunken with age. Through the gaps between the boards he could make out the door itself, held closed only by a padlock on a rusted hasp.

Gingerly he tested one of the boards. The corroded nails groaned for a second, then gave way. A moment later, two more boards lay on the ground at the boy's feet.

The boy reached out and grasped the padlock. He paused, knowing that if it gave way, he would then be committed to go inside.

He took a deep breath, tightened his grip, and twisted.

The rusted hasp held for a moment, then broke loose. The lock, free from the door it had guarded so long, lay in the boy's hand. He stared at it for several long seconds, almost wishing he had left it in place.

Then, struggling against a strange fear he could feel growing within him, the boy pushed the door open and squirmed through the gap left by the three planks he had torn away.

For a moment the deep shadows blinded him, but then his eyes adjusted to the dim light of the interior, and he looked around.

Inside, the building seemed even larger than it looked from the outside, and emptier.

Except, the boy realized, it didn't feel empty at all.

Somewhere, he was certain, there was someone—or some*thing*—lurking within these walls, waiting for him.

Almost against his will, his eyes began exploring the old building. Emptiness stretched away in all directions, and far above him, just visible in the shadowed light that barely penetrated the immense space, the tangled iron struts supporting the roof seemed to reach down to him, as if trying to grasp him in their skeletal arms.

In the silence, the boy could hear the pounding of his own heart.

Suddenly a cacophony of sound filled the enormous building, and the boy felt a scream rising in his throat. He choked it back at the last second, then forced himself to look up.

A flock of pigeons, frightened by the boy's intrusion, had burst from their nests and now wheeled beneath the roof. As the boy watched, they began settling once more into their nests.

Seconds later, silence once more cast an eerie spell over the vast emptiness.

The boy gazed into the gloom, and saw, far away at the back of the building, the top of a flight of stairs.

Beneath him, then, was not simply a solid floor. Below this floor, there was a basement.

The stairs seemed to beckon to him, to demand that he come and explore that which lay beneath.

The boy's heart began pounding once more, and a cold sweat broke out on his back.

Suddenly he could stand the silence no longer.

"*No! I won't!*"

His voice, far louder than he had intended, echoed

back to him, and once again the pigeons milled madly among the rafters, fluttering in confusion. Gasping, the boy shrank back against the reassuring solidity of the brick wall.

But when the silence came once more, the compelling fascination of those downward-leading stairs gripped him once again. He forced his fear down. Slowly, he began moving toward the back of the building.

He had moved only a few yards when suddenly the boy felt his skin crawl.

Something, he was certain, was watching him.

He tried to ignore it, keeping his eyes on the far wall, but the strange sensation wouldn't go away.

The hair on the back of his neck was standing up now, and he could feel goose bumps covering his arms. He could stand it no longer, and whirled around to face whatever was behind him.

Nothing.

His eyes searched the semidarkness, looking for something—anything!

The vast expanse seemed empty.

And then, once again, the hair on the back of his neck stood up, and his spine began to tingle.

He whirled once more. Once more there was nothing.

Yet something seemed to fill the emptiness, seemed to surround him, taunt him.

He should never have come inside. He knew that now, knew it with a certainty that made his blood run cold.

But now it was too late. Now there was no turning back.

Far away, and seeming to recede into the distance, he could barely make out the small rectangle of brightness that marked the door he had come through only a few minutes before.

The door was too far away.

It seemed as if he had been in the mysterious gloom forever, and already, dimly, he began to understand that he was never going to leave.

There was something here—something that wanted him.

Charged with the inexorable force of his own imagination, he moved once more toward the vortex that was the stairwell.

He paused at the top of the stairs, peering fearfully into the blackness below. He wanted to turn now, and run away, run back toward that distant speck of light, and the daylight beyond.

But it was too late. The gloom of the building held him in its rapture, and though there was nothing but darkness below, he knew he had no choice but to continue down the stairs.

He started down the steps, straining to see into a blackness that seemed to go on forever.

There was a mustiness in the air below, and something else—some faint odor he couldn't quite identify, but that seemed oddly familiar.

He came to the bottom of the stairs, and stopped, terrified.

Again, he wanted to turn around, turn away from the evil he felt in the darkness, but he knew he wouldn't.

Knew he couldn't.

Then he heard a sound—barely distinguishable.

He listened, straining his ears.

Was it real, or had he only imagined it?

He heard it again.

Some kind of animal. It had to be. A rat, perhaps, or maybe only a mouse.

Or was it something else, something unreal?

A voice, whispering to him so quietly he couldn't make out the words, calling to him, luring him on into the darkness and the unknown. . . .

The strange odor grew stronger, its acridity burning in his nostrils.

He stepped off the last stair, and began groping his way through the darkness.

He thought he could feel unseen hands guiding him, feel a strange force drawing him on.

And then, though he could still see nothing, he sensed a presence.

It was close to him—too close.

"Who—" he began, but his question was cut off as something struck him from behind. Staggering, he pitched forward, his balance gone, then tried to break his fall by throwing his arms in front of him.

But it was too late, and even as he fell, he knew it.

He opened his mouth to scream, but his throat felt choked, as though strangling hands held him in a deadly grip. No sound emerged from his throat.

In an instant that seemed to go on forever, he felt a coldness slide through his clothing, piercing his skin, an icy pain that slipped between his ribs deep into his chest.

The object—the thing; the unidentifiable evil— plunged into his heart, and he felt himself begin to die.

And as he died, he slowly recognized the familiar odor that had filled his nostrils.

Smoke.

For some reason, in that long-abandoned basement, he smelled smoke. . . .

Then, as the last vestiges of life drained from his body, he saw flames flickering out from beneath the stairway, and in the faint remnants of his consciousness, he heard laughter.

Laughter, mixed with screams of terror.

The laughter and the screams closed in on him, growing louder and louder, mingling with the ice-cold pain until there was nothing but blackness. And for the boy, the terror was over. . . .

# 1

Rain at a funeral is a cliché, Carolyn Sturgess reflected as she gazed abstractedly out the window of the limousine that moved slowly through the streets of Westover. Though it was June, the day was chilly, with a dampness that seemed to seep into the bones. Ahead, through the divider window and the streaked windshield beyond, she could see the car carrying her husband, her mother-in-law, and her stepdaughter, and ahead of that—barely visible—the hearse bearing the body of her father-in-law. Carolyn shuddered, feeling chilled.

Barely visible.

The words, she realized, described Conrad Sturgess perfectly, at least in his last years. For more than a decade, he had seldom left the mansion on the hill above the town, seldom been seen in the streets of the village that his family had dominated for more than a century. But despite his reclusiveness, the old man had still been a presence in Westover, and Carolyn found herself wondering how the village would change, now that Conrad Sturgess was dead.

As the long black car turned left on Church Street, Carolyn glanced back at the small crowd that still lingered in front of the white-clapboard Episcopal church that stood facing the square, its sober New England facade seeming to glare with faint disapproval at the small business district that squatted defensively on the other side of the worn patch of lawn beyond the bronze statue of a long-forgotten Revolutionary hero that gazed out from the middle of the square.

"Will any of them come up to Hilltop for the other service?"

Her daughter's voice interrupted her reverie, and Carolyn reached over to give Beth's hand an affectionate squeeze. "The interment," she automatically corrected.

"The interment," Beth Rogers repeated, her brows furrowing as she concentrated on getting the word exactly right. She pictured the look of scorn she would get from Tracy Sturgess, her stepsister, if she mispronounced it later. Not, she told herself, that she cared what Tracy Sturgess thought, but she still hated it when Tracy and her friends laughed at her. Just because Tracy was almost thirteen, and went to private school, didn't make her any better than Beth. After all, she was almost twelve herself. "How come they call it that? An . . . interment?"

"Because that's what it is," Carolyn explained. "Anyway, that's what Abigail calls it, so that's what we must call it, too. After all, we're Sturgesses now, aren't we?"

"I'm not," Beth said, her brown eyes darkening in exactly the same way her father's did when he got angry. "I'm still Beth Rogers, and I always will be. I don't want to be a Sturgess!"

Oh, Lord, Carolyn thought. Here we go again. When would she learn to stop trying to convince her daughter to accept Phillip Sturgess as her father? And why, really, *should* Beth transfer her affection to her stepfather, when her real father still lived right here in Westover, and she saw him every day? She wished, though she'd never say it, that Alan Rogers would simply disappear from the face of the earth. Or at least from Westover, Massachusetts. "Of course you are," she said aloud. "Anyway, it doesn't really matter what you call it, because an interment and a burial are the same thing. Okay?"

"Well, *are* the other people from the church coming?"

Carolyn shook her head. "The service at Hilltop is only for family and our closest friends."

"But we know everybody who was there," Beth replied, her voice reflecting her puzzlement. "Why can't they all come?"

"Because—" Carolyn floundered for a moment, knowing that whatever she said, Beth would immediately see through her words and grasp the truth of the matter. "Because they aren't all friends of the Sturgesses," she ventured.

"You mean they aren't all rich," Beth replied.

Bingo! Carolyn thought. And there was no point in trying to deny it, at least not to Beth.

The car turned again, and Carolyn glanced out the window to see the bleak form of the old shoe factory— the building everyone in Westover referred to as "the mill"—looming above Prospect Street, its soot-covered red bricks giving it an even more forbidding appearance than its bleak nineteenth-century architecture had intended.

Carolyn, as always, felt a slight shudder pass through her body at the sight of the mill, and quickly looked away. Then it was gone, and the village was left behind as the cortege moved out River Road to begin winding its way up the long narrow lane that led to Hilltop.

"Mom?" Beth suddenly asked, interrupting the silence that had fallen over the big car. "What's going to happen, now that—" She hesitated for a moment, then used the term her mother had asked her to use. Until today she had refused to utter it. "—now that Uncle Conrad's dead?"

"I don't know," Carolyn replied. "I suppose everything will go on just as it always has."

But of course she knew it wasn't true. She knew that without Conrad Sturgess silently controlling his family's interests from the privacy of his den, everything in Westover was going to change.

And she knew that she, at least, wasn't going to

like the changes. As the limousine pulled through the gates of Hilltop, she remembered the old adage about sleeping dogs.

Her husband, she knew, had no intention of letting them lie.

The six pallbearers carried the casket containing Conrad Sturgess's body slowly up a narrow path through the forest. Behind the casket, Abigail Sturgess walked alone, head held high, unmindful of the rain that still fell in a dense drizzle. Though she leaned heavily on a cane, her back was as stiffly erect as ever. Behind her walked her son, Phillip, with Carolyn on his arm. Following the couple were their two children, Beth Rogers and Tracy Sturgess. Then, bringing up the rear of the short procession, came the mourners: the Kilpatricks and the Baileys, the Babcocks and the Adamses—the old families whose ties to the Sturgesses went back through the generations.

The cortege rounded a bend in the trail, and came to a sudden stop as Abigail Sturgess paused for a moment to gaze at the wrought-iron grillwork that arched over the path.

Two words were worked into the pattern:

### ETERNAL VIGILANCE

She seemed to consider the words for a few moments, then walked on. A few minutes later, Conrad Sturgess, followed by his family and friends, arrived at the spot he had always known would be his final resting place.

Worked carefully into the earth, and covered with moss, there was a short flight of stone steps. At the top of the steps, looming out of the forest like some sort of strange temple, stood the Sturgess-family mausoleum.

The structure was circular, and made entirely of pale pink marble. There were seven columns, each of them nearly twenty feet high, topped by a marble ring that was almost fifty feet across. All around, the forest seemed to be crowding in on the strange edifice, and only a few rays of sunlight ever glinted on the polished marble. Today the lowering skies seemed to hover only a few feet above the strange monument, and the stone, slick with rain, seemed to have had its color washed away.

Six of the columns were in perfect condition.

The seventh pillar was broken; all that remained of it was its base, and the top two feet, hanging oddly from the surmounting marble drum.

In the center of the circle of columns, on a marble floor, stood a large round marble table, with space around it for seven marble chairs.

Six of the chairs were there.

The seventh place at the table, the place with the broken pillar behind it, was empty.

Beth, her eyes glued to her mother's back, climbed the steps uncertainly. She'd been here before, but always before the mausoleum had seemed to her to be nothing more than some strange ruin from the past. But today it was different, and she felt a chill pass through her as she stepped between two of the columns and found herself inside the stone ring.

She glanced nervously around, but everyone else seemed to know exactly what to do. The mourners, all of them clad in black, the women's faces veiled, had spread themselves in a semicircle around the chairs. The pallbearers placed the coffin carefully on a bier that stood at the empty seventh place. Abigail Sturgess, her face impassive, stood behind the coffin, gazing at the massive stone chair that stood opposite.

Beth's eyes shifted to the back of the marble chair upon which the old woman's eyes were fixed.

On the back of the chair, chiseled deep into the marble, was an inscription:

SAMUEL PRUETT STURGESS
MAY 3, 1822–AUGUST 12, 1890

Beth's hand reached out and took her mother's. She tugged gently, and when Carolyn leaned down, the little girl whispered in her ear.

"What's she doing?" she asked.

"She's presenting Conrad to his grandfather," Carolyn whispered back.

"Why?"

"It's a tradition, sweetheart," Carolyn replied, glancing nervously around. But it was all right—no one seemed to notice them at all.

Beth frowned slightly. Why were they "presenting" Uncle Conrad to old Mr. Sturgess? It didn't make any sense to her. She tugged at her mother's hand once more, but this time her mother only looked down at her, holding a finger to her lips and shaking her head.

Silently, wishing she were somewhere else—anywhere else—Beth watched the rest of the service. The minister's voice droned on, repeating everything he'd said about Conrad Sturgess in the church only half an hour ago, and Beth wondered if this time he was telling Samuel Pruett Sturgess about Uncle Conrad. Then she began looking around at all the unfamiliar faces of the people around her.

None of them were the people she'd known all her life, the people she'd known when her mother and father were married. They were all strangers, and she knew that they were somehow different from her.

It wasn't that they were rich, even though she knew they were. They all lived in big houses, like Hilltop, though none was quite so grand as Hilltop itself.

It was the way they acted.

Like this morning, before the funeral, when she'd been sitting by herself in the breakfast room, and one of them—she thought it was Mrs. Kilpatrick—had come in, and smiled at her. It had been a nice smile, and for a minute Beth had hoped she and the woman might be friends.

"And a good morning to you, young lady," the woman had said. "I don't believe we've met, have we?"

Beth had shaken her head shyly, and offered the woman her hand. "I'm Beth Rogers."

"Rogers?" the woman had repeated. "I don't believe I know any Rogerses. Where are you from? Do I know your mother?"

Beth had nodded. "I live here. My mother's—"

And then she'd seen the woman's smile disappear, and her eyes, the eyes that had been so warm and sparkling a minute before, had suddenly turned cold. "Oh," she'd said. "You're Carolyn's little girl, aren't you? How nice." Before Beth could say anything else, the woman had turned and silently left the room.

Now, Beth realized she must have been staring at the woman, for the woman—she was almost sure it was Mrs. Kilpatrick—was glaring at her. She felt her mother tugging at her arm, and realized that the service was over.

The pallbearers were carrying the casket down another flight of steps, and as Beth, walking beside her mother, followed Tracy and Phillip Sturgess—at old Abigail's side now—she saw that there was a tiny cemetery in the forest behind the mausoleum. An open grave awaited, and Conrad Sturgess's coffin was slowly lowered into it. Abigail Sturgess stepped forward, reached stiffly down to pick up a clod of sodden earth, and dropped it into the grave. Then she turned away, and began making her way back through the mausoleum, and down the path that led to the house.

Beth noticed that Abigail Sturgess, once she had turned away from her husband's grave, never looked back. It was very much like Mrs. Kilpatrick this morning. Beth wasn't sure why, but for some reason it bothered her.

Carolyn Sturgess stood uncomfortably in the walnut-paneled library doing her best to chat with Elaine Kilpatrick. She was finding it difficult. It wasn't anything that Elaine said, really; the woman was perfectly polite. It was just that there seemed to be a chasm between them, and Carolyn had no idea of how to bridge that chasm. It wasn't that she had no interest in the things Elaine talked about; indeed, one of the things that had attracted her to Phillip Sturgess when she'd first met him a year before had been his own interest in all the things Elaine Kilpatrick seemed to know everything about.

And that, of course, was the trouble. Elaine seemed to know everything about everything, and Carolyn was feeling, once again, like an uneducated, provincial fool.

Carolyn Rogers Sturgess was no fool. She'd graduated from Boston University with a degree in art, and even though it wasn't Smith, and the degree wasn't *cum laude*, Carolyn was proud of it.

And she and Alan had done their share of traveling, too. Of course it hadn't been Paris and London, nor had she seen the museums in Florence, but she had certainly done her share of galleries in New York.

"But of course we don't really appreciate art in this country, do we?" she heard Elaine asking earnestly, and silently chided herself for wondering if she detected a note of condescension in the other woman's tone. Certainly if it was there, it wasn't reflected in Elaine's luminous brown eyes, which seemed to concentrate on her with undivided attention.

And yet, as she nearly always did when she was with Phillip's friends, she had a feeling she was being talked down to.

"No," she said lamely, "I don't suppose we do." Then she offered Elaine what she hoped was a radiant smile. "Do excuse me, won't you?" she asked. "I see Francis Babcock over there, and there's something I have to talk to her about."

"Of course," Elaine said smoothly, immediately turning to Chip Bailey and plunging into another conversation.

As Carolyn started toward Frances Babcock, whom she secretly loathed, she wondered how Elaine did it. And worse, she wondered if she would ever learn the trick of it, or whether these women had simply been born with all the social graces bred into them over the generations. But whatever it was they had, she knew she lacked it. She lacked it, and her daughter lacked it.

She realized then that she hadn't seen Beth for more than an hour, not since the receiving line had broken up and the family had come into the library to join their guests. Beth, in fact, had not come into the library at all. Veering away from Frances Babcock, Carolyn slipped out of the library, and glanced down the broad corridor that ran through this wing of the house. It was empty.

But coming out of the living room, she saw her stepdaughter.

"Tracy?"

The girl, her blond hair twisted up in a French knot that Carolyn thought was too old for her, paused at the bottom of the broad staircase that swept from the entry hall up to the second floor. She glanced around furtively, then glared at Carolyn when she saw that they were alone. "What do you want?"

Carolyn felt a twinge of anger. If Phillip had been there, Tracy's reply would have been guardedly polite. But when they were alone, no matter what Tracy said to her, it always contained a note of challenge, as if she were daring Carolyn to try to exercise any form of control over her.

"I was looking for Beth," Carolyn replied evenly, refusing to let Tracy see her anger. "I thought she was coming into the library with the rest of us."

"Well, if she's not there, then obviously she didn't, did she?" Tracy countered.

"Have you seen her?"

"No."

"Well, if you do see her, will you tell her I'm looking for her?"

Tracy's eyes narrowed, and her lips curled in what should have been a smile, but wasn't. "Maybe I will, and maybe I won't," she said. Then she started up the stairs, disappearing from Carolyn's sight.

Ignore it, Carolyn told herself. She's not used to you yet, and she's not used to Beth, and you have to give her time. Then, guiltily, she found herself wishing that it were not June, and that Tracy were not home for the summer. It had been bad enough at Christmas, when she and Phillip had gotten married, and Tracy had refused to speak to her at all, and worse during the spring break, when Tracy had furiously demanded that she and Beth leave, telling them they had no place in this house. Tracy had been careful to deliver her ultimatum when her father wasn't around, and Carolyn had finally decided not to tell Phillip about the incident at all. But now the girl was home for the summer, and though there had been no major scenes yet, Carolyn could feel one building. The only question, she was sure, was when Tracy's anger at her father's second marriage would boil over once more. She hoped that when it did, she would bear the brunt of it, not Beth. Beth, she knew, was having a hard enough time of it already. Sighing, she started up the stairs. Perhaps, as she often did, Beth had retreated to her room.

As she reached the second floor, the imperious voice of her mother-in-law stopped her.

"Carolyn? Where are you going?"

Carolyn turned, and fleetingly wondered how Abigail Sturgess had managed to materialize so suddenly. But there she stood, her ebony cane gripped firmly in her right hand, her head tipped back as she surveyed Carolyn with her blue eyes—the same eyes she had passed on to her son and her granddaughter.

Except that Phillip's eyes were as warm as a tropical sea.

Abigail's and Tracy's were chipped from ice.

And now, as they were so often, those eyes were fixed disapprovingly on Carolyn.

"I was just looking for Beth, Abigail," Carolyn replied.

Abigail offered her a wintry smile. "I'm sure Beth is perfectly capable of taking care of herself. And a good hostess doesn't leave her guests by themselves, does she? Come. There are some people with whom I wish you to speak."

Carolyn hesitated, then, with a quick glance up the stairs, followed Abigail back to the library.

No one but Abigail seemed to have noticed that she had left.

No one but Phillip, who, spotting her from his position next to the fireplace, offered her a smile.

Suddenly she felt better, felt that perhaps, after all, she did belong here. At least Phillip seemed to think she did.

Alan Rogers leaned back in his desk chair and unconsciously ran his hand through the unruly mop of black hair that never, no matter how hard he tried, seemed to stay under control. He glanced out the window; the rain seemed finally to have stopped, at least for a while. He couldn't help smiling to himself as he pictured the scene that must have been going on up at the Sturgesses' an hour ago.

All of them dressed in black, standing in the rain, but regally ignoring it while they finally put the old bastard to rest.

If Conrad Sturgess would ever rest in peace. Alan Rogers sincerely hoped he wouldn't.

Perhaps, he thought, he should have gone to the burial. No one, after all, would have told him to leave. That wasn't their way. They would simply have looked down their patrician noses at him, and done their best to let him know, subtly, of course, that he wasn't wanted there.

And if it hadn't been for Beth, he might have done just that, and the hell with Carolyn.

She would have been furious with him, naturally, but that wouldn't really have bothered him at all. After all these years, he was used to Carolyn's fury. Indeed, sometimes he wasn't sure he could remember a time when she had not been furious with him.

There must have been a time, though, when they had loved each other. Maybe the first couple of years of their marriage, before Carolyn's ambitions for him had taken over their lives. Alan had been a carpenter and a good one, who took pride in practicing his craft, but that had not been enough. Carolyn had decided he should become a contractor, a businessman. He'd always refused, telling her he just didn't want the responsibility.

The arguments grew more bitter and, finally, had broken up the marriage.

The irony was that two years after the divorce, he'd wound up getting his contractor's license anyway. It had finally become an economic necessity. If he was going to support himself, along with Carolyn and Beth, he simply had to have more money coming in. And so he'd done what Carolyn had always wanted him to do in the first place.

And what had happened?

She'd upped and married Phillip Sturgess, and he was off the hook for everything except child support. For that matter, he didn't suppose it would matter a whit to Carolyn anymore whether he sent the monthly support check or not. Phillip, he knew, would make up the balance, and do it cheerfully.

But it was a matter of principle. Beth was his daughter, and he wanted to support her, whether she needed his support or not.

The money, he suspected, was probably going into a trust fund for her. That would be very much like Phillip—children should have trust funds from their fathers, and he would see to it that Beth had one, whether Alan knew anything about it or not.

Grinning to himself, he wondered if Carolyn knew how well he and Phillip really got along together. In fact, if Carolyn hadn't married Phillip, they would probably have become good friends, despite the difference in their backgrounds.

For Phillip, alone among the Sturgesses, had somehow managed to overcome the sense of superiority that had been bred into him from the day he was born.

He'd gone to the right schools, played with the right children, met the right women—even married one of them, the first time around—but no matter how hard his parents had tried, Phillip had never been able to put on the aristocratic airs the Sturgesses were renowned for. Now that Phillip had married Carolyn, the two men should have kept a wary distance, but, in fact, Alan could not help liking Phillip Sturgess. Now that Carolyn had what she wanted—position, money, all the comforts of life he had not been able to provide—he hoped the marriage would thrive. For one thing was certain, Phillip loved her—as much as Alan himself once had.

He wanted his ex-wife to be happy, if only for his daughter's sake, knowing that if Phillip and Carolyn found it rough going, somehow Beth would get caught in the middle.

Whatever happened, Alan would never allow his daughter to be caught in it. It wasn't Beth's fault that things hadn't worked out for him and Carolyn. In fact, if he really thought about it, it was probably the Sturgesses' own fault.

For as long as he'd known Carolyn—and they'd grown up together—she had been fascinated by the Sturgess family.

Fascinated by them, and repulsed by them.

And yet she'd married Phillip.

So maybe the revulsion of them that she'd always professed had not been quite what she'd said.

Maybe it had been envy, and a wish that she'd been born one of them.

At any rate, when Phillip Sturgess had suddenly reappeared in Westover a year ago after living abroad for nearly a decade, Carolyn had wasted no time in snaring him. Which, Alan realized, wasn't really a fair thing to say. The two of them had met and fallen in love, and Carolyn had resigned her job in the local law office when she'd married Phillip, claiming that continuing as assistant to an attorney when she was marrying his major client involved a conflict of interest.

Perhaps it did; perhaps it didn't. None of it mattered, not anymore. The fact was that Carolyn had married Phillip, and Alan hoped she would be happy.

When Abigail followed Conrad to the grave, he thought, maybe she would have a chance at that. Until then, Alan was certain his former wife had an uphill battle ahead of her.

The door opened, and his secretary walked in. She dropped a stack of mail on his desk, then surveyed him critically. "Thoughtful," she said. "Always a bad sign."

"Just thinking about the Sturgesses, and hoping they didn't all drown in Conrad's grave."

Judy Parkins snickered. "That would be something, wouldn't it? And after Carolyn worked so hard to get Phillip, too."

The smile faded from Alan's face, and Judy immediately wished she hadn't spoken. "I'm sorry. I didn't really mean that."

Alan shrugged wryly. "Well, let's just hope they're happy, and wish them well, all right?"

Judy regarded her employer with a raised brow. "How come you always manage to be so damned *good?* And if you are, how come Carolyn wanted to trade you in for Phillip Sturgess in the first place?"

"First, I'm not so damned good, and second, she didn't trade me in. She chucked me. And it's over and done with. All right?"

"Check." Judy turned, but as she was about to leave the office, Beth burst in, her face blotched and streaked with tears. She threw herself into her father's arms, sobbing. Judy Parkins, after offering Alan a sympathetic look, slipped out of the office, quietly closing the door behind her.

"Honey," Alan crooned as he tried to calm his daughter. "What is it? What happened?"

"Th-they hate me," Beth wailed. "I don't belong there, and they all hate me!"

Alan hugged the unhappy child closer. "Oh, darling, that isn't true. Your mother loves you very much, and so does Uncle Phillip—"

"He's *not* my uncle," Beth protested. "He's Tracy's father, and he hates me."

"Now who told you that?"

"T-Tracy," Beth stammered. She stared up into her father's face, her eyes beseeching him. "She . . . she said her father hates me, and that by the end of the summer, I'll have to go live somewhere else. Sh-she said he's going to make me!"

"I see," Alan replied. It was exactly the sort of thing that had happened in the spring, when Tracy had last been home from school. "And when did she tell you this?"

"A little while ago. Everyone was in . . . in the library, and I was by myself in the living room, and she came in, and she told me. She said that now that her grandfather's dead, her father owns the house, and . . . and he's going to make me go away!"

"And was anybody else there?"

Beth hesitated, then shook her head. "N-no . . ."

"Well, I'll bet if Uncle Phillip had heard Tracy say that, he'd have turned her over his knee and given her a spanking. Maybe I'd better just give him a call, and tell him."

Beth drew back, horrified. "No! If you call him, then Tracy will know I told, and it'll just be worse than it already is!"

Alan nodded solemnly. "Then what do you think we ought to do?"

"Can't I come and live with you, Daddy? Please?"

Alan sighed silently. This, too, was something they'd been through before, and he'd tried to explain over and over why it was best for Beth to live with her mother. But no matter how often he explained it to her, her reply never changed.

"But I don't belong there," she always said. "They're different from me, and I just don't belong. If you make me stay there, I'm going to die."

And sometimes, when he looked into her huge brown eyes, and smoothed back her soft dark hair—the hair she'd inherited from Carolyn—he almost believed she was right.

He stood up, and took his daughter by the hand.

"Come on, honey," he said. "I'll drive you home, and we'll talk about it on the way."

"Home?" Beth asked, her eyes suddenly hopeful. "To your house?"

"No," Alan replied. "I'll drive you back to Hilltop. That's where you live now, isn't it?"

Though Beth said nothing, the eager light faded from her eyes.

# 2

Alan Rogers turned off River Road, shifted his Fiat into low gear, and started up the drive.

"Almost there." When there was no response from Beth, he glanced at her out of the corner of his eye. She sat huddled against the door, her eyes clouded with unhappiness.

"Act as if," Alan said. Beth turned to face him.

"Act as if? What does that mean?"

"It means if you act as if things are all right, then maybe they will be. Don't think about what's wrong—think about what's right. It helps."

"How can it help? Pretending doesn't change anything."

"But it can change how you think about things. Like that apartment I lived in for a while. The one above the drugstore?"

A hint of a smile played around Beth's mouth. "You hated that place."

"Indeed I did. And why shouldn't I have? I wasn't living with you anymore, and I missed you terribly. And the apartment was small and dark and empty. It was awful. And then one day Judy came over."

"Judy Parkins?"

"The very same. Anyway, I was griping about how

bad the place was, and she asked me what I'd do with it if I liked it."

"But you didn't like it," Beth protested. "You hated it!"

"That's what I said. And Judy said, 'So pretend you like it. What would you do with it?' So I thought about it, then told her that I'd start by getting rid of the venetian blinds, and put shutters in, and I'd paint it, and cover the floor with grass mats. And the next weekend she came over, and we did it. And guess what? It turned out the place wasn't so bad after all."

The Fiat passed through the gates of Hilltop House, and Alan drove slowly along the wide circular driveway that skirted a broad expanse of lawn in front of the Sturgess mansion. He brought the car to a halt between a Cadillac and a Mercedes, then sat for a moment staring at the immense house. As always, he was struck less by its size than its strange appearance. Whoever had designed it had apparently been less interested in creating a thing of beauty than in making a declaration of power.

"All right, all right," he said, turning a deadpan face to his daughter as though she had spoken. "I'll admit that grass mats and paint won't help this place."

Built primarily of carved stone, the house spread in two flat-roofed wings from a central core, the main feature of which was an immense stained-glass window—which Alan thought more appropriate to a cathedral than a home—over the massive double front doors. The facade was nearly devoid of decoration, and the only breaks in the roof line were provided by a few chimneys, scattered haphazardly wherever the floor plan had required them.

There was something vaguely forbidding about the structure, as if the house were trying to defend itself against a hostile world.

"It's not like a house at all," Beth said. "It's like a museum. I always feel like I'm going to break something."

"You've only lived here a few months, sweetheart. Give yourself a chance to get used to it." But even as

he spoke the words, Alan wondered if it would be
possible for his daughter to be at home in a house such
as this. Certainly, he knew, he never could have. "Come
on," he sighed. "Let's get you back inside."

Beth reluctantly got out of the Fiat as Alan held
the door open for her, then slipped her hand into her
father's. "Couldn't I stay with you tonight?" she pleaded.
"Please?"

Alan pulled his daughter close, and dropped his
arm over her shoulder. "Don't make me feel like I'm
feeding you to the lions," he replied, but his attempt at
humor sounded hollow even to himself. He reached out
and pressed the bell. A moment later the door was
opened by the old woman who had been the Sturgesses'
housekeeper for as long as anyone could remember.

"Beth! Why, where have you been? Your mother's
been looking everywhere for you!"

"She came down to say hello to me, Hannah. I
guess she didn't tell anyone where she was going."

Hannah's eyes narrowed in mock severity. "Well,
you might have told me, mightn't you, young lady?"

"I . . . I'm sorry, Hannah. But I just . . . I—"

"I know," Hannah broke in. She glanced over her
shoulder nervously, then lowered her voice. "All the
swells standing around acting like they care about old
Mr. Conrad, and each other too, for that matter. Don't
see how they can stand themselves." She reached out
and gently drew Beth away from her father and into the
house. "Come on into the kitchen and have a cup of
cocoa. You too, Alan—"

"I don't think so, Hannah. I'd better—"

"Hannah?" Carolyn's voice called from inside. "Hannah, who is it?" A second later Carolyn, her face drawn,
appeared at the door. Seeing Alan, she fell silent for a
few seconds, then nodded with sudden understanding.
"She came to you again?"

Alan's head bobbed in agreement, and Carolyn
hesitated for a moment, then slipped her arms around
her daughter. "Darling, what happened? Why didn't
you tell me where you were going?"

"Y-you were busy."

"I'm never too busy for you. You know that—"

"It was just too much for her," Alan interjected. "She didn't know anyone, and—"

Carolyn glanced at him, then turned to Hannah. "Take her up to her room, will you, Hannah?"

"I was going to give her some cocoa, ma'am."

"Fine. I'll be there in a minute." She waited until Hannah and Beth were gone, then faced her ex-husband. "Alan, did something happen? Something Beth won't want to tell me about?"

Alan shook his head helplessly. "Carolyn, what can I say? If there's anything she wants to tell you, she'll tell you."

"But you won't," Carolyn said, her voice cool.

"No, I won't. We agreed long ago that—"

"We agreed that we wouldn't use Beth against each other. But if something happened that I need to know about, you have to tell me."

Alan considered his wife's words carefully, then shook his head. "If you want to know what's happening with Beth, talk to her. After all, she lives with you, not with me."

Carolyn stood at the door until Alan was gone and she could no longer hear his car. Then she closed the immense carved-oak front door and started toward the kitchen. But before she had crossed the foyer, her mother-in-law's icy voice stopped her.

"Carolyn, we still have guests."

Carolyn hesitated, torn. Then, as if drawn like a puppet on a string, she turned to follow Abigail Sturgess back to the library.

It was nearly midnight when Carolyn finally went through the house for the last time, making her nightly check to be sure the windows were closed and the doors locked. It was unnecessary—she knew that. Hannah went through the house too, as she had done each night for the last four decades, but Carolyn did it anyway. When Phillip had asked her why one night, she hadn't really been able to tell him. She'd said that checking the house helped make her feel that it was really hers, and that it was a habit left over from all the years before she'd married Phillip. But it was more than that.

Part of it was a simple need to reassure herself, for every night before she went to sleep, she listened to the old house creaking and groaning in the darkness until she could stand it no longer, and giving in to what she knew were irrational fears, got up to search through the rooms to make sure everything was as it should be. After the second month—last February—she had decided it was easier simply to make her rounds before she went to bed.

But it was more than that. There was something about Hilltop House at night—after Abigail had gone to bed—that drew her with a fascination she rarely felt in the daylight. During the day, Hilltop always seemed to her to be trying to shut her out. But at night, it all changed, and the cold stone took on a different feeling, less forbidding and chilly, cradling her, assuring her that no matter what else happened, the house would always be there.

She wandered slowly through the rooms, pausing in the dining room to gaze, as she often did, at the portraits of all the Sturgesses who had once lived in this house, and were now in the mausoleum or the small graveyard behind it. They gazed down on her, and she sometimes imagined that they—like Abigail—were disapproving of her. But of course that was ridiculous. Their expressions of vague contempt had nothing to do with her.

Nothing to do with her personally, at any rate.

Tonight she sank into the chair at the end of the immense dining table, and stared up at the portrait of Samuel Pruett Sturgess. The soft light from the crystal chandelier glowed over the old picture. Carolyn examined it carefully. For some reason she had almost expected the old man's demeanor to have softened tonight, as if meeting his grandson that afternoon had pleased him.

But if it had, the portrait gave no hint. Samuel Pruett Sturgess glowered down from the wall as he always had, and Carolyn caught herself wondering once again if the founding Sturgess had been as cruel as he seemed in the artist's depiction of him, a mean-faced, stern-looking patriarch.

Had the artist heard the rumors about Samuel Pruett, too, or had the rumors about him only begun after his death? There had been so many stories whispered about the old man, his rages, his ruthlessness, that some of them must have been true. And in Carolyn's own family . . .

She shuddered involuntarily, and was once more glad that both her parents had died long before she married Phillip Sturgess. In her family, hatred for the Sturgesses had run deep, and all the rumors had been accepted as fact. For the last child of the Deavers to have married a Sturgess would have been, for both her father and mother, the ultimate shame.

The Deavers had lived in Westover as long as the Sturgesses, perhaps longer. And in Carolyn's family, the legend had always been that Charles Cobb Deaver— Carolyn's great-great-grandfather—had been in partnership with Samuel Pruett Sturgess. Charles Deaver had been a cobbler, and the legend had it that Samuel Pruett Sturgess had used him to get the shoe mill started, then squeezed him out. As the mill had grown, and the Sturgess fortunes risen, the Deaver fortunes had declined. Charles had ended up as nothing more than a shift foreman, and found himself in the position of overseeing the labor of his own children. In the end, he had killed himself, but it was an article of faith to Carolyn's parents that Samuel Pruett Sturgess had murdered him, as surely as if he'd held the gun himself.

Looking at the portrait of Samuel Pruett Sturgess, Carolyn found it hard to doubt the legend. Certainly there was nothing in the man's face that hinted at any sort of kindness. It was a pinched face, an avaricious face, and often Carolyn wished it didn't hang in the dining room, where she had to see it every day. But at the same time, she found the portrait held a strange fascination for her, as if somewhere, buried in the portrait, was the truth behind all the legends.

She stood up, switched off the light, and made her way back through the vast expanse of the living room to the entry hall. She checked the front door once more, then started up the stairs. On the second-floor landing, she glanced down the north wing, and saw a sliver of light beneath the door to Abigail's suite. For a moment, she was tempted to go and tap on the door and say good night to the old woman. But in the end, she turned away, knowing that it would do no good. She would only be rebuffed once more. She turned the other way, and hurried down the wide hall to the suite she and Phillip occupied at the opposite end of the house.

"Are we safe for another night?" Phillip asked as she came into the bedroom. He was propped up against the headboard of the king-size bed, clad in pajamas, paging through a magazine. "No thieves or rapists prowling the corridors?"

Carolyn stuck her tongue out at him, then went to perch on the edge of the bed, presenting her back to him. "The only rapist around here is you, and I happen to like it. Unzip me?"

She felt the warmth of Phillip's fingers on her skin, and shivered with pleasure, but as he started to slip his arms around her, she wriggled away and stood up. Stepping out of the black dress, she started toward her dressing room.

"People should die around here more often," she heard Phillip say. Startled, she turned around to find him grinning at her. "I like you in black."

"I look terrible in black," Carolyn protested. "And anyway, that's a horrible thing to say."

"I like to say horrible things. And you don't look terrible in black. Anyway not in black undies."

"Well, it's still a horrible thing to say on the day we buried your father."

"Who was beginning to show signs of never dying at all," Phillip remarked dryly.

"Phillip!"

"Well, it's true, isn't it? And don't go all pious on me. As for dear old Dad," he went on, "I'm not going to pretend I'm sorry to see him go. At least not to you."

"Your father was—" Carolyn began, but her husband cut her off.

"My father was a half-senile old man who had outlived his time. My God, Carolyn, you should be the first to admit that. He never faced up to the fact that the nineteenth century ended, even though he never lived in it."

"All right, he was difficult," Carolyn admitted. "But he was still your father, and you owe him some respect."

The mischievous glint in Phillip's eyes died, and his expression turned serious. "I don't have to respect him at all," he said. "We both know how he was, and we both know how he treated you. He acted as though you were one of the servants."

"And I survived it, didn't I?" Carolyn asked. "After all, we could have moved out, if we'd really wanted to."

"Agreed," Phillip sighed. "And we didn't, which probably doesn't speak very well for either one of us. Anyway, it's over now."

"Is it?" Carolyn asked. "What about your mother? And Tracy? They haven't been a bed of roses either." Then, at the look of pain that came into Phillip's eyes, she wished she could take back the words. "I'm sorry. I shouldn't have said that, should I?"

"You shouldn't have had to say it," Phillip replied quietly. Then his eyes met hers. "Carolyn, do you want to move? We can take the girls, and go anywhere we want. Away from Westover. Without Mother's influence, Tracy will come around."

It was something Carolyn had thought about often, and always, in the end, rejected. Leaving Westover, she knew, was not the solution. "We can't, Phillip. You know we can't. We can't leave Abigail alone here—it would kill her. It's going to be hard enough for her without your father. Without you and Tracy, she'd have nothing left. Besides," she added, "this is your home."

"And your home, too."

Carolyn shook her head ruefully. "Not yet. Maybe someday, but not yet. This is your home—and your mother's. And I'm afraid I still feel . . . like a guest here," she offered hesitantly. She had almost said, "an unwelcome guest."

"You don't have to, you know."

"I know," Carolyn replied. "Lord knows you've told me to spend what I want redoing the place, but I can't. I'd be afraid of bankrupting us, and besides, I wouldn't know where to start. And I'm not about to open another front for Abigail."

"She's just set in her ways. If you just began—"

"She's not just set in her ways, and you know it. She's Abigail Sturgess, and she's frozen in time." Suddenly her voice broke. "And she thinks I'm a toy you found on the wrong side of the tracks, and brought home to play with for a while!"

Immediately, Phillip was on his feet, and his arms were around her. "Darling, don't think that. Don't think that for even a minute."

Carolyn fought back the tears that were burning her eyes and shook her head. "I don't. You know I don't. I'm just having a weak moment. Let me finish undressing, and then let's talk about something else, all right?"

Reluctantly Phillip released her, and went back to the bed. Carolyn moved through the dressing room into the bathroom, and quickly ran cold water in the sink, then washed her face, and began running a brush through her hair.

Maybe it had been a mistake to marry Phillip— maybe, no matter how badly she wanted it to work, it was an impossible situation.

But she had to make it work.

After Alan—

She tried to force the thought out of her mind, but

couldn't. The problem, she knew, was that Phillip and Alan were too much alike.

Good, kind, decent men.

And she'd lost Alan, simply because she hadn't been able to accept him as he was. She'd always wanted more.

She wouldn't make the same mistake with Phillip. Westover was his home; this house was his home. He belonged here. And no matter what happened, she wouldn't ask him to leave. She would figure out a way to deal with his mother, and she would win his daughter over. And she would never ask him to leave.

She'd married him for what he was. A large part of that identity was defined by the fact that Phillip was a Sturgess. And Sturgesses lived at Hilltop.

Suddenly fragments of the old stories flitted through her mind—stories she'd grown up with, stories about the Sturgesses. But as quickly as they came, she rejected them. They were only the unkind whisperings of people who had less than the Sturgesses and therefore envied them. Legends. And they had nothing to do with Phillip.

She put the hairbrush away, and returned to the bedroom, then slid into the bed next to her husband. Switching off the lamp on her bed table, she snuggled close, feeling the tension drain out of her body. And then a thought occurred to her.

"Phillip . . ."

"Hm?"

"Phillip, that plan you've been working on—the one to refurbish the mill?"

"Mm-hmm. What about it?"

"You're not . . . you're not thinking of going ahead with it, are you?"

Phillip drew away slightly, and looked down at her. "Don't tell me you've been talking to Mother?"

"Abigail? What made you think that?"

"Because we were talking about the mill today. On the way up here, after the church service. She asked me if the plan was ready."

Carolyn felt her heart beat faster. "What did you tell her?"

"That it was all set. Everything's on paper."

"And what did Abigail say?" Carolyn realized that she was holding her breath.

Phillip chuckled. "For once, Mother agreed with me. She said that now that Father's gone, it's time I went ahead with that project."

Carolyn lay silent for a long time, then spoke again. "Phillip, maybe you shouldn't go ahead. Maybe . . . maybe your father was right."

Now Phillip sat full upright, and turned on the light. When she looked at him, she saw his eyes flashing angrily.

"Right? All Father would ever say about the mill was that it was evil, and should never be touched. Not restored, not converted to some other use, not even torn down. Just left to rot, for God's sake! How can that be right?"

Carolyn shook her head unhappily. "I don't know. But there have been so many stories. And you don't know how everyone in town feels about the mill."

"They feel the same way I feel about it," Phillip declared. "That it's a hideous old eyesore, and that something ought to be done with it."

"But that's not it," Carolyn replied. "It's something else. It's a reminder of how things used to be here—" She stopped herself, not wanting to hurt her husband, but it was already too late: she could see the pain in Phillip's eyes.

"You mean a reminder of the bad old days, when my family used to work children to death in the shoe factory?"

Mutely, Carolyn nodded.

Phillip stared at her for a moment, then flopped back down on his pillow, averting his eyes.

"I think that's another reason to renovate it," he said tiredly. "Perhaps the best reason. Maybe all those old stories will finally be forgotten if I do something with the mill and some people in Westover make some honest money from it."

"But maybe . . . maybe the stories shouldn't be forgotten, Phillip. Maybe we always need to remember what happened there."

"My God," Phillip groaned. "You sound just like Father. Except that he'd never say exactly what he was talking about. It was always vague references, and dark hints. But nothing I could ever put my finger on." He propped himself up on one elbow, and his tone lightened. "And you know why I could never put my finger on any of it?" he asked.

Carolyn shook her head.

"Because maybe there was nothing to put my finger on! Just a bunch of stories and legends about terrible abuses in the shoe mill. But that sort of thing went on all over New England. Christ, child labor was our answer to slavery. But it's all over now, Carolyn. Why should we keep torturing ourselves with it?"

"I don't know," Carolyn admitted. "But I just can't help feeling that somehow your father was right about the mill."

Phillip reached over and turned off his light again, then drew her close. "Well, he wasn't," he said. "He was as wrong about the mill as he was about everything else. He was my father, darling, but I have to confess I didn't like him very much."

Carolyn made no reply, and lay still in her husband's arms. Here, in bed with Phillip, she felt secure and safe, and she would do nothing to threaten that security. But as Phillip drifted into sleep, and she lay awake, she couldn't help feeling that Phillip was wrong about the mill, and that old Conrad Sturgess, whom they had buried that day, was right.

The mill should be left alone; left to crumble away until there was nothing left of it but dust.

# 3

Tracy Sturgess lay in her bed listening to the faint echoes of the old grandfather clock that had stood in the entry hall for as long as she could remember. She counted the chimes, then checked her tally against the little clock on her night table.

Eleven.

She threw the covers back, put on her robe, then went into the bathroom that adjoined her bedroom. Switching on the light, she inspected herself in the mirror.

She didn't look quite right.

Carefully she mussed her hair until she was satisfied that it looked as though she'd been tossing in her bed for the last hour. Then she turned the bathroom light off and moved quickly through the darkness to her bedroom door. Opening it a crack, she peered out into the dimness of the corridor, lit only by a small nightlight that sat on the marble-topped commode midway between the stairs and her grandmother's rooms.

The hall was empty, and silence hung over the house. But at the far end of the hall, as she had known it would, light glowed from beneath her grandmother's door.

Smiling, she hurried down the hall.

She paused outside her grandmother's door, and

listened. From within, she could hear the faint sounds of her grandmother moving restlessly around her sitting room, then a silence. Tracy smiled. Composing her face into a mask of worried unhappiness, she rapped softly at the door. For a moment there was no response from within, then she heard her grandmother's voice.

"Come in."

Tracy twisted the brass knob, and gently pushed the door open just far enough to slip through. "G-Grandmother?" she asked, letting her voice tremble just the slightest bit. "I couldn't sleep. I miss Grandfather so much . . ." She reached up and brushed at her eyes.

Her grandmother's response, as always, was immediate.

"Tracy, darling, come in. Please." From her chair, Abigail held her arms wide, and Tracy, after hesitating only a second, ran across the room, dropped to her knees, and buried her face in the old woman's lap. Abigail, her own eyes flooding, gently stroked Tracy's hair.

"What is it, child? What's wrong?"

Tracy sniffled slightly, then looked up. "I . . . I just don't know what's going to happen to us, now that Grandfather's . . ." She let her voice trail off, and held still as Abigail brushed the beginnings of a tear away from her eye.

"It's going to be all right, my darling," Abigail assured her. "We have to learn to accept these things. We all die sooner or later, and it was time for your grandfather to go."

"But I didn't *want* him to die!" Tracy wailed. "I loved him so much!"

"Of course you did. We all did. But we have to understand that he's gone now, and that our lives go on."

"But without him, everything's going to be different!"

"Different?" Abigail asked. "How are things going to be different?"

Tracy hesitated for a long time, waiting for her grandmother to urge her to speak.

"Go on, Tracy. Whatever it is, you know you can tell me."

Tracy took a deep breath. "It . . . it's Carolyn. What's going to happen to me, now that Grandfather isn't here to help me? She hates me."

Abigail slipped her arms around her granddaughter, and drew her close. "How could she hate you? You're a lovely child."

Tracy allowed herself a small pout. "But she does hate me. She always tells Daddy that I'm spoiled, and that you've raised me wrong." She felt her grandmother's body stiffen.

"I've raised you precisely as your mother would have raised you," Abigail replied. "And your father knows that."

"But he married *her!* And now she's going to try to change everything!"

"Everything? How?"

Tracy's eyes clouded, and she drew a little away from her grandmother. "I . . . I guess I shouldn't talk about it tonight," she said. She stood up as if to leave, but Abigail stopped her.

"Nonsense. Whatever is upsetting you, we should deal with it. Now, what is it?"

Tracy turned to face her grandmother again. "M-my birthday party," she stammered. "Are we still going to have it next week, like we planned?"

Abigail blinked, then remembered. Tracy's party, planned for weeks, had slipped her mind when Conrad died. "Why—I don't know." Then, seeing the disappointment in Tracy's eyes, she immediately made up her mind. "But I don't see why we shouldn't have it. In fact, I'm certain your grandfather would have wanted it that way."

Suddenly Tracy brightened. "And I can invite anybody I want?"

"Absolutely," Abigail assured her. "After all, it's your party, isn't it?"

"But what about—" Tracy fell silent, as if once

again she was hesitant to tell her grandmother what was on her mind.

"What about what?" Abigail pressed.

"Beth," Tracy whispered. She hesitated as her grandmother's jaw tightened slightly, and wondered if she'd made a mistake. But when Abigail spoke a moment later, Tracy knew it was going to be all right.

"I don't think the little Rogers girl would enjoy your party."

"But what are we going to do?" Tracy asked. "Carolyn will make me invite her."

"Perhaps," the old woman said softly, but her eyes were glinting now. "Perhaps she will. But perhaps she won't, either. At any rate, we'll deal with it tomorrow. All right?"

Tracy came back, and leaned down to give her grandmother a hug. "I love you, Grandmother," she whispered.

"And I love you, too," Abigail replied. "And you mustn't worry about anything. Just because your grandfather's gone doesn't mean you're all alone. You've still got me."

A few minutes later, Tracy left her grandmother's room, and started back down the long corridor. But the smell of the room—a mixture of mustiness and too-sweet cologne as well as something else—was still with her. She took several deep breaths, trying to rid herself of that cloying scent she had always hated: it was the smell of old people.

She wondered how her grandmother could stand it. And the room, too. Though she was always careful to tell her grandmother how much she liked the old-fashioned sitting room, with its Victorian furniture and worn Oriental rugs, the truth was that she hated the look of her grandmother's suite as much as its smell. When her grandmother finally died, and Tracy talked her father into letting her move into the big suite, she'd change it all.

Everything.

But until then, she had to go on pretending to her grandmother. Grandparents, after all, had been known to cut people out of their wills. Tracy, even though she wasn't quite thirteen yet, wasn't about to let something like that happen.

Suddenly she stopped, listening. From behind a closed door she could barely make out the sounds of one of her favorite rock bands. She frowned, and listened harder.

The music was coming from Beth's room.

She listened for a moment, her body unconsciously swaying to the familiar rhythms. Then, her eyes narrowing, she strode to Beth's door, and pushed it open without knocking.

Startled at Tracy's sudden entry, Beth sat up in bed and stared at the other girl.

"What do you think you're doing?" she heard Tracy hiss.

"Tracy? What . . . what's wrong?"

"That music, stupid! Don't you know we're mourning my grandfather?"

Beth stared at Tracy for a second, trying to understand what she'd done. "But—I was playing it soft."

"You shouldn't be playing it at all," Tracy said. "How can anybody sleep, with you blaring your radio?"

"But you can hardly hear it—" Beth protested.

"*I* could hear it," Tracy insisted. "And my grandmother could, too! Shut it off!"

Beth's eyes widened, and she reached over to turn the knob on the clock-radio. "I'll turn it down—"

"Turn it off!" Tracy insisted. She marched over to the night table, and punched at the button on top. The radio went silent. Beth, her eyes frightened, stared at her stepsister.

"I don't see why I can't listen to it if it's so soft no one else can hear—"

"You can't listen to it, because I said you can't. It's my house—not yours—and if you don't like it here, you can just go live somewhere else!"

"But Mom said—"

"Who cares what your mother says?" Tracy demanded. "Just because your stupid mother married my father doesn't give you the right to—"

Suddenly Beth's anger overcame her confusion. "You take that back, Tracy Sturgess!"

Tracy, startled by the unexpected outburst, stepped back. "Don't you talk to me like that!"

"Don't you call my mother stupid!"

Tracy's eyes hardened, and her mouth set petulantly. "I'll call your mother anything I want, and you can't stop me!"

Beth stared at Tracy, fighting back her anger. "Just go away," she finally managed to say. "Just go away and leave me alone."

The, two girls stared at each other for several long seconds, Tracy's eyes glittering with rage while Beth struggled against the tears that threatened to overwhelm her. Then, at last, Tracy turned and stamped out of the room.

As soon as Tracy was gone, Beth ran to the door and locked it, then returned to her bed. Sobbing, she buried her head in the pillow.

It wasn't going to get any better, despite what her father had told her. It was only going to get worse, and it wouldn't matter what she did, or how much she pretended.

Tracy would still hate her.

Her sobs slowly subsided, and she lay in bed wondering what tomorrow would be like.

But she already knew.

It would start at breakfast.

She would sit miserably at the table in the breakfast room, trying to figure out which spoon to use for what.

Old Mrs. Sturgess would ignore her, just like she always did.

But Tracy would watch her, waiting for her to make a mistake, so that she could laugh when Beth made one.

And she would say or do something wrong. She always did.

But what if she didn't go down for breakfast? What if she got up early, and sneaked down to have breakfast with Hannah? Then she could go down to the stable and see the horses, and after that—

—What?

Tracy would come, and tell her she didn't know anything about horses, and that she should leave them alone.

And the trouble was, Tracy was right.

Beth didn't know anything about horses. She didn't know anything about anything in this house, and she'd never learn.

She snuggled deeper under the covers, and closed her eyes. Maybe, if she pretended hard enough, she could convince herself that she was back in the house on Cherry Street, where she'd lived before. And she could pretend that her parents were still married, and—

—and she couldn't do it.

Her parents *weren't* still married. Her mother was married to Uncle Phillip, and she had to get used to it.

She had to, and she would. Her mother wanted her to, and so did her father.

She turned over, telling herself that it wasn't really so bad. It was a nice house, even if it was too big, and Uncle Phillip was always kind to her.

If she could only figure out some way to make Tracy like her.

Slowly, sleep reached out to her . . .

And in the night, she dreamed of Tracy.

Tracy was trying to kill her.

Despite the June warmth in the glassed-in breakfast room, Carolyn could feel the chill emanating from her mother-in-law, and the cold hatred from her stepdaughter. Phillip, engrossed in the financial pages of *The Wall Street Journal*, appeared oblivious of the strain in the room, though she was certain that he was listening to every word spoken. And when he at last felt compelled to put an end to the argument that had been going on for the last twenty minutes, she knew that he would come down firmly on her side.

It had begun when Carolyn had first come in that morning, and seen that her daughter's place was not occupied.

"Isn't Beth down yet?" she'd asked.

Abigail had peered at her over the tops of her reading glasses.

"I believe she took her breakfast with Hannah this morning," she'd said, managing to convey that though she didn't approve of members of her family eating with the servants, she was willing to overlook the breach in Beth's case.

Beth, after all, wasn't a Sturgess, and couldn't be expected to meet the Sturgess standards of behavior.

Then she'd offered Carolyn a bright smile, and suggested that, since Beth was not present, perhaps they should discuss Tracy's birthday party.

Carolyn's guard had immediately gone up, particularly when she saw the slight smile on Tracy's lips.

Now, almost half an hour later, Tracy was glaring at her, her blue eyes glittering with barely controlled fury beneath her creased brows.

"But Beth won't even *enjoy* my party," Tracy began, taking a new tack. "She won't know how to dress, or what to say. She doesn't know any of my friends, and they don't know her!"

"Then perhaps it would be good for them to get to know her," Carolyn said placidly, unwilling to reveal her own anger. "And perhaps we ought to invite some of Beth's friends, too. It certainly seems to me that it would be good for you to get to know them. After all, you're going to be going to school with them next year."

"That has hardly been decided yet," Abigail put in, laying her napkin aside in a gesture Carolyn had long since learned to recognize as a danger signal. "After Phillip and I have discussed the quality of the Westover schools, we'll make the final decision."

"We've already talked about it, Mother," Phillip said, putting his newspaper aside. "The decision has been made. Next year Tracy goes to public school."

"I've told you, I'm quite willing to pay her tuition out of my own funds—" Abigail began, but Phillip cut her off.

"Funds are not the point. The point is that neither I nor Carolyn is pleased with Tracy's school."

"And just what would Carolyn know about Tracy's school?" Abigail asked, her voice taking on an acid quality she no longer tried to hide. "I hardly think," she went on, casting a haughty half-smile in her daughter-in-law's direction, "that your Carolyn is in any position to judge the quality of private schools."

"That is not what we are talking about right now," Carolyn replied, ignoring Abigail's frosty gaze. Then, noting the beginnings of a grin playing around Phillip's mouth, she stretched her foot under the table and kicked him. The grin threatened to grow for a split second, then he managed to suppress it. Carolyn continued, "What we're talking about is Tracy's party, and it seems to me that we're making a mountain out of a molehill. Aside from the fact that my daughter is a perfectly nice girl, whose feelings I have no intention of letting either of you trample on, I think that you, Abigail, might keep in mind that her father happens to be an Alderman, and while that doesn't make him a Sturgess—or a Babcock, a Kilpatrick, or a Bailey, either—it does give him a certain amount of power." She let her eyes bore directly into Abigail's. "Back when you were Tracy's age, the Board of Aldermen consisted of your father, Phillip's grandfather, Jeremiah Bailey, and Fred Kilpatrick. Aside from the fact that they were the Aldermen, they were also very rich."

"The people voted for them," Abigail snapped.

"Of course they did. The people worked for them, too, which might have had something to do with the way they cast their votes. But all that's over, and it's time you understood it. There are no Baileys, Kilpatricks, Babcocks, or Sturgesses on the board anymore. But the board still runs Westover, and the board still has to pass on all the permits that Phillip is going to need for future projects." She paused, noting that Abigail flinched slightly, and surreptitiously glanced at her son.

Phillip, she was almost certain, was suppressing another grin.

"Given what you want to do with the mill, Abigail, you should understand the value of being on good terms with the board. There are a lot of people—and I am among them—who feel the mill should be left as it is, or torn down. I, of course, won't fight Phillip. But others will. And snubbing Beth on Tracy's birthday isn't going to help your cause. It will hurt me, and I don't even want to think about what it will do to Beth. But it will infuriate Alan."

"I can't imagine that Alderman Rogers is even aware of Tracy's party," Abigail observed archly.

"I wouldn't count on that," Carolyn replied. "Beth talks to her father about everything. In all of the talk about Tracy's party, it was never suggested that Beth not be invited."

"*I* didn't invite her," Tracy said sullenly. "And it's my party. If I don't want her to be here that day, she doesn't have to be here! Does she, Grandmother?"

"Of course not, dear," Abigail assured her. She turned her gaze back to Carolyn. "I'm sure you understand that our family has never mixed with children like Beth, and I see no reason why Tracy should be forced to do something that is unnatural to her. As for Beth, I'm sure she won't feel the least bit snubbed. Those kinds of people rarely do—particularly the children."

Steeling herself, Carolyn managed to keep her voice level. "Since I can't imagine that you've ever been snubbed, Abigail, I'm sure you wouldn't know how it feels. I, on the other hand, know very well, since it happens to me quite regularly. I can tolerate it. But there's no reason why Beth should have to." She paused, then decided it was time to let both Abigail and Tracy see how angry she truly was. "My God," she went on.

"Beth lives here! This is supposed to be her home, and the two of you do your best to make her feel as if she doesn't belong here. And perhaps she doesn't. Perhaps neither of us does. But here we are, and here we shall stay. And Beth will be at Tracy's party, and you will both be polite to her. Is that clear?" She took a breath, and hoped Abigail couldn't see that her hands were trembling. "Now, I think we might as well talk about something else, since this discussion is over," she finished, somehow managing to force a smile. "More toast, Abigail?"

Abigail ignored her. "Phillip, I will not be treated this way. I don't understand how you can—"

"She's right, Mother," Phillip interrupted, and Carolyn breathed a silent sigh of relief. "Aside from the moral issues, which we Sturgesses have never been too strong on, I think you'd better consider long and hard before you offend Alan Rogers. Not, mind you, that I think Alan would be petty enough to hold up any permits over a birthday party." He smiled ironically. "Somehow that sort of thing strikes me as being much more our style than his. But there are a lot of projects coming up, and we're going to need cooperation from the town. It's not only Tracy who should start getting acquainted with everyone else who lives in Westover, all of us should." He turned finally to his daughter. "I'm sorry, honey, but your stepmother's right. Beth will be included in your party, or there won't be a party."

Tracy, her face twisting into a grimace of frustration and fury, burst into tears and stormed from the table. Immediately, Abigail rose to follow her, but Phillip spoke once more. "Leave her alone, Mother."

"I will *not* leave her alone," Abigail replied. "Ever since you married Carolyn, you've become insensitive to your own family. But you're making a mistake, Phillip, and you will live to regret it." She started out of the breakfast room, then turned back. "And as for the mill, Carolyn, whatever is done with it is no concern of yours. It is Sturgess property, and always has been. We shall do as we please with it, and what we please to do is to restore it as a monument to the foresight of Phillip's great-grandfather. If the people of Westover cannot appreciate that, then the people be damned." Her back ramrod straight, she swept out of the room.

There was a long silence, finally broken by Carolyn's tired sigh. "I'm sorry," she said. "I know how unpleasant that was for you. And maybe she's right. Maybe Tracy shouldn't be forced to include Beth in her party."

Phillip shook his head. "Not a chance. It's time all of us got dragged into the modern world. You've done it for me, and maybe Beth can do it for Tracy. We'll just keep on plugging, and eventually things will all work out." He glanced at his watch, then drained the last of his coffee. "And as for me, I've got to meet one of the wrong sort of people at the mill, and if I don't hurry, I'll be late."

"Wrong sort of people?" Carolyn asked archly. "Who?"

"The worst," Phillip replied, dropping his voice to a conspiratorial level. "Your ex-husband!" Then, before she could reply, he was gone.

Alone, Carolyn sat for a few minutes staring down on the village below. Always, when she'd lived down there and gazed up at Hilltop, the house had seemed to her to be the most peaceful place on earth.

Now she was here, and there was no peace.

# 4

Beth pushed open the screened kitchen door, and stepped out onto the little flagstone patio that led to the back gardens. The door slammed shut behind her, and she jumped slightly at the crash, calling a quick apology over her shoulder.

"It's all right," Hannah replied mildly from the shadows of the kitchen. "No harm done."

Beth stood in the small enclosure, feeling the early-morning sunshine, and looked around. Here, away from the vastness of the rest of the house, she almost felt at home. The patio, in fact, was almost like the one her father had built behind the house on Cherry Street.

At Hilltop, though, there was another terrace, a wide veranda that extended across most of the length of the house, filled with tables and chairs and chaise longues. It overlooked the tennis court and the rose garden, and Beth didn't really like it: like everything else here, it was too big and too ornate.

She skipped down the steps, then started along a path that led under an arbor, then skirted the edge of the rose garden. Beyond that, hidden from the house by a high hedge, was the stable.

The stable was Beth's favorite part of Hilltop. In the barn, where it was warm in winter, but cool now that summer was here, and everything smelled like horses and hay, she always felt better. In fact, she'd even made friends with one of the horses, a large black-and-white one named Patches, who always whinnied when she came into the barn, and nuzzled at her pockets looking for carrots.

She turned a corner, and almost tripped over the gardener, who was on his knees carefully digging up a border of tulip bulbs and replacing them with tiny marigolds.

"Hi, Mr. Smithers."

The old gardener looked up, then rocked back on his heels, dangling his trowel in his right hand. " 'Morning, Miss Beth. You're out bright and early today."

"I had breakfast with Hannah this morning."

Smithers's brows rose slightly, but he said nothing.

"Well, what's wrong with that?" Beth asked. "If I want to eat breakfast with Hannah, why shouldn't I?"

"No reason—no reason at all," the old man assured her. Then a little grin cracked his weathered face. "But I bet Mrs. Sturgess didn't like that."

Beth frowned uncertainly. "Why wouldn't she like that?"

Now Smithers's brows arched in a caricature of disapproval. "A member of the family eating with the servants? Tut-tut, child! It simply isn't done!"

"But I'm not a member of the family! I'm just who I always was. Remember?" Then her voice dropped. "And I wish you wouldn't call me Miss Beth, either. You never used to do that."

"And your mother never used to be married to Mr. Phillip, either," Smithers replied, his voice gentle. "Things are different now, and you have to learn what's expected of you. And part of that is that I call you Miss Beth, and you call me Ben. I'm the gardener here, and you shouldn't call me 'mister.' "

"But when we lived next door to you, I always called you Mr. Smithers."

"That was before," the gardener explained once more. "And I used to call your mother by her first name, too. But everything's changed now." Ben Smithers shrugged, shaking his head. "It's just the way of the world, Miss Beth. Everything changes, and there's not much you can do about it." Then he brightened. "Except my garden," he added. "Every year, I try to make it look just the way it always has. 'Course, even that doesn't work out, when you get right down to it. It's always a little different, and every year the soil gets a little more worn out." He smiled ruefully. "Sort of like me, I guess. Every year, a little more worn out. Now, you run along, and let me get my work done, all right?"

"I could help you," Beth offered, but even as she uttered the words, she knew what the old man's answer would be.

"Not for you to help me," he said. "It's for you and the rest of the Sturgesses to pick 'em. It's for me to grow 'em. Which is just as well, since growin' 'em is what I like to do."

His grip on the trowel tightened, and he rocked forward. A moment later a clump of tulip bulbs appeared, and Ben Smithers carefully brushed the dirt away from it before slipping it into a labeled bag. A moment later, a young marigold had replaced the tulip.

Beth watched for a few minutes, then silently continued on her way down to the stable.

Beth let herself into the stable and heard Patches whinny softly. Fishing in her pocket, she found a stump of carrot, then scratched the horse affectionately between the ears as the animal munched the treat. There was a movement at the back of the barn, and Beth quickly withdrew her hand from the horse, afraid that Tracy Sturgess was about to appear, but when she looked up, all she saw was Peter Russell, the stableboy, grinning at her.

"Hi, twerp. Come down to help me muck out the stalls?"

"Can I?" Beth asked eagerly.

Peter looked puzzled. "Why not?"

"I just—" Beth hesitated, then plunged on. "Peter, am I any different since I moved up here?"

"Jeez," Peter replied. "How would I know? Why don't you ask Peggy? She's your best friend, isn't she?" He handed a shovel to Beth, and pointed to a large pile in one of the empty stalls. Making a face, Beth let herself into the stall, and gingerly slid the shovel under the pile of manure.

"But Peggy never comes up here," Beth replied. Peggy Russell was Peter's younger sister and Beth and Peggy had been best friends since second grade. Balancing the shovel carefully, Beth moved outside and added the manure to the pile that grew steadily behind the stable each week until a truck came on Monday afternoons to take it all away. When she went back into the stall, she found Peter staring at her with the contempt he usually reserved for his kid sister.

"You know, you can be almost as dumb as Peggy sometimes. The reason she doesn't come up here is because I work here. Mom says if she came up here it would look like she was tagging along on my job, and then Mr. Sturgess might fire me."

Beth stared at Peter. "He wouldn't do that!"

"Tell that to my mom."

"I will! Peggy's my friend. Uncle Phillip wouldn't fire you just because your sister came to see me!"

"Uncle Phillip?" Peter echoed, his voice suddenly tinged with scorn. "Since when is he your uncle?"

Beth felt herself redden, and turned away. "It . . . it's what I'm supposed to call him," she mumbled.

"Why don't you just call him Dad?" Peter asked.

Beth spun around to face him again, the sting of his words bringing tears to her eyes. "He's not my father! And why are you being so mean? I thought you were my friend!"

Peter stared at his sister's friend, wondering what she was so angry about. Didn't she have everything now? She lived in a mansion, and had servants, and a tennis court, and horses. She was living a life all the other kids in Westover only dreamed about.

"We're not friends," he said finally. "You're the kid who lives in the mansion now, remember? Since when have any of the kids like you ever been friends of the rest of us? Now, if you want to help, help. If you don't, just go away. Okay? I've got work to do."

Beth dropped the shovel and ran from the stall, certain her tears were going to overcome her. She started toward the door, but before she could get out of the stable, the big black-and-white horse in the first stall whinnied again, and stretched its neck out to snuffle at her.

Beth paused, and automatically reached up to pet the horse. Suddenly she knew what she should do. If Peter was going to treat her like she was Tracy Sturgess, she would act like Tracy.

"Peter," she called; then, when there was no answer, she called again, louder. "Peter!"

The stableboy stuck his head out of one of the far stalls. "What do you want now?"

"Saddle Patches," Beth told him. "I want to go for a ride."

Peter stared at her. "Are you nuts? You don't know how to ride."

"Do it!" Beth demanded, hoping she didn't sound as frightened as she suddenly felt. "Let Patches out in the paddock, and put the saddle on!"

Peter only grinned at her, and shook his head.

"Then I'll do it myself!" Beth cried. Opening the gate, she let herself into the stall. The horse backed away, then reared up, snorting.

Beth darted across the stall and threw open the door on the other side, and the horse immediately bolted through into the paddock beyond. A moment later, Beth followed.

Outside, she paused, then reached up and took the lead rope off the nail it was coiled over. As she started toward the horse, she tried to remember what it was that Tracy did when she was going to saddle a mount.

Patches eyed her as she approached, pawing at the ground and whinnying softly. When she was only a few feet away, the horse reared up, pawed at the air, then cantered off to the other end of the paddock.

From the stable, Beth heard Peter laughing. She spun around, glaring at him.

"Don't just stand there! Help me!"

"You let Patches out—it's your problem!"

Beth looked from Peter back to the horse, and suddenly felt herself begin to panic. The animal, so friendly in the stall, suddenly looked much bigger, and somehow threatening. But she had to get the horse onto the lead. She had to!

She started forward once more, moving slowly and carefully, feeling her heart pound. Patches, apparently no longer interested in her, had reached down and torn a clump of grass up. But when Beth moved in close, the horse suddenly shied away, snorted a warning, then once more trotted away.

Suddenly Beth felt the lead rope being torn from her hand, and heard Tracy's voice.

"What are you doing, stupid? Give me that!" Then, while Beth stood watching, Tracy trotted over to the horse, grasped its halter just as it began to rear, and snapped the lead in place. She jerked sharply on the lead, and Patches came back to earth, neighing softly.

"You idiot," Tracy shouted to Beth as she led the horse back to its stall. "What were you doing?"

"I . . . I just wanted to go for a ride. And Peter wouldn't saddle him for me, so I tried to do it myself."

"Well, you can't," Tracy snapped. "You don't know anything about horses."

"I do, too—"

"You just called Patches 'him,' didn't you? Well, it just so happens Patches is a mare. If you can't even tell that, you should stay out of the stable. And besides, Patches is *my* horse!"

"Aw, come on, Tracy," Peter Russell began, but Tracy whirled around, glaring at him.

"You stay out of this, or I'll make Father fire you. And don't ever let her back in the stable again."

Peter's lips tightened, but he said nothing. When

Tracy had led the horse back into the stable and closed the door, Beth ran over to the boy.

"Peter, I'm sorry. I didn't mean to—"

"Didn't you hear her?" Peter demanded, his anger at Tracy now refocused on Beth. "Just stay away, all right?" Then he turned, and also disappeared into the stable.

Beth hesitated, then felt the tears she'd been fighting overflow. Scrambling through the paddock fence, she ran along the path back toward the rose garden, then veered off to the right, going around the end of the house, crossing the front lawn. On the far side two immense stone lions flanked the foot of the trail that led up to the mausoleum. Beth passed between them unseeingly, almost blinded by the stinging tears.

Phillip Sturgess and Alan Rogers stood on Prospect Street, gazing across at the sullen brick facade of the long-abandoned mill. Its windows, long since bereft of glass, were boarded over, and the once-red bricks bore a thick accumulation of grime that had turned them nearly black. At the top, some of the crenellations that had once been the building's sole claim to architectural interest had crumbled away, giving the abandoned factory a ruined look.

The two men stood silent for a long time. Alan finally sighed, and shook his head.

"I don't know. On paper, it all looks great, but when you look at what we really have to work with— well, I just don't know. It might be easier to tear it down and start over."

Phillip nodded. "It would be cheaper, too. But we'd lose something if we did that. There's history in that building, Alan. Almost the whole history of Westover is tied up in the mill."

"Don't you mean the history of the Sturgesses?" Alan replied.

"I'm not sure there's a difference." Then he saw the grin on Alan's face, and chuckled. "All right, so I sounded like my parents. But the whole attraction of the place will be the fact of the restoration, so we don't really have any choice, do we? And the structure's sound, believe it or not. I had an engineer survey it a few months ago."

Alan regarded the other man skeptically. "Did your father know that?"

"You know how Father felt about the mill."

"And he had a right to, after what happened to your brother."

There was a silence; then Phillip spoke again, his voice softer. "What happened to Conrad Junior was an accident, despite what Father believed." Then, when Alan said nothing, Phillip turned to face him. "Alan, you don't believe all those stories, do you?"

"The ghost stories? Of course not. But apparently your father did."

Phillip's expression tightened. "He's dead now."

"Yes." Alan paused, then chose his words carefully. "What about Carolyn? What does she think of all this?"

Phillip eyed Alan shrewdly. "The fact that you asked the question suggests to me that you know the answer."

"I just wondered," Alan replied, shrugging noncommittally. "She just always hated this place, that's all." Then, meeting Phillip's eyes, he went on. "A lot of people in Westover hate this mill, Phillip. They see it as a symbol, and the memories it evokes aren't pleasant ones. A lot of the children of Westover died in that building—"

"That was a long time ago, Alan," Phillip interrupted. "And while I'm not pretending it was right, child labor went on all over New England back then. It wasn't just here, and it wasn't just the Sturgesses."

"I'm not saying it was," Alan agreed. "All I'm saying is that a lot of people here still look at that mill, and think about what went on in it."

"Something none of them really remembers," Phillip pointed out. "Let's not forget that the mill's been closed for a century, and stories get exaggerated. If

Father had been smart, he'd have done something with the property years ago." Suddenly Phillip cocked his head, and gazed at Alan suspiciously. "Alan, is there something you're not telling me? Is the board likely to hold up the permits just because of the history of the building?"

Alan shook his head. "Nope. The permits will go through without a murmur. As far as the board's concerned, history is history. If turning this old wreck into a mall full of cute little shops will make people in Westover some money, the aldermen are all for it."

"But you doubt that it will," Phillip stated.

"I do," Alan agreed, but then smiled ruefully. "Of course, as your wife will tell you, I'm not the most imaginative son-of-a-bitch around, and never think anything will work. So why don't we go inside and have a look around, and I can tell you just why the dump will collapse when we start working on it."

"And I," Phillip laughed, "will expect you to buy me a drink when nothing collapses at all."

They crossed Prospect Street, walked to the corner of the vast building, then turned left onto a weed-choked path that paralleled the building's long northern wall. Halfway down, they came to a metal door, its paint badly weathered. But when Phillip slipped a key into the padlock that hung from an oversized hasp, it opened easily.

"Father had the lock checked every month, from the day Conrad Junior died. Sometimes he did it himself. When I was a kid, I used to beg him to bring me along and show me the inside of the mill, but he never would. I guess—well, I guess he never got over my brother's death at all."

"He really never even let you look around?" Alan asked.

Phillip shook his head. "It used to drive me nuts. Sometimes I'd lie awake nights, looking down at it from my window, plotting how I could sneak in. But then I'd think about what Father would do to me if I got caught, and I never tried it." His face twisted into an abashed grin. "Do you know, even when I came down here with the engineer, I almost couldn't bring myself to go inside? I kept thinking Father was watching me from Hilltop, and when I got home, he'd skin me. Forty-three years old, and still afraid of my father. Some tycoon, hunh?"

Alan chuckled, and thumped his friend's back. "Afraid you just don't pull off the tycoon act very well at all, Phillip, and that's the truth. You sure you're a real Sturgess?"

"I'm going to accept that little bit of snideness as a compliment, thank you very much," Phillip replied. Then he pulled the door open, and stood back. "After you."

Alan stepped through the door, and looked around curiously. It was almost pitch black in the interior, for only a little light filtered through the boarded windows. High overhead, a latticework of iron strutting supported the ceiling.

"In its day, that roof was considered quite an accomplishment. There weren't many buildings this size with no pillars for the roof. It's almost the size of a football field."

"And almost as empty, too," Alan observed. He kicked at the floor, and was surprised when there was no give.

"It's oak. Solid oak, and three inches thick. Downstairs, there are beams and pillars everywhere. The engineer said he'd never seen anything quite like it."

They prowled through the building, but Alan quickly realized there was little to see. It was simply an immense shell, with a few remnants of partitions still in place at the back, where the mill offices had been. Though it had suffered badly from neglect, the structure did, indeed, seem basically sound. After exploring the main floor, they headed toward a stairway leading to the basement.

Phillip switched on a flashlight, and they started down. At the bottom of the stairs, Phillip suddenly stopped.

"This is where they found Conrad Junior," he said softly. "Apparently he tripped, and fell on some kind of tool."

Alan frowned, then took the flashlight from the other man and cast its beam around the expanse of the basement. Shadows from the closely spaced columns were everywhere, and the beam of light finally seemed to lose itself in the distance. But except for the forest of supporting pillars, the basement, like the floor above, seemed empty.

"What was a tool doing here? It looks like the place was cleared out a hundred years ago."

"Search me," Phillip replied. "When it happened, I hadn't even been born yet. In fact," he added, his voice taking on a note of melancholy that Alan had never heard before, "I guess I was the replacement child. I don't think Mother intended having more than one, but when Conrad Junior died, they decided to have me."

"They didn't do so badly," Alan said, deliberately making his voice light. "I don't know what your brother was like, but—"

"—But he was the son my father loved," Phillip said, his voice suddenly bitter. "Father never failed to let me know that I was no substitute for my brother," he added. Then, embarrassed by what he had confided, he cleared his throat, and grasped Alan's arm. "Come on. Let's get out of here."

Though he would have liked to examine the massive wooden beams that supported the main floor, and take a closer look at the building's foundations, Alan followed Phillip up the stairs and across the barren building.

Their footsteps echoed loudly in the silence, and neither man spoke again until they had once more emerged into the bright sunlight of the summer morning.

"Well," Phillip asked, "what do you think?"

Alan once more regarded the building thoughtfully before he spoke. Then, at last, he nodded.

"It can be done. And it won't take long either. If

we get started right away, we should be able to have it open by Labor Day."

The two men stared at each other, both of them recognizing the irony at the same time.

"Labor Day," Phillip repeated softly. "Given the history of the building, that seems somehow fitting, doesn't it?"

"I suppose so," Alan agreed. "And a tad macabre, too, when you think about it."

Phillip relocked the metal door, and they started back up the path toward Prospect Street. Then, when they were once more in front of the old factory, Phillip spoke once more.

"Alan, when we were down in the basement, did you smell something?"

Alan frowned thoughtfully, then shook his head.

"It was probably nothing," Phillip went on. "But for a minute there, while we were talking, I thought I smelled smoke."

# 5

"Hannah?"

The old housekeeper looked up from the bowl of peas she was shelling, then started to pull her weight up from the battered easy chair she'd long ago moved from her room into the enormous kitchen.

"Don't get up," Carolyn told her. "I was just wondering if you'd seen Beth."

"She was right here till after breakfast," Hannah replied, sinking gratefully back into the depths of the chair. "Helped me with the dishes." She glanced up at Carolyn over the rims of her half-glasses. "She's a mighty nice girl, that daughter of yours."

Carolyn nodded absently, and Hannah's gaze sharpened slightly. "Something wrong, Miss Carolyn? Have I done something to displease you?"

"Of course not," Carolyn replied immediately. "You're wonderful, and I don't know what I'd do without you." She hesitated, knowing she should probably leave Hannah alone in her domain, then lowered herself onto one of the straight-backed wooden chairs that sat at the kitchen table. Her fingers began nervously twisting at a button on her blouse. "I . . . I'm not really sure," she went on. "It's just that . . ." She let her voice trail off, afraid that whatever she might say would sound somehow disloyal to her husband.

But Hannah, her face imperturbable, nodded wisely, and finished the sentence for her. ". . . it's just that things up here aren't like you thought they'd be, and it's not as easy as it looked?"

How did she know? Carolyn wondered. Is it all that obvious? Instinctively, without thinking about it at all, she reached out for a handful of the peas, and began shelling them.

"You don't have to do that, Miss Carolyn," Hannah said quietly, but there was something in her tone that made Carolyn look at the housekeeper. As she'd suspected, Hannah's eyes were fixed on her, as if challenging her to speak her mind clearly.

But she won't ever ask me anything, Carolyn suddenly realized. If I need to talk, I can, but she'll never initiate a conversation.

"Yes, I do," Carolyn replied, making up her mind. "I have to do something. I'm just not used to sitting around all day with no work to do. And I'm afraid I'm not good at lunches, either," she added, remembering the few times she'd accepted invitations from the wives of men her husband had grown up with, only to spend a few miserable hours listening to them chat about people she didn't know and places she'd never been.

"I'm good at fixing lunches," Hannah said mildly. "But I'm afraid I'd have to agree with you about them fancy luncheon parties. Some of us just can't abide that sort of twaddle."

"Beth couldn't abide facing breakfast with the family this morning, could she?" Carolyn asked pointedly.

Hannah's lips pursed, and Carolyn was afraid she'd asked the old servant to step beyond some invisible limit.

"She'll get used to things here," Hannah said at last. "She likes it out here because it's familiar." She glanced up again, and there was a slight twinkle in her eyes. "She tells me when she lived on Cherry Street, the family practically lived in the kitchen."

"What family doesn't?" Carolyn replied, then rolled

her eyes as she realized the ridiculousness of the question. "Never mind. That was a stupid thing to say."

"Not so stupid. Mr. Phillip used to spend a lot of time here when he was a boy. In fact," she added, "sometimes I feel like I raised him myself. Anyway, he certainly turned out the way I'd want a son to turn out, if I'd had one. And I have to say, it's nice to have a child in my kitchen again. Particularly one who already knows how to wash dishes and take out the trash."

She fell silent, and Carolyn found herself wondering exactly what the old woman was trying to tell her.

"What about Tracy?" she asked. "Doesn't she ever come out here?"

"Only when she wants something," Hannah replied, and though there was nothing condemnatory in her voice, Carolyn noticed that the old woman's eyes stayed on the bowl of peas as she spoke. "Tracy's a different kind of child. Takes after her grandmother, if you know what I mean."

"I'm afraid I do," Carolyn replied. "She—well, she seems determined to make Beth feel as if she doesn't belong here."

Hannah opened her mouth, then seemed to change her mind. But an opaqueness came into her eyes, and Carolyn knew that now she had gone too far.

"I wouldn't know about that," Hannah finally said. "But as for that little girl of yours, I have an idea of where she might be." Her eyes drifted toward the window.

Following Hannah's lead, Carolyn gazed out the window. Barely visible through the treetops, she could make out the marble ring that surmounted the mausoleum.

"The mausoleum? Why would she have gone up there?"

Hannah shrugged. "She might not have. But there was a bit of a ruckus down at the stable a while ago, and I've noticed that when people want to be alone around here, they often go up to the mausoleum." Her eyes met Carolyn's once more. "If she wants to tell you what happened, she will. But don't push her, Miss Carolyn. She's doing her best to fit in. Just let her do it her way."

Then, as Carolyn hurried out the kitchen door, Hannah went back to shelling her peas. But as she worked, she wondered if either Beth or Carolyn would ever be allowed to fit into this house. If it were up to Tracy, she knew, they wouldn't.

Tracy would die first.

Beth sat alone in the coolness that pervaded the mausoleum despite the growing heat of the morning. Her tears had long since dried, and she'd spent a few minutes reading the inscriptions on the backs of each of the chairs that surrounded the marble table. Now she was perched on the edge of Samuel Pruett Sturgess's marble chair, staring out at the village she'd grown up in.

From here, Westover almost looked like a miniature village—like one of the tiny model-train layouts her father had taken her to see at a show in Boston last year. She could see the tracks coming around the hillside, crossing the river, then disappearing behind the mill and reemerging to curve in a wide arc around the village until they disappeared into the distant hills.

But it was the mill that interested her most. From where she sat, the old brick building was framed exactly between two of the marble pillars. The town itself was mostly to the left of the mill, but from this vantage point the mill was precisely centered below her.

In fact, if the seventh pillar—the pillar that had once stood opposite Samuel Pruett Sturgess's chair—hadn't been broken, the mill would be completely invisible.

For a while, she'd sat trying to decide whether the mausoleum had been built the way it was on purpose, or if, after the whole thing was finished, someone had noticed that if one of the pillars was broken out, then old Mr. Sturgess would be able to look down at his factory from his chair.

For that's the way it had struck Beth.

It was almost as if the table was for all the dead Sturgesses to meet around, as though they were still alive, and had business to discuss, and the oldest of them—Samuel Pruett Sturgess—was sitting where he could watch over the whole town, and especially his mill.

Then, while she had been pretending to be Mr. Sturgess, she had seen it.

It was a flash, like some kind of explosion. Suddenly, it had seemed as if the mill was on fire.

At first she'd thought it was the sun, reflecting off the windows of the building.

But then she remembered that all the windows were boarded up, and there wasn't any glass in them.

Now she was staring at the old building, waiting to see if it would happen again. So far, it hadn't.

"Beth?"

She jumped, startled, and turned to see her mother coming up the steps from the path to the house. Quickly, she slid off the marble chair.

"Honey? Are you okay?"

Beth felt a sudden stab of embarrassment. Did her mother know what had happened down at the stable? Had Tracy told on her? But she hadn't really done anything—not really. Just let Patches out into the paddock.

"I . . . I'm fine," she said.

Carolyn surveyed the little girl carefully. She could see from the puffiness around her eyes that Beth had been crying, but she seemed to be over it now. Panting slightly, Carolyn eased herself into the chair next to the one Beth had been occupying, then sighed as the cool of a faint breeze touched her forehead.

"Go on," she said. "Sit down again." Then she lowered her voice slightly, and glanced around as if she was looking to see if they were being watched. "Actually, I've been dying to sit in these chairs ever since Phillip told me no one's allowed to sit in them."

Beth's eyes widened. "They aren't? I didn't know that. I didn't mean to—"

"Of course you didn't mean to do anything wrong. And you didn't, either, so don't worry about it. I, on the other hand, know perfectly well that I shouldn't be sitting in this chair, and I'm rather enjoying breaking the rules. Whose chair is it, anyway?"

Beth hesitated, then giggled slightly. "His wife's," she pronounced solemnly.

Carolyn frowned. "Whose?"

"You mean you haven't read it?" Beth said, laughing out loud now. "Go on, read it. You're going to hate it." As Carolyn rose, and moved around behind the chair, Beth stopped her. "You have to read his first, though."

Thoroughly puzzled, Carolyn studied the back of the chair that contained the ashes of Samuel Pruett Sturgess. Aside from his dates of birth and death, also etched in the stone were the facts of his life, at least those he had apparently considered important. The marble proclaimed that he had been a member of Sigma Alpha Gamma, a thirty-second-degree Mason, an Episcopalian, a Republican, and the father of four children.

After she had read through all the information, Carolyn's eyes shifted to the chair in which she had been sitting.

The inscription on the back was simple:

### HIS WIFE

"Do you believe it?" Beth giggled. "Not even her name!"

Though she tried to contain herself, Carolyn couldn't help laughing. "So much for women's lib, hunh? I wonder what the poor woman's life must have been like?"

"I bet he made her walk three steps behind him," Beth replied. "Can you imagine Daddy putting something like that on your tombstone?" Then, suddenly remembering the divorce, she reddened.

"It's all right," Carolyn assured her. "And you're right. Your father wouldn't dare put something like that on my tombstone. And neither would Phillip, for that matter."

The mischievous light that had been in Beth's eyes a moment before faded, and Carolyn wished for an instant that she hadn't mentioned Phillip's name. But now it was too late.

"Phillip loves you very much, you know," she said.

Beth nodded. "I know. It's just—" She fell suddenly silent, then shook her head. "Oh, never mind. It doesn't matter. Can we just talk about something else?"

But Carolyn could see that whatever had happened, it did matter. Beth's eyes were damp, and she could see that the little girl was struggling once more against her unhappiness. But then Hannah's words of a few minutes before came back to Carolyn. Reluctantly, she nodded. "All right. What shall we talk about?"

Beth thought for a minute, then grinned crookedly. "Let's not talk about anything. Let's go for a hike!"

"A hike?" Carolyn echoed. "Where?"

"Down the hill. Look. There's a little trail over there. See?" Beth pointed past the broken seventh pillar.

Carolyn's eyes followed her daughter's gesture, and she saw what had apparently once been a path leading down the hill, though what now remained of the trail was overgrown with weeds and brush.

"Good Lord," she groaned. "Can we even get through? Where does it go?"

"I bet it goes down to the river! Can we go down, Mom? Please? It'll be just like it used to be!"

Carolyn eyed the trail carefully. To her it looked both steep and difficult. Then she turned back to Beth, and the eager light in the little girl's eyes made her mind up for her.

"Hit it, Tarzan. I'm right behind you."

As Beth, dressed in jeans and a white shirt that Carolyn recognized as having once belonged to Alan, plunged into the brush, Carolyn had a sudden fleeting memory. There had been days like this before—days when the three of them, she and Alan and Beth, had hiked around the countryside, just following the paths and trails. Even then the strain between herself and Alan had been all too evident, festering just below the surface. Now here she was, hiking again, and once again there was something festering just below the surface.

But this time, the infection had invaded Beth.

From now on, she determined, she would spend more time with her daughter. Her daughter, right now, needed her very badly.

Abigail rapped once on Tracy's closed bedroom door, then let herself in. Tracy sat propped on her bed, her arms folded against her chest. The sophistication that sometimes lent her the look of an older girl was nowhere to be seen. Right now she looked exactly like the angry almost-thirteen-year-old she was.

"I hate her," she said. Then, again: "I hate her, hate her, hate her. I hate Beth, and I hate Carolyn, too!"

Abigail seated herself on the edge of the bed, and took one of Tracy's hands in her own. "Hate is a very unattractive emotion that we should do our best to keep out of our hearts."

"I don't care." Tracy sulked. "They hate me, too!"

"No, I don't think they do," Abigail went on, her voice soothing. "At least not Carolyn. She simply doesn't understand you, that's all. You have to remember where she came from, Tracy. She never had any of our advantages, and we should pity her, not hate her. But of course," she added, "pitying her doesn't mean we should give in to her, either."

Tracy looked up, a glimmer of hope in her eyes. "But Daddy said—"

"I know exactly what your father said. I may be eighty-three years old, but I'm neither deaf nor blind. I heard your father, and I see every day how that woman treats him."

"I just wish she'd go away."

"One day she will," Abigail promised. "Mark my words, one day your father will realize the mistake he's made, and understand that he needs a woman of his own background. But until then, all we can do is try to ignore her, and the child, too."

"She was chasing Patches," Tracy stormed. "She chased her out of the stall, and Patches was terrified."

Abigail, who had watched the incident at the stable from her sitting-room window, said nothing.

"And what about my party?" Tracy went on. "Having Beth there will wreck it! My friends will think I actually *like* her."

"Not if she isn't here," said Abigail. "Now it seems to me that all you have to do is change the day of your party. Beth always spends Saturdays with her father, so we'll simply move your party from Sunday to Saturday. You tell Hannah," she finished, "and I'll tell Carolyn." Her patrician lips curled into a smile. "I'm an old lady, and I suppose there's a chance I might just forget to speak to her, of course."

Tracy reached out to hug her grandmother. "Will you do that?" she asked. "Will you really do that for me?"

"Of course I will. What are grandmothers for?" Disentangling herself from Tracy's embrace, she stood up. "Now, I want you to go down and talk to Hannah. And don't look too pleased with yourself. While I don't question Hannah's loyalty, I sometimes think she has a tendency to talk too much to your father's wife."

Giggling, Tracy rolled off her bed and left the room. Abigail followed her slowly, then watched her as the girl hurried down the hall toward the stairs. From the back, even at her age, she looked so much like her mother that tears came to Abigail's eyes. Lorraine Kilpatrick Sturgess had been exactly the right girl for Phillip and Abigail had never quite adjusted to the fact of her death. And yet, Tracy seemed sometimes almost to be a reincarnation of the woman who had died giving birth to her. Except for the eyes. Tracy's eyes had come from her father, who had inherited that clear blue from Abigail herself. But the rest of Tracy was pure Lorraine.

And dear Lorraine would never have had anything to do with a woman like Carolyn, nor allowed Tracy to associate with a child like Beth. Abigail would see to it that Tracy never felt any differently.

When Tracy had disappeared down the stairs, Abigail retreated to her suite. Here, in the rooms that hadn't changed since she'd come here as a bride, life seemed to her to be as it should have been. Here, nothing ever changed. Whatever happened in the outside world had no meaning for her here, for in these rooms were all the portraits of her family, and of Conrad, and the mementos of times past, when the Sturgesses had run Westover.

When the mill was reopened, the Sturgesses would once again resume their rightful place. Perhaps the people wouldn't be working directly for her family, but at least they would be paying rent.

Abigail, almost against her will, glanced up at the portrait of her husband, and heard once again the words he had uttered so often in the years before he had died.

*"It is an evil place, but it must never be torn down. It must stand as it is, a constant reminder to us all. It is evil, Abigail, but it is our conscience. We must never lose it, and never change it."*

Abigail had listened to him, and pitied him, but in the end had realized that her husband had simply lost his mind.

And she knew exactly when it had started.

It had started on the day that Conrad Junior had died, and his father had refused to accept it as the accident it had been.

Instead, he had blamed the mill, insisting that the mill itself had somehow claimed their son's life.

Then, in the last few years of his life, when his mind had begun to fail as rapidly as his body, he had

become fixated on a box of old records from the last
days of the mill's operations.

He had kept them in a metal box in the closet, and
as he drew closer and closer to death, he had spent
more and more time poring over them, and mumbling
about the evil in the mill.

She took the metal box off the closet shelf now,
and went to sit in her favorite chair by the window.
Opening the box, she carefully removed the old journals with which it was filled. The pages were yellowed
with age and threatened to crumble in her fingers.
Slowly, she began reading.

Strange records of odd things happening at the
mill.

Horrible things that seemed, on a bright sunny
morning like today, far too terrible to believe.

And Abigail didn't believe, despite her husband's
fanatic ravings. She turned the pages one by one, shaking her head sadly as she thought of the manner in
which Conrad had wasted his life because of a few lines
in an ancient journal.

Even on the day he died, he had demanded that
she bring him the box, then, propped up in his bed, he
had pored over the journals for the last time, his hands
trembling as he fingered the pages, muttering to himself as he deciphered the words once more. Abigail had
watched him, knowing that his mind was no longer in
the present, that he had taken himself to another era.
Finally, late in the afternoon, his breathing had suddenly changed, and the hollow rattles of death had
gripped him as his worn-out heart began its last spas-
modic flutterings.

Abigail had pried his fingers loose from the journals, but even as she put them back in the box and
carried the box itself back to the closet, Conrad had
reached out for them, as if by grasping the past one last
time he could stave off death and prolong the final
moment.

When she had returned to his bed, he had struggled to speak, his words barely audible as they bubbled through the fluids gathering in his lungs.

"She's there," he'd gasped at last. "She's still there, and she hates us all. . . . Keep her there, Abigail. Keep her there for me. . . ."

And then, clutching at her hand, he'd died.

Abigail had pondered his last words since then, but only now, as she sat fingering the crumbling documents, did she decide that whatever he had been trying to say, the words had been nothing more than the fragmented ramblings of a dying man.

Now Abigail put the journals back in the box, closed and locked it, and returned it to its place on her husband's closet shelf. Then she went to the window, and gazed out across Westover, as she had so many times before. At the other side of the town, silent and forbidding, lay the ancient hulk of the long-abandoned mill.

When she and Phillip had finished with it, though, it would once again be the proudest building in Westover.

Nothing and no one would stop them.

Neither Conrad's insane superstitions, nor Carolyn's inane prattling, would ever convince her that the mill was anything but an ordinary building.

And it was there—had always been there—to make money for the Sturgesses.

Certainly there was nothing either shameful or evil in that.

Hannah eyed Tracy suspiciously.

"Isn't it a little late to be switching a party?"

Tracy sighed dramatically, and did her best to look as upset by the whole thing as Hannah seemed to be.

"Well, of course it is," she said. "But I *can't* have my party without Alison Babcock, and she won't be able to come on Sunday! So we'll just have to have it on Saturday, instead."

"What about the other kids? What if they can't come on Saturday?"

"They can," Tracy lied smoothly. "I've already talked

to them, and they can all come on Saturday. I don't see why you want to make such a big deal about it."

Hannah's brows arched skeptically. "And just when did you talk to Miss Alison? The phone hasn't rung here all morning."

Tracy's eyes narrowed, and glinted dangerously. Who did Hannah think she was, anyway? Didn't she know she was just a servant? "I called her. We were talking about something else, and she remembered. So I've been calling all the other kids ever since. Okay?"

Hannah's eyes went to the telephone extension on the counter, with its two buttons, one of which glowed when either of the telephone lines was in use. Then she saw Tracy silently daring her to challenge her words.

"I'll speak to Miss Carolyn about it," she said, deciding there was no point in calling the lie. The girl already knew she'd been caught, and didn't care.

"That won't be necessary," Tracy said, her voice petulant, though her eyes glowed with her apparent victory. "Grandmother's going to talk to Carolyn. And if Grandmother says it's all right to change the party to Saturday, then it is. So just do it."

"Now see here," Hannah began, but her words were suddenly cut off by a scream coming from outside.

Turning away from Tracy, Hannah squinted out the window into the brightness of the morning.

Beth was charging across the lawn, her face pale, and her hair streaming out behind her.

"Hannah!" the little girl shouted. "Hannah! Mr. Smithers! Come quick! It's Mom! Something's happened to Mom!"

# 6

Carolyn opened her eyes, and for a moment thought she was in her room in the little house on Cherry Street. But that was impossible. She'd been on a trail below Hilltop, hiking with Beth. And then—

Then what? She searched in her mind for details, and as she probed the recesses of her memory, her eyes fixed on the ceiling of the little room.

A hospital room, painted the same pale green that her room on Cherry Street had always been.

Hospital green, Beth had always called it, and now Carolyn had to admit she was right.

Something in her mind clicked.

She'd fainted.

They had been on the path leading down from the mausoleum, and then they'd turned off to the left, along a steep side trail. After a few yards, they'd come to a little clearing, and while Beth explored, Carolyn had sat down to rest.

She'd been looking out over the village, enjoying the view, and then, gradually, she'd begun to notice something at the far side of town. It seemed to her that it had crept slowly into her consciousness, but then, as she'd become aware of it, she'd found herself staring at the mill.

It was burning.

Clouds of smoke were billowing from it, and flames licked out from the windows.

And even though the entire village separated her from the mill, she could hear screams, as if people were trapped inside. . . .

The memory seemed to wobble in her mind, and Carolyn found herself struggling to keep it in focus.

Struggling.

That was it.

She had struggled to her feet, and called out to Beth, and then the whole sky had seemed to turn black, as if smoke were covering it.

And she had felt dizzy.

After that, there were only fragments.

Beth, calling to her, begging her to wake up.

Then Hannah's face, a mask of worry, looming above her.

How had Hannah gotten there?

Then hands, lifting her, carrying her.

And now she was in the hospital.

For the first time since waking, she tried to move, and immediately felt a warm pressure on her hand.

"Don't, honey."

At the unexpected sound of a voice, the memories faded out of her mind.

Phillip's voice. Why hadn't she been aware that he was here? Had he been holding her hand all along? She turned her head slightly, and saw him, sitting by the bed, his blue eyes clouded with worry.

"Phillip? How . . . how did I get here? What happened?"

"You fainted. Hannah and Ben managed to get you back to the house, then had you brought down here."

"Hannah and Ben?" Carolyn repeated. "How did they—?"

"You helped. You were half-conscious, and you kept talking about a fire. They said you seemed to think there was a brush fire or something."

Carolyn frowned. "No . . . no, it was something

else." Her hand tightened on Phillip's. "It was the mill. I saw the mill burning."

"The mill? What on earth are you talking about?"

Carolyn hesitated. Now that she thought about it, it seemed much more like a memory from a dream than something that had actually happened. "I . . . I don't know. It was all so strange . . ." Her voice trailed off, and she glanced around the room. "Where's Beth?"

"Right outside," Phillip replied. "I'll get her."

A moment later her daughter appeared at the bedside, her eyes wide with worry. "Mom? Are you okay? I . . . I was afraid you'd—"

"Died?" Carolyn chuckled, managing to lend her voice a strength she didn't feel. "Not quite yet. Your old mother has a few more years in her." She smiled, and hitched herself a little higher in the hospital bed. "But let me tell you, if that's your idea of a fun little hike, you can get somebody else to go next time."

Phillip's brows arched, and he winked at Beth. "Obviously she's feeling better. All of a sudden it's your fault."

Carolyn twisted her face into a grimace of comic indignation. "Well, you don't expect *me* to take the blame, do you? I'm the one who wound up in the hospital. The least the two of you can do is make sympathetic noises and tell me it wasn't my fault. Right?" she added, turning to her daughter.

"Oh, absolutely," Beth replied, nodding solemnly. "You were just standing there yelling at me, and pointing, so I thought, wouldn't it be fun to make Mother faint? And you fell right over."

"See?" Carolyn asked Phillip. "That's the kind of child every mother dreams of having." Then her expression turned serious. "Beth, did you see anything? Just before I fainted, did you see anything happening down in the village?"

Beth frowned uncertainly. "Like what?"

"Well, it was strange," Carolyn said. "I could have sworn that I saw the mill burning. You didn't see anything like that?"

Beth shook her head, then suddenly remembered what had happened up at the mausoleum before her mother had arrived. For a minute, while she'd been sitting in the marble chair, she *had* seen something like that. But before she could tell them about it, the door opened, and a doctor entered the room.

Phillip immediately rose to his feet, but the doctor waved him back into his chair, turning to Carolyn with a little smile playing around the corners of his mouth.

"Mrs. Sturgess," he asked, "you and your daughter wouldn't by any chance have been rabbit hunting this morning, would you?"

Carolyn blinked. Rabbit hunting? What on earth was he talking about?

"Because if you were, the hunt was a success. You've killed a rabbit. Or, if you haven't yet, I'm prepared to guarantee that you will."

Carolyn stared at the doctor, and slowly the light began to dawn. "You mean—I'm pregnant?"

"Congratulations. And to you too, Mr. Sturgess."

Phillip's eyes fixed on the doctor, then slowly shifted to his wife. "A baby?" he asked. "You and I are going to have a baby?"

Carolyn nodded, suddenly feeling almost stupidly happy. "That's what the man says," she said, grinning foolishly. "You know—little tiny critters, with ten little fingers, and ten little toes? Keep you up late at night? That's what he's talking about." Phillip looked dazed, and Carolyn's surge of happiness was suddenly tinged with fear. What if he—

But then his arms were around her, and he was hugging her close. "Who ever thought—I mean I just didn't think—we never even talked about it!" Suddenly he drew away, and his forehead creased with worry. "Honey, is it all right with you?"

Carolyn squeezed him hard. "Of course it's all right with me. I can't think of anything I'd rather do."

As Carolyn and Phillip gazed happily at each other, neither of them saw Beth slip quietly out of the room.

*        *        *

A baby.

The idea of her mother and Uncle Phillip having a baby had never occurred to her before, and as Beth left the little Westover hospital, walking slowly along Prospect Street, her eyes fixed on the sidewalk in front of her, she wasn't at all sure how she felt about it.

It was bad enough living at Hilltop already. What would happen when there was a baby there, too?

Her mother would spend all her time with the baby, and not have any time for her.

Which wasn't fair, and Beth knew it.

In fact, now that she thought about it, she knew that she'd always wanted to have a baby brother. Or a sister—it hadn't really mattered. But after her parents had gotten the divorce, she'd just sort of given up the idea.

And then, when Carolyn had married Phillip Sturgess, it had just never entered her head that her mother might have another baby.

Which was kind of a dumb thing to have thought, really. After all, lots of the kids in Westover had half-brothers and half-sisters. Why shouldn't she?

The more she thought about it, the more she liked the whole idea of it.

Suddenly she felt better, and looked up to see that she'd walked almost four blocks. In the next block, the mill stood, looking dark and threatening even in the noontime sun.

Beth stared at it for a few minutes, wondering what it was about the big old building that had always made her friends, especially the boys, talk about what might be inside it, and wonder what had really happened to the boy—Uncle Phillip's brother—who had died in there long before they had even been born.

To her, it was just an ugly building.

Or anyway it had been, up until this morning.

She started walking again, coming closer to the building, trying to figure out what the sun might have been reflecting off. But there didn't seem to be anything. The windows were boarded over, and so were

the massive doors, set back into the front of the building at the top of a short flight of stairs.

But she *had* seen something that morning, and so
had her mother.

Her mother had said it looked as if the building
were on fire.

She stepped back, tipping her head up to gaze
toward the roof line. As she reached the edge of the
sidewalk, she bumped into a car.

Her father's car.

But her father's office was several blocks away.
Why was his car here? She scanned the street, but saw
nothing.

Puzzled, she stared once more at the mill.

Could her father be inside?

She trotted up the steps, and carefully inspected
the boards over the front door. All of them were nailed
tight, and there didn't seem to her to be any way to get
in.

And yet, even as she stood there, she could almost
feel that the mill wasn't empty.

Her father *had* to be inside.

She went back down the steps, and turned toward
River Road. On that side of the building, she knew,
there was another door—a big metal door—and she knew
there was a padlock on it. Since she'd been six years
old, every week at least one of the kids she knew had
come down to check, always hoping that maybe this
time, someone had left the lock open.

She came to the corner of the building, and looked
down the long brick wall.

Halfway down to the railroad tracks, the door stood
open.

She broke into a run, and a moment later stood in
the doorway, gazing into the gloomy interior of the
abandoned factory.

The silence of the building seemed to gather around
her, and slowly Beth felt the beginnings of fear.

And then she began to feel something else.

Once again, she felt that strange certainty that the mill was not empty.

"D-Daddy?" she called softly, stepping through the door. "Are you here?"

She felt a slight trickle of sweat begin to slide down her spine, and fought a sudden trembling in her knees.

Then, as she listened to the silence, she heard something.

A rustling sound, from up above.

Beth froze, her heart pounding.

And then she heard it again.

She looked up.

With a sudden burst of flapping wings, a pigeon took off from one of the rafters, circled, then soared out through a gap between the boards over one of the windows.

Beth stood still, waiting for her heartbeat to calm. As she looked around, her eyes fixed on the top of a stairwell at the far end of the building.

He was downstairs. That's why he hadn't heard her. He was down in the basement.

Resolutely, she started across the vast emptiness of the building. As she reached the middle of the floor, she felt suddenly exposed, and had an urge to run.

But there was nothing to be afraid of. There was nothing in the mill except herself, and some birds.

And downstairs, her father.

After what seemed like an eternity, she reached the top of the stairs, and peered uncertainly into the darkness below.

Her own shadow preceded her down the steep flight of steps, and only a little light spilled over the staircase to illuminate the nearer parts of the vast basement.

"Daddy?" Beth whispered. But the sound was so quiet, even she could barely hear it.

And then there was something else, coming on the heels of her own voice.

Another sound, fainter than the one her own voice had made, coming from below.

Something was moving in the darkness.

Once again Beth's heart began to pound, but she
remained where she was, forcing back the panic that
threatened to overcome her.

Finally, when she heard nothing more, she moved
slowly down the steps, until she could place a foot on
the basement floor.

She listened, and after a moment, as the darkness
began closing in on her, the sound repeated itself.

Panic surged through her. All her instincts told her
to run, to flee back up the stairs and out into the
daylight. But when she tried to move, her legs refused
to obey her, and she remained where she was, paralyzed.

Once again the sound came. This time, though it
was almost inaudible, Beth thought she recognized a
word.

"Beeetthh . . ."

Her name. It was as if someone had called her
name.

"D-Daddy?" she whispered again. "Daddy, is that
you?"

There was another silence, and Beth strained once
more to see into the darkness surrounding her.

In the distance, barely visible, she thought she
could see a flickering of light.

And then she froze, her voice strangling as the
sound came again, like a winter wind sighing in the
trees.

"Aaaammmyyy . . ."

Beth gazed fearfully into the blackness for several
long seconds. Then, when the sound was not repeated,
her panic began to subside. At last she was able to
speak again, though her voice still trembled. "Is someone there?"

In the far distance, the light flickered again, and
she heard something else.

Footsteps, approaching out of the darkness.

The seconds crept by, and the light bobbed nearer.

And once more, the whispering voice, barely audible, danced around her.

"Aaaammmyyy . . ."

"D-Daddy?" Beth called once more, her fear surging back. "Daddy, is that you?"

The light stopped moving, and for a moment Beth felt a flash of fear. What if it wasn't her father? What if it was someone else?

And then, at last, she heard it.

"Beth? Honey? What are you doing here?"

Beth ran toward the light, and threw herself into her father's arms.

"Daddy! I—for a second, I was afraid it wasn't you!"

"Sweetheart! What are you doing here?" Alan asked again. He loosened himself from his daughter's grip, then began leading her back toward the stairs.

"I was walking home from the hospital, and I saw your car," Beth began, her voice still quavering. But Alan interrupted her.

"The hospital? What were you doing at the hospital?"

Beth's eyes widened in the darkness, and for a moment she wondered what she should say. But before she could make up her mind, she had blurted out the truth.

"It was Mom. We were hiking, and all of a sudden she fainted. She . . . she's going to have a baby!"

There was a momentary silence, and then Alan said quietly, "Well, how about that. You finally get your wish."

They were at the bottom of the stairs now, and he switched off the flashlight. In the dim light that filtered down the stairwell, he looked into his daughter's face. But instead of the happiness he had been expecting to see, there was something else. "Hey! You always wanted a baby brother or sister. Aren't you happy about your mom being pregnant?"

Beth hesitated, then seemed to come out of a reverie. But when she spoke, she wasn't looking at him. Instead, her eyes were fixed on a spot somewhere in the darkness beneath the stairs. "I . . . I guess I'm glad," she said, but Alan was sure she wasn't thinking about what she was saying.

"Beth?" he asked now. "Honey, what is it? Is something wrong?"

Beth shook her head uncertainly. "I don't know. I just—I thought I heard something—"

"Down here?" Alan started up the stairs, and Beth, almost reluctantly, followed.

"Unh-hunh. It was like a . . . a voice. Only not really, you know?"

"No," Alan chuckled. "I don't know. It was probably just a mouse or something."

Beth stopped, shaking her head, and turned back to peer once again down into the darkness of the basement.

And then, barely audible, she could hear it again.

A chill passed through her, and she concentrated, straining her ears.

"Don't you hear it, Daddy?" she asked. "Don't you hear it at all?"

Alan paused, and turned back.

For the last hour, he'd heard all kinds of noises in the basement of the mill.

Rats had scrambled out of his way as he'd poked around the foundations of the building, and at least once a snake had slithered over his hand. That time, he'd clearly heard his own muffled yelp of sudden fright.

Now he listened again, but there was nothing. "Sorry, hon. I don't hear a thing."

But still Beth hesitated, frowning deeply.

It had been there. She knew it had.

It was a voice, and it was calling out to her.

Why couldn't her father hear it?

And then, slowly, she realized what the answer was.

He couldn't hear it, because he wasn't supposed to.

The voice was calling out only to her.

A chill passed through her, and her skin suddenly felt as if something were crawling over it.

She knew she was right.

In the darkness of the basement, something had reached out and touched her.

Something in the blackness wanted her.

She had no idea what was in the basement, and part of her hoped never to find out. But another part of her felt a faint twinge of curiosity. That part of her, indeed, wanted to go back, wanted to plunge back into the darkness, and discover what was there.

She hesitated, struggling with that part of her that wanted to go back into the blackness. But the moment was gone. Her father had already turned away, going on up the stairs.

She followed him, her feet carrying her slowly, for the memory of what had happened filled her mind.

There was something there, something that wanted her.

Something that chilled her to the depths of her soul.

She hurried up the stairs after her father, catching up with him halfway across the great empty building.

"Take a good look at it," she heard him say just before they stepped out into the sunlight. "It won't look like this much longer."

Beth looked up at her father. "It won't? How come?"

Alan grinned happily. "You mean your mom didn't tell you?"

Beth frowned. "Tell me what?"

"We're going to reopen this place. Starting tomorrow, I'm going to begin partitioning it off, and putting in skylights, and sandblasting it, and by the end of the summer, it's going to be open and functioning again. We're turning it into a shopping mall."

Beth turned and stared back into the gloomy depths of the building.

She tried to picture the dark, cavernous mill as her father had just described it, but she couldn't.

Instead, her mind filled with the voice she had heard in the basement, and from deep in some part of her being she could not identify, a terrible knowledge surfaced. It was then Beth knew that what her father was saying was wrong.

They mustn't change the mill. Not ever.

For some reason she didn't yet understand, the mill should stay just as it was.

Abandoned, and empty.

But it wasn't empty, not really.

In the basement, somewhere under the stairs, something lived.

# 7

"I'm fine," Carolyn Sturgess insisted, gazing at her husband fondly, but with just a touch of annoyance. "This is all a bit ridiculous."

Phillip merely leaned down to adjust one of the pillows, and brushed her forehead with his lips. "It's not ridiculous. You heard what Dr. Blanchard said."

"Of course I heard what he said," Carolyn groused. "He said I should take it easy, which I fully intend to do. And I'm perfectly willing to admit that I probably shouldn't have gone blundering through the underbrush, given my condition. But I didn't know about my condition, did I?"

"No, you didn't," Phillip agreed. "But now you do, and I intend to see to it that you don't go against doctor's orders."

Carolyn glanced around the big bedroom, and fleetingly wondered if Phillip really intended her simply to lie here for the next seven months, forcing Hannah to carry her meals up the stairs three times a day. But of course, she realized, he wouldn't intend that at all.

He'd bring the meals himself.

And an ambulance to bring her home from the hospital. That, too, was just like Phillip.

She'd felt perfectly capable of walking out of the hospital, getting into the car, and driving herself home, but Phillip had insisted on a wheelchair and an ambulance, and it had been easier to give in than to argue with him.

Once they'd arrived at Hilltop, though, she'd wished she *had* argued, for there was Alan, just leaving the house after driving Beth home. The look of concern on his face when he'd first seen her had quickly given way to amusement, and she'd waited for him to make some allusion to *Camille* or *Wuthering Heights*. The fact that he'd confined himself to an arched eyebrow hadn't made her feel any less foolish.

Now, she looked up at Phillip and shook her head. "I won't do it, you know. You can't stand guard over me through an entire pregnancy, and as soon as your back is turned, I'll be up and about my business. All that happened was that I fainted. Even Dr. Blanchard didn't think I was in any danger of losing the baby."

"We're not going to take any chances—" Phillip protested, but Carolyn didn't let him finish.

"I don't intend to take any chances," she insisted. "If I'd known I was pregnant, I wouldn't have gone with Beth." Then she narrowed her eyes mischievously. "Or are you trying to say that I'm too old to be having a baby?"

Phillip reddened. "I didn't mean—"

"Of course you didn't," Carolyn broke in, suddenly unable to contain her laughter any longer. "It's all just too silly, darling. I'm starting to feel like I'm stuck in a movie or something. I keep expecting you to start using phrases like 'in a family way' or refer to my 'delicate condition.' It's just all so Victorian, that's all."

"I suppose we should expect you to feel that way," another voice said, and Carolyn looked up to see Abigail Sturgess standing in the doorway. "But after what happened to our dear Lorraine, you can't really blame Phillip for being concerned, can you?"

Carolyn's mouth tightened in anger as she saw the misery that came over Phillip's face, and she reached out to take his hand in her own. "I know you're concerned for me, Abigail," she said smoothly. "But I have no intention of losing the baby, or of dying in delivery."

"Of course not," Abigail agreed, her thin lips curving in a cool smile. "And you needn't worry about anything. I shall see to it that everything in the house runs exactly as it should."

For a moment the two women's eyes met, and then Carolyn sighed, and allowed herself to sink into the pillows. "I'm sure you will, Abigail," she said softly. "I'm sure you'll run everything exactly as Lorraine would have wanted it." Through eyes that were nearly closed, she saw the old woman watching her, and felt for a moment like a mouse being examined by a coiled cobra. But then, her appetite apparently satisfied for the moment, Abigail turned, and stiffly left the room. Only when Carolyn was sure that Abigail was out of earshot did she speak again.

"I'm sorry, Phillip. I shouldn't have mentioned Lorraine."

Her husband's forehead wrinkled into a sympathetic frown. "She's the one who brought Lorraine up, not you. Now, just get some rest, and don't worry about anything. Promise?"

"I promise. And you have to promise not to start mother-henning me. Hannah's perfectly capable of doing that."

As if to prove the point, the old housekeeper elbowed the door open, then came into the room, a pot of tea balanced on a bed tray. "See?" Carolyn asked, then hitched herself back into a sitting position as Hannah set the tray over her legs. "Thank you, Hannah. But please don't start treating me as if I'm sick."

"Who says you're sick?" Hannah retorted. "Being pregnant and being sick are two different things—despite what some people think. But a nice pot of tea never hurt anybody." She poured two cups, and handed one to Phillip. "And as for Miss Tracy's party, I don't want you to worry about anything. I can take care of it all. Although I must say," she added, making no attempt to keep the grumpiness out of her voice, "changing it from

Sunday to Saturday isn't going to make my life any easier."

"Changing it?" Carolyn asked. "Hannah, what on earth are you talking about?"

Hannah peered at Carolyn for a moment; then her eyes narrowed slightly. "You mean Mrs. Sturgess didn't talk to you about it?"

"She hasn't talked to me about anything," Carolyn replied.

"But Miss Tracy said—" Hannah began, then abruptly fell silent, her lips closing tightly.

"Said what, Hannah?" Phillip urged. "It's all right. What did Tracy say?"

"I don't like to talk out of turn," Hannah mumbled. She busied herself refolding the already perfectly folded bedspread.

Phillip opened his mouth to speak again, but Carolyn held up a restraining hand. "Hannah, telling us about a change in Tracy's birthday plans is hardly speaking out of turn. Now, what is this about changing the party from Sunday to Saturday?"

Hannah hesitated, then repeated what Tracy had said in the kitchen that morning. "She told me that Mrs. Sturgess was going to talk to you," she finished. "It just must have been forgotten in all the excitement. Now, if there's nothing else, I'd better get back to my kitchen."

She bustled out of the room. Neither Carolyn nor Phillip said a word for a moment. Finally Phillip spoke.

"Did Mother talk to you about switching the party?"

"No," Carolyn replied. "She didn't."

"Well, I'm sure there was a reason for the change—" Phillip began, but fell silent as Carolyn pushed the tray to the foot of the bed and threw back the covers.

"There was a reason," she agreed, swinging her feet off the bed and getting shakily to her feet. "And I intend to put a stop to it right now."

Phillip set his teacup on the bed table, and rose to steady his wife. "Hey, take it easy. Whatever it is can wait. Let me deal with it."

"But it can't wait," Carolyn insisted. "And I have to deal with it myself." She began struggling into her robe, then met her husband's eyes. "Don't you see? There's a very simple reason why they changed the party, and why Abigail didn't tell me. Oh, I'm sure she would have—on Saturday morning, right after Beth left to spend the day with Alan!" Her eyes blazed with anger, and her mouth twisted into a parody of Abigail's supercilious smile. "I can hear her now: 'Oh, Carolyn dear, didn't I tell you? Tracy's party is going to be today. Such a pity Beth will miss it.' Only it's not going to happen that way!"

"You don't think—"

"Of course that's what I think, Phillip. And if you think about it, you'll know I'm right. Tracy doesn't want Beth at her party, and Abigail's figured out a way to give Tracy what she wants."

Now it was Phillip's eyes that glittered with anger. "I'll deal with Mother myself. In fact, I'll deal with both of them. This has all gone far enough." He turned and started out of the room, but Carolyn stopped him.

"No, Phillip. I've got to do it myself. What's happening in this house is between Abigail and me, and I can't hide behind you. Abigail will only see that as weakness, and hate me more than she already does."

"And what about Tracy? Isn't she part of it?"

"Tracy takes her lead from your mother. I'm not going to say a word to her about it. I'm going to let Abigail do that."

Phillip smiled. "It'll be the first time in years that Mother's had to go back on a promise to Tracy. Maybe it'll be good for both of them. But you're sure you don't want me to take care of it?" he added, his voice anxious. "You should be in bed."

"I'll be fine," Carolyn promised him. Tying the belt of her robe firmly around her waist, she left Phillip alone in the bedroom.

Carolyn found Abigail in the library, sitting placidly in a chair by the window, a book open on her lap.

The old woman glanced up, then, surprised, put the book aside.

"Why, Carolyn," she said. "Shouldn't you be in bed?"

"Perhaps I should," Carolyn replied. "But right now, I'm afraid you and I need to have a little talk, Abigail." For the first time in her memory, Carolyn saw uncertainty flicker in the old lady's eyes.

"I'm sure whatever it is can wait," Abigail began.

"No, it can't," Carolyn said softly. She closed the door behind her, then moved across the room to lower herself into the chair opposite her mother-in-law. "We'll talk now, Abigail."

"Very well," Abigail said. Her voice was chilly, but her eyes darted nervously toward the closed door. "And just what is it you'd like to discuss? The weather? It seems to be a nice afternoon—"

"Nice enough for a birthday party," Carolyn interrupted, matching the old lady's smile. "I do hope the weather holds until Sunday, don't you?"

Abigail's eyes widened for a split second, but then she recovered herself. "I meant to talk to you about that," she said. "But of course after what happened, I didn't want to worry you with something so petty."

"'Petty' does seem to be the right word, I suppose," Carolyn mused, letting her eyes drift around the room. For once, she knew, Abigail was on the defensive.

"I'm sure I don't know what you're talking about," Abigail replied, but her nervousness betrayed her.

"And I'm sure you do." Carolyn's eyes moved back to the old woman. Abigail sat stiffly in the armchair, her posture rigidly erect. "Abigail, all this has to stop. I know what you think of me, and I know what you think of Beth. But I am married to Phillip, and that's not going to change. I am also Tracy's stepmother, and I would like that to be a pleasant relationship for both her and myself. I'd appreciate it if you'd stop interfering."

Abigail expertly feigned puzzlement. "Carolyn, I don't know what all this is about, and I do wish you'd explain it to me. Whatever has happened, I'm sure we

can straighten it out. Now, why don't you just start at
the beginning—"

"No, Abigail. I've already taken care of it. I was
just in the kitchen, where I told Hannah that Tracy's
party will be on Sunday afternoon, as planned. I do
hope it won't inconvenience Tracy, having to call all her
friends again." Now Carolyn saw the cold fury in the
old woman's eyes, which Abigail made no attempt to
hide.

"Except that Tracy will not be calling them again,"
Abigail rasped. "The fact that I failed to mention the
change to you is my fault. There's no reason why Tracy
should suffer. All the plans have been made, and Hannah has everything under control. I really fail to see the
problem."

"The problem is that Beth will be with her father
on Saturday afternoon, as she always is. A fact both you
and Tracy are perfectly aware of."

"Are we?" Abigail replied, allowing her voice to
turn venomous. "I think you lend your child's activities
an importance they don't deserve, my dear."

Carolyn smiled benignly, betraying none of her
inner fury. "The same might be said of your attitude
about Tracy, Abigail. At any rate, that's not the issue.
The fact of the matter is simply this: Tracy's party will
take place on Sunday afternoon, or it will not take place
at all."

Abigail's eyes flashed with pure hatred now. "If
that's what you and Phillip have decided, I'm sure
there's nothing I can do about it," she said. "Perhaps
you'd better tell Tracy about the change in plans. I
believe she's outside playing tennis."

"I'll tell her," Carolyn replied. "And I'll be sure to
be as careful about telling her as you were about telling
me."

"I had intended to tell you!" Abigail fumed.

"All right," Carolyn sighed. "Have it your own
way, if it's so important to you. But you're wasting your
time, and making life harder for all of us."

"Am I?" Abigail asked, her voice icy. She rose to

her feet and, grasping her cane, started toward the
French doors. "Perhaps I am. But perhaps I'm not. I
don't know why Phillip married you, Carolyn, but I do
know that he is still my son, and still a Sturgess. In
time, he will come to his senses. As to the party, I shall
explain things to Tracy myself, and we shall deal with
the situation. And hereafter, I shall do my best to
protect Tracy, and bring her up in a manner of which
Lorraine would approve." Leaving Carolyn still sitting
in her chair, Abigail swept regally out of the room.

*But she's dead*, Carolyn wanted to scream. *Don't
you understand that Lorraine is dead?* But, of course,
it wasn't Lorraine at all. It was Abigail herself, desperately trying to hang on to a way of life that had all but
disappeared. Carolyn sighed once more, feeling suddenly worn out. She allowed herself to sink deeper into
the chair.

Like so much of the furniture in the old house, the
overstuffed wing chair needed reupholstering. Nothing
had been repaired or refurbished here for years, for
Abigail refused to see how threadbare it had all become. The old woman saw only the splendor of her
youth, when the house had been staffed by a butler,
five maids, a cook, and a gardening staff.

Now all that was left were Hannah and Ben
Smithers, who did their best to cope with all the work
that had to be done, aided occasionally by a few people
who came in part-time when things could be put off no
longer.

But Abigail wouldn't see it. Sometimes, as now,
when she was feeling dispirited by the constant battle,
Carolyn thought that nothing would change until the
day Abigail finally died.

And sometimes Carolyn was certain that Abigail
would live forever.

Abigail flung open the French doors, stepped out
onto the terrace, and looked down toward the tennis
court, where Tracy, dressed in spotless whites, was
playing with Alison Babcock. Abigail watched the game

for a few minutes, remembering the days before concrete courts, when the young ladies and gentlemen of her own generation had played genteel lawn tennis here—days long ago that Abigail still missed sorely. How much more civilized life had been then. Life went on, some things never changed. That was what Carolyn would never understand. She would never understand that being a Sturgess was something special, with rights and privileges that had to be protected. To Carolyn, the Sturgesses were just like anyone else.

Abigail knew better, and always had.

And Tracy knew it, too.

The game ended, and Tracy, grinning joyfully, was running toward her.

"Three sets, Grandmother," she crowed. "I won three straight sets!"

"Good for you," Abigail told her. "Why don't I have Hannah bring us some lemonade, and we can sit for a while?"

Tracy's face immediately crumpled. "But Alison and I wanted to go to the club. Her mom's picking us up."

"Well, I'm sure a few minutes won't matter, and I want to talk to you about something."

"What?" Tracy asked. "Why can't we talk about it later?"

"Because I think we'd better talk about it now," Abigail replied in a tone that warned Tracy not to push her luck too far. Reluctantly, the girl accompanied her grandmother to a small wrought-iron table surrounded by four chairs, and sat down.

"I'm afraid our little plan didn't work out quite the way we intended," Abigail began. "Carolyn has changed your party back to Sunday."

Tracy's eyes flared dangerously. "But she can't do that! I've already told everyone it's Saturday!"

"I know, and I'm sorry," Abigail replied. "But there doesn't seem to be anything we can do. Beth is going to be here. And," she added, smiling tightly, "I

shall expect you and your friends to treat her exactly as
I would myself."

Tracy's eyes clouded threateningly, but then, as
she began to understand, a smile spread over her face.
"We will, Grandmother," she replied. A horn sounded
from the front of the house, and Tracy leaped to her
feet. "Is it okay if I go now, Grandmother?"

"Of course," Abigail replied. Tracy bent over, and
the old woman gave her a quick peck on the cheek.
"You have a good time, and don't worry about the
party. I'm sure you know exactly what to do."

When Tracy was gone, Abigail suddenly had a
sense of being watched, and turned.

Standing at the French doors, looking at her
thoughtfully, was Carolyn.

It doesn't matter, Abigail told herself. Even if she
heard, she won't know what I was telling the child. The
woman doesn't even speak our language.


Beth retreated to her room right after dinner that
evening. The meal itself had been horrible—her mother
hadn't come down at all, and she'd had to sit at the
table, picking at her food, while Tracy glared at her and
old Mrs. Sturgess ignored her. Uncle Phillip had been
nice to her, but every time he started to talk to her,
Tracy had interrupted him. Finally, pretending that she
didn't feel well, she'd asked to be excused.

Now she lay sprawled on her bed, trying to read a
book, the radio playing softly in the background. Suddenly there was a knock at the door, and Beth rolled
over and guiltily switched the radio off. A second later
the door opened. With relief, Beth saw that it was not
Tracy this time.

Phillip stuck his head inside. "Okay if I come in?"

Beth nodded. "I'm sorry the radio was too loud. I
didn't think anyone could hear it."

Phillip's brow knit into a frown. "It isn't even on, is
it?"

"I turned it off. I was afraid Tracy—" Then she fell
silent, suddenly embarrassed.

"Tracy's downstairs, listening to the stereo in the music room," Phillip replied. "If you want the radio on, turn it on."

"I don't want to bother anyone."

Phillip hesitated, then crossed the room and sat on the edge of the bed. "How come it's not all right for you to bother anyone, but it's all right for everyone else to bother you?"

Beth regarded her stepfather shyly. "But it's Tracy's house."

"It's your house too, Beth," Phillip told her. "And it seems to me you ought to be sticking up for yourself a little more. Your mother can't fight all your battles for you."

Beth looked away, then felt Phillip's hand on her shoulder. She started to pull away, but couldn't. Finally she turned to face him again. "I . . . I just don't know what to do," she said. "I want to do the right thing, but all that ever happens is that I mess it up. Like this morning, down at the stable."

"All that happened down there was that you didn't know what you were doing. And whatever Tracy might have said, there wasn't any harm done. In fact, I'll bet Patches was happy to get out of the stall, even if it was only for a couple of minutes. Most of the time, all she does is just stand there." He smiled reassuringly. "Would you like to learn how to ride her?"

Beth's eyes widened eagerly. "Could I?"

"I don't see why not. In fact, if you want to, we could go out tomorrow morning. We can both get up early and have breakfast with Hannah, and be back before anyone else even knows we're gone. What do you say?"

"That would be neat!"

"Then it's a date," Phillip said. He stood up, and started toward the door. "And for God's sake, turn the radio back on. This place is too big, and too quiet." Then he was gone, and Beth was alone again.

She switched the radio back on, then flopped over onto her back, staring up at the ceiling. Suddenly, for the first time since Tracy had come home, she felt a little better. Maybe if Uncle Phillip really would teach her to ride . . .

With the radio playing softly, she drifted into sleep.

When she woke up, the dream was still clear in her mind.

She lay still, thinking about it, reliving it, then rolled over to switch off the radio that was still humming softly on the nightstand.

She had been back in the mill, but it hadn't been at all the way she remembered it from this afternoon.

Instead, it had been filled with people working at all kinds of machinery she'd never seen before. But they hadn't seemed to be able to see her, and she'd wandered around for a long time, watching them work.

And then, faintly, she'd heard someone calling to her. The voice had been muffled at first, and she'd barely been able to hear it. But as she'd wandered toward the back of the building, the voice had grown stronger. She'd suddenly realized that it was coming from downstairs.

She'd gone to the top of the stairs, and listened, hearing faintly but distinctly, the voice, calling to her again.

But then, as she'd started down the stairs, a hand had fallen on her shoulder.

"You can't go down there," a man's voice said.

She had stared up into the face of the man, and realized that he looked strangely familiar. His hair was iron gray and there was a hardness in his eyes that frightened her.

"But I have to," she'd protested weakly. "Someone's calling me."

"You can't go down there," the man had said again.

Then the voice had called to Beth again, and she'd struggled with the man, trying to twist away from his grip. But it hadn't done any good. The man's hands had only tightened on her, and begun dragging her away from the stairs.

And then, with the voice from the basement still ringing in her ears, she'd awakened.

Now, in the silence of the room, with the darkness of the night gathered around her, she could almost hear the voice again, still calling to her, even though she was awake.

She got up from the bed, and went to the window, peering out into the night.

A full moon hung in the sky, and the village, its lights twinkling, lay spread out below. In the distance, almost lost in the darkness, was the dark silhouette of the mill.

Beth waited, half-expecting to see the same strange light glowing from it that she'd seen from the mausoleum this morning, but tonight there was nothing.

She watched for several long minutes, then finally turned away and began undressing. But when she finally slipped under the covers and closed her eyes, the memory of the dream came back to her once more. Once more she heard the strange voice calling out to her, a strangled, needy cry.

"Beeettthhh. Beeettthhh . . ."

And in the depths of her memory, the same voice echoed back, calling out the other word, the word she had seemed to hear in the mill that afternoon.

"Aaaaammmyyy . . ."

Amy.

Amy was calling to her. Amy needed her.

But who was Amy?

As Beth tossed in her bed, trying to fall back into sleep, she knew that somehow she would have to go back to the mill. She had to find out.

# 8

Tracy Sturgess woke up early on Sunday morning, her eyes going immediately to the open window.

Outside, the day was bright and sunny, without a cloud in the sky. That meant they'd be able to play tennis and croquet that afternoon, two games Tracy was an expert at and that Beth Rogers could barely play at all.

Tracy smiled to herself as she thought about it. She could picture Beth now, clumsily running around the tennis court—barely able to return a serve—while the rest of them watched, clucking sympathetically while they tried to keep from giggling out loud. Maybe they'd even play doubles, and Tracy would get Alison Babcock to be Beth's partner. Alison was almost as good at tennis as Tracy herself, and the two of them had already planned it out. Alison would act as if she was going for the ball, then step aside at the last minute, telling Beth that she was only giving her more room. And Beth, not knowing what was going on, would keep on trying harder, and it would get funnier and funnier. And the best part of it was that even if Carolyn was watching, she wouldn't be able to do anything about it, because it would look like they were all doing their best to help Beth have a good time.

Tracy stretched, then lazily got out of bed and

wandered over to the window to look out onto the grounds. On the lawn, Ben was setting up the croquet court, laboriously studying a book, then measuring the distances with a tape measure. Tracy had insisted on an English court, with a single stake in the center and six wickets arranged around it. She and Alison had planned this, too, then practiced the unfamiliar layout with Jeff Bailey and Kip Braithwaite. Tracy could hardly wait until she saw the look on Beth's face, particularly when Beth had to ask how the game was played.

"Oh," she'd say, pretending to be surprised. "I thought you said you knew—" And then she'd pretend she'd suddenly remembered, and offer Beth her best sympathetic expression. "You meant the *American* game, didn't you? None of us plays that." Then, while Beth squirmed in embarrassment, and her friends looked politely bored, she'd carefully explain to Beth the sequence of the wickets, graciously allowing her to go first.

And then, of course, all the rest of them would use Beth's ball to get around the court fast.

As Ben placed the last wicket into the lawn, Tracy's eyes wandered down toward the stable, and suddenly her happy mood vanished. Her father and Beth were in the paddock, saddling Patches. Next to Patches, already saddled, was her father's favorite horse, an enormous black Arabian gelding named Sheik.

Tracy's chin trembled with fury. She turned from the window and began struggling into a pair of jeans and one of her father's old shirts. Ignoring the tangled mess of her hair, she slammed out of her room, and started toward the stairs.

"Tracy?" she heard her grandmother call from the far end of the corridor. "Tracy, darling, what on earth is wrong? Where are you going?"

Tracy spun around, her eyes glittering with anger. "He's doing it again! He's down in the paddock with her, and he's going to let her ride my horse again!"

Abigail, framed in the door of her room, frowned

in puzzlement. "Peter?" she asked. "But I thought you'd told him not to let Beth anywhere near the stable."

"I did. But it's not Peter—it's Father! He's down there with her, and he's going to take her riding. Just like day before yesterday!"

Abigail's brows arched, and she started toward Tracy, but Tracy had already turned away. And then, when Abigail was halfway to the landing, she heard a muffled thump and a scream. Hurrying forward, she reached the landing, and peered down over the railing.

Near the bottom of the stairs, Carolyn sat nearly doubled over, clutching herself in pain, while Tracy glared at her furiously.

"What were you doing there?" she heard Tracy demand. "You could see me coming down! Why didn't you get out of my way?"

"And you could see me, too, couldn't you?" Carolyn replied. "If you hadn't been running, it wouldn't have happened at all."

"I can run if I want to," Tracy said, fixing a malevolent stare on Carolyn now. "And you can't stop me! You'd better just watch where you're going."

Carolyn pulled herself painfully to her feet, then reached out and grasped Tracy's wrist just as the girl began to turn away. When she spoke again, her voice was level, but carried an edge that made Tracy turn back and face her.

"That will be quite enough, young lady. You may be thirteen years old today, but you're not so old that I can't turn you over my knee and give you a good spanking. I've put up with just about as much from you as I intend to tolerate, and I suggest you think long and hard before you speak to me again that way. Me, or anyone else. And as for running up and down the stairs, I don't really care if you do it or not, so long as you don't run into people. You could have hurt me very badly, you know. You might even have made me lose my baby."

Tracy's mouth quivered, and she suddenly twisted loose from Carolyn's grip. "I wish I *had* hurt you," she hissed. "I wish I'd killed you and your baby, too!" Then she spun around. She charged through the French doors at the rear of the foyer, and dashed across the lawn to push her way through the hedge to the paddock. But when she got there, it was too late.

The paddock was empty.

Carolyn, shocked at the hatred in Tracy's voice, sank back down onto the stairs, burying her face in her hands.

Abigail remained where she was, watching her daughter-in-law silently. After nearly a minute had passed, she spoke.

"Carolyn? Carolyn, are you all right?"

Carolyn stiffened, then looked up to see Abigail gazing down at her from the landing above. She managed a weak smile, and got once more to her feet. "I'm all right, Abigail. I just had a bad moment, that's all."

The old woman's lips curved into a tight line of disapproval. "I thought I heard a scream. You didn't fall, did you?"

Carolyn hesitated, then shook her head. "No. No, I'm really perfectly all right."

"Perhaps you're trying to do too much," Abigail suggested, her voice taking on the slight purring quality that Carolyn had long since learned to recognize as a danger signal. "Why don't you spend the rest of the day in your room? After all, you'd never forgive yourself if something happened to the baby, would you? And I hate to think how Phillip would feel."

*She heard!* Carolyn suddenly knew. *She heard every word we said!* And she doesn't care. She knows what happened, and what could have happened, and she won't say a word to Tracy, or a word to Phillip. She feels the same way as Tracy. She hopes I lose my baby.

Her heart was thumping now, and when she spoke she had to make an effort to keep her voice from trembling. "But nothing's going to happen to my baby, Abigail. It's going to be perfectly all right."

The two women gazed at each other for a moment;

then, at last, Abigail turned away, and started slowly
back down the corridor toward her rooms.

Only when she was gone did Carolyn gingerly
touch her abdomen once more, hoping to feel a movement that would tell her the baby was all right.

But it was too early to expect any movement from
the life within her, and finally she moved painfully
across the wide entry hall to the telephone and called
the hospital. Despite the fact of Tracy's party that afternoon, she made an appointment to see Dr. Blanchard
at two o'clock.

Phillip and Beth dismounted, and Beth carefully
tied Patches's reins to a low branch before flopping
down onto the soft grass of the little meadow. Then she
sat up, and looked around, remembering the last time
she'd been here.

"This is where Mom fainted, Uncle Phillip. Right
over there by that big rock."

Phillip's eyes followed Beth's pointing arm, then
he stood up and wandered over to the rock on which
Carolyn had been sitting that morning a few days earlier. A moment later Beth was beside him. "Remember
what Mom said that morning? About it looking like the
mill was on fire?"

Phillip glanced down at Beth, nodding. "And she
asked you if you'd seen the same thing."

"And I did," Beth said, her voice suddenly shy.
"At least, I think I did." Slowly, trying to reconstruct
the memory, she told Phillip what she'd seen that day
from up at the mausoleum. "I thought it was an optical
illusion at first," she said when she was finished. "But
Mom saw the same thing."

"Maybe you both saw an illusion," Phillip replied.
"From up here, the sun can play funny tricks on you. It
reflects off the roof of one building and lights up another. And sometimes when it catches the windows just
right, it looks as though the whole village is on fire."

"But it wasn't the whole village," Beth protested.
"It was just the mill. And it couldn't have been reflec-

tions, because all the windows at the mill are boarded up."

Phillip nodded thoughtfully, and looked once more at the old building at the far side of the town. Already it had changed. The boards were torn away from the windows now, and scaffolding had been constructed around it. Already the sandblasting had begun, and here and there areas of bright red brick were beginning to show through the thick layers of grime that had built up over the decades. In his mind's eye, Phillip began to picture the mill as it would be in a few more months, with shutters softening the stark rows of evenly spaced windows, a porte cochere extending from the front entrance out over the sidewalk, and wrought-iron tracery decorating the roof line.

"How come it was closed?" he suddenly heard Beth ask. He glanced down once more, and saw her looking back at him with earnest curiosity.

"Economics," he replied. "The place just wasn't making any money anymore."

"But what about all the stories?" Beth pressed.

"What stories are those?" Phillip countered, though he was fairly certain he knew.

"About the children that used to work there. I thought something happened, and they made your family close it up."

"Well, those stories certainly aren't anything new, are they? I've heard them all my life. And I suppose there's some truth to them, too."

"You mean children really did work in the mill?"

"Absolutely. And it wasn't just this mill, either. There were mills and factories all over the Northeast where children worked. And it wasn't much fun, either. Most of the children your age had to work as much as twelve hours a day, six days a week."

"Th-that's what Mom told me," Beth stammered. "And she said that a lot of the children died."

Phillip's eyes clouded slightly. "Yes, I suppose that's true, too. But it's all over now, isn't it? All that happened a hundred years ago."

But Beth didn't seem to be hearing him. Instead, she was once more looking out over the town. Even without following her gaze, Phillip knew that her eyes were fixed on the mill.

"Uncle Phillip? Did . . . did the mill ever catch on fire?"

"On fire?" Phillip echoed. "What on earth makes you think that?"

"It just—I don't know," Beth floundered. "I was just thinking about what Mom and I saw the other day, that's all."

"I thought we'd agreed that was just an optical illusion," Phillip said carefully.

"But what if it wasn't?" Beth asked. Her eyes brightened, and the beginnings of an eager smile came over her face. "What if we were sort of looking into the past? What if it did burn, and sometimes you can still see it?"

"Now, that," Phillip chuckled, "is a story I haven't heard before. How on earth did you come up with that one?"

"But what if it's true?" Beth pressed, ignoring her stepfather's question. "Could something like that happen?"

Phillip shrugged. "It depends on whom you ask, I suppose. If you ask me, I'd say no. But there are plenty of people who claim that whatever happens in a building never goes away. That's the whole idea of ghost stories, isn't it? That people die, but instead of going to heaven they stay around the place they died, scaring people?"

Beth fell silent, thinking about what Phillip had said. Was that what had happened to her the other day? Was that what she had heard? A ghost?

Beth didn't believe in ghosts.

Still, she'd heard something in the mill, and she had seen something from the mausoleum that same day.

And there was the dream, too. . . .

She turned away from the view of the town, and

wandered back into the meadow. From the tree where she was tied, Patches whinnied softly, and pawed at the ground. Beth started across the meadow toward the horse, then stopped as something caught the corner of her eye.

She looked around, and frowned slightly.

A few yards away, a small depression, almost barren of the lush grass that filled the rest of the meadow, dipped slightly below the clearing's floor. In the morning light, it almost looked as if the grass on that spot had been burned away.

And from where she stood, the spot looked exactly like a grave.

Suddenly she became conscious of her stepfather standing next to her.

"Beth? What is it?"

"Over there," Beth said, pointing. "What's that?"

Phillip's eyes scanned the meadow, but he saw nothing unusual. It looked exactly as it had always looked. "What?" he asked.

Beth hesitated, then shook her head. "Nothing," she replied as she untied Patches and remounted the big mare. "I just thought I saw something, that's all." Then she grinned. "It must have been another optical illusion."

"Either that," Phillip laughed, "or you're seeing things. Come on. We don't want to be too long, or you'll be late for Tracy's party." He swung easily up onto the Arabian, and cantered out of the meadow onto the trail that led around the hillside to the paddock. But before Beth followed him, she looked once more around the little meadow.

The strangely sunken area was still there, and the more she looked at it, the more certain she became that it was, indeed, a grave.

And in her own mind, she decided whose grave it was.

It was Amy's grave.

By the time lunch began, Beth wished the floor would open up, and she could just fall through.

It had begun after she'd spent almost an hour trying to decide what to wear for the party, and finally settled on a green dress that she'd found in the thrift shop almost a year ago. Now, of course, she never shopped at the thrift shop, but she missed it. The thrift shop was an adventure. You never knew what you were going to find there, and she and her mother used to spend hours rummaging around, looking for things they wouldn't have been able to afford new. The green dress had been one of their best discoveries. It had been almost new, and her mother had had it cleaned and pressed, and then they'd put it away for a special occasion. And today, Beth had decided, was the special occasion.

But when she'd gone downstairs after all Tracy's friends had arrived, she'd realized her mistake.

All the other kids, Tracy included, were dressed in jeans and Lacoste shirts.

Beth had burned with humiliation as Tracy had eyed the dress scornfully, then said, "I guess I should have told you it was informal, shouldn't I? I mean, how could you have known?" Beth had flinched at the slight stress on the word "you," but said nothing.

Then Tracy began making introductions, and Beth squirmed miserably as Tracy's friends asked her questions that weren't really quite questions.

"You go to school right here in Westover? How can you *stand* it?"

"Where do you go during the summer? My family's always in Maine, but it gets *sooo* boring up there, don't you think?"

"You mean you've never *been* to Maine? I thought *every*body went to Maine."

"How come you never go to the country club? Everything else here is so tacky!"

It was a boy named Jeff Bailey who delivered the final blow. He looked at Beth with large blue eyes, and a smile on his face. "I like your dress," he said. Then his smile turned into a malicious grin. "I even liked it when my sister bought it three years ago."

That was when Beth had suddenly fled back upstairs and quickly changed her clothes, shoving the offending green dress back into a corner of the closet where she'd never have to see it again. Finally, after washing her face and recombing her hair, she'd gone back downstairs.

Tracy and her friends were playing croquet, and when they offered to start over again so she could play, she should have known what was going to happen.

Instead, she'd thought they were being nice to her.

Half an hour later, she had still not made it through the first wicket, and all the rest of them were finished.

"In croquet, you never want to go first," Tracy had told her after it was all over, then dropped her voice and glanced around to see if Carolyn was within earshot. "But you wouldn't know *that* either, would you?"

When they had asked her to play tennis, Beth had only shaken her head.

Now all she had to do was get through lunch and the movie Tracy had talked her father into getting for them, and it would all be over.

Tracy opened the curtains over the library windows, then turned and grinned maliciously at Beth. "You were scared, weren't you?" she asked.

"N-no," Beth replied, not quite truthfully. Even though she had kept telling herself it was only a movie, she *had* been scared. Horror movies always frightened her, no matter how much she told herself they weren't true.

"Well, I think you were," Tracy insisted. "If a silly old movie scares you so much, I don't see how you can stand to live in this house."

Beth frowned uncertainly. "What are you talking about? There isn't anything so scary about this house." That wasn't really true, but Beth wasn't about to admit that when she'd first moved into Hilltop, she'd spent several nights lying awake listening to the strange sounds that had seemed to fill the old house.

"Isn't there?" Tracy asked. "What about the ghost?"

Beth's frown smoothed out as she realized that Tracy just wanted her to look stupid again. "What ghost?" she asked, trying to make her voice as scornful as Tracy's.

"We're not sure." Tracy's voice took on a tone of smug self-importance, and she glanced at Alison Babcock. "But we think she's friendly. She's an old lady, dressed in black, and she prowls around the house late at night, looking for something."

"That's your grandmother," Beth ventured, but nobody laughed, and Tracy only shook her head.

"No, it's not," she replied. She turned to Jeff Bailey. "It isn't Grandmother, is it?"

"It didn't look like her to me," Jeff said, picking up the game. "She's real old, and her eyes are all sunken in, like she's blind or something. And she carries a candle," he added, in his most sepulchral tone.

"When did you see her?" Beth demanded.

"Last year," Jeff replied. "There were a bunch of us here for the weekend, and we all saw her. Isn't that right?"

Brett Kilpatrick nodded. "I saw her the same time Jeff did. She was in the upstairs hall, right by the top of the stairs. And when we spoke to her, she disappeared."

Beth looked around at the rest of Tracy's guests. All of them were nodding agreement and looking a little bit frightened. Maybe, after all, it was true. Then, slowly, an idea began to form in her mind. "Maybe . . . maybe she was looking for Amy," she said.

Tracy Sturgess's eyes clouded uncertainly. "Amy?" she repeated. "Who's Amy?"

"The ghost who lives in the mill," Beth replied, her confidence beginning to grow. "Don't you know about her?"

Tracy shook her head slowly, glancing at her friends out of the corner of her eyes. "Tell us about her."

Beth shrugged. "She's a little girl," she improvised. "And she's lived in the mill practically forever."

"Oh, sure," Jeff scoffed. "But have you ever seen her?"

Beth felt herself flush. "No," she admitted. "But . . . but I've heard her."

"Really?" Tracy asked. She was smirking now. "What did she say?"

"She said—" But before Beth could think of anything a ghost might have said, Jeff and Brett looked at each other and broke into loud laughter.

"She believes it!" Brett crowed. "She really believes there's a ghost in the mill."

As the boys' raucous whoops filled the room, Beth felt her face flush with humiliation once again. "Well, if there's a ghost here, why couldn't there be one in the mill?" she demanded, her face scarlet and her voice desperate as the laughter grew among Tracy's friends.

"Because there *isn't* any ghost here," Tracy said triumphantly. "I just made all that up! And you believed it, just like I thought you would. You really *are* stupid, aren't you?"

Beth stood up, her chin quivering. "Not as stupid as you and your dumb friends, Tracy! There *is* a ghost in the mill, and I know who it is! And I'm leaving!"

"So leave," Tracy taunted, dropping the last vestige of politeness from her voice. "Who wants you here anyway?"

Beth fled from the room, intent on finding her mother.

And then she remembered.

Her mother had made an emergency appointment to go see Dr. Blanchard. Neither she nor even Uncle Phillip was home.

Her father.

She would go and see her father.

Tears welling from her eyes, she hurried out the front door, and started toward the driveway.

And then, as she came to the lawn, she remembered the trail leading down the hill.

It was a shortcut, and would get her to the village much faster. She ran across the lawn, and plunged through the brush until she came to the trail from the paddock, then hurried along to the path that led down the hill.

It was when she was halfway down the hill that the idea came to her.

She wouldn't go see her father after all. Instead, she would go to the mill, and find a way to get inside.

And once she was in the mill, she would find out if Amy was truly there or not.

But even as she started on her way again, she knew what she would find in the mill.

Amy would be there—because Beth wanted her to be there.

# 9

Jeff Bailey and Brett Kilpatrick presented an odd contrast as they walked along River Road. Though they were distant cousins, Jeff was blond and gangling, while Brett's thatch of dark curly hair gave the same clear evidence of Celtic descent as did his compact body. They were approaching the point at which River Road crossed the railroad tracks, where they would turn right, cross the trestle over the river, and head north toward their homes near the country club. It was the long way around from Hilltop, but neither of them had felt like taking the shortcut directly down the hillside to the river.

"How come she was even there?" Jeff asked, casually kicking a battered beer can that lay by the road. It arced into the air, then dropped back into the drainage ditch. "Tracy hates her."

"She lives there," Brett replied. "Tracy tried to switch the party, but her stepmother found out. She's sure a creep, isn't she?"

"She's a local—they're all like that." Jeff watched idly while Brett took careful aim on the beer can, then snickered when it rolled only a few feet ahead. "And you think you're going to make the soccer team next year?" At St. Francis Academy, where both of them spent nine months of each year, the soccer team was *the* team to be on.

Brett ignored the gibe. "Can you believe the dress she was wearing?" he asked, bringing the subject back to Beth Rogers. "It looked even uglier on her than it did on your sister. And when Tracy started telling that story about the ghost, and she *believed* her, I thought I was gonna piss my pants."

Jeff skidded down the shoulder into the ditch, and kicked the can neatly back up onto the road. Then, as they came to the railroad tracks, he glanced across the street, his eyes falling on the scaffold-covered walls of the mill.

"What about the ghost she claimed lives in there?" he asked.

"Give me a break," Brett groaned. "She was just trying to look smart. Or she's so dumb she really believes there's something in there."

Jeff eyed his friend, a mischievous grin playing around the corners of his mouth. "Want to go in and take a look?" he challenged.

Brett hesitated. All his life he'd heard stories about the mill, and he knew as well as everyone else in Westover that Mr. Sturgess's older brother had gotten killed in the building years earlier.

And according to Brett's father, no one had ever found out exactly what had happened to Con Sturgess. It was supposed to have been an accident, but everyone knew that old man Sturgess had always claimed it wasn't.

Then he saw Jeff watching him, a smirk on his face. Ignoring the knot of fear in his gut, he nodded. "Why not?" he asked, aiming one last kick at the battered can and missing completely. He followed Jeff down the tracks toward the back of the mill. "How do we get in?"

Jeff surveyed the building, then shrugged. "It's got to be a cinch. I bet they aren't even keeping it locked up."

Brett's eyes followed Jeff's, but he didn't feel nearly as confident as Jeff sounded. "What if someone catches us?"

"So what? All we're going to do is look around. What's the big deal? Besides, they're working on it, right?"

Brett nodded.

"So everybody pokes around buildings that are being restored. If anybody catches us, we'll just tell them we wanted to see what was going on. Come on."

They followed a spur from the main line that led to the long-abandoned loading dock at the rear of the mill, skirted around a pile of trash that had accumulated against the dock itself, then scrambled up to try the freight door. It was securely locked, as was the door to what had once been the dispatcher's office. After trying two more doors, they jumped off the dock, rounded the corner of the building, and started walking along a newly cleared path that paralleled the side of the building. Halfway to Prospect Street they came to the metal door that had always before been carefully locked.

Today the lock was open, hanging loosely from the hasp.

"See?" Jeff asked. "What'd I tell you? It's not even locked up. We can just walk in." He reached out and grasped the knob, then twisted it.

It turned easily.

"H-how *come* it's not locked?" Brett asked, his voice dropping to a whisper. "S'pose someone's inside?"

Jeff's eyes raked him scornfully. "It's not locked because the workmen were too stupid to lock it," he said. He pushed the door open, and stepped through, but Brett still hung back. "You coming, or not?"

"Maybe we shouldn't," Brett suggested. He glanced to the west, where the sun was sinking toward the horizon. "Isn't it pretty dark in there?"

"You can see fine." Jeff sneered. "Either come in, or stay out, but I'm gonna look around."

Struggling against his fear, Brett stepped through the door and closed it behind him. For a moment the deep shadows blinded him, but then his eyes adjusted to the dim light of the interior, and he looked around.

Somehow, he had expected it to be empty.

But it wasn't.

Already, the floor had been subdivided by the skeletal shapes of newly constructed framework, and in the roof, several holes had been cut for skylights. Now, in the late afternoon, little light came through the holes, and it seemed to Brett that all they did was make the place even spookier than it already was.

And the framework, he realized, was almost like a maze. Almost anywhere, there could be someone hiding.

In the silence, Brett could hear the pounding of his own heart.

"Hey!"

The sudden sound jabbed Brett like a needle, and he felt his whole body twitch with a sudden release of tension. Then he realized the sound had come from Jeff. "Jeez!" he whispered loudly. "What did you do that for?"

Jeff gazed at his friend with disgust. "Because," he explained, "if anybody had answered, we could have said we were looking for someone, and then left. No one ever thinks you're sneaking in somewhere if you make a lot of noise." He called out once more: "Anybody here?" A pair of pigeons, frightened by the sudden disturbance, burst from their nests in a flapping of wings.

When silence had fallen once more, Jeff raised his hand, pointing toward the rear wall. "If there's anything in here, I bet it's back there," he said.

Brett gazed into the gathering gloom, and saw the top of the stairs that led down into the basement below. It was in the basement, his father had told him, that Con Sturgess's body had been found. Brett's heart pounded harder, and he felt a cold sweat breaking out on his back. "I bet there's nothing there at all," he said, though his voice quavered slightly in spite of his efforts to keep it steady. Jeff, catching the slip, grinned.

"Scared?"

"Hell, no," Brett lied. "What's to be scared of?"

"Ghoooosts," Jeff intoned, then snickered. "Come on."

They started toward the back of the building, with Brett following reluctantly. They had gone only a few yards when Brett felt his skin crawl.

He had the eerie feeling of unseen eyes watching him.

He tried to ignore it, keeping his eyes on Jeff's back, but the feeling wouldn't go away.

Instead, it got worse.

There was something else in the mill—he was sure of it. But he couldn't be sure where it was. It seemed to be all around him, following him. Suddenly he could stand it no longer, and whirled around to face whatever was stalking him.

Nothing.

His eyes scanned the tangle of structural supports, searching for a movement, but there was nothing there. Nothing, at least, that he could see.

And then, once again, the hair on the back of his neck stood up, and his spine began to tingle.

There was a sudden feeling of movement behind him. His stomach lurched. Something touched his shoulder.

Screaming, he jerked free, and whirled once more.

Jeff was staring at him, laughing. "Gotcha!"

"Jesus Christ! You scared the shit out of me!"

Jeff regarded him with knowing eyes. "You were already scared, weren't you?"

"I . . . I thought I heard something," Brett lied again.

"Well, you didn't, 'cause there's nothing here," Jeff replied. "Let's go see what's downstairs."

Without waiting for Brett to reply, Jeff headed once more for the staircase. Brett, unwilling to stay where he was, or admit by leaving that he was frightened, followed close behind. But when Jeff started down the stairs, Brett stopped, peering fearfully into the blackness below. "I'm not going down there."

"Chicken," Jeff taunted.

This time, Brett ignored the taunt. "It's dark down there, and you can't see anything."

"I can see all the way to the bottom of the stairs, and I'm going down whether you come or not."

Brett said nothing, only shrugged. He was staying where he was.

Jeff started down the stairs, but with each step he took, a little more of his confidence slipped away.

He began to wonder what might actually be waiting in the darkness below.

According to Beth Rogers, there was a ghost here.

But that was ridiculous. He didn't believe in ghosts.

He tried to remember how funny the ghost story had been a couple of hours ago, when they'd all been lying around on the floor of Tracy's library.

But it didn't seem so funny now, not with the dank gloom of the old building gathering around him.

In fact, now that he thought about it, the darkness itself was almost like something alive, reaching out for him.

He stopped near the bottom of the stairs, and tried to shake the feeling off.

He wasn't scared of the dark. He'd never been scared of the dark, at least not since he was a baby.

But now, here, he found that the dank blackness below was something very much to be afraid of.

Here, he didn't know what the darkness concealed. It wasn't at all like being in the dark at home, where you knew everything that was in the room around you, and could identify every sound you heard.

Here, the darkness seemed to go on forever, and the sounds—the little rustling sounds he was beginning to hear now—could be anything at all.

Mice. They could be mice, or even rats.

Or something else.

Something you couldn't touch, but that could touch you.

He wanted to go back now, but it was too late. Brett was waiting above, and he'd laughed at Brett. If he came back up now, and admitted he'd been afraid to go any farther, Brett would never let him forget it.

Holding his breath, he took another step.

He listened to the noises, and began to imagine that they were voices.

Voices, whispering so quietly he could barely hear them.

He took another step, which brought him to the basement floor. Bracing himself, he edged into the horrible blackness around him.

And then, out of the darkness, he sensed something coming for him.

He opened his mouth, but fear choked his throat and no sound came out. From behind him, he felt himself being pushed. He staggered in the darkness, and reached out to find something to brace himself with.

There was nothing.

Now, as he realized what was happening to him, his fear released him, and a scream erupted from his throat—cut off a moment later as he pitched forward and fell.

In a flash, he remembered the story he'd heard about how Tracy's uncle had died, long before he had even been born. It's happening again, he thought. Just like it happened before.

In an instant that seemed to go on forever, something hard and sharp pressed against his chest, so cold it seemed to burn as it punctured his shirt, then his skin.

His own weight as he fell thrust the object into his heart, and he heard himself gasp, felt the final racking stab of pain, then heard his own blood bubbling into his lungs.

As he died, a draft of cool air blew around him, and then he smelled a familiar odor.

Smoke.

To Jeff Bailey, death smelled like smoke. . . .

Brett heard the soft thump of something falling, then silence closed around him once more. "Jeff?"

There was no answer. He called out again, louder,

sure that his friend was trying to scare him as he had before. "Come on, Jeff. Quit fooling around."

Still there was no answer, and Brett took a tentative step down the stairs.

And then, a chill passing through him, he was suddenly certain that Jeff was not fooling around. Turning, he dashed toward the door they had come through twenty minutes earlier, hurled it open, and charged out into the gathering dusk.

"Help!" he yelled. "Somebody help me!" In panic, he began running toward the street in front of the mill.

"All right, son," Sergeant Peter Cosgrove said a few minutes later. "Just try to calm down, and tell me where your friend is."

"D-down there," Brett quavered. He pointed down the stairs, now brightly lit by the worklights that were strung throughout the building. "Something happened to him. I . . . I don't know what."

Cosgrove's partner, Barney Jeffers, trotted down the stairs, a flashlight in his hand. A moment later, as he flashed his light around the darkness of the basement, they heard him swear. At the same moment, brakes squealed outside, then an ambulance crew with a stretcher hurried through the door.

"Over here," Cosgrove called. He turned his attention back to Brett. "You stay right here, son. I'm gonna find a light for the basement. Okay?"

Brett nodded mutely, his eyes fixed on the staircase. What seemed like an eternity later, the lights in the basement suddenly flashed on, and he could see Jeff lying on the basement floor. Blood, mixed with dirt, soaked his shirt, and the stillness of death lay over him like a shroud. Brett's stomach heaved, and he turned away.

"What do you think?" Cosgrove asked Jeffers half an hour later. The ambulance was gone, and they were standing at the top of the stairs while a crew worked below, photographing the site and searching for evidence. Cosgrove was ninety-percent certain they wouldn't find anything.

"Same as you," Jeffers replied. "I think the Kilpatrick kid was telling the truth. Looks to me like the boy went down to look around, couldn't see anything, and tripped. If he'd been anywhere else, he might have skinned his knee. As it was, he landed on that pick."

"What the hell was it doing lying there?" Cosgrove muttered angrily.

"You want to charge someone with criminal negligence?" Jeffers inquired.

"I'd love to," Cosgrove replied, his voice tight. "But who do you charge? Might just as well charge the Bailey boy. If he hadn't been trespassing—"

"It was an accident," Jeffers interrupted. "Sometimes things happen, Pete. There's nothing we can do about it."

Cosgrove sighed, letting the tension drain from his body. "I know," he agreed. "But it's weird, too, you know?"

"Weird?" Jeffers echoed.

Cosgrove looked around, his eyes surveying the interior of the mill. "Yeah," he said. "Weird. All my life, I've heard stories about this place, and how dangerous it is. Stupid stories. So now they're fixing it up, and what happens? They aren't even done, and we already got someone dead. That's what I call weird."

Jeffers looked at his partner curiously. "You're not saying what I think you're saying, are you?"

Cosgrove shrugged. "I don't know," he said softly. "You didn't grow up here, like I did. Something like this happened once before. Must have been forty-odd years ago. That time it was Phillip Sturgess's brother. Conrad Junior."

Barney Jeffers frowned. "You mean he died? Here in the mill?"

"Not just in the mill, Barney," Cosgrove said darkly. "Right here. At the bottom of the stairs."

Jeffers uttered a low whistle. "Jesus. What happened?"

"That's the thing," Cosgrove went on. "No one ever found out. No one ever knew if it was an accident, or murder, or what. But it was just like this one." He fell silent for a few seconds, then shook his head. "Weird," he muttered. "It's just—well, it's weird, that's all."

Then, his face grim, he started toward the patrol car, bracing himself for what was ahead. He was about to call Jeff Bailey's parents to tell them their son had died in the mill, a pickax through his heart.

# 10

Hannah was in the midst of serving dessert when the telephone rang. Carolyn slid her chair back and started to stand up, but Abigail's voice, quiet yet firm, made her sink back into her chair. "Hannah will get it." Silently, Hannah placed the pie she had been serving on a sideboard, and left the room. A moment later she came back.

"It's for Mr. Phillip. It's the police, and they say it's an emergency. I explained you were in the middle of dinner, but they insisted—"

"It's all right, Hannah," Phillip said. "I'm sure it's important." He turned to his mother. "If you'll excuse me?"

Abigail glared at her son. "Really, Phillip, it's most impolite of them to call you now. I simply don't understand—"

"Maybe you will, after I talk to them," Phillip interrupted. "Go ahead with dessert."

When he was gone, Abigail turned her attention to Carolyn. "You simply must learn a few rudimentary things, Carolyn. First, it's very impolite to call people during the dinner hour. There is, however, little we can do to stop *that*. It seems that *no one* has manners anymore. But if the phone does ring while we are dining, Hannah will answer it."

From the corner of her eye, Carolyn saw Tracy's smirk, but ignored it. Beth, intently studying her plate, appeared suddenly to have found something fascinating in her pie. Smiling tightly, Carolyn patted Abigail's hand. "I'll try to remember that, Abigail," she promised as the old woman jerked away as if she'd been burned. "But suppose Hannah weren't here? Suppose it were her day off?"

"One of the other servants—" Abigail began, then abruptly fell silent as she remembered that there were no other servants. "In that case," she finally admitted, her voice stiff, "I suppose one of us would have to answer it."

Score one for our side, thought Carolyn as Tracy's smirk faded and a tiny smile played around the corners of Beth's mouth. In silence, the four of them began eating their pie. After four or five minutes that seemed to Carolyn like an eternity, Phillip returned, his expression grim.

"I have to go downtown," he informed them.

"Now?" Abigail immediately asked. "Surely whatever it is can wait until we've finished dinner?"

"What's happened?" The look on Phillip's face told Carolyn that something was terribly wrong.

"An accident," he replied. "A couple of kids got into the mill after the party this afternoon."

Beth's eyes widened, and her fork stopped in mid-air. Then, as her hand began to tremble, she carefully put the fork back on her plate.

"And what happened?" Abigail Sturgess asked. Her voice, normally strong and commanding, suddenly sounded hollow. When Carolyn looked at her, the old woman was pale, and there was an anxiety in her eyes that Carolyn had never seen before. "Tell me, Phillip," she insisted. "What has happened?"

Phillip hesitated a fraction of a second. "Jeff Bailey," he said at last. "He's—well, I'm afraid he's dead."

There was a sudden shocked silence as the name sank in. It wasn't a stranger—not even someone they had known only casually. It was a boy they all knew, who had been in their home only that afternoon.

"Jeff?" Tracy echoed. "Jeff's dead?"

"But—how?" Carolyn asked. "What happened?"

Phillip shook his head. "I'm not sure exactly. I have to go down there immediately."

Abigail rose to her feet. All the blood had drained from her face now, and she was swaying, as if she might faint at any moment. "My God," she whispered. "It's like your brother. He was the same age as Jeff when he—when he—" She fell suddenly silent, unable to continue.

Phillip stared at his mother. "Like Conrad?" he echoed. "Mother, what on earth are you talking about? We don't even know what happened yet—"

But Abigail was shaking her head, and her eyes had taken on a strangely empty look, as if she were seeing something far removed from the dining room. "Your father," she whispered. "He always said something like this would happen. He was always afraid—"

"Mother, please," Phillip said, taking her arm and guiding her back into her chair. "We don't even know what happened yet," he repeated.

"What did they say?" Abigail demanded. "Phillip, tell me what they said about Jeffrey."

Phillip swallowed, and glanced at Tracy and Beth, reluctant to repeat what he had been told in front of the girls. But both girls were staring at him, Tracy's eyes glinting strangely, Beth's wide and frightened. "Apparently he tripped," he said quietly. "There was a pick lying on the floor. He fell on it."

"Oh, God," Carolyn moaned.

Abigail gasped, and sank limply into her chair. "Like Conrad," she whispered. "It's just like Conrad." Her eyes seemed to focus again, and fixed on her son. "Phillip, maybe your father was right about the mill. Maybe we've made a mistake. Perhaps we should simply board it up again."

But Phillip shook his head, his face setting grimly. "For heaven's sake, Mother," he began. "It was an accident. It wasn't anybody's fault. Jeff shouldn't have been in there in the first place. He was—" And then he broke off his own words, the look in Abigail's eyes telling him she wasn't listening. Once again she seemed to have disappeared into another world. "I'll be back as soon as I can," he told Carolyn. He kissed her quickly on the cheek, then was gone.

"I must call Maggie Bailey," Abigail said suddenly. "I must try to apologize to her for what we've done." She started from the dining room, but before she reached the door, Carolyn blocked her path.

"No," Carolyn said. "If you call Maggie Bailey, it will only be to tell her how sorry you are about Jeff. But you will not begin filling her head with any superstitions about the mill."

Slowly, Abigail turned to face her. "Superstitions?" she echoed. Then she smiled bitterly. "Well, I suppose that's easy for you to say. But you don't remember the last time something like this happened, do you? Of course not—you weren't even born then. But it was an evening very much like this. And the telephone rang, and the police told us that Conrad Junior had been found in the mill. He'd tripped, they said. Tripped, and fallen on an old tool." Her voice dropped to a whisper. "It was the same thing, Carolyn. My husband always said that what happened to our son was not an accident, but I never believed him. But now? What do you expect me to think? It's happened again, just as my dear husband was afraid it would."

Almost in spite of herself, Carolyn felt a flicker of sympathy for the old lady. "Abigail, what you're saying just doesn't make any sense. The mill is dangerous—we all know that. And it was locked up precisely in order to prevent any more accidents like the ones that happened to your son and Jeff Bailey."

"But what if it wasn't an accident?" Tracy suddenly asked. "What if there was someone else in there?"

Carolyn glanced at Tracy, then felt her stomach tighten as she saw that although Tracy had directed the question to her, the girl's eyes were fixed on Beth.

"Just what are you suggesting, Tracy?" she asked, her voice cool.

"Nothing," Tracy replied with exaggerated innocence. "I was just asking a question."

Before Carolyn could reply, Abigail spoke again. "Conrad's last words," she said so quietly that Carolyn wasn't sure if she was speaking to them or to herself. "He said, 'She's still there. She's there, and she hates us. . . .'"

Tracy's eyes brightened. "Who, Grandmother? Who hates us?"

But Abigail shook her head. "I don't know," she whispered. "It was the last thing he said. I . . . I didn't think it meant anything. But now—"

"And you were right," Carolyn declared. "It didn't mean anything. As it happens, I agreed with your husband about the mill—I don't think it should be reopened. It was an evil place, a place where people were exploited, worked till they dropped, and I think it should be torn down and forgotten. But let's not start inventing ghost stories. All right?"

Abigail hesitated, then shook her head. "And what if you're wrong?" she asked. "What if my husband was right? What if there *is* something about the mill, and the only way we can keep it safe is by keeping people out of it?"

"For heaven's sake, Abigail, don't start filling the children's heads with a lot of nonsense."

"But I *want* to hear," Tracy protested.

"And I *don't* want to hear," Carolyn said firmly. "And neither does Beth. The mill is nothing but an old building that's been an eyesore in this town for nearly a hundred years. Frankly, I can't understand why it wasn't torn down years ago." Her eyes fixed on Abigail. "In fact, Abigail, I'd like to know why your husband didn't tear it down years ago when your son died there."

Abigail's strength seemed to flow back into her, and she gazed imperiously at Carolyn. "He didn't tear it down because he always said that it *mustn't* be torn

down. He always said that it must stand as a reminder
to us."

"A reminder?" Carolyn replied. Suddenly she had
had enough, and did nothing to conceal the fury that
welled in her as she stared at the old woman. "A
reminder of how big a fortune your family once made in
that building? A reminder of all the children who spent
their lives in that building, working twelve hours a day
for next to no money at all so that your family could
build this monstrosity of a house and staff it with the
few people in town who weren't working in your mill?
Was that it, Abigail? Did he want the mill to stand
there forever to remind us all of the good old days?
Well, for my family, those days weren't so good, though
I'm sure you're not aware of that!"

Abigail remained silent for several long seconds,
then finally said, "I don't know what Conrad thought at
the end, Carolyn," she began quietly. "But I do know
that he was terrified of the mill. Until tonight, I paid no
attention to it. But now I think perhaps we all ought to
rethink the matter." She walked from the dining room,
her back straight, her proud old head held high.

A moment later Tracy followed her grandmother,
leaving Carolyn and Beth alone in the dining room.
There was a long silence, and finally, for the first time,
Beth spoke.

"Mom? What . . . what if she's right? What if there
is something in the mill? What would it mean?"

Carolyn sighed, and shook her head. "It wouldn't
mean anything, sweetheart," she said. "It wouldn't mean
anything, because it's not possible. It doesn't matter
what old Mr. Sturgess thought, or what Abigail thinks
now. There's nothing in the mill." But even as she said
the words, a memory flashed through Carolyn's mind—a
memory of that morning the day after the funeral, when
she'd been out hiking with Beth.

For a moment, just before she'd fainted, the mill
had looked as if it were burning.

But that was silly. The mill hadn't been on fire,

and she hadn't actually seen anything. It had simply been a delusion, caused by the fainting spell.

She put the memory out of her mind, and began helping Beth and a silent Hannah clear the table. Surely there was a reasonable explanation for what had happened in the mill that day. When Phillip came home, they would know what it was.

Phillip Sturgess sat in Norm Adcock's office, facing the chief of the Westover Police Department over a desk that looked even more worn than Phillip felt. In the chair next to him, Alan Rogers sat, his eyes grim as he waited for Phillip to finish reading the report Cosgrove and Jeffers had filed. They'd already listened to Brett Kilpatrick's story.

For Phillip, there was a dreamlike quality to the whole thing, as if something out of the past were being replayed. And, of course, it was—the events of that afternoon were an eerie replay of what he'd heard about the day his brother had died.

The police, he was beginning to understand, were much more interested in the minutiae of what had happened than in the death of Jeff Bailey. Of course, he knew why that was. Jeff Bailey, like Phillip himself, was one of "them" to Norm Adcock. One of the rich ones— the ones who lived in Westover but were seldom seen in the town. Not, to Adcock, really a part of the town at all. Had it been this way when his brother had died?

Undoubtedly it had.

He finished reading the report, and put it back on the police chief's desk. "But the door *had* to be locked," he said now, in response to the question he'd heard Adcock asking Alan Rogers. "I can't believe no one checked it before the workmen left Friday."

His eyes went to Alan, who shook his head. "I'm sorry, Phillip. I'm almost sure I checked the lock myself, but I suppose it's possible I didn't. At any rate, it doesn't matter now. The lock was open, and doesn't show any signs of being forced. So part of the responsibility for what happened is mine."

Adcock shrugged. "Or maybe one of the kids had a key that fit. It's unlikely, but it's a possibility."

"What about charges?" Phillip asked. "Will there be any?"

Adcock shrugged noncommittally. "That's not really up to me, Mr. Sturgess. That'll be up to the prosecutor. I s'pose he could make a case that the mill is an attractive nuisance, and probably a few other things, too." He leaned back in his chair, his fingers fiddling with a ballpoint pen. "And I think you can probably count on being sued by the boy's folks."

"Which is between their attorneys and mine," Phillip said tightly. Then, hearing how cold his own words sounded, he tried to recover: "I couldn't feel worse about this if Jeff had been my own son."

Adcock nodded, though the expression of contempt in his eyes didn't change. He laid the pen back on the desk. "Then you won't object to fencing the place off, will you?" he asked, making no attempt to disguise the fact that his words had not been a question but an order.

"You don't even have to mention it," Phillip replied. "Alan, you can start the work tomorrow, can't you?"

"Of course."

"I'll post a guard on the place until the fence is finished," Phillip added.

"I already put a man out there for tonight," Adcock said. "I know it seems like closing the barn door after the horse is gone, but things like this have a way of gettin' out of hand. Unless I miss my guess, there's already kids in town planning to try to sneak in there tonight."

Phillip nodded. "Bill us for your man's time, Chief. The mill's my responsibility, not yours."

"I wasn't planning to do anything else," Adcock observed coolly. He stood up. "Well, I guess there isn't much else we can do tonight. I better get back home before Millie comes looking for me." He shook his head as he fished in his pocket for his car keys. "Hell of a thing," he said. Then, again: "Hell of a thing."

The three men walked together through the small police station, Adcock greeting each of his men by his first name.

All of them replied to the chief, all of them spoke to Alan Rogers.

For Phillip Sturgess, there were no greetings, not even a nod of the head.

Then they were outside, and the chief had gone. Alan and Phillip stood for a moment next to Alan's car. Silence hung over them until finally Alan reached out and put his hand on the other man's shoulder.

"I really don't know what to say, Phillip."

"There's not much *to* say, is there?"

"If you want to fire me, I'll understand. In fact, I've already written a letter withdrawing from the contract."

Phillip said nothing for a moment, then shook his head. "No. I can't see how that will solve anything. It won't bring Jeff Bailey back, and the job still has to be finished."

Alan nodded, then got into his car. "Can I buy you a drink? I know I could use one."

Again Phillip shook his head. "Thanks, but not tonight. I think I'd better go home and start taking care of things."

"Okay." He turned the key in the ignition. The engine of the old Fiat coughed twice, then caught. "Phillip, try not to let this get to you. What happened today was just an accident, nothing more. But people are going to talk—it's all too much like what happened to your brother. All I can tell you is, don't listen to them. Don't listen to any of them." Then, before the other man could answer, Alan put his car in gear and drove off into the night, leaving Phillip Sturgess alone on the sidewalk.

Phillip parked his car on Prospect Street, and sat for a few minutes, staring at the mill, wondering what his father had meant all those years when he'd insisted over and over that it was an evil place. Though Phillip had pressed him to explain, Conrad Sturgess had gone on pronouncing his dire words as though the statement itself were sufficient, adding only that someday he would understand.

But it was all nonsense. There was no such thing as a building that was evil, not even a building as ugly as the mill, with its stark facade and unadorned utilitarian lines.

He switched off the ignition, then reached into the glove compartment for the flashlight he always kept there. Locking the car, he crossed Prospect Street, and started toward the side of the building and the metal door.

"Hold on there, mister," a voice said from behind him. "Just where do you think you're going?"

Phillip turned, and was immediately blinded by the bright beam of a halogen light. Two seconds later the light went out. "Sorry, Mr. Sturgess," the voice went on. "I didn't recognize you." A man stepped forward. Phillip recognized his police uniform, but not his face.

"It's all right. I was just going home, and thought I'd stop to have a look around."

The officer hesitated, then reluctantly nodded. "Well, I suppose you can go in if you want to. It's your building." Another hesitation, and then, with even more reluctance: "Want me to go with you?"

"No, thanks," Phillip immediately assured him. "I'll only be a few minutes." Then, with the officer still watching him, he used his key to open the door, and stepped into the black emptiness of the mill. He stood still, listening, then reached out and groped for the light switch. The darkness was washed away by the big worklights suspended from the roof.

Phillip glanced around, then headed toward the back of the building, and the stairs leading downward.

He paused at the top of the stairs, looking into the blackness below, and wondered if perhaps he shouldn't leave now, and simply go home.

But he couldn't.

A boy had died here today, and it had happened down below, in the black reaches of the basement.

For some reason—he wasn't really certain why—he had to see the place where Jeff Bailey had died.

Turning on the flashlight, he started down the stairs.

At the bottom, he paused again, and shone the light around the basement.

Nothing.

As far as the weak beam of the flashlight could penetrate, there was nothing. Only a worn wooden floor, covered with dirt, and a scattering of tools.

He turned the light onto the area beneath the stairs.

There, the dust had been disturbed by many feet. In the midst of the footprints, Phillip saw a brownish smear.

The stain left by Jeff Bailey's blood.

Swallowing hard in an attempt to quash the wave of nausea that threatened him, Phillip turned away, switched off the flashlight, and started up the stairs.

Halfway up, he stopped.

From the darkness below, he was certain he had heard something.

He listened, waiting for it to come again.

All he could hear was the pounding of his own heartbeat.

Once more, he started up the stairs.

And he heard it again.

It was faint, almost inaudible, but he was nearly certain that it was there.

It was a crackling noise, almost as if something were burning.

He froze again, straining his ears, struggling to hear the sound once more, hear it clearly.

It didn't come.

The minutes passed, and his heart finally slowed to a normal pace. In the mill, there was only silence. At last, Phillip went on up the stairs, and walked slowly toward the door. He paused one final time, his hand poised over the light switch, and looked around.

Everything was as it should be.

He switched out the lights, plunging the building back into darkness, then carefully locked the door. From a few feet away, the policeman spoke. "Everything all right, Mr. Sturgess?"

Phillip nodded, about to start back toward his car. Then: "You didn't hear anything, did you?" he asked. "While I was in the mill?"

The cop frowned in the darkness. "Hear anything, Mr. Sturgess? No, I don't think so."

Phillip thought for a moment, then nodded once again. "All right," he said. "Thanks."

He walked quickly to his car, unlocked it, and got in. Then he put the flashlight back in the glove compartment, started the engine, and shifted the gears into drive.

He looked at the mill once more.

He decided he hadn't heard anything. It had only been his imagination, and the stress of the day.

Phillip Sturgess drove away into the night.

Beth woke up just after midnight, screaming.

The dream was still vivid in her memory, and her pajamas were soaked with perspiration. Her heart pounded as her scream faded away.

The door to her bedroom flew open, and the light went on.

"Beth?" she heard her mother's voice asking. "Beth, what is it? Are you all right?"

Beth shook her head, as if the gesture would shake the hideous images from her mind. "I saw it," she breathed. "I saw it all!"

"What?" Carolyn asked, crossing the large room to sit on the bed and gather Beth into her arms. "What did you see, honey?"

"Jeff," Beth sobbed. "I saw what happened to him, Mom."

"It was a nightmare, sweetheart," Carolyn crooned,

gently stroking her daughter's forehead. "It was only a dream."

"But I *saw* it," Beth insisted. "I . . . I was in the mill, downstairs, and there was someone else there. And then there was a sound, and I could hear Jeff's voice."

She broke off, sobbing, and Carolyn cradled her. "No," she whispered. "It was a dream. Only a dream."

It was as if Beth didn't hear her. "And then the wall slid away, and all of a sudden I could see Jeff. And then—and then someone pushed him!"

"Pushed him?" Carolyn asked. "What do you mean, honey?"

"I . . . I don't know," Beth stammered. "But someone pushed him, and he fell onto the pick. He didn't trip, Mom! She pushed him. She killed him!"

"No, sweetheart," Carolyn insisted. "All that happened was that you had a bad dream. And what happened to Jeff Bailey today was an accident."

Beth looked up at her mother with worried eyes. Carolyn brushed the hair back from the child's forehead with gentle fingers. "A dream?" Beth asked. "But . . . but it was so real—"

"I know," Carolyn assured her. "That's what makes nightmares so scary, honey. They seem so real that even when you wake up, sometimes they seem as if they're still happening. Is that what happened to you?"

Beth nodded. "I woke up, and it was dark, and it seemed like I was still in the mill. And I could still see it, and . . . and— "

"And now it's all over with," Carolyn finished for her. "Now you're all wide-awake, and you know it was just a dream, and you can forget all about it." She eased Beth back onto the pillow, and carefully tucked her in. "Do you want me to leave the light on for a few minutes?"

Beth hesitated, then nodded.

"Okay. Now, you just try to go back to sleep, and I'll come back in later, and turn the light off. How's that?"

"C-can't we leave it on all night?" Beth asked.

Carolyn hesitated, thinking about the nightmares that had plagued Beth in the months after she and Alan had separated, and how the only thing that had finally solved them was leaving the light on through the night. It had been less than a year since Beth had finally been able to start sleeping in darkness once again. Was it all about to start over? "All right," she said. "For tonight, we'll leave the light on. But just tonight. All right?"

Beth nodded, and Carolyn leaned down and kissed her on the cheek. "Now, go back to sleep, honey, and if you have another bad dream, you call me."

Beth said nothing, but turned over and drew the covers tightly around her. Carolyn straightened up, and looked at her daughter for a moment, wishing she could simply take Beth in with her and Phillip. But of course that could never happen. No matter how bad the nightmares had been, Beth had always refused to leave her own bed for the safety of her mother's. That would have been giving in to her fears, and Beth would never do that.

Giving the little girl a reassuring smile, Carolyn kissed her again, then quietly left the room, pulling the door closed behind her.

Alone, Beth rolled over again, and lay staring at the ceiling in the soft glow of the bedlamp.

She knew what had happened now; knew what had taken place during the time that had disappeared from her day.

She'd been on her way to visit her father, running away from the party—the horrible party where everything had gone so wrong—and she'd stopped at the mill.

Stopped just for a moment, hoping to find out if Amy was really there or not.

And then she'd gone on her way, but something had been different. The light had changed, and the sun had dropped over the horizon.

It was suddenly much later than she'd thought.

So instead of going to see her father, she'd come back home, climbing back up the trail on the hillside.

No one had even missed her; no one had even known she was gone.

But now, after the dream, she knew exactly what she'd done.

She had found Amy, and told her what had happened at the party, told her how mean Jeff Bailey had been to her.

And Amy had gotten revenge.

It hadn't been she who had killed Jeff; she was sure of it.

If Beth had killed him, she would have remembered it.

So it had to have been Amy who killed him.

Beth reached up and switched out the light.

The darkness no longer frightened her, for now she had a friend. A friend named Amy, who liked the dark.

From now on, Beth wouldn't be alone anymore. There would be someone to talk to, someone to confide in.

Someone who understood her.

# 11

The morning was bright and cool, and as Beth came slowly awake, she had a strange feeling of peace. Her nightmare of a few hours earlier was almost forgotten, and she lay comfortably in bed, her eyes closed, planning the day. Maybe she and Peggy Russell—

And then, as always happened on mornings when she woke up feeling happy and relaxed, the feeling of contentment fled.

She remembered where she was.

She wasn't back home in her bedroom on Cherry Street. She was still at Hilltop.

She was still at Hilltop, and she'd had a bad dream last night, in which she'd seen Jeff Bailey die.

Suddenly a shadow fell across her, and Beth's eyes snapped open. A few feet away, between her and the window, stood Tracy Sturgess.

"I know what you did," Tracy said, her voice so low that for a moment Beth wasn't quite sure she'd spoken at all.

She sat up in bed, and instinctively pulled the covers up around her chest.

Tracy was glaring at her angrily, but there was something in the half-smile on her lips that Beth found even more frightening than the words she had spoken.

"D-did what?" she stammered. The clock on her

nightstand told her that it was only seven A.M. "What are you doing here?"

"I know what you did," Tracy repeated, louder this time. Now the smile widened into a malicious grin. "You killed Jeff, didn't you? You sneaked into the mill yesterday, and when he came down the stairs, you killed him."

Beth's eyes widened. "No—I—"

"I heard you," Tracy pressed. "Last night, when you were talking to your mother, I was out in the hall. And I heard everything you said!" There was a taunting lilt to her voice now that made Beth cower back against the headboard, clutching the covers even tighter.

"But I didn't do anything," she protested. "It was only a dream."

Tracy's eyes narrowed. "It wasn't either a dream. You just made that up to tell your mother. And she's dumb enough to believe you. But I'm not. And wait'll I tell my father!"

"Tell him what?" Beth asked.

"That you're crazy, and you killed Jeff Bailey just because he was teasing you at my party."

"But I didn't kill him," Beth said, her heart suddenly beating harder. "It . . . it was Amy who killed him."

Tracy's lips twisted into a scornful sneer. "Amy? You mean the ghost in the mill you were talking about?"

Beth nodded mutely.

"There's no such thing as ghosts," Tracy told her. "All you did was make up a story. But no one's going to believe you!"

"But it's true," Beth suddenly flared. "Amy's real, and she's my friend, and all she did was just try to help me. And if you don't watch out, maybe she'll kill you, too!"

The grin faded from Tracy's face. "Don't you say things like that," she hissed. "Don't you ever say things like that to me."

"I can say what I want," Beth replied, her fear

washed away by her anger. "And you get out of my room."

"It's not your room," Tracy replied. "This is my house, and if I wanted to, I could take this room away from you. You shouldn't even be on this floor anyway— you should be upstairs where the servants used to live, because that's all you're good for."

"You take that back!" Beth shouted. She was out of the bed now, standing in her pajamas, her fists clenched.

"I won't take it back!" Tracy shouted. "I hate you, and I hate your mother, and I wish both of you were dead!" Suddenly she threw herself at Beth, her fingers reaching out to grab Beth's hair.

Beth ducked and tried to twist away, but it was too late. Tracy's body hurtled into her own, and she fell to the floor with Tracy on top of her. Then she felt Tracy's hands grabbing at her hair, pulling and jerking at it. With a violent lurch, she managed to roll over, and covered her face with her arms.

"I'll kill you!" she heard Tracy screaming.

And then, just as she was expecting Tracy to start clawing at her, she heard another voice.

"Beth? Beth, are you all— My God, what's happening in here?" A second later she felt Tracy's weight being lifted off her and opened her eyes to see her mother staring down at her.

And beyond her mother, she saw her stepfather, his hand clamped tightly on Tracy's forearm. Wiping at her face with one hand, she pulled herself together, then got to her feet.

"What on earth were you doing?" she heard her mother demand. "What's going on?"

Beth glanced at Tracy out of the corner of her eye, then shook her head. "Nothing," she said. "She . . . she wanted me to shut off my radio, and I wouldn't do it."

Carolyn turned to Tracy. "Well? Is that true?"

Tracy's chin jutted out, and she glared at Carolyn. "I don't have to answer you! You're not my mother!"

Then she winced as her father's hand tightened on her arm.

"You do have to answer Carolyn," Phillip said, his voice calm but firm. "It's true that she's not your mother, but she's my wife, and you will respect that. Now, is what Beth said the truth?"

Tracy remained silent for another few seconds, her eyes flashing venomously at Beth. "No!" she said at last. "She didn't even have her dumb radio on! She was threatening to kill me, just like she already killed Jeff Bailey!"

As Beth's eyes widened, and her skin turned ashen, a silence fell over the room. Both Phillip and Carolyn stared at Tracy in shocked horror.

It was Phillip who finally spoke. "The only threat I heard was yours. Now, go to your room, and stay there until either Carolyn or I tell you to come out. And in the future, stay out of Beth's room unless she invites you in."

"It's not her room—" Tracy protested, but her father let her go no further.

"That's enough, Tracy!"

Tracy's eyes glittered angrily, but she said nothing more. She stamped out of the room, slamming the door behind her. When she was gone, Carolyn sat down on the edge of the bed, and motioned Beth to join her.

"Did you threaten to kill Tracy?" she asked.

Beth hesitated, then nodded silently.

"But why?"

Beth's chin trembled, but she managed to keep herself under control. "B-because she said I killed Jeff Bailey," she whispered. "She came in, and said she knew what I did, and that she was going to tell Uncle Phillip."

"But you didn't do anything," Phillip interjected. "What did she think she knew?"

"She was listening last night when I was talking to Mom," Beth explained. "She heard me telling Mom about my dream, and said I was just making it all up."

Phillip's eyes darkened. "I see," he said. Then:

"Excuse me, Carolyn. I think it's time my daughter and I had a private talk."

Before Carolyn could protest, he was gone. Beth, her eyes damp, looked up at her mother. "I'm sorry, Mom."

"So am I, darling," Carolyn replied. "I wish you and Tracy didn't fight and I'm sorry she's so mean to you. I guess you'll just have to do the same thing with Tracy that I do with Abigail. No matter what she says, and how much it hurts, you have to ignore it. After a while, if you don't react, it won't be any fun for Tracy anymore, and she'll stop."

"But why does she hate me?" Beth asked. "I never did anything to her."

Carolyn put her arms around her daughter, and drew her close. "It's not you, honey. That's what you have to understand. Right now, she'd be just as mean to anybody else who was living here. She's afraid we're going to take her father away from her, that's all."

"But I don't want to do that," Beth replied. "I already have a father. Doesn't she know that?"

"Of course she does." Carolyn rose from the bed and started toward the door. "But you have to understand that what Tracy knows doesn't really matter right now. It's what she feels. And she's still very angry that her father married me. So she's taking it out on you."

"But . . . but that's not fair," Beth said, unconsciously echoing the words Tracy had used only a few moments before.

"I know it," Carolyn agreed. "But that's the way life is. It isn't always fair, and it doesn't always make sense. But we still have to do the best we can." She smiled fondly at the little girl. "So why don't we forget all this and get dressed and go down to breakfast. Okay?"

Beth nodded. She said nothing, but when her mother had gone, instead of going to her closet to begin dressing, she went to the window, and gazed down over the village to the mill.

In the depths of her mind, Tracy's words still reverberated.

*I know what you did.*

Was it possible? Was it possible that just as she had seen Amy in the dream last night, seen Amy pushing Jeff, making him fall on the pick . . .

She shuddered slightly, and turned away from the window.

But still the thought lurked in her mind.

What if Tracy was right? What if there were no Amy?

But there had to be. If Amy wasn't real, if she hadn't heard her, if she hadn't seen her in the dream, then that meant—

She shut the thought out of her mind, for if there were no Amy, then maybe Tracy was right.

Maybe she, Beth, really had killed Jeff.

But she wouldn't have . . . she *couldn't* have. . . .

Alan Rogers glanced at his watch, then signaled to the foreman to call the lunch hour. As the workmen moved from the heat of the day into the relative coolness of the mill itself, Alan began his normal twice-daily inspection of the job. He had found out long ago that it was impossible to hire workers with standards as high as his own, but he'd also understood that he couldn't demand as much of his crews as he demanded of himself. They, after all, were working for an hourly wage, and didn't share his fanaticism for getting things done right. To them, a job was a job, and what counted was the hours put in. For Alan, the work itself was more important than the money he earned. His satisfaction in getting the job done right usually outstripped his interest in squeezing out the last dollar of profit.

Today the work was going well. Already all the fence posts were in place, and by this afternoon, with any luck at all, the fence should be complete. It wouldn't be pretty—nothing more than sheets of plywood hastily nailed to the posts and stringers, but it would be effec-

tive. Tomorrow they could get back to the real work—
the reconstruction.

He had come to the last post, and was about to join
the rest of the crew in the shadowy interior, when he
heard Beth calling to him. He looked up to see his
daughter pedaling her bicycle furiously along River Road,
leaning into the turn at Prospect Street with a lot more
courage than Alan himself would have had, then
jumping it up the curb as she barreled onto the grounds
of the mill itself. As he watched, the rear wheel of the
bike lost its traction and began to skid out of control,
but Beth merely put a foot down, pivoted the bicycle in
a neat Brodie, and came to a stop in front of him,
grinning.

"Pretty good, hunh?"

Alan nodded appreciatively. "Very neat. But if you
break your neck, don't coming whining to me. You're
nuts."

"Didn't you ever Brodie your bike when you were
a kid?"

"Of course I did," Alan agreed. "And I was nuts,
too. So what brings you down here?"

"I came down to have lunch with you," Beth replied,
holding up a brown bag that she'd fished out of the
pouch slung under the racing seat on the bike. "Hannah made me some sandwiches. Peanut butter and
jelly. Want one?"

"I might swap you for a tuna fish."

Beth made a face. "I hate tuna fish. Is that all you
have?"

Alan chuckled. "Don't get picky. It may be tuna
fish, but I made it myself."

"Big deal," Beth replied, rolling her eyes. "You
probably icked it all up with mayonnaise, didn't you?"

Alan regarded his daughter with mock exaspera-
tion. "If you only came down here to pick on me, you
can go right back home. I don't need any grief from any
eleven-year-old smart-asses, thank you very much!"

Beth stuck out her tongue, but when Alan started
back toward the mill, she followed along behind him.

Grabbing a hard hat from the portable site shack, Alan dropped it over her head, then stepped aside to let her precede him through the door into the vast building. Beth promptly took the hat off, adjusted the headband so it wouldn't sink down over her eyes, then put it back on.

As soon as she stepped inside, her eyes went to the stairs at the far end of the mill.

"No," Alan said, as if reading her mind. "You can't go down there."

Beth's brow furrowed. "Why not? I just want to look."

"Because it's morbid," Alan told her. He opened his lunchbox and pulled out a sandwich, offering Beth half. She shook her head.

"But all I want to do is see where it happened," she pressed. "What's wrong with that?"

Alan sighed, knowing there was really no way to explain it to her. If he'd been her age, he'd have been dying to see the spot where the accident had happened, too. This morning, as he'd expected, there had been a steady stream of kids coming by the mill, some of them stopping to stare, others trying to look as though the last thing in the world they had come to see was the place where someone had died the day before. "There isn't any reason for you to see it," he said. "There's nothing there, anyway."

"Not even any blood?" Beth asked with innocent curiosity.

Alan swallowed, then concentrated on the sandwich, though he was suddenly losing his appetite for it. "Why don't we talk about something else? How's everybody up at your house?" Beth's eyes clouded, and Alan immediately knew that something had gone wrong that morning. "Want to talk about it?"

His daughter glanced at him, then shrugged. "It wasn't any big deal," she said. "I just had a fight with Tracy, that's all."

"Is that why you came down here? 'Cause things got too rough up there?"

"I don't know. Anyway, there isn't anyone home. They went over to the Baileys'."

"All of them?"

"Mom and Uncle Phillip. Tracy's got some friends over. And they're all talking about what happened to Jeff."

So much for changing the subject, Alan thought. And then, suddenly, he thought he understood. "Might be kind of neat if you could go back and tell 'em all what the spot looks like, hunh?"

Beth's eyes widened slightly. "Could I? Could I go down there just for a minute?"

Helplessly, Alan gave in. "All right. After lunch, I'll take you down. But just for a minute. Promise?"

Beth nodded solemnly. "I promise."

With the darkness washed away by the blazing worklights, the basement looked nothing like it had before. It was simply a vast expanse of space, very much like the main floor, except that down here the space was broken by the many columns that supported the floor above. As she looked out into the basement, Beth could hardly remember how terrifying it had been when it was dark. Now there was nothing frightening about it at all.

Except for the spot on the floor.

It was a slightly reddish brown, and spread from a spot a few yards from the bottom of the stairs. It looked to Beth as though someone had tried to clean it up, but there was still a lot left, soaked into the wooden floor.

Still, if her father hadn't told her what it was, she wasn't sure she would have known. Somehow, she had sort of expected it to be bright red, and glistening.

She stared at the spot for several long seconds, searching her mind for a memory.

But all that was there was the memory of the dream.

Surely, if she had killed Jeff herself, seeing the place where she had done it would have brought it all back.

And then, as she was about to turn away, her eyes scanned the rear wall, under the stairs. She frowned, then tugged at her father's arm. "What's that?" she asked.

Alan's eyes followed his daughter's pointing finger. For a moment he saw nothing—just a blank wall. Then, as he looked again, he realized that under the stairs the wall wasn't made out of concrete.

It looked to him like it was made out of metal.

He stepped into the shadows below the stairs, and took a closer look.

"Well, I'll be damned," he said softly.

"What is it, Daddy?" Beth asked. Suddenly her heart skipped a beat and she felt a slight thrill of anticipation.

"It looks like some kind of fire door," Alan replied. He reached up and felt in the darkness, and his fingers found a rail bolted to the concrete behind the metal. Moving his hands along the rail, he came to a metal roller.

He pounded on the metal, and heard a low echoing sound.

"Is it hollow?" Beth asked.

Alan nodded. "It sure seems like it's some kind of fire door. Give me a hand, and we'll see if we can open it."

Gingerly, Alan felt for the end of the door nearest the staircase, and curled his fingers around its edge. Then he leaned his weight into it, and tugged.

The door didn't budge.

Frowning, he stepped back, surveyed the door, then moved to the other end.

Near the ceiling, he found what he was looking for. A metal pin, protruding from the concrete. When he tried to remove it, it too held fast.

"What is it, Daddy?" Beth asked.

"Don't know," Alan muttered. "And it's going to take a couple of wrenches to find out."

"Is there another room back there?"

"That's what's weird," her father replied. "Accord-

ing to the plans I have, all that's back there is the
loading dock, and it's supposed to be solid concrete."

"Then why would they need a fire door?"

"Good question. Unless it's not a fire door. It
might be something else entirely. I'll be back in a
minute."

As her father trotted up the stairs, Beth stared at
the strange, barely visible door in fascination.

There was a room behind the door—she was sure
of it.

And she knew what the room was.

It was Amy's room.

It was the room where Amy lived, and that's why,
when she'd heard the strange voice the other day, it
had sounded so faint.

It had been muffled by the door.

She moved closer to the door, letting her imagination run free.

There could be anything behind the door. She
imagined an old forgotten room, still filled with the
kind of furniture they sold in antique stores. It was
probably an office of some kind, so there would be
desks, and maybe a big black leather chair. There might
even be one of those old-fashioned braided rugs still on
the floor.

It would all be covered with dust, but there would
still be papers on the desks, and stuff in the wastebas-
ket, for in Beth's mind she was sure the room had
simply been closed up one day, and forgotten. And
then, when the mill had been closed, no one had even
remembered that this room was there.

Suddenly she heard footsteps on the stairs, and her
father reappeared, carrying a large monkey wrench.

"This should do it," he said, giving her a conspiratorial wink. "All set?"

Beth nodded, and stood back while Alan adjusted
the wrench to the pin, then applied pressure to it.

The pin held for a moment, then squealed, and
slowly began to turn. With some further effort, it fell

away, and once more Alan gripped the end of the metal door and leaned his weight into it.

This time the door groaned and moved slightly. After two more pulls its rusty rollers screeched in protest, and it slid reluctantly to one side.

Instantly, a rush of ice-cold air flowed out of the gap.

Beth froze, the chill seeming to cut through her, and she could feel goose bumps rippling her skin as the hair on her neck stood on end. It was as if something physical had emerged from whatever lay behind the door. Beth's first instinct was to turn and run.

And then the blast of icy air stopped, almost as if it had never happened. She looked up at her father.

"What was that?" she asked, her voice trembling slightly.

"What?" Alan replied.

"The cold," Beth explained. "Didn't you feel the cold coming through the crack?"

Alan frowned slightly, then shook his head. "I didn't feel anything at all." He pulled on the door again, opening it far enough for them both to peer inside.

Alan shone his flashlight into the darkness beyond the metal door.

It was a room, perhaps twenty feet long and fifteen feet deep.

Its walls were blackened, and the floor was covered with a thick layer of dust.

It was completely empty.

Then, as Beth gazed around the long-forgotten room, she noticed a familiar odor in the stale air.

The little room smelled strongly of smoke.

# 12

There was nothing comfortable about the silence that reigned in the Mercedes-Benz as Phillip maneuvered it up the long drive and brought it to a stop in front of Hilltop. It was as if, by mutual consent, all of them were waiting until they were once more inside the mansion before they faced the argument that all of them now knew was inevitable.

For Carolyn, it was particularly difficult, for she was in the unique position of finding herself in agreement with her mother-in-law, albeit for reasons that Abigail would never understand. Still, the fact remained that for the first time Carolyn was about to side with the woman who hated her, against the husband who loved her.

She waited for Phillip to come around and open the door for her, and offered him an uncertain smile that was part gratitude and part apology. Getting out of the car, she started up the front steps. Hannah opened the door for her, and she nodded a greeting to the old woman before crossing the foyer to turn right down the wide corridor that led to the library. Beyond the French doors and the terrace outside, she could see Tracy and three of her friends playing tennis.

Beth was nowhere to be seen.

She dropped her purse on a table, and glanced at

the fireplace, where—as always—a fire was laid, ready to be lit. For a moment she was tempted to put a match to it, despite the warmth of the day. But warming the room even further would do nothing to alleviate the chill that was emanating from Abigail.

"It won't help," Abigail said as she entered the room, apparently reading Carolyn's mind. Then, stripping off her gloves and expertly removing the pin from her veiled hat, she turned to her son. "I don't think there can be any question now of continuing with your project. We shall order Mr. Rogers to begin closing the mill tomorrow."

Phillip's brows rose a fraction of an inch, and his arms folded over his chest. He leaned back against the desk that had once been his father's. "Indeed?" he asked. "And when did it become my project, Mother? Until yesterday, it was our project, unless I'm suddenly getting senile."

Abigail's sharp eyes raked over her son, and her lips curved into a tightly cynical smile. "If that remark was intended to suggest that I'm losing my grip, I don't appreciate it. I've simply changed my mind, and in light of what happened to Jeff Bailey—"

"What happened to Jeff Bailey was an accident, Mother. We've seen the reports, and there's nothing to suggest there was anything more to it than the simple facts. He tripped, and fell on a pick. That's that."

"He tripped and fell on a tool on the precise spot where your brother tripped and fell on a tool. Don't you consider that a bit more than a coincidence?"

"No, Mother, I don't," Phillip replied, his voice and manner clearly indicating that his mind was made up on the subject.

But Abigail was not about to give in so easily. "I'm sorry you can't see that which is perfectly clear," she went on. "But it doesn't really matter, does it? I shall speak to Mr. Rogers myself."

"Will you?" Phillip asked. There was a hardness in his tone that neither Carolyn nor Abigail had ever before heard. Carolyn gazed curiously at her husband, while Abigail's eyes suddenly flickered with uncertainty. "You may certainly speak to Alan if you wish, but I hope you understand that he won't act on your orders. He's working for me, not for you."

The uncertainty vanished from Abigail's eyes. She regarded her son with undisguised fury. "You?" she asked, making no effort to conceal her contempt. "Working for you? How dare you suggest that my wishes will not be obeyed. Particularly when all I am doing is seeing to it that your father's own wishes are honored."

"Enough, Mother," Phillip said, his voice suddenly sounding tired. "You might be able to buffalo everyone else that way, but it won't work with me. I've read Father's will. He left me in charge of all Sturgess business enterprises, and it is my decision to go ahead with the mill project. If you want to give in to Father's superstitions, that's up to you. But don't expect me to go along with them."

"Your brother's memory should mean something to you," Abigail flared.

But Phillip only shook his head. "My brother's memory?" he repeated. "Mother, I wasn't even born until a year after Conrad Junior died. And I wouldn't have been born at all if he hadn't died."

Abigail, looking as if she'd been struck, sank into one of the wing chairs. "Phillip—that isn't true!"

"Isn't it?" Phillip demanded. "I'm not a fool, Mother. Don't you think I know that I was nothing more than a replacement for Conrad? God knows, you and Father certainly never let me forget it. I grew up being compared to a brother I never even met! And now you want me to close down the restoration of the mill, simply because there have been two accidents there in the space of forty years? Well, you can forget it, Mother. What you choose to do is your own decision, but I won't be bound by Father's superstitions."

Abigail sat coiled in her chair like a serpent ready to strike. "I'll stop you," she hissed. "I'll use everything in my power to stop you from finishing that mill."

"Fine!" Phillip said in a mild tone. "Start calling

your lawyers, and mobilizing your forces. But you won't get anywhere. The power resides in me. Or have you forgotten that particular Sturgess tradition?"

Carolyn, who had said nothing throughout the exchange, preferring to remain as invisible as Abigail sometimes made her feel, suddenly spoke for the first time. "Tradition?" she asked. "Phillip, what are you talking about?"

Phillip turned to face her, a glint of triumph playing in his eyes. "Something I'm sure Mother's never mentioned to you. In my family, while the women have always been strong—we Sturgesses seem to attract strong women—there has always been a carefully drawn line. And that line, as Mother knows perfectly well, is the line where personal affairs stop, and business affairs begin. There has never been a female Sturgess who has had anything to say about our business affairs. That is always left up to the men. So when Father died, sole control over the family's assets passed to me. In short," he finished, smiling grimly, "Mother can make my life as miserable as she wants, and scream to her lawyers as much as she wants. But in the end, there isn't a thing she can do. When it comes to the mill, or anything else outside of this house, she is totally without power. Indeed, Mother," he added, his voice taking on the same chill Carolyn had felt so often from the old woman, "if I chose to, I could throw you out of this house."

Abigail was on her feet again, her eyes blazing. "How dare you?" she demanded of her son. "How dare you speak to me that way? And in front of her, of all people?" She wheeled around, and the full force of her anger was focused on Carolyn. "This is all your fault," she went on. "Before Phillip met you, he never would have talked to me this way. He would have asked for my advice, and heeded my words. But not anymore. You've hypnotized him! You've come into our lives— you and your common little daughter—and done your best to take Phillip away from us. But you won't succeed! Do you understand me? Somehow, I shall find a way to stop you!" She started toward the door, her anger making her stagger slightly, even though she leaned heavily on her cane. Carolyn took a step toward her, wanting to reach out to her, to steady her. But Phillip shook his head, and made a gesture that kept Carolyn where she was.

A moment later they were alone, with Abigail's fury hanging between them like a cloud.

"I'm sorry," Phillip said. "She shouldn't have attacked you and Beth. But she knows there's nothing she can do to stop me from finishing the mill project, so she had to turn elsewhere. And you were convenient." He moved toward her, his arms spread wide, but instead of stepping forward to meet him, Carolyn turned away, and sank into the chair Abigail had vacated only seconds earlier.

"Maybe she's right," Carolyn replied. Conflicting emotions were battering at her now. All the control she'd developed so carefully in the months since she'd moved to Hilltop seemed to be deserting her at the moment she needed it most. "Maybe our marrying *was* a mistake, Phillip. Maybe you should never have met me. Maybe you should have stayed away from Westover for the rest of your life."

"You don't believe that," Phillip said, his face ashen, his eyes pleading. "Darling, you can't mean that!"

"Can't I? I don't know what I mean. But I can't go on much longer living with a woman who hates me. And it isn't just me. It's Beth, too. Phillip, Beth knows how Abigail and Tracy feel about her. Even though she tries to pretend it isn't happening, she feels every slight they inflict on her! I'd hoped we could be a family—all of us. But it's not like that! As long as we've been married, it's been like a war, with Beth and me on one side, and Abigail and Tracy on the other. And you're caught in the middle."

"Well, at least the sides are balanced," Phillip said in a wry but futile attempt to defuse the situation. "At least you're not ganging up on me!"

Suddenly Carolyn laughed, but it was a high-pitched, brittle parody of her normal laughter, and

Phillip realized how close she was to slipping into hysteria. "Aren't we?" she asked. "Abigail made a mistake just now, but I don't think she knows it. On the subject of the mill, I would have sided with her. Isn't that funny? Isn't that just about the funniest thing you ever heard?" And then she crumpled in her chair, sobbing.

Phillip came to her then, kneeling by the chair and gathering her into his arms. Carolyn neither resisted him nor moved closer to him, and even as he held her, he could sense the loneliness she was feeling.

"It's all right, darling," he whispered, stroking her hair gently. "We'll get through this. Somehow, we'll put all of this behind us. But you mustn't even think of leaving me—without you, I'd have nothing."

"Nothing?" Carolyn echoed. "You'd have your mother, and your daughter, and Hilltop, and all the rest of everything the Sturgesses have always had. You'd hardly miss me at all."

Phillip groaned silently, and held her closer. "It's not true, darling. The only thing that matters to me is you. You and our baby."

Carolyn stiffened in his arms. For that moment—that moment of overwhelming anguish—she'd forgotten about the baby. She drew back slightly, and tipped her face up to look at Phillip. In his eyes, she could see his love for her, and she felt a glimmer of hope.

"You do love me, don't you?" she asked, the need for his reassurance gripping her once more.

"More than anything," Phillip replied.

"And the baby? You really do want the baby? You haven't just been saying that for my sake?"

Phillip smiled fondly at her. "How could I not want the baby?" he asked. "It's going to be our baby. *Ours!* It won't be anything anyone can use to try to drive us apart. In fact, it might even help. It will be Mother's grandson, and she'll fall in love with him the moment he's born."

Deep in Carolyn's mind, a warning sounded. "Son?" she asked. "What makes you so sure it will be a boy?"

"What else can it be?" Phillip asked. He was grinning broadly now, the crisis behind him. "I've already got a daughter, and so have you. And I need a son. After all, if it's not a boy, who will there be to carry on the Sturgess line?"

*The Sturgess line.*

The phrase echoed in Carolyn's mind. She tried to tell herself that he hadn't meant anything by it, that he'd meant it as a joke. But deep inside, the warning sounded stronger.

*He wants an heir. He wants a boy, to name after himself, and to raise in his own image. Abigail's right. He's a Sturgess, and I mustn't ever forget it.*

"And what if it's a girl?" she asked, careful to keep her tone as lightly bantering as his had been.

"Then I'll spoil her," Phillip assured her. "I'll give her everything she wants, and treat her like the princess she'll be, and she'll be the happiest little girl who ever lived."

But she'll be a girl, Carolyn said to herself. And to the Sturgesses, girls just aren't quite as good. Nice to have around, but just not quite as good.

She kissed Phillip on the cheek, and stood up. "Well," she said as blithely as possible, "I shall certainly do my best to produce a boy for you. But if I fail," she added, "it will be your own fault. As I understand it, the gene that determines sex comes directly from the father. If the Sturgesses want boys, their chromosomes better be able to handle it."

Phillip nodded affably, and his eyes once again took on the gentleness that Carolyn had fallen in love with. There wasn't a trace left of the cold anger with which he had told his mother that she was little more than a guest in her own home. "And what about the mill?" he asked. "Are you really planning to form some kind of unholy alliance with my mother?"

Carolyn hesitated, then shook her head. "I suppose not," she said. "For one thing, in their own way, my reasons for keeping it closed are just as superstitious as hers. And I have a feeling that she'd change her position before accepting support from me anyway. So

I'll just stay out of it, bite my tongue, and hope for the best."

But as she slowly climbed the stairs and started toward the master suite at the end of the hall, Carolyn wondered, once more, what the best would be. Perhaps, indeed, she had been right in her hysterical outburst, and the marriage—no matter how much she and Phillip loved each other—was doomed to failure already.

Or perhaps (and much more likely, she told herself) she was simply suffering from her pregnancy, which, despite her insistence that she was feeling fine, was beginning to bother her. Though she wouldn't admit it to Phillip, she was secretly glad that Dr. Blanchard had insisted that she get at least two hours' rest every day.

If nothing else, at least it provided her with an escape from the tensions of the house.

She slipped into the bedroom, and closed the door behind her. Lying down on the bed, she stretched luxuriously, and then let her eyes wander out the window to the enormous maple that stood a few yards away, its leaves completely blocking out the sunlight.

Concentrating on the cool peacefulness of the greenery, she drifted into sleep.

At the other end of the house, in her rooms that were almost an exact mirror image of those her daughter-in-law occupied, Abigail Sturgess was wakeful and wary. She was staring out the window, her eyes focused angrily on the forbidding building that had represented so much tragedy for her family.

More and more, she was becoming convinced that her husband had been right.

There was something evil about the mill, and though she wasn't yet sure what it was, she had made up her mind to find out.

Beth pedaled away from the mill, but instead of heading out River Road to start the long climb back up to Hilltop, she turned the other way, riding slowly along Prospect Street, then turning up Church toward the little square in the middle of the village. Once there, she slowed her bike, looking around to see if any of her old friends might be playing softball on the worn grass. But the square was empty, and Beth rode on.

Almost without thinking about it, she turned right on Main Street, then left on Cherry. A minute later she had come to a halt in front of the little house in which she'd lived until she had moved to Hilltop.

The house, which had always seemed big to her, looked small now, and the paint was peeling off its siding. In the front yard, weeds were sprouting in the lawn, and the bushes that her mother had planted along the front of the house didn't have the neatly trimmed look of the gardens at Hilltop.

But still, it was home to Beth, and she had a sudden deep longing to go up to the front door, and ask whoever lived there now if she could go into her own room, just for a few minutes.

But of course she couldn't—it wasn't her room anymore, and besides, it wouldn't look the same as it had when she had lived there. The new people would have changed it, and it just wouldn't feel right.

She got back on the bike, and continued down the block, looking at all the familiar houses. At the corner, she turned right again, then left on Elm Street.

In front of the Russells' house, Peggy was playing hopscotch with Rachel Masin, and Beth braked her bike to a stop.

"Hi," she said. "What are you guys doing?"

Peggy, whose lager was in one corner of the number-four square, was concentrating hard on keeping her balance in the number-five, while she leaned down to pick up the key chain she had won from Beth herself last summer. Finally, snagging the chain with one finger and taking a deep breath, she hopped quickly down the last three squares and out of the pattern.

"Playing hopscotch," she announced. "And I'm winning. Rachel can't even get past number three."

"But I'm using a rock for a lager, like you're supposed to," Rachel protested. "Anybody can do it with a key chain. They always stay right where you throw them."

"Can I play?" Beth asked. She leaned the bike against a tree, and fished in her pocket for something to use as a lager. All she came up with was the key chain—identical to the one she had lost to Peggy—that held her house key. "I'll start at one."

Peggy looked at her with open hostility. "How come you're not out riding your horse? Peter says you go out every day now."

Beth's heart sank. Why couldn't Peter have kept his mouth shut? Now Peggy thought she was just like Tracy. "I don't have a horse," she said. "It's Uncle Phillip's horse, and all he's doing is teaching me to ride it. And we don't go out every day. In fact, we've only been out a couple of times."

"That's not what my brother says," Peggy challenged, as if daring Beth to contradict her big brother.

"Well, I don't care what Peter says," Beth began, and then stopped, realizing she sounded just like Tracy Sturgess. "I . . . I mean we don't really go out every day. Just sometimes." Then she had an idea. "You could go with us sometime if you want to." Peggy said nothing, but her face blushed pink, and Beth belatedly remembered what Peter had told her. "Uncle Phillip wouldn't fire Peter," she blurted out. "Really he wouldn't."

The red in Peggy's face deepened, and her eyes brimmed with tears. "Why don't you just go away?" she demanded. "We were having fun until you showed up!"

"But we're supposed to be friends," Beth protested. "You're supposed to be my best friend!"

"That was when you lived on Cherry Street. You were just like us then. But now you live up on the hill. Why don't you be friends with Tracy Sturgess?"

"I hate Tracy!" Beth shot back, on the verge of tears herself now. "I hate her, and she hates me! And I'm not any different than I ever was! It's not fair, Peggy! It's just not fair!"

Rachel Masin, looking from Peggy to Beth, then

back to Peggy, suddenly stooped down and picked up her lager. "I gotta go home, Peggy," she said hurriedly. "My—" She searched around for an excuse, and seized on the first one that came to mind. "My mom says I have to baby-sit my little brother." Without waiting for either of the other girls to reply, she ran off down the street and around the corner.

"Now look what you did," Peggy said, glowering at Beth. "We were having a good time till you came along."

"But I didn't do anything. How come you don't like me anymore?"

Peggy hesitated for a moment, then planted her fists on her hips, and stared at Beth.

Beth stared right back.

The two girls stood perfectly still, their eyes fixed on each other, each of them determined not to be the first to blink. But after thirty seconds that seemed like ten minutes, Beth felt her eyes beginning to sting.

"You're gonna blink," Peggy said, seeing the strain in Beth's face.

"No I'm not!"

"You are too. And if you do, you owe me a Coke. That's the rules."

Beth renewed her concentration, but the harder she tried not to blink, the more impossible it became. Finally giving up, she closed her eyes and rubbed at them with her fists.

"You owe me a Coke," Peggy crowed. "Come on— you can ride me down to the drugstore."

The spat forgotten, Peggy climbed onto the rack that was mounted over the back fender of the bike, and wobbling dangerously, Beth pedaled them away. Ten minutes later they were in their favorite booth in the rear corner of the drugstore, sipping on cherry Cokes.

"What's it really like up there?" Peggy asked. "I mean, what's it like living in that house? Isn't it scary?"

Beth hesitated, then shook her head. "It's not really scary. But you have to get used to it. The worst part is Tracy Sturgess."

Peggy nodded wisely. "I know. Peter says she's the meanest person he ever met."

"She is," Beth agreed. "And she really hates me."

"How come?"

Beth shrugged. "I don't know. I guess she thinks Mom and I are just hicks. She's always acting like she's better than everybody." Then she grinned. "But wait till next year—she's going to be going to school right here!"

Peggy's eyes widened in astonishment. "You mean she isn't going back to private school?"

"That's what I heard."

"Wow," Peggy breathed. "Wait'll the other kids hear about that!" Then she snickered maliciously. "And wait till the first day of school. I bet everybody cuts her dead."

"I hope they do," Beth said, her voice edged with bitterness. "I hope they're all just as mean to her as she is to me."

Peggy nodded, then sighed despondently. "But they prob'ly won't be. They'll prob'ly start kissing up to her just because she's a Sturgess." She sucked the last of the Coke through the straw, then tipped the glass up so that the crushed ice slid into her mouth. She munched on it for a minute, then looked across the table at Beth again. "Do you know what really happened to Jeff Bailey?"

Beth felt a slight chill go through her. "I—he just tripped and fell, didn't he?"

"Search me," Peggy replied. "But I heard my parents talking about it last night, and they kept talking about the other boy that got killed in the mill—"

"Uncle Phillip's brother," Beth put in.

Peggy nodded. "Anyway, my mom said that she didn't think it was a coincidence at all. She said there's always been stories about the mill, and she thinks maybe there's something in there."

Beth hesitated, then nodded. "There is," she said.

Peggy stared at her. "How do you know?" she asked.

Beth hesitated, then made up her mind. "Come up to Hilltop tomorrow, and I'll show you something. And I'll tell you what's in the mill. But you have to promise not to tell anyone else, all right? It's a secret."

Peggy nodded eagerly. "I promise."

"Cross your heart?"

"Cross my heart," Peggy repeated. "Cross my heart, and hope to die."

# 13

Eileen Russell looked at her daughter doubtfully, then shook her head as she slid two perfectly fried eggs out of the skillet onto the child's plate. "I don't know. I just don't like the idea of Peter getting into trouble over it."

"But Peter *won't* get in trouble," Peggy insisted. "Beth promised. She even said I could go riding with them sometime, if I wanted to. With her and Mr. Sturgess!"

Eileen's gaze shifted to her son. "Well?" she asked. "Does that sound like Mr. Sturgess to you?"

Peter shrugged noncommittally, but at the pleading look in his sister's eyes, he nodded his head. "He's pretty nice, and he takes Beth riding sometimes. I don't think he'd care if Peg went along." Then he grinned. "But Tracy'd piss her pants. She hates it bad enough when her dad goes riding with Beth. If Peg was along, she'd shit."

"Watch your language, young man," Eileen said, more out of habit than any particular prudery. She turned the matter over in her mind once more. She knew how much Peggy had missed Beth over the last few months, but her main concern was still that nothing threaten Peter's job. Jobs, particularly in the summer, were scarce, and they needed the money. Her job

hostessing at the Red Hen barely covered the bills, and
if something should happen to Peter's job—

Finally she decided to compromise, and call Carolyn Sturgess. Except that even something as simple as
that suddenly presented a problem. It was stupid, and
Eileen knew it. After all, when they'd been growing up
together, Carolyn Deaver had been one of her best
friends, and after Dan Russell walked out on her about
the same time Carolyn had divorced Alan Rogers, they'd
become even closer.

But then Carolyn had married Phillip Sturgess,
and moved up to the mansion on top of the hill, and
everything had changed.

Still, Eileen had to admit that part of the problem
was her own fault. She'd gone up to Hilltop a couple of
times, but the very size of the house had made her
uncomfortable, and old Mrs. Sturgess had been bla-
tantly rude to her. Finally she'd stopped going, telling
herself that from now on, she'd invite Carolyn to her
own house.

Except she'd never really done it. She'd tried to
tell herself that she just kept putting it off because she
was busy, but she knew that the real reason was that in
comparison to Hilltop, her house was little more than a
slum. And after getting used to the splendor of the
mansion, Carolyn would be sure to notice the short-
comings of Eileen's place. So the invitation had never
been issued, and as the months went by, Eileen thought
about it less and less.

Still, there was no reason why Peggy and Beth's
friendship should end simply because their mothers'
had withered. She picked up the receiver and dialed
the number that was still written in pencil on the wall
next to the phone. To her relief, Carolyn herself answered the phone on the second ring, sounding sleepy.
With a sinking heart, Eileen realized that there was no
longer any reason for Carolyn to be up by seven A.M.

"It's Eileen," she said. "Eileen Russell. Did I wake
you?"

Instantly, the sleepiness was gone from Carolyn's voice. "Eileen! It's been months!"

"I know," Eileen replied. "And I'm sorry. But—well, you know how it goes."

There was an instant's hesitation before she heard Carolyn's reply, and some of the enthusiasm seemed to have gone out of her voice. "Yes," she said. "Of course. I . . . I understand, Eileen."

"The reason I'm calling," Eileen plunged on, "is that Beth ran into Peggy yesterday, and invited her to come up to Hilltop this morning. I just wanted to be sure it wouldn't be any problem."

"Problem?" Carolyn echoed. "Eileen, it would be wonderful. Beth's missed Peggy so much, and so have I. You know she's welcome here anytime."

Suddenly Eileen felt ashamed of herself. Carolyn hadn't changed—hadn't changed at all. Why had she been so sure she had? Or was she herself busy being a snob, attributing to Carolyn airs that she herself would have taken on in the same situation? She had to admit that the possibility existed.

"Okay," she said. "She'll be up sometime in the middle of the morning." She hesitated, then went on. "And maybe this afternoon I could come up myself. We haven't had a talk for a long time."

"Could you?" Carolyn asked. "Oh, Eileen, that would be wonderful. What time?"

Eileen thought quickly. "How about three-ish? I have to do lunch at the Hen, but it's a split shift. I don't have to be back until seven."

"Great!" Carolyn agreed.

When she hung up a moment later, Eileen grinned happily at Peggy. "Looks like the drought's over," she said. "You can go up anytime you want."

Peggy, winded from the hike up the hill, paused when she came through the gates of Hilltop, and stared at the mansion while she caught her breath. It still seemed to her impossible that anybody could really live in it. But Beth? That was really weird. Beth should still

be living on Cherry Street, where they could run back
and forth between each other's houses four or five times
a day. Up here, just the driveway was longer than the
whole distance between their houses used to be.

She started toward the front door, then changed
her mind, and skirted around to the far end of the
house. Somewhere, she knew, there had to be a back
door, and all her life she'd been used to using her
friends' back doors. You only went to the front door on
special occasions.

Finally she found the little terrace behind the
kitchen, and knocked loudly on the screen door. A
moment later, Beth herself appeared on the other side
of the door. "I knew you'd come around here," she
said, holding the door open so Peggy could come into
the kitchen. "Want a doughnut or something?"

Peggy nodded mutely, and Beth helped herself
from the plate on the kitchen table, handing one to the
other girl. "Come on," she said. "Let's get out of here.
I want to show you something." They pushed the screen
door open, and let it slam behind them, Beth calling
out an apology even before Hannah could admonish
her. Then, with Peggy following behind, Beth led her
back around the corner of the house, and across the
lawn toward the trail to the mausoleum.

Patches snorted, pawed at the stable floor, then
stretched her neck out over the half-door, whinnying
eagerly.

"Not yet," Tracy Sturgess told the big mare. "Not
till I'm done grooming you." She gave the horse's lead a
quick jerk, but instead of obediently backing away from
the door, the horse only snorted again, and tossed her
head, jerking the lead from Tracy's hand.

"Stop it!" Tracy snapped, grabbing for the lead,
but missing. "Peter! Come make Patches hold still."

"In a minute," Peter called from the other end of
the stable.

"Now!" Tracy demanded. She moved carefully
around Patches, then grasped the horse's halter, and

tried to pull her back into the stall. Again, the horse snorted, reared slightly, and tried to pull away.

"What's wrong with you?" Tracy asked. Then, her hand still clutching the halter, she looked out into the paddock to see what had attracted the mare's attention. The paddock, though, was empty.

Tracy raised her eyes, and then, past the rose garden, saw the movement that had distracted the horse.

It was Beth, walking across the lawn with someone else, a girl Tracy didn't recognize. Tracy frowned, then jerked the horse's lead again. Patches whinnied a loud protest, but a moment later Peter came into the stall, took the lead from Tracy, and gently pulled the animal away from the door. Tracy remained where she was, staring out at the retreating figures of the two girls.

"Who's that?" she asked, her back still to Peter.

"Who?"

"That girl with Beth."

Peter shrugged. "My sister. Her name's Peggy."

Now Tracy turned around to glare angrily at the stableboy. "Who cares what her name is? What's she doing up here?"

Peter reddened slightly. He'd known this would happen. Now he'd be in trouble for sure. "Beth invited her up."

"Who said she could do that?" Tracy demanded. "This isn't her house. She doesn't have the right to invite people up here."

"Her mom said it was okay. She said Peggy could come up anytime she wanted to."

"Well, she can't!" Tracy exclaimed. "And I'm going to tell her so!" She stamped out of the stall, leaving Peter to finish the job she'd begun, then ran through the rose garden and around the corner of the house just in time to see Beth and Peggy starting up the trail toward the mausoleum.

She was about to call out to them, and tell Peggy Russell to go home, when she changed her mind. Maybe it would be more fun to follow them, and find out what they were doing.

\*    \*    \*

Peggy stood staring in awe at the strange marble structure that was the tomb of the Sturgesses. "Wow," she breathed. "What is it?"

Beth explained the mausoleum as best she could, then pulled Peggy away. "But this isn't what I wanted to show you," she said. "It's down here. Come on."

They started down the overgrown path on the other side of the mausoleum, walking carefully, their feet crunching on the thick bed of fallen leaves and twigs that covered the old trail. Here and there the path seemed to Peggy to disappear completely, and several times they had to scramble over fallen trees. And then, just as Peggy was sure the trail was coming to an end, it suddenly branched off to the left. Peggy looked around. At the place where the two paths converged, she spotted a sign, old and rusty, its paint peeling away, hanging crookedly on a tree.

**PRIVATE PROPERTY**
**NO TRESPASSING**

"Maybe we'd better go back," Peggy said, her voice dropping to a whisper as she glanced around guiltily.

"It doesn't mean us," Beth replied. "It's just marking the place where Uncle Phillip's property starts. It's for people coming up the hill, not going down. Come on."

With Peggy following somewhat reluctantly now, Beth started along the track that would lead to the little meadow.

"Where are you going?" Peggy asked.

"You'll see," Beth replied. "Don't worry."

"But what if we get lost?" Peggy argued. "How do you know which trail to follow?" More and more, she was wishing they hadn't come down here at all. It seemed to her that the woods were closing in around her. She wished she were back up on the top of the hill, where at least everything was open.

"I've been down here before," Beth replied. "Mom

and I came down here one day, and Uncle Phillip and I came out here on the horses. Stop being chicken."

Peggy hesitated, wondering what to do. Maybe she should turn around, and try to find her own way back. But if she did that, she'd have to go by herself.

Making up her mind, she followed Beth. They had gone only about a hundred yards when Beth stopped. "Look," she said softly. "Here it is."

Peggy stared around the little meadow. Saplings stood here and there in the clearing, and the underbrush came nearly to her waist. But there didn't seem to her to be any difference between this meadow and any of the others that dotted the woods around Westover.

"What's so special about this?" Peggy complained. "It's just a clearing, isn't it?"

Beth shook her head, and led Peggy across the meadow to the place where she'd found the small depression last time she had been there.

She pointed to it silently, and Peggy frowned in puzzlement. "What is it?"

"It's a grave," Beth said.

Peggy's eyes widened. She glanced around nervously, wishing she were somewhere else. "H-how do you know?" she breathed.

"I just know," Beth replied. "I found it the other day."

"Whose is it?" Peggy whispered, her wide eyes fixed on the odd depression. "Who's buried here? Is it one of the Sturgesses?"

Beth shook her head. "They're all buried up in the mausoleum. I think—" She hesitated, then took a deep breath. "I think this is where Amy's buried."

"Amy?" Peggy repeated blankly. "Who's Amy? What's her last name?"

"I . . . I don't know," Beth admitted.

The two girls stood silently for a moment, their eyes fixed on the odd sunken spot.

"Maybe it isn't a grave at all," Peggy suggested. "If it was a grave, wouldn't there be a headstone or something?"

Beth's eyes flicked up the hill, toward the spot where the mausoleum lay hidden in the woods. "There isn't any headstone because they didn't want anyone to know," she said in a whisper. "They didn't want anyone to know who she was, or that she's even here."

"But who is she?" Peggy pressed.

Beth turned to look at Peggy, and there was something in her eyes that made Peggy feel suddenly nervous.

"She's my friend," Beth said.

"Y-your friend?" Peggy repeated. "But . . . but I thought she was dead."

"She is," Beth agreed. "But she's still alive, too. She lives in the mill."

"The mill?" Peggy echoed. Suddenly she felt a small knot of fear forming in her stomach.

Beth nodded, her mind racing now. "I think she must have worked there," she said, her voice quiet. "I think something terrible happened to her, and they buried her up here. But she's not up here. Not really. She's still in the mill."

Peggy watched Beth warily. Something seemed to have come over her now. Though Beth was looking at her, Peggy wasn't sure her friend was seeing her. And what she was saying didn't make any sense at all.

In fact, it sounded crazy.

"B-but what's she doing in the mill?" Peggy finally stammered. "What does she want?"

Beth's eyes darkened. "She wants to kill them," she said at last. "Just like she killed Jeff Bailey."

As the words sank into Peggy's mind, the knot of fear grew, reaching out into her arms and legs, making her knees tremble.

"Why?" she whispered. "Why would she kill Jeff?"

Beth heard the words, and as her eyes remained fixed on what she was now certain was Amy's grave, she began to understand. She remembered the party, and the way Tracy and her friends had treated her.

She remembered the humiliation, and the pain.

"Because he was mean to me," she said softly. "He

was mean to me, so she killed him." The words became the truth in her own mind even as she spoke them. For her, Amy was real now. "She's my friend, Peggy. Don't you understand? She's my best friend."

Peggy felt her heart beating faster. "But she's dead, Beth," she protested. "She's not even alive, and you don't even know who she is. How can she be your friend?"

But Beth wasn't listening to her. In fact, Peggy wasn't even sure Beth could hear her anymore. Slowly, one step at a time, Peggy began backing away. If Beth noticed, she gave no sign, for her eyes were still fixed on the depression in the ground that she had decided was a grave.

But it wasn't anything, Peggy told herself. It was just a little dip in the ground where the grass seemed dried up, not bright green like the rest of the meadow, and there wasn't anything there. Nothing at all.

She backed up another three steps, then turned and fled from the meadow back into the woods, hurtling back along the path toward the "No Trespassing" sign. But when she got there, she didn't turn right, up the hill toward the mausoleum.

Instead, she turned left, and began thrashing her way down the hillside toward the river below.

Beth stood rooted to the spot, staring at the grave. Unaware that Peggy was gone now, she began telling Peggy about the dream she'd had—the dream that was like a memory.

"I saw it," she said. "I was in the mill, under the stairs. And I heard something, and waited. And then Jeff came down the stairs, and he . . . he died. But it wasn't me that killed him. It was Amy. There's a little room under the stairs, and that's where Amy lives. But she came out of the room, and she killed Jeff. And I wasn't scared," she finished. "I watched Amy kill Jeff, and I wasn't scared at all."

And then, as she tore her eyes away from the grave

and looked around for Peggy, the silence of the forest was shattered by the sound of laughter.

Tracy Sturgess stepped into the little clearing, her mocking eyes fixed on Beth.

Beth, her own eyes suddenly clearing, felt herself flushing red with humiliation. Had Tracy just gotten there, or had she been following them all along, listening to them and watching them? "How long have you been there?" she asked, her voice quavering now.

Tracy laughed cruelly. "Just long enough to find out you're crazy!" she said.

"I'm not crazy," Beth flared. "There's a grave here, and Peggy saw it too! Didn't you, Peggy?" She turned around, and discovered that Peggy was no longer there.

Tracy snickered. "She left. And you better get out of here, too. If you don't, the ghost might get you!"

Beth looked frantically around, searching for Peggy, but there was no sign of her. "Where is she?" she demanded. "Where's my friend?"

"She isn't your friend." Tracy sneered. "When she found out how crazy you are, she ran like a scared rabbit." Then, her mocking laughter echoing strangely in the bright morning sunlight, she disappeared back into the woods.

Beth stood still, her eyes flooding with tears of anger and humiliation. Then she sank down into the coolness of the grass, drawing her knees up to her chest.

They didn't believe her. Peggy didn't believe her, and Tracy thought she was crazy.

But it was true.

She *knew* it was true!

Her sobs slowly subsided, and finally she sat up. Her eyes fixed on the small depression in the earth, and she tried to figure out how she could prove that she was right.

But there wasn't any way. Even if she dug up the grave and found Amy's bones, they still wouldn't believe her.

Almost unconsciously, her fingers began probing at

the soft earth, as if looking for something. And then, a moment later, her right hand touched something hard and flat, buried only an inch below the surface.

She began scraping the dirt away, exposing a weathered slab of stone. It was deeply pitted, its cracks and crevices packed with the rich brown soil, and Beth at first had no idea what it might be. But then, as she scraped more of the earth away, the slab began to take shape.

One edge was rough and jagged, but from that edge, the stone had been worked into a smooth, clean semicircular curve, its edges trimmed in a simple bevel. After a few minutes, Beth had cleared the last of the dirt off its surface, and managed to force her fingers under the stone's edge. When she tried to lift it, though, it held fast, and all she succeeded in doing was to break a fingernail, and bare the knuckles of her left hand. Wincing with pain, she wiped her injured hand as clean as she could, then held the smarting knuckles to her mouth. While she waited for the pain to ease, she searched the clearing for a stick, and finally found one that looked thick enough lying a few feet from the mouth of the trail.

She picked it up, and returned to the stone slab. Forcing one end of the stick under its edge, she pressed down on the other end. For a moment, nothing happened. Then the stone came loose. Dropping the stick, Beth crouched down and turned the slab over.

The other face had been polished smooth, and Beth knew immediately that her first feeling about it had been right—it was the top of what had once been a headstone.

With growing excitement, she rubbed the dirt away from the shallow engraving just below the upper curve. The letters were fuzzy, almost worn away by the ravages of time. But even so, she was able to read them:

**AMELIA**

There was nothing else, nor could she find the rest of the broken gravestone.

But it was enough.

Amy was real.

Beth thought about Tracy, and her mocking laughter.

And Peggy, who hadn't believed her, and had run away from her.

But she had found the proof. Now, no matter what they said, they wouldn't be able to take Amy away from her.

If they tried, she knew what would happen to them. Amy would do to them what she had done to Jeff Bailey.

For Beth and Amy were friends now—best friends— and nothing would ever be allowed to come between them again.

# 14

Tracy let herself in through the French doors leading to the foyer, and started up the stairs to the second floor. All the way back from the clearing in the woods, she'd been trying to figure out the best way to use what she'd overheard Beth saying, but she still hadn't made up her mind.

Of course, she'd tell all her friends, starting with Alison Babcock.

But who else? What if she told her father? If he believed her, maybe he'd send Beth away somewhere.

But what if he didn't believe her? What if he thought she was just making up a story? Then he'd get mad at her.

Her grandmother.

That's who she'd tell. Her grandmother always believed her, no matter what she said. And if she had to, she'd make her grandmother walk all the way out there, and show her where Beth had been, standing over that stupid sinkhole, talking about a ghost like it was something real.

She hurried on to the top of the stairs, and started down the hall toward the far end. Just as she got to her grandmother's closed door, she heard Carolyn's voice calling her name. But instead of turning around, or even acknowledging that she'd heard, she simply ig-

nored her stepmother, turned the knob of her grandmother's door, and let herself in.

Abigail sat in a chair by the window. Her eyes were
closed, and one hand rested in her lap. The other one
hung limply at her side, and a few inches below her
hand, a book lay open, facedown, on the floor.

Tracy stared at her grandmother. Was it possible
she'd died, just sitting there in her chair?

Tracy's heart skipped a beat.

She edged slowly across the room. How could you
tell if someone was dead?

You had to feel for a pulse.

Tracy didn't want to do that. It had been horrible
enough having to look at her grandfather when he was
dead. But to actually have to touch a dead body . . .
she shuddered at the thought.

She paused. Maybe she should go and get her
father, or even Carolyn.

But then, as she was about to back away, her
grandmother's eyes flickered slightly, and her hand
moved.

"Grandmother?" Tracy asked.

Abigail's eyes opened, and Tracy felt a surge of
relief.

Relief, and a twinge of disappointment. Telling
Alison Babcock about finding her grandmother's body
would have been even better than telling her about
how crazy Beth Rogers was.

"Tracy?" Abigail said, coming fully awake, and
straightening up in her chair. "Come give me a kiss,
darling. I must have dozed off for a moment."

Tracy obediently stepped forward and gave her
grandmother a reluctant peck on the cheek.

"What are you doing here, child?" Abigail asked.
"Why aren't you outside? It's a beautiful morning."

"I was," Tracy said. She searched her mind, trying
to figure out how to tell her grandmother what she'd
heard without admitting that she'd followed Beth. "I
. . . I went for a walk in the woods," she went on,

deliberately making her voice shake a little. As she'd hoped, her grandmother looked at her sharply.

"Did something happen?" she asked. "You look as though something frightened you."

Tracy did her best to appear reluctant, and, once again, the ruse worked.

"Tell me what happened, child," Abigail urged her.

"It . . . it was Beth," Tracy began, then fell silent once more as if she didn't really want to tell on her stepsister.

Abigail's eyes darkened. "I see. And what did Beth do to you?"

"N-nothing, really," Tracy said.

Abigail's sharp eyes scanned her granddaughter carefully. "Well, she must have done something," Abigail pressed. "If she didn't, why do you look so worried?"

Still Tracy made a show of hesitating, then decided it would be better to let her grandmother pull the whole story out of her. "Grandmother," she said, "do you think maybe Beth could be crazy?"

"Crazy?" Abigail repeated, her brows arching slightly. "Tracy, what on earth happened? What would make you say such a thing?"

"Well, I was out in the woods, just hiking around, and all of a sudden I heard something," Tracy explained. "It sounded like Beth—like she was talking to someone, so I went to find her. But when I got there—" She paused, wondering if she should mention Peggy Russell at all. She decided not to. "Well, she was talking to herself. She was out there in the woods, and she was talking to herself!"

Abigail's forehead wrinkled into a frown. "And what was she saying?" she asked.

Slowly, as if struggling to remember every fragment of what she'd heard, Tracy repeated the words she'd heard Beth speak. "It was weird, Grandmother," she finished. "I mean, she was talking like there was really a ghost. She had a name for her, and everything. She called her Amy, and she said the ghost killed Jeff!

She said it killed Jeff, and she watched it happen! Doesn't that sound like she's crazy?"

Abigail sat silently for several long minutes, feeling the erratic pounding of her heart.

Amy.

"Amy" was a corruption of "Amelia."

And Amelia was a name she'd heard before.

Her husband had used it sometimes, when he was muttering to himself about the mill, and about Conrad Junior.

"Where?" Abigail finally asked, her blue eyes fixing intently on Tracy. "Where did all this happen, child?"

"In a little clearing," Tracy replied. "Down the hill from the mausoleum. There's a trail to it." She hesitated, then went on. "Do you want to go down there, Grandmother? I can show it to you. I can even show you the thing Beth thinks is a grave. Only it's not a grave. It's just a little sunken spot." She fell silent for a moment, but when her grandmother didn't say anything, she spoke again. "Well? What do you think? Is she crazy?"

Abigail glanced up at her, and Tracy suddenly realized that her grandmother was no longer listening to her.

"What?" Abigail asked.

Tracy's expression tightened into an angry pout. "Nothing," she said. "Nothing at all." Then she turned and stamped out of her grandmother's little parlor, slamming the door behind her.

Abigail, sitting thoughtfully in her chair, ignored the slam of the door. Indeed, she didn't even hear it.

Her mind was occupied with other things.

Eileen Russell parked her five-year-old Chevy in front of Hilltop, and wished once more that she hadn't agreed to come up here. She'd considered calling Carolyn and asking her to come down to the village instead, pleading a heavy workload and suggesting they just get together for a quick drink in the bar. She'd quickly rejected that idea; what she had to talk to Carolyn about couldn't be discussed in a public place.

Perhaps it couldn't be discussed at all, given the fact that they hadn't seen each other for several months, and Carolyn's life had changed so radically in the interim.

Still, for old times' sake, she had to try.

She got out of her car, slammed the door shut, and strode up the broad steps to the front door. She pressed the bell, and, when she heard nothing, pressed it again. Then, assuming it must be broken, she raised the huge brass knocker, and let it fall to its anvil with a resounding thump.

After what seemed an eternity, the door opened, and Hannah peered out. She blinked in the sunlight, then nodded a greeting. "Peter's out in the stable," she said. "You can just go around the back if you want to."

"I'm not here for Peter, Hannah," Eileen replied. "I came to see Carolyn."

Hannah looked momentarily taken aback, then recovered herself. "I'm sorry," she said. "She didn't tell me to be expecting anyone. Come on in, and I'll go find her." She held the door wide, and Eileen stepped into the huge entry hall. "Just make yourself at home," Hannah went on, closing the door and starting the long climb to the second floor.

After what seemed an eternity to Eileen, Carolyn appeared at the curve of the stairs. "Eileen! Come on up. If I'd been thinking, I'd have had Hannah send you right up, but I forgot to tell her." As Eileen climbed the stairs, Carolyn smiled ruefully. "I'm afraid I can't get used to the idea of having someone to answer the door for me. It seems so decadent. I'd have answered myself, but I never heard the bell. I was resting and I must have fallen asleep."

Eileen frowned, studying her old friend. "If you're not feeling well, I can—"

"I'm fine," Carolyn broke in. "But unfortunately, I can't convince either Phillip or Dr. Blanchard that there's no problem having a baby at my age."

They were halfway down the corridor now, and

Eileen came to an abrupt stop, staring at Carolyn. "A baby?" she repeated.

Carolyn nodded happily.

"Well, for heaven's sake." Then a thought occurred to her, and she blurted it out before she had considered it. "Does Alan know?"

Carolyn stared at her for a moment, then burst out laughing. "Of course he knows! Beth told him right off the bat." Her smile faded slightly. "I'm afraid Beth was a little upset at first, but she's used to the idea now. In fact, I think she's looking forward to having a baby brother. Anyway, I hope she is."

She opened the door to the master bedroom, then stepped back to let the other woman go in ahead of her. Eileen surveyed the room quickly, taking in the rich antique furnishings, the sheer size of the room, then whistled appreciatively. "If this were my bedroom, I'd never leave it. My God, Carolyn, it's bigger than my living room."

"I know," Carolyn sighed. "And if you want to know the truth, sometimes I hate it." She saw the skepticism in Eileen's eyes, and shrugged helplessly. "I think you have to be born to this kind of thing. Sometimes I feel so out of place, all I want is to be back on Cherry Street."

Eileen said nothing, but crossed to the window and looked out. The view took in the entire estate, the village, and the countryside beyond. Indeed, if she looked carefully, she could pick out the roof of her own little house, looking from here like nothing more than a speck in the landscape. "What about Beth?" she asked without turning around. "How's she handling living up here?"

Carolyn started to make a casual reply, but there was something in Eileen's voice that stopped her. "What do you mean?" she asked instead. "Eileen, did something happen this morning? With Peggy?"

Now Eileen turned to face Carolyn, her expression serious. "I almost didn't come up here," she confessed. "Peggy showed up at the Red Hen about eleven. First she told me nothing was wrong, but I didn't believe her. You know Peggy—she can't hide her feelings at all. And she was pretty upset."

Carolyn sank into one of the twin love seats that faced each other in front of the window. "What happened?"

"Beth didn't say anything?" Eileen countered.

Carolyn shook her head. "But I haven't seen her. In fact, I thought Peggy was still with her, and they were out on the grounds somewhere."

"They went for a hike," Eileen explained. "Apparently yesterday Beth told Peggy there was something she wanted to show her, and today she showed it to her."

"What was it?" Carolyn asked.

"That's the thing," Eileen went on, perching nervously on the couch opposite Carolyn. "From what Peggy said, it didn't sound like anything. Just a sort of a depression in a little clearing somewhere down the hill. But Peggy says that Beth insisted that it was a grave, and that it belonged to some little girl who used to work at the mill."

Carolyn studied Eileen for a moment, trying to decide if her old friend was pulling her leg. But Eileen's eyes were serious, and her brow was furrowed with worry. "I . . . I'm not sure I understand," Carolyn said at last.

"I'm not sure I do, either," Eileen replied. "At first, it sounded as though Beth was playing a joke on Peggy—telling her a ghost story. You know Peggy—she believes everything anybody tells her. But when she told me what happened up there, she said it wasn't as if Beth was even talking to her. She said it sounded crazy, that Beth really seemed to believe there was some kind of ghost living in the mill."

"But that's ridiculous," Carolyn said. "Beth knows there's no such thing as ghosts—"

"We all know that," Eileen agreed. "And ordinarily I wouldn't have thought anything about it. But Peggy was so frightened by the whole thing, that I thought I'd

better come up here and tell you about it. And I guess I
wanted to find out if it really happened."

"I don't know," Carolyn replied. "But—well, I'm
sure there's a reasonable explanation for whatever happened." Then, when Eileen said nothing, Carolyn had
a sudden feeling that there was something the other
woman wasn't saying. "Eileen? What is it? What's
wrong?"

Eileen looked away, and when she spoke, her eyes
were fixed on something outside the window. "Peggy
said that the way Beth was talking, it sounded as though
Beth was at the mill the night Jeff Bailey died. Peggy
got the feeling that maybe Beth had killed him herself."

"Oh, my God," Carolyn groaned, suddenly understanding. Quickly she told Eileen about the dream Beth
had had that night, and how real it had seemed to her.
"That's all she was doing," she finished. "She was just
telling Peggy about the dream."

Eileen hesitated, then rose to her feet. "Well," she
said, "I hope you're right—I hope that's all it was. But
I'm not sure there'll be any convincing Peggy of that.
I'm afraid—" She hesitated, then decided to go ahead.
"Well, I'm afraid Peggy doesn't want to see Beth
anymore."

"Not see her anymore!" Carolyn exclaimed. "But,
Eileen, that's crazy. They're best friends. They always
have been."

Eileen stood silently for a moment, then shook her
head. "They were best friends," she said quietly. "But
not anymore. Everything's changed now, Carolyn. Things
aren't the way they used to be. I'm sorry." As she
started toward the door, Carolyn rose to her feet, but
Eileen waved her back onto the couch. "I'll let myself
out," she said.

Then she was gone, and Carolyn knew that she
would never be back

But it had nothing to do with Beth. Of that, she
was absolutely positive.

It had to do with the fact that she herself had
married Phillip Sturgess, and Eileen, like all her other

old friends, didn't believe she hadn't changed, didn't believe she was the same Carolyn they'd known for years. They were sure that since she had married a Sturgess, she had taken on the airs of a Sturgess, and her daughter had, too.

Peggy's story was just that—a story.

The real reason Peggy Russell didn't want to play with Beth anymore, Carolyn insisted to herself, was nothing more than simple resentment of the way Beth lived now.

And there was nothing Carolyn could do about that. It was just a matter of time. In time, Beth would adjust to her new life, and make new friends.

Soon, too, there would be a new baby in the house. That would help. The baby would be a half-brother to both Beth and Tracy, and maybe, at last, the two of them could be friends.

As for the story of the ghost that Peggy was so certain Beth believed in, Carolyn dismissed it from her mind.

Her daughter, she knew, was far too sensible ever to believe in something like a ghost.

Abigail Sturgess stood in the mausoleum, gazing down through the fading afternoon sun at the foreboding silhouette of the mill. Earlier, when she'd first come up to the mausoleum, the newly sandblasted bricks had glowed red in the sunlight, and for a moment it had looked to Abigail as if the building were on fire. But it was, she knew, only an illusion.

Abigail Sturgess didn't believe in illusions.

Still, somewhere inside the mill there was something that her husband had believed in, and that now she, too, was beginning to believe in.

Coming to a reluctant decision, she turned and began making her laborious way down the steps to the forest path. Abigail moved steadily along until she emerged onto the lawn in front of the house, but instead of going into the house, she crossed to the garage, and entered it through a side door. Turning on the

lights, she reached into her purse and found the keys to
the old Rolls-Royce that her husband had steadfastly
refused to sell, though he hadn't driven it in years.
Instead, he had kept it in the garage, insisting that it be
taken out on a monthly basis, to be driven a few miles,
gone over by a mechanic, then returned to the garage,
where it would be available on the day when he finally
decided to take it out himself. That day had never
come. When he died, he hadn't been behind the wheel
of the car for nearly a decade. But it was in perfect
condition, ready for Abigail now.

She got stiffly behind the wheel, found the slot for
the key, and twisted the starter.

Immediately, the engine purred into nearly silent
life. Abigail reached up and pressed the button attached to the sun visor, and the garage door opened
behind her. Putting the car in gear, she backed carefully out into the driveway, changed gears, and rolled
sedately around the lawn and out the gates.

A few seconds later, she had left the estate, and
was starting down the hill into Westover.

She parked the car on Prospect Street, across from
the mill, and sat for a long time, wondering whether or
not she was doing the right thing.

On the day nearly forty-five years before, when
they had buried Conrad Junior, Abigail had accompanied her husband to the mill. There, she had watched
as he placed the padlock on the door, then turned to
her and made her swear never to set foot inside the
building again. To humor him she had agreed. And
though she had helped Phillip plan the reconstruction,
she had not toured the building with him. Now, as she
steeled herself to her task, the oath came back to her
and she felt herself shiver slightly.

But it was ridiculous. She was going into the mill
this time not to violate Conrad's wishes, but to imple-
ment them.

She left the car, and crossed Prospect Street, unaware that the men who were finishing up their day's

work on the scaffolding covering the mill's facade were staring at her.

She made her way down the path along the northern wall of the mill, ignoring the stream of workmen coming the other way, making them step off the path to make way for her. Finally she stepped through the open door that broke the wall halfway to the end.

She paused. The worklights glittered with a surprising intensity that cut away the gloom she had expected. Almost immediately, she heard a voice behind her. She turned to see Alan Rogers emerging from the construction shack. "Mrs. Sturgess," he was saying. "Can I do something for you?"

Abigail's lips tightened slightly, and she regarded him with open contempt. "I have decided that we shall stop work," she said without preamble. "You may dismiss your crew, Mr. Rogers. I have changed my mind."

Alan stopped abruptly, and stared at the old woman. What the hell was she talking about? "I beg your pardon, Mrs. Sturgess," he said aloud. "Did you say you'd changed your mind?"

"I did," Abigail replied.

"About what?" Alan asked, deciding to buy some time while he decided how to handle her.

"Don't pretend to be more of a fool than you are, Mr. Rogers," Abigail said coldly. "I have decided not to go ahead with the reconstruction. I want the mill sealed up again."

Alan licked his lips uncertainly. The last thing he wanted to do right now was get into a fight with Abigail Sturgess. "Well, I'm afraid it isn't quite that simple, Mrs. Sturgess," he began, but Abigail cut him off.

"Of course it's that simple," she snapped. "It's my mill. You will be paid, of course. But the work is to stop immediately."

Alan said nothing, but shook his head.

Abigail's eyes flashed dangerously. "Did you hear me, Mr. Rogers?"

Alan sighed, then nodded. "I did, Mrs. Sturgess. But I'm afraid I can't stop the work on your authority.

It was Phillip who signed the contract. If he's changed his mind, he'll have to tell me himself. He was here this morning," he added with elaborate casualness, "and he didn't say a word about stopping the project. In fact, just the opposite. We were figuring out ways to speed the job up."

Abigail was silent for a moment, then nodded curtly. "I see." She turned away, and started back into the cavernous interior of the building. Before she had taken two steps, though, she felt Alan's hand on her arm.

"I'm sorry, but you can't go in there."

She brushed his hand away as if it were an annoying insect. "Of course I can go in," she snapped. "If I wish to inspect my property, I have the right to do so." Her eyes met his, as if challenging him to stop her. "The men are gone, Mr. Rogers," she went on. "I'll hardly be in the way."

Alan nodded a reluctant agreement. "All right. But I'll go with you."'

"That's not necessary," Abigail replied.

"I'm afraid it is," Alan told her. "You may own the mill, Mrs. Sturgess, but right now I'm responsible for it. I don't leave in the afternoon until I know that it's empty, and locked. And I'm not about to allow you to wander around by yourself."

Abigail's nod of assent was almost imperceptible. "Very well."

Twenty minutes later they stood at the top of the stairs to the basement. Without looking at Alan, Abigail spoke. "Give me your flashlight, Mr. Rogers. I wish to go downstairs."

"Mrs. Sturgess—" Alan began, but Abigail cut him off.

"Mr. Rogers, one of my sons died down there many years ago, and my dearest friend's grandson died in the same place two days ago. I wish to visit the spot where the tragedies occurred, and I wish to visit it alone. You will give me your flashlight, and then you will wait for me at the door."

Alan hesitated. "Let me at least turn on the lights down there." He started toward the electrical panel, but Abigail stopped him.

"No," she said. "I wish to see it the way my son and Jeff Bailey saw it." When Alan still hesitated, she allowed the faintest note of pleading to enter her voice. "I have my reasons, Mr. Rogers. Please."

Reluctantly, Alan turned his flashlight over to the old woman, then, as she started slowly down the stairs, headed back to the site shack. He would give her twenty minutes, no more.

Only when she reached the basement, and the darkness of it had closed around her, did Abigail turn on the flashlight and let its beam wander through the dusty expanse of the cellar.

There seemed to be nothing there.

Only piles of crates and stacks of plasterboard.

She stepped onto the floor of the basement, and turned right. She took five more steps, then turned right again, so that she was facing the area below the stairs.

Holding the flashlight firmly, she played its beam into the darkness there.

Abigail's thoughts were fueled by the memory of her husband's strange fixations about this place, and her eyes began to play tricks on her.

A face loomed out of the darkness, pale skin stretched over sharp cheekbones, the mouth drawn back in a grimace of terror.

Eyes glared at her, sparkling with hatred.

Another face, twisted in agony.

A mouth, hanging in the blackness—open—screaming silently.

Abigail's heart began to pound as the faces surrounded her, all of them hanging in the darkness, all of them staring at her, accusing her, judging her.

Laughter began to ring in Abigail's ears. Then the laughter turned to screams of agony and anguish.

A stabbing pain shot through Abigail's left arm, up into her shoulder, and through her chest.

The flashlight dropped to the floor, its lens and bulb shattering on the hard concrete.

Her knees buckled beneath her, and she began to sink to the floor.

But still the faces—faces of children—loomed in the darkness, coming closer, closing in on her. Their screams echoed through the old building, and rang in her ears, louder and louder, until the screaming seemed to be inside her head. Then, as she felt herself losing consciousness, she thought she saw a flash of light, a glow, thought she saw flames licking from the edges of the fire door.

*It's true*, she thought, as the flames receded and blackness engulfed her, *Conrad was right. It's all true. . . .*

# 15

Abigail Sturgess sat propped up in bed, three pillows behind her back, her frail shoulders covered with the cashmere afghan that was the first thing she had demanded after awakening to find herself in the hospital. Her skin, almost translucent, seemed to sag around her features, but her eyes were as bright as ever as she regarded her family with something that Carolyn felt was very close to disdain.

"It's nothing more than a minor inconvenience," the old woman insisted. "If anyone sends flowers, I shall have them thrown away—flowers are for funerals, and a slight heart attack hardly qualifies me for the grave."

"There was nothing slight about it, Mother," Phillip replied. "You're probably going to be here for a while."

"I'd rather be dead, and I shall tell that to the first doctor who suggests that I can't rest just as well in my own home as I can here." But despite her words, Abigail knew she would stay in the hospital until her strength returned, however long it took. And right now she felt much worse than she was prepared to admit.

"But what happened, Grandmother?" Tracy demanded. "What were you doing down there?"

Abigail turned to smile at her granddaughter. "Why,

I wasn't doing much of anything, darling. I simply went
down to see just what it was that your father is doing to
the old place, that's all."

Tracy's eyes narrowed suspiciously. "After everybody had gone home, Grandmother?"

"Mr. Rogers had not gone home," Abigail sniffed.
"Although had I wished to go in alone, who was to stop
me?"

"The liability laws, and the fine print in the contract might have given you a certain amount of pause,"
Phillip observed dryly, "had you bothered to read them.
But Tracy's right—whatever possessed you to go down
there today? And why didn't you ask me to take you? I
would have been more than glad to show you around."

"And bore me with a lot of technical claptrap I care
nothing about," Abigail said with more peevishness than
she truly felt. "I was up in the mausoleum and suddenly I had an urge to go down to the mill and have a
look around." She glanced at Tracy, who was watching
her with more shrewdness than she would have expected from a girl of thirteen. "At any rate, it doesn't
really matter, does it? All that happened was that I
went down to the basement, and I had a heart attack.
I'll grant you it was inconvenient, and it would have
been a lot easier for us all if I'd done this at home, but I
didn't, and that's that."

Phillip gazed at his mother speculatively. "The
mausoleum," he repeated. "Why did you go up there?"

Abigail's eyes hardened slightly. "Your father is
buried there, Phillip. Do you need more of an explanation as to why I might go there?"

"Under the circumstances, Mother, I think I do,"
Phillip replied. "You've never been in the habit of
walking up that trail by yourself, and you certainly
haven't driven a car in years. Yet today you not only
hiked up to the mausoleum, but you then took the car
and drove yourself down to the mill, where you pro-
ceeded to have a heart attack."

"Perhaps," Abigail grated, "the walk and the drive
were simply too much for me."

"And perhaps," Phillip shot back, "there's something else going on. Something you're not telling us about."

Abigail glared at her son. "I do not intend to be cross-examined by you, Phillip." Then, appearing to relent, she eased herself back against the pillows. "I was thinking about Conrad, that's all. So I went up to the mausoleum to be nearer to him. I find it peaceful up there." She smiled bitterly. "One day, I suppose, I shall find my peace there on a more permanent basis, shan't I?"

No one said anything.

"As for the mill, today I simply decided to go down there and see if I could discover what it was about it that so upset your father."

The door opened, and a smiling nurse bustled in. "I'm afraid our time's up," she announced with exaggerated cheer. "Doctor made us promise to keep our visit short this evening, and now we need our nap."

Carolyn rose from her chair, and picked up her purse, while Tracy leaned over to kiss her grandmother. Abigail accepted the kiss, but her eyes remained fixed on the nurse. "I made no such promises," she announced. "Furthermore, I have no intention of taking a nap. I intend to talk to my son for a few more minutes."

"Mrs. Sturgess—" the nurse began.

"It won't work, Nurse," Phillip said, sighing and lowering himself into the chair his wife had just vacated. "Better to give her a few more minutes than waste your time arguing with her, and end up giving in to her anyway."

"But Doctor said—"

"Doctor was a stupid child, and I can't imagine that he's grown into a much brighter adult," Abigail announced. "Now please leave me alone with my son."

The nurse hesitated, then gave up. Besides, she privately agreed with Abigail Sturgess's assessment of the doctor, and from what she'd seen of Mrs. Sturgess in the two hours since she'd arrived in the hospital, she suspected the old woman was a lot stronger than the doctor thought. "All right," she said. "But please, Mrs. Sturgess, not all night, okay?"

Abigail nodded slightly, and offered her hand to Carolyn when the younger woman made as if to kiss her on the cheek. "I expect to be home in a few days," she said. "I shall have to trust you to supervise Hannah until then. Please tell her—"

"I'm sure Hannah knows exactly what to do, Abigail," Carolyn interjected. "Just try to relax, and get well, all right?"

Abigail's lips tightened, but she didn't speak again until Carolyn and Tracy had followed the nurse out of the room and the door was shut. "As if she really wants me to get well," she began, but this time Phillip cut her off.

"Of course she wants you to get well, Mother," he said. "But sometimes I can't imagine why, considering the way you treat her. Now, what is it you want to tell me that you wouldn't say in front of Carolyn?"

"And Tracy," Abigail pointed out.

"Indeed?" Phillip asked. "Somehow I thought it was mostly Carolyn you wanted to be rid of."

Abigail shook her head. "Not this time. What I have to say, I shall say only to you." Her head turned, and her eyes fixed on her son with an intensity Phillip had rarely seen. "Phillip, you must close the mill."

Phillip groaned. "For God's sake, Mother. This is absolutely ridiculous. I thought when Father died, we could be done with all that nonsense. Please don't you start in on it now. Besides, it's far too late to change our minds. The investment is too big, and the contracts have been signed. I couldn't cancel them, even if I wanted to, which I don't. There's no way—"

"If you don't close the mill, more people will die there," Abigail interrupted. "It isn't going to stop, Phillip—don't you see? It happened to Conrad Junior, and now it's happened to Jeff Bailey—"

"Jeff Bailey's death was an accident—nothing more. It's been investigated, and there's no evidence of anything other than the fact that he tripped, and fell on a pick."

"Which is almost exactly what happened to your brother," Abigail replied.

"And that was more than forty years ago, Mother. We've been through all this before."

Abigail reached out and clutched Phillip's hand. "And what about me?"

Phillip eyed her impatiently. "You? Mother, you yourself said that what happened to you could as easily have happened at home or anywhere else."

"I lied," Abigail said softly.

Phillip leaned forward. "You *lied?*"

"I didn't want to frighten Tracy, or talk about it in front of your wife, but something happened today." She looked at Phillip again, and he thought he saw something in her eyes that he'd never seen there before.

Fear.

"I saw something down there, Phillip. I can't tell you exactly what it was, because I can't truly remember it. But I know that this afternoon, when I was in the basement of the mill, I was in the presence of death. I could see it, and I could hear it, and I could feel it. It's there, Phillip. Death lives in the mill, and if you don't close it, it will kill us all."

Phillip sat still, wondering what to say to his mother. Was it possible that her age was finally catching up with her, and she was beginning to suffer from delusions? But her voice was so strong, and she seemed so sure of what she was saying. "Mother, I'm sure you believe you felt something today, and there's no reason why you shouldn't. My God! You had a heart attack! It must have been terrifying." He smiled sympathetically. "In a way, you *were* in the presence of death, as you put it—"

"Don't patronize me, Phillip," Abigail rasped. "I know what I felt, and I know when I felt it. It had nothing to do with the heart attack, except to cause it. Oh, I was frightened all right. What do you think brought the attack on? It was fear, Phillip. Pure, un-

adulterated fear. I've never been a coward, but I saw
something in that basement that frightened me more
than anything has ever frightened me in my life. Whatever it is, it killed Jeff Bailey, and it tried to kill me.
And there's no way to get rid of it. Your father was
right. The only thing you can do is close the mill."

Phillip rose to his feet, knowing that arguing with
his mother was useless. "I'll think about it, Mother," he
said softly as he leaned over to kiss her. "I can't promise you anything right now, except to think about it."

Abigail turned away from Phillip's kiss, her head
sinking tiredly into the pillows. "Not good enough," she
whispered so quietly that Phillip could barely make out
her words. "It's just not good enough." She closed her
eyes, and for a moment Phillip thought she had fallen
asleep. But then her eyes blinked open, and her body
stiffened. "Beth," she said.

Phillip stared at her. "Beth?" he repeated.

Abigail's eyes narrowed slightly, and she nodded.
"Where is she?"

The question threw Phillip into confusion. What
on earth was she thinking of now? "She's with her
father," he replied. "Alan was still here when we arrived, and we asked him if he'd take Beth for the
evening."

"I want to see her," Abigail announced. "Get her,
and bring her to me."

Phillip's eyes widened. "Now? Tonight?"

"Of course, tonight!" the old woman snapped. "If
I'm as sick as you'd like to think, I could be dead by
tomorrow!"

Phillip felt a sudden uneasiness. "Mother, what is
all this about? I know how you feel about Beth—"

"You know nothing," Abigail whispered in a voice
as venomous as Phillip had ever heard her use. "Apparently you're as much of a fool as your father always said
you were."

Anger surged through Phillip, and he felt a vein in
his forehead begin to throb. "I hardly think you'll get
my cooperation this way, Mother," he replied, biting

the words off one by one. "And if you think I'll expose
Beth to you while you're in a mood like this, you're
quite wrong."

Abigail glared at him for a moment, her entire
body trembling as if it were palsied. Then, slowly, she
eased herself back down, and when she spoke, her
voice was calm.

"I'm sorry," she said, though there was no hint of
regret in her voice. "I suppose I shouldn't have spoken
to you that way. But I wish to see Beth, and I wish to
see her tonight." When Phillip said nothing, she went
on. "If she doesn't wish to see me, I shall understand,
Phillip. And you may tell her that she may feel free to
walk out of this room at any time."

"But why, Mother?" Phillip pressed. "Why do you
want to see Beth?"

Abigail hesitated, then shook her head. "I can't tell
you," she said quietly. "It wouldn't make any sense to
you." Then she turned her head away, and closed her
eyes once more. Phillip watched her for a moment,
then slipped out of the room to join Carolyn and Tracy
in the reception area.

"What did she say, Daddy?" Tracy immediately
demanded while Carolyn asked the same question with
her eyes.

"Nothing much," Phillip replied, his voice pen-
sive. "She told me she wanted the mill closed, and she
. . ." His voice trailed off, and there was a long moment
of silence.

"What, Phillip?" Carolyn finally asked. "What else
did she say?"

Phillip glanced at his daughter, then his eyes fell
on his wife. "She says she wants to see Beth. Tonight."

Carolyn's eyes widened in surprise. "But—Phillip,
she always acts as if Beth doesn't even exist!"

"I know," Phillip agreed. "Don't ask me why she
wants to see her—she wouldn't say. All she said is that
she wants to talk to Beth, but that if Beth doesn't want
to come, she doesn't have to."

As confused as her husband, Carolyn slipped her

hand into his, and let him guide her out of the reception room onto the street.

In their preoccupation with Abigail's strange request, neither of them noticed the look of pure hatred that came into Tracy's eyes as soon as her stepsister's name was spoken.

# 16

"What do you say we have supper at the Red Hen?"
Alan asked dolefully as he stared into the nearly empty
refrigerator. He hadn't expected to have Beth with him
that evening, so hadn't stocked up on the food he knew
she liked. Nor had he bothered to stop at the store on
the way back to his apartment from the hospital. He
was too tired, and he'd known from Beth's silence that
something was wrong. Now, when she didn't answer
his question, he decided to face the issue directly.

"You might as well tell me what's up," he said,
closing the refrigerator door and moving into the tiny
living room of the apartment. He dropped down onto
the sofa next to Beth, and slipped his arm around her.
"If you can't tell your old dad, who can you tell?"

Beth looked up at him, her eyes filled with worry.

"I . . . I think I know what happened to Mrs.
Sturgess," she said after a silence that had threatened
to stretch into minutes. "I think Amy must have done
something to her, just like she did to Jeff Bailey."

Alan frowned thoughtfully, and wished—not for
the first time—that he knew more about psychology.
Then he reminded himself that parents had dealt with
children for centuries before psychologists had ever
invented themselves, and decided that his own instincts
were all he needed. Right now, his instincts told him

not to challenge the existence of Beth's imaginary friend. "Why would Amy want to do something to Mrs. Sturgess?" he asked.

"I'm not sure," Beth replied. "I think she hates the Sturgesses, though. And I think she hates all their friends, too."

"But why?" Alan pressed. "That doesn't really make sense, does it?" But of course he knew that it did. Amy, as Beth's "friend," would be angry at all the people who had hurt Beth, but whom Beth would not let herself hate. But how could he explain that to his daughter now, after what had happened that morning? She was already feeling friendless, and taking Amy away from her—trying to explain to her that the child didn't exist outside her own imagination—seemed to him as if it would be too much.

He'd heard about what had happened up on the hill that morning. At least he'd heard what Peggy Russell had had to say when she'd come bursting into the Red Hen while Alan was having lunch that afternoon.

But he hadn't, he now realized ruefully, connected Peggy's wild tale with Abigail Sturgess's unexpected visit to the mill. He should have, especially when the old woman insisted on going into the basement, but he hadn't.

Beth, obviously, had, and now it was up to him to try to find a way to convince his daughter that what had happened to Abigail was nothing more than a heart attack brought on only by her age. But it was certainly not connected to the presence in the mill of any sort of being, either real or imaginary. He was trying to figure out how to explain this to Beth when the doorbell rang. To his surprise, he found Phillip and Carolyn, with Tracy between them, standing in the hall.

Instinctively, he stepped out of the apartment and closed the door behind him, rather than invite them all inside. As Phillip began to explain the reason they were there, Alan's feeling of apprehension grew. There could only be one possible reason why Abigail wanted to talk to Beth, and the last thing he wanted to do was discuss that subject in front of Tracy. Why, he wondered, couldn't they have left her at home?

"Beth and I were just going out for supper," he said at last, not really intending the statement as anything more than an attempt to buy some time to think. But Phillip immediately suggested that they all go together, and Alan, taken off guard, was unable to invent a polite way to refuse.

It was a mistake.

Alan realized it was a mistake even as he pulled into the parking lot at the Red Hen, to be greeted warmly a few moments later by Eileen Russell. When the Sturgesses appeared behind him, Eileen's welcoming smile all but disappeared, and Alan felt a distinct chill between Carolyn and Eileen as Eileen led them to a large round table near the fireplace, that, even on this warm early-summer evening, was ablaze with the false warmth of poorly designed gas logs.

"This is totally tacky," Tracy announced as they spread themselves around the table. "No wonder Grandmother never comes here."

"How *is* Mrs. Sturgess?" Alan asked immediately. Out of the corner of his eye, he'd seen Phillip opening his mouth to admonish his daughter, and all his instincts told him that if he let that happen, Tracy would do her best to make the meal as difficult as possible for all of them. And for Beth, it would become sheer misery. As if to confirm his feeling, he saw Carolyn shoot him a grateful look.

"Much better," Phillip replied, his attention diverted from Tracy. "In fact, she's doing her best to make life miserable for everyone at the hospital, which, for Mother, is a good sign."

"Did she say what happened?" Alan asked warily, still certain the woman's experience in the mill had to be the reason she now wanted to talk to Beth.

Phillip hesitated, but shook his head. "Not really. She said something in the basement frightened her, but she couldn't say exactly what."

A nervous silence fell over the table, which Alan finally broke with an attempt at a lightness he didn't feel. But he still wasn't ready to discuss Abigail's request with Beth, so he tried to put it off with black humor. "Aside from the darkness, the smell, and the rats that live down there, what's to be scared of?"

It didn't work. Beth, who had said nothing until then, turned serious eyes to him. "Smell? What kind of smell?"

Alan winked at his daughter. "The smell of dirt, damp, and age. That place was closed up so long, I'm not sure I'll ever be able to get it aired out."

"Of course you will," Phillip replied. "It's just a matter of getting a decent furnace in, and letting it dry out."

"It might not be that simple," Carolyn said quietly. "With the mill, it seems that nothing is as simple as it appears, doesn't it?"

Alan eyed his ex-wife carefully. "Do I hear a note of skepticism?" he asked. "Don't tell me you've joined forces with your mother-in-law and decided the mill shouldn't be reopened."

Carolyn shot him a look of annoyance, but then decided that under his bantering tone, he'd meant the question seriously. "It has to do with a lot of things," she replied. "Aside from the history of the place, it just seems to me that Westover isn't big enough to support the kind of shops that always go into places like Ye Olde Mill." In an attempt to take the sting out of her words, she purposely pronounced the final E in "olde," and was relieved when Phillip joined in Alan's chuckle.

But then Phillip's laughter died away, and when he spoke, his voice was serious. "I'm afraid that despite what everyone else thinks—including my wife—I'm still convinced it'll be a success. If it turns out the way Alan and I have planned it, I'm hoping it will draw people from the whole area. And that could give the entire town a boost."

"Well, God knows Westover could use that," Alan

sighed. He picked up his menu, and glanced at the list of appetizers. "How does escargots sound?"

"*Here?*" Tracy asked. "You've got to be kidding." Her father shot her a warning glance, but Tracy ignored it. "Why couldn't we have gone to a nice restaurant?"

"There's nothing wrong with this place, Tracy," Phillip said quietly.

Tracy's eyes narrowed, and her mouth set into a sullen pout. "If Grandmother weren't in the hospital, we wouldn't have had to come here at all."

"We're here because we want to be," Phillip replied, and though his voice remained quiet, it had taken on a certain edge.

Carolyn seemed to be doing her best to ignore the exchange, and Alan, certain that anything else he said—no matter how innocuous—would only exacerbate the situation, concentrated on his menu even though he was quickly losing his appetite. And this, he thought as he began eliminating entrées to narrow his choices, is what Carolyn and Beth have to put up with every day. He felt a flicker of sympathy for Carolyn, and wondered if this marriage, like their own, was also going to be a failure for her. If Tracy had anything to do with it, he was certain it would be.

And more and more, it was becoming clear to him why Beth had found it necessary to invent a friend.

Surreptitiously, he stole a glance at his daughter. She seemed to be trying to disappear behind the menu. But she couldn't disappear all the time. How did she cope with Tracy's constant hostility and snobbery?

And why should she have to? Maybe, after all, he should try to find a way to make it possible for her to come and live with him. "Anything look good to you, honey?" he finally asked when the silence at the table began to become uncomfortable.

"I like the shrimp," Beth replied, but when she tried to tell Tracy how they were cooked, Tracy merely glared at her, and turned away. Beth once more fell silent, and as the meal wore on, the conversation became increasingly strained.

Then, over coffee, Phillip Sturgess suddenly came
to the point of their unannounced visit to Alan's apartment. Without a word to Alan, he turned to Beth.

"Beth, Tracy's grandmother would like to see you."

Carolyn stiffened slightly, as Beth's eyes widened
in surprise. Alan, who had been sipping his coffee, set
his cup down as he felt his daughter staring at him
accusingly from across the table.

"Is that why they came to the apartment?" she
asked.

"Well, we didn't come because we wanted to see
you," Tracy hissed, then fell silent when her father
glared at her.

"I'm afraid so, honey," Alan confessed. He turned
to Phillip. "But I really don't understand why she wants
to see Beth," he went on. "I thought—" Then he stopped
himself, embarrassed to utter the words that had been
on the tip of his tongue.

"That Mother isn't particularly fond of Beth?" Phillip finished. Then, when everyone except Tracy—whose
mouth was now twisted into a smug smile—seemed as
embarrassed as Alan had been, he went on. "I don't
think there's any reason for any of us to pretend the
truth doesn't exist. But today she specifically asked to
see Beth. I don't know why—she wouldn't tell me. But
she did say that Beth doesn't have to come if she
doesn't want to." He turned to Beth, who was now
looking at him with a mixture of fear and curiosity.
"And she also told me that if you do decide to come and
see her, you can leave anytime you want to."

Alan frowned. "What in the world did she mean by
that?"

Now it was Phillip who looked uncomfortable. "I'm
not sure about that either," he replied. "But I have to
assume that Mother is well aware of how she's treated
Beth, and this is her way of apologizing for it."

Alan felt a sudden surge of anger for his daughter.
"It seems to me," he said tightly, "that your mother is
still busy acting like the queen of the world. If she's
been mean to Beth—and I think we all know damned

well that she has—then I see no reason for Beth to go see her now. Frankly, I'm surprised you'd even ask, Phillip."

Tracy's eyes flashed angrily. "Don't you talk about my grandmother that way—" she began, but Alan had finally had enough.

"Shut up, Tracy," he said, not even glancing at the girl, but instead keeping his eyes on Phillip, as if challenging him to try to defend his daughter's rudeness. Out of the corner of his eye, he saw the shock on Tracy's face. Apparently her own father had never spoken that way to her.

"Of course you're right," Phillip said quietly, his shoulders slumping. "Mother's treated Beth shamefully—and Carolyn too, for that matter. And perhaps I should have simply told her it was out of the question." He turned to Beth. "I'm sorry," he said. "I shouldn't have even brought it up."

"I don't see why Grandmother even wants to talk to Beth at all," Tracy said as her father fell silent.

Beth, who had been sitting silently as the others talked, turned to face her stepsister. "Why not?" she asked. "Why wouldn't she want to talk to me?"

Tracy glared malevolently at Beth. "Because you're nothing but trash," she said, her voice quivering with anger. "You should be living with your stupid father in that crummy apartment, and you never should have come to Hilltop in the first place."

"Tracy!" Phillip interrupted. He put his napkin aside, and for a split second, Alan thought he might actually be about to strike the girl. But suddenly Carolyn, her voice low, stopped him.

"Leave her alone, Phillip," she said. "We might as well let her speak her piece." She turned to Tracy. "Go on," she said.

The reasonableness of Carolyn's voice only seemed to fuel Tracy's fury, and her eyes flashed dangerously. "Don't you talk to my father like that," she said, her voice rising to fill the room so that people at other tables turned to stare. "All you ever do is try to tell us

what to do. Well, why don't you do something about
Beth, instead of picking on me all the time? She's the
one who's crazy, and everybody knows it!"

A deathly silence fell over the entire restaurant.
After a moment Alan laid his napkin aside and stood up.
"Come on, sweetheart," he said to his daughter. "I
think we've heard all we need to hear."

But Beth didn't move. Instead she stared silently
at Tracy for a moment, then shook her head. "It's all
right," she said quietly. "I'll go see Mrs. Sturgess. And
I don't care what you think, Tracy. I don't care what
you think, and I don't care what you say. I'm not crazy,
and your grandmother knows it." She said the words
with as much bravado as she could summon up, but it
wasn't enough to still the pain Tracy's words had caused
her.

The only way she could shut out that pain was to
concentrate on something else, on something that
wouldn't hurt her.

And right now, the only thing that wouldn't hurt
her was Amy.

From now on, she would concentrate on Amy, and
then she would be safe from whatever Tracy might say
or do.

Beth glanced nervously down the corridor to the
waiting room where her mother, Phillip, and Tracy
were waiting. Phillip nodded to her, and her mother
gave her an encouraging smile, and she reached out
and shyly knocked at the closed door. From inside,
Abigail Sturgess's voice weakly called out for her to
come in. She opened the door, and slipped inside.

The room was much bigger than she'd thought it
would be, and there were flowers everywhere. It seemed
as if there should have been a second bed in the room,
but it wasn't there. She wondered if they'd really taken
it out just for Mrs. Sturgess. Finally, after taking in the
room, she made her eyes go to the bed. There, propped
up against two pillows, and looking much smaller than
Beth remembered her, was the old woman.

For her own part, Abigail surveyed the child with more interest than she ever had before. Until today, Beth had been nothing more to her than an unwelcome intrusion in her life, one best ignored until such time as Phillip finally came to his senses and left Carolyn.

Now, as she studied the girl, she slowly came to realize what a pretty child she truly was. Not that she wasn't perfectly familiar with Beth's features; she was. But today, for the first time, she really looked at Beth. There was a softness to her face, she realized, that was totally lacking in Tracy's face. Indeed, there was an innocence in Beth's eyes that she couldn't remember having seen in a child for years. Until now, she'd simply attributed the sophistication of Tracy and her friends to the hardening effect of growing up in the modern world. But in Beth, there was no trace of a knowing glint in her eyes. Rather, they appeared to be totally guileless.

"Come here, Beth," she said softly, patting the edge of the bed. "I—" She hesitated, almost unable to speak the words. "I want to thank you for coming to see a sick old lady," she finally managed.

Slowly, like a nervous animal, Beth approached the bed, but stopped short before she was within range of Abigail's hands. "I'm sorry you're sick," she offered shyly, then stood as if waiting to have her sympathy rebuffed.

"Well, perhaps I'm not that sick," Abigail replied. Then she twisted her lips into a grimace that was intended to be a warm smile. "Don't you want to know why I asked that you be brought here?"

Beth hesitated, then nodded silently.

"I want to talk to you about your friend," Abigail went on. She searched Beth's face for a reaction, but saw none. "Amy," she added.

For a moment, she thought Beth was going to turn around and flee from the room. But instead, Beth's eyes only showed the hurt of betrayal. "Tracy shouldn't have told you," she said. "She wasn't even supposed to know about Amy."

"I agree with you," Abigail said evenly, then watched carefully to see what Beth's reaction would be. As she'd hoped, Beth's eyes brightened slightly. "But since she did tell me about Amy, I thought we might talk about her." When Beth's forehead creased into a worried frown, Abigail hastened to reassure her. "It will be our secret. I promise not to tell anyone else about Amy, unless you say it's all right."

Beth chewed thoughtfully on her lip, then looked warily at the old woman in the bed. "Wh-what do you want to know about her?" she stammered.

Abigail let herself relax. It was going to be all right. "Well, to start with, how old is she?"

Beth hesitated. She wasn't quite sure. "My age," she said at last. "I think she's eleven, going on twelve."

"Eleven," Abigail repeated. "And do you know what she looks like?"

Beth shook her head.

"But I thought she was your friend," Abigail pressed. "Haven't you ever seen her?"

"Y-yes—"

"Then you must know what she looks like, mustn't you?"

"It . . . it was dark."

"Dark. Like it is in the mill?"

Beth nodded.

"And is that where you saw her? In the mill?"

Once more, Beth nodded.

"What does she do there?"

"She . . . she lives there," Beth replied, then stepped back almost as if she expected to be punished for what she'd said.

"But I thought—I thought she was dead," Abigail said.

Beth's eyes widened once more, and again Abigail was afraid she was going to run from the room. But instead, she swallowed hard, and stood her ground.

"She *is* dead," she said. "She used to work in the mill a long time ago, and something terrible happened to her. And she's still there."

"I see," Abigail breathed. "Do you know what happened to her?"

Beth thought, and then remembered the smell she'd noticed when she'd been in the basement of the mill with her father. "I think there was a fire," she whispered. "I think there was a fire, and she couldn't get out."

Abigail gasped, suddenly sitting up in the bed. Her hand shot out, clutching Beth's arm. "How do you know that?" she demanded. "How do you know there was a fire?"

Beth, suddenly terrified, wrenched herself loose from Abigail's grip, and ran to the door. Then she turned back to face the old woman once again,.

"I know!" she said, her voice reflecting her sudden desperation. She wished she hadn't come here after all, wished she hadn't agreed to come and see this old woman who hated her for reasons she couldn't understand at all. "I just know, that's all!" she repeated.

She reached for the door handle, but just as she was about to pull on it and run from the room, Abigail spoke again.

"I can tell you about Amy," the old woman said. "I can tell you everything about her that you want to know."

Beth froze, and then, very slowly, turned away from the door. Abigail's eyes seemed to reach out to her, gripping her, drawing her inexorably back toward the bed. . . .

Tracy sat in the waiting room, her fury growing inside her.

It should have been *her* her grandmother wanted to see, not that stupid Beth. What could they possibly be talking about? Her grandmother didn't even like Beth—in fact, she hated her almost as much as Tracy herself did.

Then she remembered the conversation she'd had that afternoon when she'd told her grandmother how

crazy Beth was. And her grandmother hadn't really said
anything.

But she'd gone down to the mill later on.

Was it possible that her grandmother didn't believe Beth was crazy? Could she actually believe what
Beth had been saying?

It wasn't fair.

None of it was fair!

Everyone was paying attention to Beth, and no one
was paying attention to her!

In fact, her own father hadn't even done anything
when that horrible Alan Rogers at dinner had told her
to shut up. Instead of defending her, he'd actually
apologized to Beth, like he was Beth's father, instead of
her own.

And now her grandmother was acting like Beth
was her grandchild, instead of herself.

All of a sudden, Tracy knew what was happening.
Beth was stealing her family. She was stealing her
father, and she was stealing her grandmother.

Tracy clutched at the magazine she was pretending
to read, and saw her knuckles turn white as her anger
turned her hands into tight fists.

Well, she wouldn't put up with it, and if any of
them thought she would, they were wrong!

She'd get even. She'd get even with them all!

# 17

Beth sat silently in the back seat of the Mercedes, staring out the window, watching the darkness outside as the big car made its ponderous way along Prospect Street toward River Road. As it came abreast of the mill, though, she stirred slightly, and leaned forward, as if by the slight movement her eyes would be able to pierce the brick walls of the ancient building, and see into its depths.

It was impossible, though. All she saw was the blank facade of bricks. But still, as Phillip turned left onto River Road, her eyes remained on the great mass of the building, then fixed on the loading dock that extended out from behind the mill.

There.

It was in there, in the dark cold room beneath the loading dock, that Amy had died.

Unless old Mrs. Sturgess had been lying to her.

Ever since she'd left the hospital room, she'd been trying to decide if the old woman had been telling her the truth or not, and she still hadn't made up her mind. But eventually she'd know.

Amy would find a way to tell her.

The mill disappeared into the darkness as the car moved on, and finally Beth let herself sink deep into the seat. Then, feeling eyes on her, she glanced over to where Tracy, her lips tight with anger, sat glaring at her.

"I want to know what my grandmother told you," she whispered so quietly that Beth was certain no one in the car but herself could hear it. But from the front seat Phillip Sturgess spoke.

"That's enough, Tracy. If she wants to tell us, she will. But she certainly doesn't have to."

"Why not?" Tracy demanded. "And why did Grandmother want to talk to her instead of to me?" Her eyes, which had never left Beth, grew angrier. "I'll find out," she said. "I'll get my grandmother to tell me."

Beth said nothing, only turning away to face the window once more. But this time her eyes were closed. She didn't open them again until she heard the familiar crunching noises of the car's tires on the gravel of the circular driveway. Wordlessly, she got out of the car the moment Phillip stopped, hurried up the steps, and was the first one through the front door.

Hannah—waiting in the foyer—spoke to her, but Beth went past the old servant as if she hadn't seen her, and ran up the stairs. A moment later Hannah turned puzzled eyes to Carolyn as the rest of the family came into the house.

"Is Miss Beth all right?" she asked, her voice anxious.

"She's fine," Tracy replied before either her father or her stepmother could say anything. "Aren't you going to ask about my grandmother?"

Hannah reddened slightly, but nodded. "I was just going to, Miss Tracy. How is she? Is she better?"

"She's doing very well," Phillip said before Tracy could go on. "In fact, she'll probably be home in a few weeks."

Hannah's brows rose. "Shall I get one of the downstairs rooms ready?"

"Don't bother. Mother won't budge from her rooms until the day she dies, and that doesn't look like it's going to be for quite a while yet." Then, understanding what Hannah was really saying, he reached out and patted her shoulder. "Don't worry, Hannah—if Mother needs extra help, we'll bring in a nurse. I'm not going to ask you to spend all day running up and down the stairs."

"Thank you, Mr. Phillip. I'm not as young as I used to be, I'm afraid. Would you like a nice pot of tea?"

Phillip and Carolyn glanced at each other, then shook their heads at the same time.

"I'll have a Coke, Hannah," Tracy said. "You can bring it to my room." She started toward the stairs, but Carolyn stopped her.

"If you want a Coke, Tracy, you can get it for yourself."

Tracy turned, her chin trembling. "I don't have to. It's Hannah's job."

"It is not Hannah's job," Phillip said quietly, but with a firmness in his voice that silenced Tracy. "Things are going to be difficult enough around here when your grandmother comes home, and it will be appreciated if you will do your part without making life even more difficult for us. All of us," he added, nodding pointedly toward Carolyn.

Tracy said nothing for a moment, and Carolyn could almost see her calculating the effects of various responses. In the end, she produced an apologetic expression, and looked shyly at the floor. "I'm sorry, Daddy," she said. Then, the Coke she had wanted apparently now forgotten, she dashed up the stairs two at a time. A moment later her door slammed loudly.

Carolyn sighed. "I'm sorry," she said. "I suppose I should have overlooked that, shouldn't I?"

"Why?" Phillip asked. He led her into the library, and poured each of them a stiff drink. "If you ask me, she was just testing, to see how far she could go. And I have to confess I'm getting just as tired of it as you are." Handing her the drink, he smiled ruefully. "I'm afraid I wasn't much of a father to her, which isn't an excuse— only an apology."

"Nothing to apologize for," Carolyn replied. She held the drink up in a silent toast, but as Phillip drank from his glass, she put her own back on the bar. "Pregnant ladies shouldn't drink." Then, feeling the built-up strain of the evening, she lowered herself tiredly into one of the wing chairs. "Do you want to tell me what's going on?" she asked.

Phillip looked at her quizzically, but said nothing.

"Come on," Carolyn pressed. "Your mother said something to you that you didn't want Tracy to hear. What was it?"

Phillip said nothing, but wandered over to the fireplace, where he stood leaning against the mantel, staring into his glass. Finally, instead of answering her question, he asked one of his own. "You don't think I should go ahead with the mill project, either. Is it just because of the way it used to operate, or is it something else?"

Carolyn frowned, wondering what, exactly, he was getting at. And then, slowly, the pieces began falling together in her mind. But what it added up to made no sense. It was as if Conrad Sturgess had suddenly risen from his chair in the mausoleum, and come back into the house with all his superstitions, and ramblings of evil in the mill. "It's the history," she said at last. "My great-great-grandfather was driven to suicide because of the mill. That my family blamed old Samuel Pruett is something you know, Phillip. It's been a sore spot in my family for generations."

"And yet you married me," Phillip pointed out.

"I love you," Carolyn replied.

Phillip nodded perfunctorily, and Carolyn had the distinct feeling that he hadn't really heard her, that his mind was on something else. "Was your family afraid of the mill?" she finally heard him ask.

Carolyn hesitated. Again, more pieces fell into place. "There were stories," she said, almost reluctantly.

"What kind of stories?"

"There was a story that several children disappeared from the mill. And right after that, your family closed it."

"Disappeared?" Phillip asked, his eyes reflecting a

genuine puzzlement that told Carolyn he'd never before heard the story.

"That's what I was told. One day some of the children went to work, and didn't come home again. The story the mill put out was that they'd run away. And I suppose it was plausible, given the working conditions. But a lot of people in Westover didn't believe it. My great-grandparents certainly didn't."

Phillip's forehead furrowed into a deep frown, and he refilled his glass. "What did they think happened?"

"They thought the children had died in the mill, and that the Sturgesses covered it up." She hesitated, then went on. "One of the missing children was a member of my family."

Phillip was silent for a moment. "Why didn't you ever tell me that story before?"

"There didn't seem any point," Carolyn replied. "It all happened so long ago, and I've never been quite sure whether to believe it or not." She smiled ruefully. "Well, to be perfectly honest, I was more than ready to believe it until I met you. Then I decided no one as nice as you could have sprung from a family that would have done something as awful as that, so I decided that the tales my grandmother told me must have been exaggerated. Which they probably were," she added, attempting a lightness she wasn't quite feeling. "You know how old family stories go."

"Don't I just," Phillip agreed, smiling thinly. "So now you don't believe the story?"

Carolyn shrugged. "I don't know that I ever believed it, truly. And I don't know that I disbelieve it now. It's just there, that's all. And whether I believe it or not, I'll never be comfortable about that mill. It gives me the willies, and it doesn't matter what you do to it, it always will."

Phillip sighed heavily. "Well, if what Mother said is true, it gave her considerably more than the willies this afternoon." Then, as Carolyn listened in silence, he repeated what Abigail had told him at the hospital. When he was finished, she picked up her glass from the bar, took a large sip, then firmly replaced it. "She really said it was the fear that brought on the heart attack, not the other way around?"

Phillip nodded. "She was very positive about it. And you know how positive Mother can be," he added archly. "Anyway, right after that, she asked me to bring Beth to her."

Carolyn's heart sank as she remembered the conversation she'd had with Eileen Russell that very afternoon. Had Eileen spent the rest of the day spreading Peggy's story all over town? She must have, since apparently Abigail had already heard.

"So that's why your mother went to the mill today," she said out loud, then repeated her conversation with Eileen to Phillip. "It must have gotten back to your mother," she finished, suddenly angry. "So she tied it all together with your father's nonsense and Jeff Bailey's accident, and went down there looking for something. But there's nothing there—only Beth's imagination, and your father's craziness!"

"And your family's stories," Phillip added. "If you mix it all together, it gets pretty potent, doesn't it?"

"But it's just stories," Carolyn insisted, her eyes imploring her husband. "And besides, Beth never heard them. My family all died before she was even born, and I never told them to her."

"But Beth's grown up in Westover," Phillip observed. "Everyone in town must know those stories, and she's probably heard them in one version or another all her life." He left the fireplace, and sank onto a sofa. "Maybe Mother's right," he said. "Maybe you're both right. If everybody in Westover's heard all those stories, probably no one will come anywhere near the mill. Wouldn't that be something?" he added wryly. "All that money, and I'll wind up boarding the place up again."

"No!" Carolyn suddenly exclaimed. "Phillip, we're being ridiculous. And I've been ridiculous right along. But it's going to stop right now. I don't believe in ghosts, and neither do you. There's nothing in the mill.

And as soon as it's opened, all the old stories will be forgotten!"

Before Phillip could make a reply, they both heard the screams coming from upstairs.

Tracy had appeared at Beth's door five minutes earlier, letting herself in without knocking. Beth, lying on the bed staring at the ceiling, had not moved, and for a minute Tracy had thought she was asleep. But then she'd seen that Beth's eyes were open.

"Look at me!" she'd demanded.

Beth, startled, had jumped up, then, when she saw who it was, sat back down on her bed. "What do you want?"

"I want to know what my grandmother said," Tracy told her. She advanced across the room a few steps, then stopped, still ten feet from the bed.

Beth hesitated. She could see the anger in Tracy's eyes, and was sure that if she tried to make something up, Tracy would know she was lying.

Maybe she should call her mother. But what good would that do? Tracy would just wait until they were alone, then start in on her again.

"She . . . she wanted to talk about Amy," she finally blurted.

Tracy looked at her scornfully. "You're crazy," she said. "There's no such person as Amy."

"There is, too," Beth shot back. "She's my friend, and your grandmother knows all about her."

"She only knows what I told her." Tracy sneered. "And I told her everything you were saying to that stupid Peggy Russell."

"Peggy's not stupid!"

"Maybe she's not," Tracy conceded. "At least she's not stupid enough to believe all that junk you were telling her. And neither am I, and neither is my grandmother!"

"You don't know anything," Beth replied. Tears were welling up in her eyes now, and she was struggling to keep them from overflowing. "You think you're so smart, but you don't know anything, Tracy Sturgess!"

"You shut up!"

"I don't have to!" Beth cried. "I live here too, and I can say what I want to say! And I don't care if you don't believe me! I don't care if anybody believes me. Now, go away and leave me alone!"

Tracy's eyes glowed with fury. "Make me! Just try to make me, you stupid little bitch!"

"You take that back!"

"I don't have to, 'cause it's true! You're stupid, and you're crazy, and when I tell my father, he'll make you go away. And I'll be glad when he does!"

Beth's tears overflowed now, but they were tears of anger, not of pain. "Who wants to live in your stupid house anyway! I never wanted to come here!"

"And nobody ever wanted you to come here!" Tracy screamed. "Don't you know we all hate you? I hate you, and my grandmother hates you, and my father hates you! I bet your mother even hates you!"

The blood drained from Beth's face, and she lunged off the bed, hurling herself at Tracy. But Tracy, seeing her coming, spun around, yanked the door open, and dashed down the hall. Beth caught up to her just as she was opening the door to her room. Grabbing Tracy's hair, she tried to pull her back out into the hall.

"Let go of me!" Tracy screamed. Her arms flailing, she tumbled into her room, with Beth on top of her. "Daddy! Daddy, help me! She's trying to kill me!"

She was lying on her stomach, Beth astride her, pummeling at her shoulders. With a violent wrench, Tracy twisted herself over onto her back, and, still screaming, began clawing at Beth's face.

And then, just as she was sure she was going to be able to throw Beth off her and give her the thrashing she deserved, her father suddenly appeared, his hands sliding under Beth's shoulders, lifting her up.

"Get her away from me," Tracy wailed, her hands immediately falling away from Beth to cover her face. "Get her off me, Daddy! She's hurting me!"

With a quick tug Phillip pulled Beth to her feet, then let her go. Sobbing, she ran to her mother, who was now standing just inside the door, and threw her arms around her. Carolyn knelt down, pulling her daughter close.

"Beth! Honey, what happened?"

But before she could reply, Tracy's voice filled the room. "She's crazy!" Tracy yelled. "I was just lying on my bed, and all of a sudden she came in and jumped on me! I didn't do anything, Daddy!"

Carolyn, bewildered, looked from Tracy to Beth. "Beth? Is that true?"

Beth, tears streaming from her eyes, shook her head. "She came into my room," she replied. "She came in and started telling me I was crazy, and that everyone hates me. And . . . and—" She broke off, choking back her sobs.

"That's not true," Tracy said hotly. "I didn't go anywhere near her room!"

"That's enough!" Phillip declared. "It doesn't matter who started it. You're both quite grown up enough not to be fighting like this. Now I want you both to apologize to each other."

"I won't!" Tracy shouted. "I didn't do anything, and I don't have to apologize to anyone! Why don't you make Beth apologize? She started it!"

Phillip took a deep breath, and silently counted to ten. When he spoke, his voice was quiet, but there was an edge to it that cut through his daughter's fury. "I don't care who started it, Tracy. All I'm interested in is ending it. Now, apologize to Beth."

Tracy's eyes narrowed. "I'm sorry," she whispered in a voice that was barely audible.

Phillip turned to the other girl. "Beth?"

Beth hesitated, then sniffled. "I'm sorry," she said at last. "I shouldn't have jumped on you."

"See?" Tracy crowed. "She admitted it!"

"She apologized, Tracy," her father replied. "That's all. Now get into bed, and I'll be back in a little while to say good night."

Tracy glanced at the clock, then decided not to
press her luck by protesting that it wasn't even ten yet.
Instead, she looked up at her father appealingly. "Is it
all right if I watch television?"

"For an hour," Phillip agreed. "Say good night to
Carolyn and Beth."

Tracy hesitated, then spoke the words while she
looked at the floor.

"Good night, Tracy," Carolyn said quietly, then
led Beth out of the room and back to her own. Neither
mother nor daughter said anything while Beth undressed,
put on her pajamas, then slipped under the covers.
Finally Carolyn leaned over, and kissed her daughter's
forehead.

"I'm sorry, honey," she said.

Beth looked up at her mother. "Do you believe
me, Mommy?" she said so quietly that Carolyn could
barely hear the words.

"Of course I do," Carolyn assured her. "Why would
I ever think that you'd pick a fight with Tracy?" She
forced herself to grin. "After all, she's bigger than you."

"But why does she hate me?" Beth asked.

"I don't know," Carolyn replied, the smile fading
from her lips. "And I don't know what we can do about
it, either. But we'll think of something. I promise." She
kissed Beth once more, then went to the door. Then, as
she let herself out, she heard Beth speak once more,
almost as if she were talking to herself.

"Sometimes I wish Amy would just kill her."

Chilled, Carolyn said nothing, but pulled Beth's
door closed behind her.

Phillip glanced up as Carolyn came into their bedroom. "You look white as a sheet," he said. Taking her
hand, he led her to the bed, but she pulled away from
him and went to sit at her vanity instead.

In the mirror, she could see that he was right. Her
skin looked ashen, and there seemed to be dark circles
under her eyes. Helplessly, she shook her head.

"I just don't know how much more of it I can

stand," she said, her voice trembling with the tears that were suddenly threatening to overwhelm her. "It's not getting any better, Phillip. And I don't think it's going to!"

Phillip came to stand beside her, his strong hands resting gently on her shoulders. "But what can we do?" he asked. "They're our children." Then he smiled tightly. "Maybe I was wrong," he suggested. "Maybe I shouldn't have stopped the fight. In the end, they may just have to fight it out."

"That's boys," Carolyn said. She reached for a Kleenex, and blew her nose, then threw the tissue into the white wicker basket at her feet. "Girls don't do that sort of thing."

"Ours do," Phillip said quietly.

Carolyn shook her head hopelessly. "And what's it going to be like when the baby comes? Phillip, I just don't think I can cope with it all."

"Of course you can," Phillip began, but Carolyn shook her head again.

The last words Beth had spoken before Carolyn had left her room echoed in her mind. Should she repeat them to Phillip? But she couldn't. It would be almost like betraying Beth. Besides, the words hadn't meant anything—they'd been nothing more than the venting of childish anger.

"I . . . I've been thinking maybe I ought to let Beth go live with Alan for a while," she finally said. "At least until the baby is born." In the mirror she could see her husband's worried frown. "And she'd like to go—I know she would."

"What about Alan?" Phillip asked. "Don't you think you ought to ask him about it?"

"I don't have to," Carolyn sighed. "You know as well as I do that he'd take her in a minute. He'd rearrange his whole life for her."

There was a melancholy note in her voice that made Phillip wonder if Carolyn was having more second thoughts about their marriage. "And I wouldn't?" he asked quietly, hoping he didn't sound defensive.

Carolyn patted one of his hands gently. "You'd do anything for anybody, if you could," she told him. "In that way, you and Alan are very much alike. And I know how much you've tried to do for Beth. But you have Tracy and Abigail to worry about, too."

"And you," Phillip added.

"And me, and in a few months, a new baby as well. And I just keep thinking maybe I'm being unfair to Beth. She's so unhappy here, and it doesn't seem to matter what you or I do. Sometimes I feel as though we're both caught in the middle."

"I know," Phillip agreed. Giving her shoulders one more squeeze, he wandered over to the window, and looked out into the night. From here, at the front of the house, he could barely make out the upper ring of the mausoleum, glowing softly in the moonlight. Up there, at least, it looked peaceful. If only they could make the house peaceful, too.

"Let's not make any decisions now," he said. "Let's give it a little more time, and see what happens. I hate giving up. Another few days, all right? And then we'll talk to Alan."

Carolyn nodded, and looked at herself in the mirror once more.

She not only looked tired now, she thought. She looked defeated as well.

In the corridor outside, Tracy padded silently away from the door to her father's bedroom.

She hadn't heard every word—the wood was too thick for that—but she'd heard enough.

They were thinking about sending Beth away. That was exactly what Tracy wanted. But it wouldn't be forever.

When the baby came, they'd bring her back, and then it would be worse than ever.

She had to figure out how to convince them that Beth was crazy so they'd send her away and never let her come back again.

She went back to her room, and got into bed. The

television was on, and though she was looking at it, she wasn't really seeing it. She was thinking.

By the time her father came in to say good night twenty minutes later, she had figured it out. When he leaned over to kiss her, she slipped her hands around his neck, and hugged him tightly. "I love you, Daddy," she said quietly. "I love you, and I really am sorry about what happened with Beth tonight. From now on, I'll do my best to be nice to her. All right?"

She felt her father's body stiffen for a moment, then relax as he returned her hug. "Thanks, Princess," he said into her ear. "That would really help out."

"Then I'll do it," Tracy whispered, giving him one more kiss, then rolling over in bed. "Good night, Daddy."

When he was gone, she rolled back over and lay staring at the ceiling. When the house was silent and she was sure everyone had gone to sleep, she got out of bed, and quickly dressed.

A minute later, she was down the stairs and out of the house, moving across the terrace, then disappearing into the night.

# 18

The warmth of the morning woke Beth early, and she
stretched luxuriously, then kicked the covers off and
got out of bed. But a moment later, as she came fully
awake and remembered last night's fight with Tracy,
her good feeling vanished.

It would be another day just like all the rest—a day
of trying not to make any mistakes, of trying to stay out
of Tracy's way, of not knowing what to do next.

Maybe she should go down to the village and find
Peggy.

Or maybe, instead of looking for Peggy, she should
go to the mill. Maybe, if she promised to stay out of
everyone's way, her father would let her spend the day
at the mill. Then, while everyone was busy, she could
go down into the basement, and sneak into the little
room under the stairs. And Amy would be there, waiting for her.

They could sit in the dark together, and Beth could
talk to her. It would be nice, Beth thought, to be alone
in someplace cool and dark and quiet, with no one around
except a friend who wouldn't laugh at you, or tease you,
no matter what you said. That's the kind of friend, she
was sure, that Amy would be to her. Someone for her to
talk to when she got so lonely she felt like no one in the
world wanted her, or understood her, or cared about her.

She began dressing, then looked at the clock. It was only seven-thirty. Hannah would be in the kitchen, starting breakfast, but neither Peter nor Mr. Smithers would have come to work yet.

Maybe she should go down to the stable and visit Patches before Peter got there. Because Peggy, she was sure, would have told Peter what happened yesterday. Peggy always told everybody everything, and by now Peter probably would have decided she was crazy, too.

What if he told her she couldn't come to the stable anymore? That, she decided, would be awful. Going down to see the horses in the morning was the best part of every day. Still, it hadn't happened yet, and even if it did, she could just start getting up earlier every day.

She tied her tennis shoes, then quickly made her bed and put away the clothes she'd been wearing last night. Then she left her room, and glanced down the hall in both directions, listening. She heard nothing. Both Tracy's door and her mother's door were still closed. Everybody but her was still asleep. She scurried down the stairs, and through the long living room, then slowed down as she crossed the dining room. She could almost feel the portraits of all the dead Sturgesses glaring disapprovingly down on her, even though she always did her best not to look at them. When she came to the butler's pantry, she let out an almost audible sigh of relief. Here, in Hannah's territory, she always felt more comfortable. Finally she pushed open the kitchen door.

"Must be a quarter to eight," Hannah said without turning from the stove where she was scrambling some eggs. "You're getting to be as regular as clockwork. Orange juice is in the refrigerator, and the eggs'll be done in a minute."

"I could have made my own eggs," Beth said as she reached into the refrigerator and brought out the pitcher of freshly squeezed orange juice. Even though she hated the pulp in it, she wouldn't hurt Hannah's feelings by telling her so, so she poured a big glass, then took a deep breath, squeezed her eyes shut tight, and tried to drink it all in one gulp. When she was finished, she opened her eyes to see the housekeeper shaking her head sympathetically.

"Don't see how you can do that," Hannah said, her face serious but her eyes twinkling. "The pulp in that stuff makes me gag. I always have to strain it, myself."

Beth's eyes widened in surprise; then she giggled, and sat down at the table to dig into the plate of eggs that was now waiting for her. When she was finished, she scraped the leavings into the sink, rinsed the plate, then picked up the waiting bag of garbage and headed out the back door. She dumped the trash in the barrel as she crossed the little terrace, then waved to Ben Smithers, who was busy in the rose garden.

She ran all the way to the door of the stable. As soon as she stepped inside, she knew that Peter, as she'd hoped, was not there yet. There was a stillness in the little barn—a quiet that was broken only by the soft snufflings of the horses as they became aware that someone had come into the stable.

Beth let herself relax as she closed the stable door behind her, and started down the aisle toward Patches's stall. The big mare was stretching her neck out as far as she could, and whinnying softly.

"Hi, Patches," Beth whispered, reaching up to scratch the horse's ears. "Have you had breakfast yet?"

The horse snuffled, pawing at the floor of her stall, then tried to poke her nose into the pocket of Beth's jeans. Across the stall, the feed trough was empty.

"I don't see why Peter can't leave you something to eat during the night," Beth told the big mare, scratching her affectionately between the ears. "What if you get hungry?"

The horse snorted softly, and her head bobbed as if she had understood every word Beth said, and agreed with her. That, Beth decided, was the neatest thing about Patches—she could say anything to her, and never have to worry about whether the horse believed her or not.

It wasn't at all like it was with people. With people, if you said something that sounded just a little bit strange, they started calling you crazy.

Either that, or they didn't believe you were telling them the truth.

Beth sighed, hugged Patches's neck, then started down the aisle toward the feed bins to find something for the horse to eat. The hay wasn't down yet, but there was a big sack of oats beneath the hayloft.

As she found a pail and began filling it with oats, Beth wondered if anyone would ever believe that Amy was real.

So far, it didn't seem like anyone would.

Except for old Mrs. Sturgess.

But had the old lady really believed her, or was she just pretending to for some reason that Beth couldn't understand? Yet if she was only pretending, why would she have said that when she came home from the hospital she'd show Beth something that proved there really was a girl named Amy? And why would she have asked Beth what Amy wanted?

Beth didn't think Amy wanted anything. All she wanted was for them to be friends.

She took the pailful of oats back to Patches's stall, opened the door, and let herself inside.

"Look what I've got for you," she said, holding the pail up close to the big mare's nose.

The horse sniffed at the pail, then backed away, tossing her head.

"It's only oats," Beth said, moving slowly forward until she could reach out and take hold of Patches's halter. "You like oats, remember?"

She offered the pail once more, but the horse, sniffing at it again, tried to pull her head away. But Beth, prepared for it, tightened her grip on the halter, and held Patches in place.

"Maybe she doesn't want any," she heard a voice say from behind her. "Maybe she's not hungry."

Beth felt herself redden, and whirled around to see Tracy standing at the stall door, smiling in that superior way of hers that never failed to make Beth feel stupid.

"She likes oats," she said. "She just wants me to feed her, that's all."

"She doesn't want you to feed her." Tracy sneered. "She doesn't even like you. She just wants you to go away!"

"That's not true!" Beth flared, stung. "Watch!"

Still holding on to the horse's halter with one hand, she set the pail on the floor, then took a handful of the grain and held it up for Patches's inspection.

The big horse eyed the grain, then tentatively opened her mouth and licked. Beth raised her hand, and the horse's lips curled out, closed, and pulled in the oats. As she munched slowly, then swallowed, Beth reached down for another handful.

"That's the way," she crooned softly as the horse ate the second handful. "See how good they are?"

"Big deal," Tracy replied, her voice scornful. "A horse will eat anything, if you shove it into its mouth." Snickering, she turned away, and left the stable as silently as she'd come.

Beth felt a sudden stinging in her eyes, and glared after Tracy. "But you do like me," Beth said to Patches when she was once again alone with the horse. "You like me better than anyone, don't you?"

She picked up the pail, and held it while Patches, snuffling with apparent contentment, finished off the oats. Then, patting the horse on the neck, Beth let go of her halter and left the stall to take the bucket to the sink, wash it, and return it to its place by the tackroom door.

She was just about to turn Patches out into the paddock when she heard her mother's voice calling her to come in. She hesitated, then patted the horse once more. "I'll be back later," she promised. "And maybe we can go for a ride. Okay?" The horse whinnied softly, and her tail flicked up. Then her tongue came out to give Beth's hand a final lick. "Who cares what Tracy thinks? Who cares what anyone thinks?"

But as she left the stable, Peter Russell was coming

in, and Beth could tell by the way he looked at her that Peggy had, indeed, told him all about yesterday morning. And though he said nothing, Beth felt herself redden.

She did, after all, care what people thought.

Beth was just coming back into the stable an hour later when she heard Patches's first high-pitched whinny, followed by the crash of hooves against the wooden walls of the stall.

She raced down the broad aisle between the two rows of stalls and got to the big mare just in time to see the horse rear up, her forelegs lashing at the air, then drop back down. She stamped her feet, then once more reared, her teeth bared and her mouth open as if she were trying to bite some unseen enemy.

Terrified, Beth backed away from the stall. "Peter!" she yelled. "Come quick!"

But Peter was already there, coming out of the stall that belonged to the big Arabian stallion named Thunder. He stared at Patches in amazement for a moment, then dashed down the aisle between the two rows of stalls, climbed the fence into the paddock, and hurried back toward Patches's stall. As the mare, her eyes glazed now, bolted out of the stable, Peter made a grab for her halter, but missed. Bucking and snorting, Patches moved out into the center of the paddock, then stopped for a moment, glancing around wildly, as if searching for the unseen attacker. Then she dropped to the ground, and began rolling over, her legs thrashing violently. A moment later Beth, her face ashen, appeared at the open stall door.

"Peter, what's wrong with her?"

Peter hesitated, his eyes fixed on the agonized horse. "I don't know," he said. "Get me the lead, then go up to the house and have someone call the vet."

Beth darted back into the stable, grabbed a lead, then ran back outside and gave it to Peter. She stared at Patches for a moment, then dashed to the paddock fence, climbed over it, and charged up the slope toward the house.

A moment later she burst through the back door, calling out for Hannah.

"What is it, child?" Hannah asked, bustling out of her room.

"It's Patches," Beth gasped. "Hannah, we have to call the vet right away. Something's wrong with Patches! I . . . I think she's dying!"

As Beth and her mother, together with Phillip and Tracy Sturgess, looked on, Paul Garvey shook his head, and slid a large needle into a vein in Patches's right foreleg. He pressed the plunger on the hypodermic home, and a moment later Patches shuddered, seemed to sigh, then lay still.

"It's better this way," the veterinarian said softly, rising to his feet. "There wasn't any way to bring her out of that."

"But it was colic, wasn't it?" Phillip asked, his eyes leaving the dead horse to fix anxiously on Garvey.

"I never saw a case that violent before," Garvey replied. "If I had to bet, I'd put my money on poison."

"Poison?" Carolyn echoed, her eyes widening. "But who—"

"I'd like to check her feed," Garvey interrupted, his attention shifting to Peter Russell. "Any of the other horses showing any symptoms like this?"

Peter shook his head. "They hadn't even been fed yet. At least not Patches. I'd just filled Thunder's trough, and Patches would have been next."

The vet frowned. "The horse hadn't eaten anything?" he asked, his voice conveying his doubt.

It was Tracy who answered him. "It was Beth," she said, her voice quivering with apparent fury. "Beth was feeding her oats this morning."

Garvey's frown deepened. "Oats?" he echoed. "How much?"

"A whole bucketful," Tracy said. "They're in that bag over there." She pointed to the big feedsack that still sat against the wall beneath the hayloft, and Garvey walked quickly over, reached deep into the sack, and pulled out a handful. Holding the feed close to his nose, he sniffed deeply. Garvey frowned, then sniffed again.

"Well?" Phillip asked.

"Doesn't smell right," Garvey said. "I'll take some of this back to my lab. In the meantime, don't let any of the other horses anywhere near this stuff."

There was a moment of silence as the import of his words sank in, and then suddenly Tracy's voice, shrill and angry, sliced through the stable once more. "She poisoned her! She poisoned my horse!"

Beth gasped, and turned to look at Tracy, who was pointing at her accusingly. "I didn't do anything—" she began, but Tracy cut her off.

"You killed her!" she screamed. "Just because you hate me, you killed my horse! She didn't even want those oats! I saw you, and you were making her eat them. You were shoving them right into her mouth!" She lunged toward Beth, but her father grabbed her, holding her back.

"Tracy, nobody would try to kill Patches—"

"She did!" Tracy wailed. "She poisoned the oats, and then made her eat them."

Beth stared at Tracy for a moment, and suddenly remembered the way Patches had snorted, and tried to pull away from the pail. It wasn't until she'd taken the food in her own hand, and almost shoved it into the horse's mouth, that the animal had finally eaten it. Bursting into tears, she wheeled around and fled from the barn.

As Phillip held his crying daughter close, he and Carolyn exchanged a long look. Finally, after what seemed an eternity of silent decision-making, he spoke.

"I'll call Alan," he said quietly. "I guess maybe it's time we did something."

As he spoke the words, he thought for a moment that he felt Tracy relax against his body, and her sobbing seemed to ease.

Tracy Sturgess emerged from the swimming pool at the Westover Country Club, grabbed a towel, and flopped down on the lawn, shaking the water out of her hair. She'd been at the club for an hour, and even though no one had told her, she was almost sure she knew why her father had suddenly suggested—even insisted—that she come here this afternoon.

They were going to move Beth out of the house while she was gone.

And almost as good as that was the fact that her father had promised her a new horse, and even given in when she'd demanded an Arabian just like Thunder. She'd had to cry, of course, and act as though losing Patches was the worst thing that had ever happened to her, but that was easy. She'd always been good at things like that.

Now she propped her head up on one arm, and grinned at Alison Babcock, who was her best friend this summer. "What's everybody talking about?" she asked.

"Your grandmother," Alison replied. She rolled her eyes toward Kip Braithwaite, who was sprawled on a towel next to her. "Kip thinks someone tried to kill her."

Tracy's eyes widened, and she turned to stare at Kip. "Why would anyone want to kill Grandmother?"

"Well, someone wanted to kill Jeff Bailey, and they did it, didn't they?"

"Aw, jeez," Brett Kilpatrick groaned. "Nobody killed Jeff. He tripped and fell on a pick."

"That's what you think," Kip replied.

"Well, I ought to know," Brett shot back. "I was there, wasn't I?"

"But what did *you* see?" Kip taunted. "You were too chicken even to go downstairs."

"But what about Grandmother?" Tracy demanded. "How come you think someone tried to kill her?"

Kip shrugged. "Well, she had her heart attack right on the same spot where they killed Jeff, didn't she?"

"So what?" Alison Babcock asked. "That doesn't prove anything."

"And it doesn't disprove anything, either," Kip taunted.

"Well, if you're so smart, who did it?" Brett asked.

Kip glared at his friend. "What about Beth Rogers?"

Brett began laughing. "Her? You gotta be kidding. Didn't you see her at Tracy's party? She almost wet her pants just watching that movie!"

"But she was talking about a ghost in the mill," Kip pointed out. "Maybe she went looking for one."

"Are you kidding?" Alison giggled. "Beth Rogers? Give me a break."

"Well, I think she killed Jeff," Kip insisted. "And I think she tried to kill Tracy's grandma, too."

"Big deal." Alison sneered. "So that's what you *think*. But how do you *know*?"

"Well, I know she killed Tracy's horse," Kip shot back. "Tracy says that's why they're kicking her out. She's crazy."

"Oh, come on," Alison started, but Tracy interrupted her.

"But she is crazy, Alison," she insisted. "I was hiking up near the mausoleum yesterday, and she was up there. I heard her talking about someone named Amy that she thinks killed Jeff."

Alison stared at her. "Amy?" she repeated. "Who's she supposed to be?"

Tracy rolled her eyes. "She's the ghost! And I heard her talking about how this Amy killed Jeff because he was teasing her at my party."

The other three fell silent, eyeing each other uneasily, and Tracy could see that she hadn't yet convinced them. "Well, she *is* crazy," she insisted. "And I bet Kip's right. I bet she's so crazy that she killed Jeff, and doesn't even know it. I bet she really believes a ghost did it."

Alison's eyes narrowed, and she stared suspiciously at Tracy. "What about your grandmother?" she asked. "Do you think Beth tried to kill her too?"

Tracy hesitated, then nodded.

"Why?" Alison demanded. "What did your grandmother ever do to her?"

"Nothing," Tracy replied. "Except she can't stand

Beth, either, and Beth knows it. But crazy people don't need a reason to do things—they just do them." Then she had an idea. "And my grandmother was acting real weird last night, too. First she talked to Daddy, and then she made us go get Beth and bring her to the hospital. And afterward, Beth wouldn't tell any of us what she and Grandmother talked about."

"Think maybe she saw Beth down there yesterday?" Kip asked.

"If she'd seen her, why would she want to talk to her?" Alison asked. "I mean, if somebody tried to kill me, the last thing I'd want to do is *talk* to them!"

"Maybe she wasn't sure it was Beth," Kip suggested. "Maybe she wanted to talk to her to see if she could trap her, like they do on TV all the time."

Alison rolled her eyes impatiently. "Oh, who cares what they talked about? There's no way we can find out, anyway."

There was a momentary silence, and then Tracy grinned conspiratorially. "I bet I can find out."

"How?" someone asked.

"I'll go visit Grandmother," Tracy went on. "And I'll bet I can pry whatever she told Beth out of her. I can always get Grandmother to do whatever I want, because she hates Carolyn so much."

"I bet she doesn't hate her as much as you do," Alison said, rolling over onto her back, and closing her eyes.

"I bet she doesn't, either," Tracy agreed. She, too, flopped back and closed her eyes. "In fact, I wish I could figure out a way to get Daddy to throw her out, too. Or maybe I could even get Beth to kill her. Wouldn't that be neat? Getting her to kill her own mother?" She giggled maliciously, and after a moment, the others joined in.

Tracy left the club at four o'clock, deciding it was better to walk the two miles into town than to ask her father to take her to the hospital when he came to pick her up. He'd want to know why she suddenly wanted to visit her grandmother, and she wasn't about to tell him.

She started along River Road, wondering how she would get the information she wanted out of her grandmother. She couldn't just ask her—she already knew that. If she'd made Beth promise not to talk, she wouldn't just start talking herself. And then, as she approached the railroad tracks, she knew the answer.

Get her talking about the past. If there was anything her grandmother liked to do, it was to talk about the "good old days" before Tracy was born. And then, when she had her grandmother's guard down, she'd figure out how to lead her into talking about what had happened last night.

She was crossing the railroad tracks on River Road when she suddenly felt as if she was being watched. Turning, she saw Beth Rogers standing a few yards away, staring at her.

She froze, wondering what was going to happen. What if Beth had already figured out what she'd done to the oats? Would she have the nerve to say anything? But it wouldn't happen—Beth, she was sure, was too dumb to figure out what had really happened to Patches, just as Patches had been too dumb to refuse the poisoned oats. Raising her chin defiantly, and studiously ignoring Beth, she continued on to Prospect Street, then turned right past the mill toward the hospital that lay a few blocks further on.

Ignoring the sign announcing that visiting hours were from six until eight P.M., Tracy made her way to her grandmother's room, and let herself inside. Lying in the bed, her eyes closed and her breathing regular, Abigail Sturgess slept peacefully.

Tracy gazed at the frail form in the bed for a few moments, then reached out and shook her grandmother.

"Grandmother? Wake up."

Abigail stirred slightly, and tried to roll over.

Tracy shook her again. "Grandmother! It's Tracy. Wake up!"

Abigail started slightly, coughed, and opened her eyes. Squinting against the light, she peered up into her granddaughter's face. "Tracy?" she asked weakly. "What are you doing here?"

Tracy wreathed her face in a smile. "I came to visit you, Grandmother. I thought you must be lonely."

Abigail struggled to sit up. "Well, aren't you sweet," she said, as Tracy stuffed an extra pillow behind her. She blinked, then reached unsteadily for a glass of water on the table next to the bed. "Did your father come with you?"

Tracy shook her head. "I walked. I was afraid if I told anyone I was coming, Carolyn would have stopped me."

"She probably would have," Abigail agreed. "She's a hard one, that woman." Then she smiled. "Not like your mother at all."

Sensing an opening, Tracy smiled again. "Tell me about her," she said. "Tell me all about Mommy!"

Abigail sighed contentedly, and her eyes took on a faraway look as she let her mind drift back into the past. "She was a wonderful woman, your mother. Pretty as a picture, and just like you." She reached out to Tracy, squeezing her hand affectionately. "And she knew her place in the world. You wouldn't find her working in the kitchen, except once a week to give Cook the menus. But I suppose those days are gone forever . . ." Her voice trailed off, and she fell silent.

Tracy gazed at the shriveled form of her grandmother, wondering if she'd gone back to sleep again. "Well, if the mill starts making money again—" she began, and Abigail's eyes snapped open.

"It won't!" she said, her voice suddenly strong. "We don't need the money, and I told your father to close it. I intend to see that he does!"

Tracy grinned to herself. "But why?" she asked. "Why should he close it?"

Abigail's head swung slowly around, and her eyes fixed on Tracy's, but Tracy had the eerie feeling that her grandmother wasn't really seeing her.

"Because she's evil," the old woman whispered,

almost to herself. "She killed my son, and she killed Jeff Bailey, and she tried to kill me!"

Tracy's heart beat faster. It was exactly what she'd wanted to hear, even though her grandmother was confused. Beth couldn't possibly have killed Uncle Conrad—she hadn't even been born yet. But it didn't matter. So what if her grandmother had part of it wrong? She did her best not to show her excitement. "She tried to *kill* you?" she whispered. "Who?" Then, when her grandmother made no reply, she decided to gamble. "You saw her, didn't you?" she asked. "You saw her down there, and she did something to you, didn't she?"

Abigail's eyes widened, and she felt her heart constrict as her mind suddenly opened and the memories of the previous night flooded back to her. Again her hand reached out to Tracy, but now that hand was a claw, and when she grasped the girl's wrist, Tracy felt a stab of pain.

"The children," Abigail gasped. "Yes . . . I saw the children."

"Beth," Tracy whispered excitedly. "You saw Beth Rogers, didn't you?"

Abigail was nodding now, and her jaw began working as she struggled to speak again. "Children," she repeated. "I saw them. I saw them just as if they were really there. . . ."

Tracy's heart was thumping now. "You did, Grandmother," she said. "You saw her, and she tried to kill you."

"Dead," Abigail whispered. "She's dead, and she wants to kill us." Her grip on Tracy's arm tightened, and the girl winced with pain. "She wants to kill us all, Tracy. She hates us, because of what we did to her. She hates us, and she'll kill us if we let her."

Tracy tried to pull away, but Abigail seemed to find new strength as her words rambled on. "Stay away, Tracy. Stay away from there. Promise me, Tracy. Promise me you'll stay away."

Suddenly frightened by her grandmother's surge of power, Tracy twisted her arm loose from the old woman's grip. As if she'd been disconnected from her source of strength, Abigail went limp, her arm falling by her side as she sank back into the pillows.

"Promise me," she muttered softly as her eyes, clouded now with her years and infirmities, sought out Tracy's.

Tracy began edging toward the door. "I . . . I promise," she mumbled. Then she was gone, pulling the door closed behind her, wanting to shut out the image of the ancient woman in the bed.

As she left the hospital, she turned her grandmother's words over in her mind, and decided that, after all, she had been right.

Her grandmother *had* seen someone in the basement of the mill last night, and whoever she had seen had tried to kill her.

And Tracy knew who the old woman had seen.

Beth Rogers.

She walked back along River Road until she came to Prospect Street, where she stopped to stare curiously at the old building that was suddenly coming back to life. What, she wondered, had really happened there so many years ago?

Nothing, she decided.

Her grandmother was old, and sick, and didn't know what she was talking about.

And promises made to her, Tracy also decided, didn't really count. In fact, Tracy had long ago figured out that promises didn't mean anything. If you wanted something, you made promises in order to get it. Then you went ahead and did what you wanted, and nobody ever said anything. At least her father and her grandmother didn't, and that was all that mattered.

If she felt like going into the mill and looking around, she would, and no one was going to stop her.

# 19

The somnolence of summer had settled into Westover, and by August the town had taken on a wilted look. People moved slowly in the damp warmth of July, and slower still as August's heat closed oppressively down on them.

For Beth, life had taken on a strange routine, each day much like the day before.

At first it had all been terribly confusing. The memory of Patches dying while she watched was still fresh in her mind—etched indelibly there, still waking her up in the middle of the night sometimes.

But the rest of that day had taken on a dreamlike quality. The sudden arrival of her father; the explanation that it had been decided that for a while, at least, she should live with him; the hasty packing of her bags; her departure from Hilltop with her father, barely aware of what was happening while she tried to figure out *why* it had happened.

Her father had tried to explain it to her, tried to tell her that while no one was blaming her for what had happened to Patches, it had just seemed better to all of them for her to live with him for a while. Mrs. Sturgess would be coming home, and her mother was pregnant, and Tracy . . .

His voice had trailed off after he'd mentioned Tra-

cy's name, but Beth had known what he meant. Hilltop
was Tracy's house, not hers, and they both couldn't live
there anymore. So she had to move out.

It wasn't fair, but it was the way things were, and
even at her age, Beth already knew that life was not
always fair.

But living with her father had not turned out to be
quite what she'd thought it would be, either. Before
she'd moved in with him, they'd always gone out to
dinner on the evenings she'd spent with him, and he'd
always seemed to have lots of time to spend with her.

But now, when she was there all the time, it was
different. She understood why—he had to go to work
every day, and he couldn't afford to take them both to
restaurants every night. So they stayed home most
evenings, and he cooked dinner for them, and the food
wasn't as good as the food Hannah had fixed at Hilltop.
And her room was a lot smaller, and didn't look out
over the whole village. Instead, it looked out over a
parking lot, and only a little corner of the mill was
visible through a gap between two buildings across
Fourth Street.

But at least Tracy wasn't there, and that was good.

What wasn't good was what had happened when
she'd gone to see Peggy Russell. Peggy had only opened
the door a few inches, and she hadn't invited Beth to
come in. Instead she'd said that she couldn't play with
Beth anymore, and that Beth better stay away from her
house.

Beth, her eyes blurred with tears, had gone back
home, but the emptiness of her father's little apartment
had made her feel even more lonesome than Peggy's
rejection. So she'd gone down to the mill, and spent
the rest of the day there.

As the days had turned into weeks she'd tried to
make friends again with the kids she'd known before
she moved up to the top of the hill, but it hadn't
worked. All of them had heard about what had happened to Patches, and all of them had heard Peggy's
story about the grave up on the hillside, and about the

fact that Beth thought the person who was buried there still lived in the mill. At first, they'd simply ignored her when she tried to make friends with them, but when she'd persisted, they'd started calling her names, and invented a nickname for her.

Crazy Bethy.

They called it out at her when she walked down the street, and if their parents were with them, and they couldn't yell it out loud, they'd whisper to each other, and point at her.

Her father told her not to worry about it—that in a few weeks something else would come along, and the kids would forget all about it.

But Beth wasn't at all sure that would ever happen.

She started spending more time at the mill, and finally it got so that the workmen expected her to be there, and stopped worrying about her every minute. They were always friendly to her, and she wandered around anywhere she wanted, watching them work, bringing them tools, sometimes even helping them.

It wasn't so bad, really, except on the days that Phillip Sturgess came to inspect the progress of the work, and brought Tracy with him.

Phillip was always friendly to Beth, interested in how she was, and what she was doing.

But Tracy never spoke to her. Instead she just stared at her, a little smile on her mouth that told Beth she was laughing at her. Beth tried to pretend she didn't care, but of course she did.

Sometimes, during the afternoons, she'd see Tracy outside, just standing there watching the mill, and Beth knew what she wanted.

She wanted to come inside, and go down into the basement.

But she couldn't. All day there were people there, and at night, when everyone had gone home, the building was carefully closed up, and the padlock on the one gate in the fence was always checked twice.

But for Beth, going down to the basement, and the little room under the loading dock, was simple. No one

ever missed her, and part of every day she spent sitting
alone in the darkness of that room, feeling the presence
of Amy, who was now her only real friend.

At first it had been a little bit scary being down
there by herself. For a long time she'd always left the
door open and kept her flashlight on, using its beam to
search out every corner. But soon she'd decided there
was nothing to fear in the darkness of the room, and
began closing the door behind her, turning off the light,
and imagining that Amy—a real Amy—was there with
her.

After a while even the strange smoky odor of the
room didn't bother her anymore, and in late July, she'd
brought an old blanket to the mill. Now she kept it in
the little room, where sometimes she'd spread it out,
then lie on it while she daydreamed about Amy.

She knew a lot about Amy now. She'd gone to the
library, and found books about what the towns like
Westover had been like a hundred years ago when Amy
had been alive.

She'd read about children like Amy, who'd spent
most of their lives in buildings like this, working all day
long, then going home to little houses that had no heat,
and no electricity, and no plumbing.

One day, she'd wandered around Westover, trying
to decide which house Amy might have lived in.

Finally, in her own mind, she'd decided that Amy's
house was the one on Elm Street, right by the railroad
tracks. Of course she knew that part of the reason she'd
decided on that house was that her mother had showed
it to her a long time ago, and told her that the house,
abandoned now, its roof sagging and its windows broken, with weeds growing wild around its weathered
walls, had once been her own family's home, long ago,
even before she herself had been born.

As Beth had stood on the cracked sidewalk that
day, staring at it, imagining that this was where Amy
had lived, she'd thought she could hear Amy's voice
whispering to her, telling her that she was right, that
this was the place which had been her home.

Then she'd begun dreaming about Amy. The dreams came to her only when she was in the little room behind the stairs, and she wasn't even sure they were really dreams, for she couldn't remember being asleep when they came to her, nor could she remember waking up when they were over. Indeed, she decided that they weren't dreams at all.

They were visions.

They were visits from Amy, who came to show her things, and tell her things.

She never talked to anyone about Amy's visits. She'd learned by now not to talk about Amy to anyone. The one time she had, no one had believed her. And now everyone thought she was crazy.

Everyone, that is, except old Mrs. Sturgess, and Beth hadn't seen her since the day after she'd gone to the hospital. Once Beth had gone back to visit her again, but the nurse had told her that there was a list of people who were allowed into the old woman's room, and her name wasn't on the list.

So Amy had become her secret, and it didn't really matter to Beth anymore if old Mrs. Sturgess could prove that there had really been someone named Amy or not.

To Beth, Amy was as real as anyone else.

Amy was a part of her.

And then one day late in August, in the little room in the basement of the mill, she actually became Amy for a little while, saw what Amy saw, felt what she felt.

It was a particularly hot afternoon, but down there, in the darkness, it felt different. It felt cool, almost as if it were a perfect morning in spring. Beth spread the blanket out on the floor, then lowered herself down onto it, switched off the flashlight, and let the visit happen. . . .

*It was the kind of spring morning Amy had long since learned to dread: the sun was shining brightly, and the air was warm even at a little before six. By ten, she knew, it would be getting hot, but there would be just enough breeze to make lying in the square and staring—daydreaming—up into the spreading maples the most alluring experience she could think of. And in the afternoon, when the heat reached its peak, and the air was getting so muggy that breathing was hard, there would be the stream, just a few yards away, its cool waters beckoning to her.*

*Yes, today was the kind of day she had come to dread, because for some reason, this kind of day never seemed to come on a Sunday, when she might have had at least a few minutes to enjoy it. On Sundays, even though she didn't have to go to work, there was too much to do at home, taking care of her sisters and brothers, keeping out of her father's way, helping her mother with all the things she never had time to do during the week.*

*Almost unconsciousiy, she slowed her pace, as if by taking a few more minutes now, she could put off the inevitable. But she knew it was impossible. As she turned off the railroad tracks to make her way up the path toward Prospect Street, and the shadow of the shoe mill blotted out the sunlight, she began steeling herself for the hours ahead. Long ago her mother had taught her the trick of survival in the mill. All you had to do was shut everything out, until the little room you worked in was your whole world, and nothing beyond that little room could enter your head at all. Then all you thought about was the work: cutting the little pieces of leather out of the tanned hides, making sure they were all exactly the same size, stacking them carefully but quickly in neat piles so that when they went to the assembly room upstairs the assemblers would have the right pieces at the right time. And you had to work fast, because you got paid by the piece.*

*You had to ignore the smells, too, or you'd quickly get sick and not be able to work at all. Sometimes Amy wondered which smells were the worst—the acrid odor of the lye used for tanning the hides, or the sour smells of the dyes used to color the leather after it was tanned. Or maybe, she sometimes thought, the worst smell was the smell of the people themselves, all of them sweating in the heat, their eyes fastened on their work for fear that if they looked toward the filthy windows the light and air outside would overpower them, and they'd drop their work and run away from the mill forever.*

*But they couldn't do that—Amy least of all. This was 1886, and there weren't many jobs, and at home her mother, who had no job at all, always told her how lucky she was to have a job in the middle of the depression. And even though Amy wasn't quite sure what a depression was, she knew that she couldn't give in to her impulse to run away from the mill, because if she did, there wouldn't be any money at all, and her mother and sisters and brothers would have nothing to eat.*

*The door of the mill loomed a few steps ahead of her now, and she paused. According to the clock on the church steeple above the square, she still had four minutes before the morning whistle blew and everyone had to be at the tables, ready to work. Her eyes darted around, as if gathering images to put away for examination later, but then fixed on a group of three children— children her own age—who were walking along the other side of the street. She knew their names, but had never spoken to them, as they had never spoken to her.*

*Fleetingly, she wondered if they knew her name.*

*Probably not, since they didn't work at the mill.*

*They didn't work at all.*

*They were the lucky ones, whose fathers ran the mill, and who lived in nice houses, and went to school in the winter and played outside all summer. And they had pretty clothes, clothes that never looked as though someone else had worn them before; never looked as though they needed mending two or three times a week. Involuntarily, Amy's hands dropped down and ran over her own dress, as if by some unseen force she could make the stains on it disappear, or smooth over the rough stitches that held its tattered pieces together.*

*For a moment, she wondered where they were going today, then decided it didn't matter. The only thing that mattered, really, was that now she had only* one minute to get to her table, and if she was late, the shift supervisor would yell at her; might even fire her. And if that happened—

She put the thought out of her mind, and hurried through the door into the dimness of the mill, doing her best to put the rest of the world out of her mind.

A few people spoke to her as she started toward the stairs at the far end of the building, and she nodded a brief response. But most of the people were already hard at work, their fingers moving quickly in unchanging routines that had long since become automatic as they assembled shoes from the piles of leather around them. The people seemed to have a sameness about them: their eyes were vacant, and their skin seemed to have the look of worn leather. Their clothes, shabby and ill-fitting, all looked alike, and marked them for what they were—millworkers. For a fleeting instant, she wondered if they, like herself, dreamed of getting out of the mill, but then she decided they didn't. For most of them, the mill was their life, and they would be here until they died.

As the whistle sounded, its piercing scream slashing through her like a knife, Amy hurried down the stairs and into the little room under the loading dock where she worked with the other children her age, cutting the freshly dyed hides into the many pieces that went into the shoes.

It was here she had started working three years ago, when she was eight, tending to the vats in which the hides were soaked, then moving on to the dyeing itself. Finally, she had begun training as a cutter, and now she worked her twelve-hour shifts, six days a week, cutting soles from the rough leather, training herself to work as the others worked, without thinking.

Even as she put on her apron and took up her position at the cutting table, she began the process of closing down her mind.

She started with her eyes.

She had to keep her eyes on her work, even though it had been months since she really needed to watch *every move she made. But if her eyes stayed on the leather, and the hypnotically moving knife in her right hand, they wouldn't stray to the children around her, and she wouldn't see things she didn't want to see. She wouldn't see her cousin, who worked only a few feet away, and whose face was always streaked with tears. She knew why her cousin cried while he worked, but he had sworn her to secrecy, knowing that if anyone found out he was allergic to the dyes he worked with he would lose his job. So he worked on, and even though the dyes hurt him to the point where he cried all day, he never said anything, and turned away whenever the foreman was in the area.*

*Amy closed her ears as well, for if she didn't, she would hear the other children talking, and if she let herself listen, she would soon begin talking, too. And if she talked, she would think, and if she thought, she didn't know what might happen.*

*The only way to get through it was to close herself down, let herself be hypnotized by the dull routine of the work, and get through the hours one at a time.*

*She picked up the knife, and began cutting. Within thirty seconds, she was into the rhythm of movement that would carry her through the day. Hold the hide down with her left hand, cut straight through with her right, cutting off a strip exactly three inches wide. Pick up the three-inch-wide strip in her left hand, and give a quick cut, twisting the knife slightly to turn the curve of the heel. Flip the heel over, repeat the cut. Put the heel piece in the box, and start the next one. Slowly, as happened every day, her senses began closing down, until all she was aware of was her tiny area of the workbench, the knife in her hand, and the leather in front of her. Soon time would have no meaning for her, and she would continue to work, oblivious not only of what was going on around her but also of the pain in her arms and shoulders, the pain that would creep up on her every day. She would not allow herself to feel it until the evening whistle had sounded, and she was on her way home. Then, as her senses came back to her,* the pain would come too, and by the time she got home she would be unable to move her arms. But her mother would have a tub of hot water waiting for her, water she'd been heating on the wood-burning stove, and she would sink into it, waiting for the pain to turn to numbness, and then the numbness to turn into the tingling sensation that meant soon she would be able to move her arms again.

But during the day, the only thing she could do was shut the pain out, as she had learned to shut everything else out. Shutting things out was the only way to get through it.

And then, when things were shut out, and she was no longer aware of the mill, she would live in her own world for a while, a world where there was no mill. In her world, she would live outside, in the warmth of the sun, with the breezes blowing through her long hair, caressing her skin. The air would be filled with the scent of flowers, and she would lie by the stream for hours, letting the water play over her fingers. And someday, she knew, she would go to live in that world. Someday, she would find a way to leave the mill, and then she would never have to shut things out again. And when that day came, she would take her cousin with her, and all the other children who, like her, were slowly dying in the mill. . . .

She had no idea what time it was when something encroached on her closed senses. Indeed, for the first few minutes, she wasn't even sure what it was that was playing around the edges of her mind. All she knew was that something wasn't quite the way it should be. Something, somewhere, was disturbing her protective trance.

Slowly, almost imperceptibly, she began opening her mind to the world around her.

It was the smell.

The room, always airless, always choked with fumes and the sour odor of sweat, contained something new. Hesitating at her work, the knife poised in mid-stroke, she sniffed at the air.

There was an acrid smell, somehow familiar, but out of place.

And her eyes were stinging.

Her senses coming fully alert now, she felt tears welling in her eyes, running down her cheeks. She dropped the knife, and painfully raised her right hand to wipe away the tears.

The smell was stronger now, and she turned, forcing herself to look around the room.

And then she saw it.

In the corner near the door a pile of rags, stained dark with oily dyes, had burst into flames.

Amy stared at the flames for a moment, uncertain they were really there. And then she looked around.

The other children, the children she thought spent their days talking among themselves while they worked, were standing at their stations, their expressions glazed over as their hands moved in the same metronomically regular rhythm she herself experienced every day.

A few yards away, his eyes streaming, her cousin stood at one of the dye vats.

And even though he was crying, she knew immediately that he, too, had retreated into a private world where the mill could not penetrate. He, like herself— like all the children—had escaped into another world, oblivious of the world in which his body toiled.

The fire was spreading now, sending tongues of flame out across the floor as billows of smoke rose from the rags and filled the room with a choking fog.

And then, from beyond the little room, she heard the sounds of people calling out: "Fire! Fire in the cutting room!" And then the voices were cut off by the scream of the whistle, this time not signaling the end of the morning shift, but blaring out in short, urgent bursts, alerting the workers to the danger. In a moment, the fire squad would appear, and begin dousing the flames.

All around her, she could feel the other children coming alive, hear them begin coughing, hear the first sounds of their terror.

Out.

She had to get them out.

She crossed to her cousin, and took his hand. The boy, a year younger than herself, stared at her for a moment, then tried to pull away.

"Come on," Amy begged. "Willie, we have to get out of here." But Willie, staring beyond her, only shook his head, and tried to pull away. Turning, Amy saw what her cousin had already seen: the door, barely visible now, was blocked by the rising flames.

"Through!" she yelled. "We have to go through the fire! Come on!" Grasping Willie's hand, she began dragging him toward the door, the heat of the growing fire searing her face, singeing her hair.

But there was no other way out. She pressed on, two of the other children following her. And then, just as she was about to charge through the flames, she heard a voice on the other side.

"Close that door, dammit! Do you want the whole place to go up?"

She froze, recognizing the voice, and knowing its command would be obeyed. Then, helplessly, she watched as the heavy metal fire door slid quickly into place. Just as it slammed shut, she saw the face of the man who had issued the order. He was looking at her, but in his eyes she saw nothing. No love, no pity, no sorrow for what he had done.

Then the face disappeared and she was trapped.

Barely comprehending, she stepped backward, then let Willie pull her away from the angry flames.

Finally, she turned away, and stared into the terrified eyes of the other children. All of them seemed to be looking at her, waiting for her to do something. But there was nothing she could do.

Finally, one of the children came to life, and, screaming, ran into the flames to pound on the closed fire door, begging someone to open it, to let them out, to save them.

Amy knew that even if someone heard the screaming child, the door would not be opened.

The child's screams began to fade, and as the girl watched, he sank slowly to his knees, his clothes on fire, his hair burned away. Then he slid lower, and the last thing the girl saw before she turned away was his hand, outstretched, still reaching toward the safety that wasn't there.

Willie was clinging to her now, and with the other children close around her, she stumbled to the far side of the room. But even as she moved away from the fire, she knew it was useless.

Except for the window.

Above her, high up, was a small window.

If she could get to the window, break it . . .

Closing her mind against her rising panic, as she had learned to close it against her life in the mill, she looked around for something to stand on.

A stool. In the corner, there was a stool.

She let go of Willie's hand, and dragged the stool over until it stood beneath the window. Climbing up, she could barely reach the sill.

The window was locked.

And then one of the other children gave her a mallet, and, ignoring the pain in her arms and shoulders, she swung it at the glass.

As the glass shattered, she realized her mistake.

Fresh air rushed into the vacuum created by the fire, and, with new oxygen to feed on, the fire exploded with new life.

Instantly, the room filled with smoke and flames, and the screams of children who knew they were about to die.

For a moment, time seemed to stand still, and the girl watched as the fire came to consume her. Then, as her dress caught fire, and she began falling toward the floor, she heard Willie calling out her name.

"Amy!" he screamed. And then once more. "Aaaa-mmyyyy!"

It was the last word Willie spoke, the last word Amy heard. And his was the last face she ever saw.

But the last memory that flashed through her mind,

the memory she died with, was the memory of another voice, and another face.

A voice ordering the fire door to be closed.

A voice ordering her death.

A voice commanding that she never leave the mill.

And the face she saw, the face that went with that terrible voice that had ordered her death, was the face of the man she knew was her father.

As Amy died, she knew that she never would leave the mill. But as it had killed her, so would she kill others.

She would have her revenge.

# 20

For Alan Rogers, that late-August afternoon had been
the day on which, for the first time, he'd finally begun
to see the results of the summer's labors. The outside of
the mill was finished. Its surfaces, stripped clean of
their layers of grime, were now the warm dark red of
old brick, set off with white trim around the windows.
The windows themselves, formerly no more than sym-
metrically placed holes in the otherwise blank facade
of the building, had been widened with shutters, and
now gave the building a vaguely colonial look.

The fence, no longer serving any useful purpose,
had been torn down a week ago.

The main entrance on Prospect Street was done, a
broad flight of steps leading to a rank of glass doors that
opened directly onto the main concourse of the first
floor. Halfway down, the concourse widened into a
huge skylit atrium, above which a rainbow-hued dome
of stained glass had been installed. Beyond the atrium,
the concourse continued to the end of the building,
where a waterfall would eventually cascade down to a
small pool. The old offices had long since been torn out,
but the staircase to the basement still remained—one of
the last vestiges of the original structure still to be
replaced.

Above him, the construction of the open mezza-

nine was two weeks ahead of schedule, and already the
dividing walls of the second-level shops were in place.
Their facades, like those on the main level, would not
be completed until the tenants had signed their leases
and submitted designs for completion of their store-
fronts. All of them would be different, but there were
strict guidelines within which the tenants could exercise their imaginations. In the end, Alan was now certain, the mill would look exactly as Phillip had hoped it
would—an ornate nineteenth-century arcade of the sort
one would be likely to run across in London, but that
one could scarcely hope to discover in a fading indus-
trial town fifty miles outside of Boston.

Until today, Alan had not been certain that the
September 1 deadline would be met. Even now he
wasn't positive that every detail would have been completed. But it would be close enough for the Labor Day
dedication ceremony to take place, and for the Old Mill
to be opened to the public. Some of the stores would
be occupied, and the rest of them would have intrigu-
ingly painted wooden fronts, announcing the names of
their future tenants, and hinting at what the contents of
the shops might eventually be.

The construction crew was gone, and silence hung
over the building. But in his mind, Alan could almost
hear the murmur of a crowd of shoppers, and the faint
gurgling of the waterfall. He walked slowly around the
main floor, inspecting the work that had been done that
day, and reinspecting what had been accomplished over
the previous weeks.

He did this every day, correcting as many of the
mistakes as he could himself, and making copious notes
with exact instructions on what was to be done the
following morning so that no time would be wasted
while he had to accompany the men from place to
place, giving them verbal instructions. But for the most
part, the work was perfect—the men had long since
discovered that Alan Rogers would allow nothing to slip
by, and that he would not appreciate having to pay
their wage while they corrected their own mistakes. It

hadn't hurt that Alan had let it be known that the bonus for early completion would be divided equally among the workers, rather than going directly into his own pocket.

His inspection of the first floor completed, he mounted the stairs to the mezzanine.

Up here, although ahead of schedule, the work had not progressed as quickly as it had downstairs, but that was only to be expected. No one expected the mezzanine to be open by Labor Day.

Still, it was coming along faster than he'd dared hope, and the subdivisions were all but completed. Now the lowered ceiling that would cap the shops was being installed. Though to the casual observer that ceiling would appear to be supported by the walls it surmounted, it was actually being suspended from the spiderlike struts that held up the roof of the building itself. Almost ten feet would separate the false ceilings of the shops from the intricate ironwork above them, and from the main concourse on the first floor, all the old strutwork would be clearly visible, framing the new skylight in the center.

Alan gazed up at the skylight, admiring it once more. Though it was massive, it appeared to be light as a feather, the effect of lightness achieved through the artist's use of pale greens and blues and almost pastel reds and oranges.

Then, as his eyes scanned the intricate glasswork, he suddenly frowned.

One of the panes, near the base of the dome, appeared to be cracked.

He hesitated, started to make a note of it, then wondered if perhaps he was mistaken. It might not be a crack at all—it could be nothing more than an imperfection in the glass, magnified by the angle of the slowly setting sun.

He moved closer, but even then he couldn't make the crack out clearly. Glancing around, he saw a ladder propped up against the strutwork, left there by one of the workmen for use again in the morning.

Alan moved quickly to the ladder, and a moment later was up in the ironwork, moving carefully out above the concourse toward the dome.

He'd never been afraid of heights—indeed he'd always rather enjoyed them—and before he moved all the way out to the center of the roof, he looked down. As always, the distance between floor and ceiling was amplified by the angle of viewing it from above, but for Alan there wasn't even the slightest feeling of dizziness or tightening in his groin. He glanced around the empty building, enjoying the new perspective on his work, then moved confidently onward toward the dome.

When he was directly beneath the spot where he thought he'd seen the cracked glass, he looked up, but the angle was far too acute. The pane in question was almost invisible, extending almost straight up from where he was.

He leaned out, his full weight suspended above the floor below by the strength of his fingers alone.

Still, he couldn't quite see the pane. But if he stretched upward, reaching with his left hand, perhaps he could feel it.

He clutched one of the crosspieces tight in his right hand, and groped upward with his left.

His fingers touched the cool surface of the glass, and carefully explored it.

Nothing.

He reached further, his left foot leaving the iron beam on which he stood.

And then, with only one foot on anything solid, and only his right hand checking his balance, it happened.

Time seemed to stop as the small piece of wrought iron in his right hand suddenly cracked in his grip, then gave way.

Instinctively, he looked down.

The distance seemed to telescope away from him, the floor, forty feet below, receding quickly into the distance. Now, for the first time in his experience, the dizziness of heights came upon him, he felt an almost sexual tightening in his groin, and a sudden wave of fear washed over him. His entire body broke out in an icy sweat.

What was happening to him wasn't possible.

The ironwork had all been examined, the badly rusted pieces replaced weeks ago.

And yet, somehow, this piece had been missed. This very piece on which he had depended today.

His fingers, acting independently from his brain, clutched desperately at the broken piece for a moment, then, too late, dropped the fragment and reached for the solid bar that was suddenly just out of his reach.

He felt himself teeter, and slowly arc away from the I-beam.

Then he was plunging downward, his eyes wide open, his arms stretched out as if to break his fall.

He opened his mouth, and screamed.

It was the scream that jerked Beth back into the present. For just the smallest instant she was sure it was Amy's scream, that last, horrible sound as she'd died, but then Beth knew it was more. For a second she could still hear it, even now that the vision was gone, and she was once more alone in the cool darkness of the room behind the stairs.

And then the scream was cut short by a loud thumping noise, followed by the kind of empty silence that Beth had never experienced before.

The silence of death happening suddenly, unexpectedly.

She sat frozen, and slowly the silence was intruded upon by her own heartbeat.

"Daddy?" she whispered softly. Even as she spoke the word, she knew instinctively there would be no answer.

She rose slowly to her feet. The pleasant cool of the room had shifted to a bone-chilling cold, and she reached down without thinking, picked up the blanket, and wrapped it around herself.

She moved slowly toward the door, but then hesitated, something in her not wanting to leave the safety and isolation of the little room, wanting rather to stay there in the darkness and isolation, as if that alone could protect her from whatever waited for her outside.

But she had to go out, had to go and see for herself what had happened.

She slid the door open just far enough to slip through, then slid it closed again behind her. Then, using the flashlight to guide her even though she knew the steps by rote, she crept out from under the stairs and started upward.

She could see him as soon as her head came above floor level.

He lay in the center of the mill, beneath the stained-glass dome. Sunlight, streaming in from one of the high side windows, illuminated his body, and motes of dust danced in the air above him.

He was very still, lying facedown, his arms out-stretched as if he was reaching for something.

Beth froze.

It couldn't be real.

She was imagining it. Or she was seeing something else, something out of the past like the things Amy had shown her.

It wasn't her father on the floor. It was someone else—someone she didn't know—someone she didn't care about.

As she forced herself to move slowly forward, she kept repeating it to herself.

*It isn't Daddy.*

*It isn't Daddy, and it isn't even real.*

*It's only a dream.*

*It's only a dream, and I'll wake up.*

But then she was there, standing beneath the dome, her father's body at her feet. Beneath his head, a pool of blood had formed.

She knew it was real, and that she wasn't going to wake up.

She felt her body go numb as her mind tried to reject it all. But that was impossible. He lay there, not moving, not breathing, with the stillness that only death could produce.

And slowly, almost against her will, the connections in her mind began to form.

It was Amy.

Amy had killed her father.

It had happened at the same time, to the very instant.

She'd been in that room with Amy, been there when the fire broke out, been there when Amy died.

She had felt Amy die, felt as though she was dying with her. She'd felt the heat of the flames, felt the despair when she knew there would be no escape.

And she'd felt the fury—Amy's fury—in that final moment when she'd heard again the words of her father, and seen his face.

*Not my father. Amy's father.*

But the wish—the dying wish for vengeance—had been hers as well as Amy's.

And now her own father was dead.

She pulled the blanket, filthy with soot, closer around her body as if its warmth could shut out the chill she was feeling, and sank slowly to her knees. She reached out with one arm, the tips of her fingers touching the flesh of her father's face.

It was still warm, but despite that warmth, she could feel that there was no life there.

He was gone.

She wasn't even aware of the sound that began emanating from her throat, the high, thin wail of anguish, that built slowly until it was the scream of a wild animal caught in the vicious jaws of a trap.

A scream that was part agonizing pain, part stark terror.

The scream built, filling the enormous building, echoing off the walls and roof, building on itself until it almost seemed the walls themselves must give way under its force.

"NNNNOOOOOOOOOOOO—"

She was prone now, stretched out over her father's body, her fingers clutching at him, poking him, prodding him, pulling at him, as if at any moment he might respond, might move beneath her, then turn over, put his arms around her, and tell her that everything was all right, that he was alive, that he loved her and would still be there to take care of her.

And still, the scream built. . . .


Phillip was driving the Mercedes at no more than fifteen miles an hour, and doing his best to avoid the worst of the potholes in Prospect Street. Beside him, Carolyn was staring straight ahead through the windshield, but he could see a slight smile playing around the corners of her mouth as she listened to Abigail's diatribe pour forth from the back seat.

"There's hardly a need to proceed at the pace of a snail, Phillip. I'm not going to break, and I shall be much more comfortable back in my own room than I am trapped in the back seat of this car."

"I asked you to use an ambulance, Mother," Phillip reminded her, but was silenced by an indignant sniff.

"Ambulances are for sick people. If I'm still sick after six weeks in that terrible place, then I should be dead. And, if I may say so, Phillip, it is a miracle that I'm not. One would think that considering the amount of money we have given that wretched little clinic, the least they could have done was serve me decent food. And as for the doctors, I can't imagine how any of them even qualified for medical school, let alone graduated. In my day—"

"I know, Mother," Phillip interrupted. "These days they're letting just anybody be doctors, aren't they?"

Abigail's lips tightened as she heard Tracy snicker from the seat next to her. She glared at her son in the rearview mirror. "Are you mocking me, Phillip?" she asked, her voice cold.

Phillip did not answer her. He slowed the car to a complete halt in front of the mill, and pressed the button that would lower his window. "Well, there it is," he said proudly. "I thought you might want to see it."

"I do not," Abigail declared, turning her head away. "All I want is to be taken home—" And then she fell silent. A strange sound was filling the air, and it seemed to be coming from the mill.

The sound grew louder, and within seconds all four of them knew what it was.

Inside the mill, someone was screaming.

Carolyn froze in her seat; her heart had begun pounding. From the back, she heard Abigail's voice, uncertainly asking what the scream could be. Then she heard her husband's voice.

"I'll go see."

"I'll go with you," Carolyn said immediately. Phillip's voice had the effect of releasing her from her paralysis, and she opened the car door, then hurried around to the sidewalk.

The scream was getting louder, sending a chill through Carolyn's very soul.

"You'd better not," Phillip told her. "Take Tracy and Mother home. I'll find out what's happened, and call you as soon as I can." When Carolyn seemed to hesitate, he gripped her arms tightly. "Do it!" he said. Then he released her arms and started toward the steps that now rose to the newly installed front doors.

Carolyn remained where she was for a moment, then, reluctantly, got into the driver's seat of the Mercedes, and closed the door.

Phillip, even as he mounted the steps, realized it would be pointless. The doors would be locked, and he had no key.

He should abandon the steps, and head for the side door. But he couldn't. He had to look now.

With the unearthly scream still ringing in his ears, he came to the top of the steps, shielded his eyes, and peered through the glass doors.

One hundred and fifty feet away, barely visible in the dim light within, he saw a shape huddled on the floor. Then, as he watched, the shape moved, and a face appeared.

Caught in the strange light of the sun, he saw Beth, her features twisted into a mask of anguished grief. Blood smeared her face, and her hands seemed to be clawing spasmodically at the air.

Phillip felt his stomach tighten for a moment, and fought against the nausea that was threatening to overwhelm him.

Then he felt a movement at his side, and heard another voice.

"What is it?" Tracy asked. "What's happening in there?"

Almost against his will, Phillip looked down. Tracy, her eyes glinting with malicious curiosity, looked back at him. "She killed someone, didn't she?" he heard his daughter saying. But there was no fear in Tracy's voice, nor so much as a hint of compassion or pity.

Only eagerness, and a strange note of satisfaction.

Clamping his hand on Tracy's wrist, Phillip jerked the child away from the door.

"Stop it!" Tracy screeched as Phillip dragged her down the steps. "You're hurting me!"

Phillip shoved Tracy into the back seat, slammed the door, then spoke through her open window. "Don't say anything, Tracy," he commanded. "If you say one word, I swear that the next time I see you I will give you a thrashing you will never forget!"

Then, at the look of anguish in Carolyn's eyes, he shook his head. "It looks bad," he said quietly. "Just get them home. I'll be there as soon as I can." Then, as Carolyn put the car in gear and drove away, he dashed around the corner of the building and started toward the side door.

Phillip recognized Alan's car parked next to the construction shack, and had an instinctive feeling of relief. Whatever had happened, Alan would already be taking care of it.

Then he was at the door, and even before his eyes

had fully taken in what he was seeing, he recognized the body that lay broken on the floor.

He rushed into the area beneath the dome, and dropped to his knees, his arms instinctively going around Beth, trying to draw her away.

She fought him for a moment, clutching at her father's body, but then let go, burying her face against Phillip's chest, her arms encircling his neck, her hysterical screams dissolving into a series of racking sobs that shook her entire body.

Phillip reached out and laid his fingers on Alan's neck, feeling for a pulse.

As he had expected, there was none.

His breath caught, and he rose to his feet, staggering back a step. Beth still clung to him, and he made no attempt to set her down, or try to get her to stand on her own legs. Instead, he hoisted her higher, his right arm supporting her while he caressed her gently with his left hand.

"It's all right," he whispered as he turned away and started back toward the door. "I'm here, and it's going to be all right."

In the shack, he picked up the phone and quickly dialed the number of the police station.

"There's been an accident," he said as soon as the phone was answered at the other end. "This is Phillip Sturgess. I'm at the mill, and we've had a terrible accident. Get some men and an ambulance down here right away." Without waiting for an answer, he hung up the phone, then stepped out of the shack and sank to a sitting position on its steps.

In his arms, Beth continued sobbing, and for a moment that was all he could hear in the quiet of the afternoon.

Then, in the distance, he heard a siren begin wailing, then another, and another.

In less than a minute the sirens had reached a crescendo, then cut off abruptly as brakes squealed and dust rose up around him.

As if from nowhere, two police cars and an ambulance had appeared, and people seemed to be everywhere.

Two men in uniform, followed by a pair of white-clad paramedics, dashed past him, disappearing immediately into the cavernous interior of the mill.

Then there was someone beside him, and he looked up to see Norm Adcock's craggy face gazing down at him.

"It's Alan," he said quietly. "I don't know what happened to him. I—" He fell silent, unsure what else to say.

In his arms, Beth stirred, her sobbing having finally subsided a little. Then he felt her arms tighten around him once more, and heard her speak, her voice distorted, barely audible as it passed through a throat worn raw from her screams of a few moments ago. But still, the words themselves were clear.

"I killed him," she whispered. "I didn't mean to—really I didn't."

Then, as Phillip Sturgess and Norm Adcock exchanged a long look, her sobs overtook her once more.

# 21

"Well?" Phillip Sturgess asked. "What do you think?"

It was past ten o'clock, but to look at the little Westover police station, anyone would have thought it was the middle of the day. Most of the force was there, and people filled the small lobby, asking questions of anyone whose attention they could get. But everyone on the force had been told to reply to all questions in the same way. Over and over again the answer was repeated: "We don't know yet exactly what happened. As soon as we have some information, there will be an announcement."

The rumors, of course, had been running rampant, feeding off one another, passed from person to person.

All of them, naturally, centered on Beth Rogers, and all of them were variations on the same theme.

"Mr. Sturgess found her right over the corpse. It wasn't even cold yet, and she was covered with blood." Then there would be a falsely sympathetic clucking of the tongue, and a heavy sigh. "She's always been an odd child, though, and these last few weeks—well, I don't like to repeat the stories I've heard."

But of course the stories *were* repeated, and embellished, and exaggerated, until by nightfall there were few people in Westover who hadn't heard that

Beth had already killed Jeff Bailey, but had been protected by the power of the Sturgesses, who hadn't wanted a scandal.

And, of course, there was the horse—Phillip Sturgess's prize mare—that Beth had slaughtered in its stall. Would a sane person kill an innocent animal? Of course not.

And they'd all seen Beth, hadn't they? Seen her wandering around town by herself? And talking to herself? Certainly they had.

The kids had known, of course, and their parents had been foolish not to have listened to them. Children always know when something's wrong with someone—they have a sixth sense about those things. In a way, the more sanctimonious citizens declared, Alan's death was the responsibility of them all, for they'd all seen the signs of Beth's illness, but no one had done anything about it.

They came and went from the police station, gathering in the square to enjoy the warmth of the summer evening, and speculate on what would happen next. Some of them dropped in at the Red Hen to have a drink, and listened with serious faces as Eileen Russell repeated over and over again what had happened to Peggy the last time she had gone to visit Beth. All of them agreed that Peggy Russell had been lucky to escape with her life.

Bobby Golding, who was an orderly at the clinic, got off shift at eight, and went directly to the Red Hen, where he reported that Beth was currently being held in a locked room, where she was held into a bed with restraints, and would be transferred to the state mental hospital in the morning. And, he added, she would never stand trial for what she'd done, because schizophrenics never did.

And that, of course, wasn't fair, someone argued. There wasn't really anything crazy about Beth at all. She was just damned clever. All she really wanted to do was get back up to Hilltop, and she couldn't do that as long as her father was still alive. So she'd pretended to be crazy, and killed him, knowing perfectly well that they'd just put her in a hospital for a couple of months, then let her go. And when she came back to Westover, then nobody would be safe.

And so it went, until by ten o'clock Beth had been charged, tried, and convicted.

Except by Norm Adcock, who now leaned back in his chair and rubbed his tired eyes, then tried to stretch the knots out of his aching shoulders. "Only way I can figure it is an accident," he said in reply to Phillip's question. He gestured to the reports that sat in a neat stack on his desk. "We found the broken brace three feet away, and there were traces of both paint and rust on Alan's hands and shoes that match what we got off the girders. I suppose the rust could have come from anywhere, but the paint was only used on the struts supporting the roof. Couldn't have come from anywhere else. Besides, we even found his fingerprints on the glass over the spot where that brace broke. He must have been up there checking the dome for something, and his own weight broke the brace."

Phillip nodded. "And what about Beth? Is there any way she could have been up there, too?"

"I don't see how. You know as well as I do that Alan wouldn't have let her start climbing around up there. He wouldn't have let anybody do that, let alone his own daughter."

"But he'd do it himself," Phillip commented, not really expecting a reply.

"That was Alan. He wouldn't let anyone else take a risk like that, but he'd never think about it himself."

There was a silence, while Phillip turned it over in his mind. "What if he was already up there, and she climbed up without his permission?"

"Already thought of that," Adcock replied. "If traces of the paint showed up on Alan's shoes, then they would have shown up on hers, too. And they didn't. There's no way she was up there, and no way she had anything to do with what happened to Alan."

Phillip felt the tension he'd been unconsciously

building up in his body suddenly ease. He hadn't yet told Carolyn about the strange words Beth had uttered when she'd finally been able to speak that afternoon, and now he wouldn't have to. But he still didn't understand them.

"What do you think about what she said?" he asked.

"Not my department," Adcock replied, shrugging. "You'll have to ask the docs about that one. But offhand, I'd say it was nothing more than shock. She was the only one there, Mr. Sturgess, and she's a little girl." He stood up, stretched, and once more rubbed at his shoulders. "I'd better get out there and talk to the folks. Hope I can convince them that I'm telling them the truth. And you," he added, "might want to think about going out the back way."

Phillip frowned, wondering what the police chief was getting at. "Why?"

"Because if you're with me, someone's bound to suggest that you've pressured me to gloss over what happened." He smiled bitterly. "People are like that. They don't want a simple answer. They'd rather have a scandal, and they're about to be disappointed." He hesitated a moment, then went on, but his tone of voice had changed slightly, become less official. "Alan was a friend of yours, wasn't he?"

"He was," Phillip replied. "In other circumstances, I suspect he might have been my best friend. We—well, we understood each other, Alan and I."

Adcock's lips pursed thoughtfully. "He was my friend, too. So I guess, in a strange sort of way, you and I should be friends, Mr. Sturgess."

Phillip hesitated, uncertain what the chief was getting at. "Friends usually call each other by their first names," he observed quietly. "And mine's Phillip."

The chief's head bobbed. "And mine's Norm. And if you want my opinion, I'd say you're going to be in for some very rough times."

"I'm not sure I follow you—"

"Beth. What do you plan to do about her?"

"Do about her?" Phillip repeated. "I'm going to

take her home, and do whatever I can to help her get through all this."

"Six weeks ago you kicked her out of your house."

Phillip's eyes narrowed, and he felt sudden anger make a vein in his forehead throb. But before he could speak, he realized that there had been nothing condemnatory in the chief's voice. Adcock had spoken as if he were simply delivering information. "Is that what people have been saying?" he asked.

"That's what they've been saying. And all evening I've been getting reports from my boys." Briefly, he told Phillip about the gossip that was already sweeping through the town. "I can't tell you what to do, but if Beth were my daughter, I'm not sure I'd want her to stay here. It's not going to matter what I say, Mr. —Phillip. People are going to talk, and the stories are going to get worse and worse."

"But Beth hasn't done anything—"

"What about the horse?" Adcock asked bluntly. "Are you going to tell me the poison got into those oats all by itself?"

Suddenly, unbidden, a memory flashed into Phillip's mind. A memory of his daughter, looking up at him earlier that afternoon, and asking him if Beth had killed someone.

She hadn't cared.

He'd seen it in her eyes.

She hadn't cared that someone had died. All she'd cared about was that once more Beth Rogers might be in trouble.

"Beth didn't poison the oats," he said now, the pain of the truth wrenching at him. "But I know who did." He turned, and started out of the office, but Adcock's voice stopped him.

"Mind telling me?" the chief asked.

Phillip didn't turn around. "Yes," he said quietly. "I mind very much." He pulled the door open and stepped out into the squad room. Glancing around, he spotted the back door that led out to the alley behind the building, and started toward it. He could feel the eyes of everyone in the room following him, but no one spoke.

Phillip slipped quietly into the room at the clinic. Carolyn, her face pale, looked up at him from her chair next to the bed in which Beth lay sleeping, but made no attempt to rise. He could see by the redness of her eyes that she had been crying. A damp handkerchief was still clutched in her left hand. With her right, she held her daughter's hand. He moved around the bed, and leaned over to kiss his wife's forehead.

"How is she?" he asked.

"Asleep," Carolyn sighed. "Finally. They had to give her a shot. She didn't want one, but she finally gave in."

Phillip's sympathetic smile slowly faded into a look of grim determination. "And maybe that's the problem," he muttered to himself. "Maybe she's always given in too easily."

Carolyn looked up at him dazedly. "Given in? Phillip, what are you talking about?"

Phillip shook his head as if trying to clear it of unwanted thoughts. "I'm not sure," he said. "I've just been thinking, that's all. And I'm not liking what I'm thinking." He hesitated, then decided there was no point in putting it off. "We were wrong to send her to Alan," he said.

Carolyn swallowed, and for a moment Phillip was afraid she was going to start crying again, but then she recovered herself. "Phillip, will you please tell me what you're talking about? I just don't understand. Alan's dead, and Beth keeps saying she killed him, and now you say—" And then a thought struck her, and her face paled. "Phillip," she whispered, "you don't believe she had anything to do—"

"Of course not," Phillip assured her immediately. "I didn't from the first minute she said it, and I'd hoped you hadn't even heard it. Norm Adcock is positive it was an accident. He says there's no way Beth could have caused Alan's fall. But that's not exactly what I'm talking about."

Carolyn relaxed just a little. "Then what *are* you talking about?"

Phillip replied, "The more I think about it, the more I keep thinking that this whole mess might not have happened if Beth weren't so damned determined to try to please everyone. Which," he added bitterly, "is a trait she inherited from her father, God rest his soul."

Now Carolyn's tears did overflow. "Will you please tell me what you're talking about?" she begged.

Suddenly Beth stirred in the bed, and Phillip reached down to stroke her forehead. Still asleep, she reached up and clutched his hand in her own for a moment, then let it go and rolled over. After a few more seconds had passed, she was sleeping peacefully once again.

"Come on," Phillip said quietly, drawing Carolyn to her feet. "Let's find someplace where we can talk."

He led her out of the room, then spoke to the duty nurse, who let them into a vacant office. Phillip guided Carolyn to a chair, then paced the little room for a moment, wondering where to start.

"I keep wondering why they were there at all, at that time of the afternoon," Phillip finally said. "The men had gone home an hour earlier, but they were still there. Anybody else would have knocked off, but not Alan. I'd asked him to rush the schedule, and instead of telling me he couldn't, he just went ahead and did it. He's been working late every day, and working on weekends, too. And on top of that, we dumped Beth on him."

Carolyn gasped, her eyes widening. "We didn't dump her," she protested. "You know what the situation was like at home. And it was just getting worse."

"I know," Phillip agreed. "But did either of us stop to think about the situation at Alan's? Carolyn, we know what's been going on, and all we've done is tell ourselves it would blow over. But what can the last six weeks have been like for Beth? No friends—every kid in town down on her—spending all her time in the mill because she had no place else to go! My God, she must have been out of her mind with loneliness. And she wouldn't complain, either. Not her. All she ever wanted was for people to love her, but none of us ever managed to have time for her."

"That's not true!" Carolyn objected. "I always had time for her, and you used to get up and take her riding."

"Three times, maybe," Phillip replied. "But you know as well as I do that we were both walking on eggs, trying to be fair to everyone. You were trying to fit in just as hard as Beth was. And then when Patches died, we were both willing to believe that she'd poisoned the oats."

"We didn't," Carolyn breathed, but Phillip held up a hand in a silencing gesture.

"Maybe we didn't. But we let it be the last straw, and we didn't try too hard to find out what really happened. It was easier just to avoid the situation by letting Beth move in with Alan."

"We thought it was best," Carolyn insisted. "We talked it over, and we agreed that it would be best for all of us. It wasn't just ourselves we were thinking about! It was Beth and Tracy, too!"

"Tracy," Phillip breathed. He'd been standing at the window, looking out into the darkness, but now he turned and faced Carolyn. "It was Tracy who poisoned Patches," he said.

Carolyn stared at him. "No . . . even Tracy wouldn't—"

"Wouldn't she? Try this—what if Tracy heard us talking the night before?" He knew he was guessing, but even as he spoke the words, he knew they were the truth. "What if she knew that if anything else happened—anything at all—we'd decided to let Beth go live with Alan? You know as well as I do that she's always resented Beth."

"But she loved that horse—"

Phillip shook his head tiredly, feeling the exhaustion of the conflicting emotions that had been boiling within him over the last hour. "It wasn't the horse she loved," he said. "It was having the horse. I . . . . I'm not sure Tracy is really capable of loving anything or anyone. This afternoon—" He fell silent for a moment, then made himself tell Carolyn what had happened in front of the mill that day. "She didn't care about Alan being dead," he finished, his own eyes flooding with tears now. "All she cared about was that it might be blamed on Beth. And she hoped it would be. I could see it in her eyes."

Carolyn groaned softly, her eyes fixed on the floor as her hand unconsciously kneaded the limp handkerchief. Then, finally, she looked up.

"But what do we do?" she asked. "What can we possibly do?"

"I don't know," Phillip confessed. "But we can take Beth home, and try to make it up to her some way. Somehow, we have to make her understand that she's not alone. We have to make her know that we love her very much."

Carolyn nodded mutely. And then, after a long moment she spoke the other question, the question that was in both their minds.

"What about Tracy? What do we do about her?"

Phillip had no answer.

# 22

Phillip left the hospital a few minutes later. Carolyn, unwilling to leave her daughter alone that night, had asked for a cot to be brought into Beth's room, and phoned Hannah to pack an overnight case for her.

Phillip walked slowly along Prospect Street, feeling the aura of tension in the village around him. There was still a crowd of people gathered in front of the mill, talking quietly among themselves, but they fell silent as he approached. There was something condemnatory in their glances, though none of them seemed willing to look directly at him. But he was all too aware of the eyes that raked over him, then quickly looked away. He wondered if he should stop and talk with them, then decided there was nothing he could say.

As he made his way quickly through the small crowd, and came to the north side of the old brick structure, his instincts told him to walk on, leaving the mill and all thoughts of it until tomorrow. But he couldn't do that. There were decisions that had to be made, and he couldn't allow himself to put them off. At the corner of the building, he turned left, starting once more toward the side entrance.

He used his key to open the construction shack, then rummaged around in Alan's battered desk until he found a spare set of keys to the building. In the darkness of the evening, he opened the door and slipped inside the mill itself. He stood still for several seconds, rejecting once more the strange urge to turn his back on the old building and simply walk away.

He told himself that the anxiety he was suddenly feeling meant nothing. It wasn't the building itself he was reacting to, but rather the tragedy that had occurred there only a few hours ago. The mill was only a building, and there were practical decisions to be made.

And yet his anxiousness began to congeal into something like fear, gathering around him, challenging him. He answered the challenge by reaching for the switch by the door that would turn on the naked bulbs of the worklights, certain that by banishing the darkness he would alleviate the irrational panic that was threatening to overwhelm him now.

At first it worked. Harsh white light flooded the building, and the familiar forms of the new construction reassured him. There was, after all, nothing to fear.

As his eyes scanned the progress Alan had made, Phillip realized immediately that there could be no reasonable argument for abandoning the project now. It was all but complete, needing little more than a few days' work on the mezzanine level.

And yet he still had an uneasy feeling that there was something here that he had yet to fully comprehend. Even with the worklights on, it was as if some dark shadow lingered in the vast spaces beneath the roof.

He moved forward to the spot where Alan Rogers had died only a few hours before. Though the floor had already been washed clean, and there was no evidence of the tragedy that had occurred there, still he could see Alan's broken body all too clearly in his mind's eye, and see Beth, her face ashen, crouching brokenly over the corpse, keening her grief into the echoing spaces above.

He paused for a moment, then, almost against his will, turned to face the front of the mill. On the steps, separated from him by the glass of the front doors, were the curious people of Westover, watching him with what he imagined to be suspicion. Suddenly he felt like an actor on a stage, caught unexpectedly in the spotlight without having rehearsed his role.

And then, as he stood alone in the mill, he realized that he had not come here tonight simply to make a decison about the future of the mill.

It was something else.

There was something he was looking for.

He turned away, and started toward the back of the mill, pausing at the enormous lighting panel that had been completed only a week ago. A moment later every light in the mill blazed into life, washing the shadows cast by the worklights away, suffusing the entire building with the even illumination of hundreds of fluorescent tubes.

When he looked down the stairs into the basement, the darkness there was gone too, driven away by the surge of electricity.

He started down the stairs, moving slowly, for still the light had not completely freed him from the near-panic that had threatened him when he'd first entered the building.

At the bottom of the stairs he gazed out into the far reaches of the basement, but there was nothing there that seemed the least bit unusual. It was as it had always been, nothing more than a vast expanse of space interrupted at regular intervals by the huge wooden columns that supported the floor above. There was nothing that Phillip could see that would induce the unease that was again growing within him.

He looked down at his feet, at the spot where his brother had died, and Jeff Bailey had died, and his mother had nearly died.

This, he realized, was the true reason he'd come here tonight. To stand alone at this spot, waiting to see if the fear his mother had described to him six weeks ago would come to him now, threaten him as it had threatened her.

Was it the same fear that had killed his brother?

He had to know.

And yet, as the seconds stretched into minutes, there was nothing.

He turned finally, and for the first time saw the little room tucked away behind the stairs. Its door stood slightly agape, but beyond the door there was only darkness.

It was from that darkness that tentacles of true fear finally began to reach out to him.

He told himself that what he was feeling was irrational, that there was nothing beyond that door but an empty room. And yet, as he approached the door he found himself stepping to one side so that the door itself separated him from whatever might lie beyond. His pulse rate suddenly rising, he reached out, grasped the door, and began sliding it to the left until it was fully open. Now the space was nearly six feet wide, and the light from the basement spilled into the room, only to be swallowed up by the blackness of the walls beyond.

There seemed to Phillip to be nothing unusual about the room. A simple rectangle, with a single small window high up on the far wall, and barren of furniture. The only sign that anyone had been in here in years was the area on the floor where the accumulated dust of a century had been recently disturbed.

All that set the room apart from the rest of the basement was its smell.

Emanating from the room was a strong odor of smoke, as if there had recently been a fire here.

As the smoky odor filled his lungs, Phillip began to feel a strange roiling of emotions that seemed to come not from within himself, but from the room.

The fear was stronger now, but mixed with it there was a sense of pent-up rage. It was almost as if the room were coiling in upon itself, preparing to strike him.

And yet there was a strange feeling of longing, too. A deep melancholy, tinged strongly with sadness. As he stood staring into the room, resisting a compelling urge to step inside and meet whatever was truly there, Phillip found his eyes flooding. A moment later the tears overflowed, and ran unheeded down his cheeks.

He took a tentative step forward, his arms reaching out as if to touch whatever was in the room, but then he suddenly veered away, and instead of entering the room, grasped the edge of the door and quickly rolled it shut.

As it slammed home, he imagined that he heard a short cry from within, a childish voice calling out to him.

*"Father!"*

He hurried up the stairs, turned off the lights, and started toward the side door.

And then, at the far end of the mill, he saw the faces.

They were still there—the people of Westover, their faces pressed to the glass, their features distorted into strange grimaces. Their hands seemed to be reaching out to him, and at first he had the feeling that they were beseeching him. Then, as he moved into the rotunda beneath the soaring glass dome of the building, he perceived something else.

The faces, though vaguely familiar, were unrecognizable. The men, clad in shabby clothing, all wore caps low on their foreheads, and their faces were unshaven.

The women, all of them gaunt with what seemed to be hunger, were also dressed shabbily, in long thin dresses that covered them from their wrists to their ankles and were buttoned high on their necks. They all wore their hair alike, twisted back into buns at the napes of their necks.

And they were not beseeching him.

They were reaching out to him not because they wanted anything of him.

They wanted *him*.

Their eyes showed it clearly. The eyes, all of them fixed on him now, glittered with hatred. He could almost feel it radiating out from them, surging through the glass of the doors—rolling toward him in an angry wave down the broad corridor of the mill.

He froze for a moment, his panic building within him, then turned and ran to the side door, reaching out to the switch and plunging the mill back into the darkness that had filled it a few moments earlier. He stepped through the door, closed it, and locked it.

He glanced toward the front of the mill, half-expecting to see an angry crowd moving toward him. Instead, there was nothing. Only a single man, silhouetted against a streetlight, waving to him.

"Mr. Sturgess?" he heard a voice calling. "Are you all right?"

Phillip hesitated. "I'm okay," he called back softly. "I just wanted to take a look around." Then he raised his hand, and returned the man's wave. But instead of going back to Prospect Street, he turned the other way, walking down the path until he came to the railroad tracks.

As he hurried through the night, he tried to convince himself that what he'd seen had existed only in his imagination.

When he got home twenty minutes later, Phillip found Tracy waiting for him. She was sitting on the stairs, halfway up, and when the door opened, she stood up and looked eagerly down at him. He glanced up at her, then dropped his keys in the drawer of the commode that sat near the front door. Neither of them said anything until he started toward the library, intent on fixing himself a drink. As he was sure she would, his daughter followed him into the big walnut-paneled room.

"Well?" she demanded as Phillip poured a generous slug of Scotch into a Waterford tumbler, then added a couple of ice cubes and some water. Only when he finished making the drink did he turn to face her.

"Well what?" he asked evenly.

Tracy hesitated. There was something in her father's eyes she'd never seen before. Though he was looking at her, she had the funny feeling that he wasn't seeing her. "Well, did she kill him?" she asked at last.

Phillip frowned, swirling his drink in his glass, then went over to the French doors to stare out into the night. "Why would she do that?" he asked, his back to Tracy.

"Well, isn't that obvious?" he heard his daughter say. "She wants to come back here. So she killed her father, because if he's dead, there's no place else for her to live."

Phillip felt his eyes flood once more, and suppressed the groan that rose in his throat. "Is this place really that wonderful?" he asked so softly that Tracy had to strain to hear him. "Is it really worth killing someone— your own father—just to live here?" Then, when he'd waited long enough for his words to sink in, he swung around and faced Tracy, who was standing in the center of the room, her eyes wide as she stared at him. "Well?" he asked. "Is it really worth all that?"

"It is to her—" Tracy began, but Phillip didn't let her finish.

"How could it be?" he asked. "What would have been so wonderful for her here? Ever since you came home from school you've done your best to make her miserable. You didn't even try to be friends with her. You treated her like a servant, ignored her, snubbed her—"

"So what?" Tracy demanded. Her face had flushed with anger, and her blue eyes glinted in the light of the chandelier. "She's nothing but trash, just like her mother. She doesn't belong here, and she doesn't fit in here, and if she comes back here, I won't live here anymore!"

"I see," Phillip said calmly. "And just where do you propose to live?"

Tracy's eyes widened, and the color suddenly drained from her face. What was he saying? He couldn't mean what she thought he meant, could he? "I . . . I'll go live with Alison Babcock."

Phillip nodded thoughtfully, and sipped once more at his drink. "Tracy," he said quietly, "I think you'd better sit down. It's a good time for the two of us to have a talk, since Carolyn won't be home."

"I hope Carolyn never comes back here again," Tracy declared, dropping into one of the wing chairs and draping her left leg casually over its arm.

"I'm sure that's what you hope," Phillip replied, sitting down opposite her. "But I'm telling you right now that it's a hope I want never to hear expressed in this house again. You may think anything you like, but you will keep your thoughts to yourself from this moment on."

His words hit Tracy like a physical blow. For a moment she was too stunned to say anything at all. Then she swallowed, and widened her eyes. "Daddy—"

"Put your feet on the floor, and sit up like the lady you think you are," Phillip said.

Tracy's leg came off the arm of the chair, and dropped to the floor. She stared at her father, trying to figure out what had happened. "You're going to let her come back here, aren't you?" she finally asked, her voice heavy with accusation. "Even after what she did to my horse."

"Ah," Phillip said, draining his glass and rising to his feet to fix himself another drink. "The horse." As he passed Tracy he glanced down, and could see by her eyes that his suspicion was correct. "The Babcocks have some pretty good stock in their stable," he commented. He said nothing more until he was once more facing her. "I wonder how safe they'd feel with you living in their house."

Tracy's heart was pounding now, and she had to grip the arms of the chair to keep her hands from shaking. "I didn't do it—" she began, but when her father shook his head, she fell silent.

"I don't believe you, Tracy," she heard him say. "I don't believe you, and I don't know what to do." His eyes flooded with tears once more, and this time he made no effort to hide them. "I guess I haven't been much of a father, have I? I've always tried to give you everything you wanted, but it wasn't enough."

"But I love you, Daddy," Tracy ventured.

"Do you?" Phillip asked. "I suppose you do, in your own way. But it's the wrong way, Tracy. I can't live my life for you. I can't decide whom to fall in love with simply on the basis of what you want. And I can't let you dictate who will live in my house and who won't."

In her own mind, Tracy mistook the sadness in Phillip's words for weakness. "But they don't belong here, Daddy," she protested once more. "I don't see why you can't see that. Carolyn and Beth don't even like it here. All they want is our money!"

The tenseness in her father's jaw told Tracy she had made a mistake, and she instinctively shrank back in her chair. Her father's eyes were coldly furious now.

"I'm not going to hit you," he told her. "Perhaps I should, but I won't. I don't believe in that sort of thing. But I will tell you this now, Tracy, and you had better listen and you had better understand, because I won't tell you again. From this moment on, you will treat Carolyn with all the respect you would give your own mother, or any other adult woman. I don't care anymore how you feel about her. The only thing I care about is how you treat her. From now on, you will be friendly and helpful and polite, whether I am in the house or not. As for Beth, yes, she will be coming back here to live. And it won't be because she has no other place to go. It will be because both her mother and I love her very much. And you will treat her the same way you will treat Carolyn. You will go even further. You will make friends with Beth, unless she's not interested in being friends with you. In that case, you will simply be polite to her, and stay out of her way. When she comes home tomorrow, you will tell her you are sorry about what happened to her father, and you will apologize for having poisoned her horse—"

"It was *my* horse," Tracy exploded. Suddenly she was on her feet, glaring at her father with naked fury. "It was my horse, and I had the right to do anything I

wanted to it! And it's my house, and I can act any way I
want to here, and you can't stop me. I hate you!"

Phillip rose to his feet. "Very well," he said softly.
"If that's the way you feel, there's only one thing I can
do. In the morning, I'll make some calls and find a
school for you."

"Good!" Tracy shot back, her feet planted wide
apart on the carpet, her face a mask of angry belligerence.
"And I hope it's as far away from here as you can get!"

"Oh, it will be," Phillip replied. "But of course
since you'll be there year-round from now on, we'll
have to find one that has no vacations. Also, of course,
one that has no horses." He looked down, his eyes
fixing on his daughter. "No privileges of any sort, I
should think," he said softly. "It appears that you've
already had far too many of those."

Tracy searched her father's face, trying to see if he
really meant what he was saying. "I . . . I'll run away!"

Phillip shrugged. "If you do, then you do. But if I
were you, I'd think about it pretty hard. I understand
life can be pretty rough out there for a girl of your age."
Then he turned and left the library, closing the door
quietly behind him. Tracy, frozen with rage and disbe-
lief, stood perfectly still for a moment, then went to the
bar and began throwing the glasses at the door, one by
one.

Phillip and Hannah met at the bottom of the stairs
as the first crash of breaking crystal emanated from the
library. The old woman's eyes widened, and she almost
dropped the small overnight case she carried in her
right hand. She said nothing, but her eyes questioned
Phillip.

"It's Tracy," he said mildly. "She's a little upset
right now, but I imagine she'll calm down when she
runs out of glasses. If she asks you to clean up the mess
for her, please do me the favor of playing deaf." He
thought he heard her gasp as her head bobbed dutifully. "Oh . . . and, Hannah," he added as he started
up the stairs. "From now on, there will be no need for

you to do anything about Tracy's room. She'll be cleaning it up herself, starting tomorrow."

Hannah's brows arched, and she eyed Phillip shrewdly. "Is that what this is all about?" she asked, tilting her head toward the library.

"I'm afraid not," Phillip replied. "She doesn't even know about having to clean her own room yet."

"In that case, sir, I'll lock up the rest of the crystal and the china as soon as I get back from the hospital."

"Thank you," Phillip said, and found himself grinning as he went up the stairs and turned toward his mother's suite. He found Abigail sitting in her favorite chair, a book facedown in her lap. The moment he came into the room, her sharp old eyes fell on him suspiciously.

"What in the name of God is that racket, Phillip?" she demanded.

"It's Tracy, Mother," he replied. "I have finally put my foot down with her." As briefly as possible, he explained to his mother what he had told his daughter, and why. When he was done, the old lady gazed at him from beneath hooded eyes.

"You're making a terrible mistake, Phillip."

Phillip shrugged, and dropped into the chair opposite her. "It seems to me I've been making a series of terrible mistakes with Tracy all her life." His mother, though, didn't seem to have heard him. She was staring at him now with the disapproval a mother reserves for a wayward child. What, he wondered, was she angry about now? And then he realized that the chair he had unconsciously sunk into had never been occupied by anyone but his father. "He's dead, Mother," he said quietly. "Is the chair in the mausoleum not enough? Is this supposed to be a shrine as well?"

He immediately regretted the words, but there was no recovering them.

"Sit where you wish," Abigail replied, her voice cold. "Since you seem intent on taking over his place in this house, you might as well take his chair as well. But as for Tracy, you can't simply change the rules on a child like her. She's far too sensitive."

"I'm afraid I can't agree with your assessment of her sensitivity," Phillip observed dryly. "And as to the rules, I haven't changed them. I've simply established some."

"And you expect me to allow it?" Abigail asked, her expression hardening.

"It's not a question of your allowing anything," Phillip replied. "I'm simply setting some limits and rules on my daughter, that's all."

Abigail's lips twisted with scorn. "Your daughter? I suppose you have a biological right to say that, but I'd hardly say you've fulfilled the functions of a father with her."

Phillip refused to rise to the bait. "And of course you'd be right in saying it," he agreed. "But that's not the point. The point is that it's time she learned that being a Sturgess does not make her anything special, and I intend to teach her that."

"By punishing her for being naturally resentful of the wrong sort of people intruding into her life?"

"That's enough, Mother," Phillip said, rising to his feet. "I simply wanted to find out how you were. I didn't come in here to debate with you."

Abigail's voice took on the coldness that Phillip had long since learned to recognize as the ultimate sign of his mother's rage. "And you presumed that I would simply acquiesce?"

"I don't presume anything, Mother," he replied, struggling to retain control of his own anger. "But it does occur to me that you might be just the slightest bit interested in how Beth is doing. Her father died this afternoon. Is protecting Tracy's selfishness really more important than Beth's welfare?"

"There's nothing I can do for Beth Rogers," was Abigail's acerbic reply. "But there is a great deal I can do for my own granddaughter. Not the least of which is preventing you from moving young Beth back into this house."

"Because she's 'the wrong sort of person,' Mother?"
Phillip asked wearily.

"Not at all," Abigail shot back. "I do not want her
here because I regard her as a danger to us all."

"Oh, for heaven's sake, Mother. You're sounding
as paranoid as Father was just before he died."

"I am not the least bit convinced that your father
did not have all his faculties intact," Abigail stiffly replied.

Phillip sighed. "All right, Mother. There's obviously no point in discussing it anymore. If you need
anything, I'll be in my rooms."

"If I need anything, I shall ring for Hannah, just as
I've done for the last forty years."

"Hannah's not here. She's gone to the hospital to
take some things to Carolyn."

Tracy stared angrily at the empty bar, looking for
something else to throw. But there was nothing. The
last of the three dozen crystal tumblers that had sat on
those shelves for as long as she could remember now
lay smashed at the bottom of the library door. The door
itself was marked with a series of crescent-shaped scars
where the glasses had struck it, and Tracy, even in her
rage at her father, was sure that those marks would
never be removed. For the rest of her life they would
be there in the door, a constant reminder of this day
when her father had turned against her.

But there was still her grandmother.

Her grandmother would take her side, and convince
her father that he was wrong, that instead of letting
Beth come back to Hilltop, they should make Carolyn
leave. They could go back to their crummy little house
on Cherry Street. Her father could buy it back for
them.

She pulled the library door open, ignoring the
broken glass that ground into the polished surface of
the floor, leaving deep scratches. Hannah could clean
up the mess tomorrow, and call someone to fix the
floor.

She hurried up the stairs, glancing down the corridor to see if her father's door was closed. Then she turned and started toward her grandmother's rooms.

She didn't bother to knock; she simply pushed the door open and stepped inside. At first she thought the room was empty. Her grandmother was no longer in her chair, and Tracy started toward the bedroom.

Then, from the window, she heard Abigail's voice. "Tracy? Are you all right, child?"

Tracy turned and saw the old woman, leaning heavily on her cane, a robe wrapped tightly around her. She looked much smaller than Tracy ever remembered, and she looked sick. Her skin seemed to hang in folds from her face, and her hands were trembling. "Daddy wants to send me away," she said.

Abigail hesitated, then slowly nodded her head. "I know," she sighed. "He told me."

"You have to make him change his mind."

"I've already tried," the old woman replied. "But I don't think I can. He's decided I spoiled you, I'm afraid. If your mother were alive—"

"But she's not!" Tracy suddenly shouted. "She's dead! She went away and left me, just like you did!" She started across the room, her face contorting as her fury, which she'd been holding carefully in check, rushed back to the surface. "You went to the hospital and left me here with them! They hate me! Everybody hates me, and nobody cares!"

Abigail felt her heart begin to pound in the face of the girl's anger, and instinctively turned away. She tried to close her ears to Tracy's fury, and made herself concentrate on the night beyond the window.

She shouldn't even be standing here. The doctor had insisted that she stay off her feet, but after her conversation with Phillip, she'd had to get out of her chair, had to pace the room while she tried to decide how to handle the situation. And finally she'd gone to the window, where she'd looked out toward the mill that was always, inevitably, the source of all her family's troubles.

She concentrated once more on the mill, still trying to shut out the shrill sounds of Tracy's angry voice.

And then, as she stared out into the black night, the dark form of the mill seemed suddenly so close she could almost touch it.

She could see the front doors, and the windows, neatly framed with their shutters, as clearly as if she were only across the street.

It was her imagination; it had to be. It was far too dark, and the mill much too far away, for her to see what she was seeing.

Her heart pounded harder, and once more she felt the bands begin to constrict around her chest.

And then, as the mill seemed to grow ever larger and closer, she saw the strange glowing light of a fire. At first it was only that, a strange glow emanating from the stairs to the basement.

But as she watched, and felt her ancient heart begin to burst within her, the glow turned bright. Flames rose up out of the stairwell, licking at the walls, then reaching out beyond the blackening brick as if they were searching for something.

Searching for her.

"No!" she whimpered. With an effort of pure will, for the pain in her chest was consuming her now, she turned from the window and groped for a chair. "Tracy!" she said, hearing the gasp in her own voice. "Tracy, help me!"

"Why?" Tracy said in a low voice, indifferent to her grandmother's pain. "Why should I help you? What do you ever do for me?"

"My heart—" Abigail whispered. She reached out, but as the pain clamped down on her breast, then began shooting down her arms toward her fingers, she dropped the cane and pitched forward, crumpling to her knees. She stretched out her left arm, and just managed to touch Tracy's leg.

Tracy's breath caught, and she pulled away from the strange apparition on the floor. She scrambled from the room, screaming for her father.

"It's Grandmother!" she yelled. "Daddy, come quick! Grandmother's dying!"

Phillip found his mother on the floor of her parlor. She lay on her side, her hands clutching at her breast as if trying to free herself of the demon that possessed her. He dropped to his knees, and reached down to take her hands.

Her eyes, death already taking possession of them, fixed on him, and she reached up to touch his face.

"Fire," she whispered. "It's burning again. You have to stop her, Phillip . . . you have to . . ."

For a moment Phillip thought his own heart would stop. "Who? Who has to be stopped, Mother?"

The old woman gasped for breath, then made one final effort. "Amy," she croaked. "Amy . . ."

And then she was gone.

# 23

Almost everyone in Westover went to the funeral for Alan Rogers or to the funeral for Abigail Sturgess.

Only a handful went to both.

For a few fleeting moments, Carolyn and Phillip had considered the possibility of combining the two services, but quickly rejected it. There had been no relationship between the two people who had died, nor did their circles of mourners overlap. So, in the end, they had decided that services for Alan would be held in the morning, three days after he died, and for Abigail the following afternoon.

What Carolyn had noticed most as the two long days wore on were the differences between the two services.

For Alan, the little church had been packed full with all the people she had been close to during her childhood and the years she had been married to Alan. The minister, who had grown up with Alan, had talked for forty minutes about the friend he had lost, and carried them all back into the past. It was, for Carolyn, a time of memories shared with people she hardly knew anymore, and she found herself missing all the old friends she had unwittingly cut herself off from when she married Phillip. Alan, for those forty minutes, had come back to life for everyone in the church, and

Carolyn had found herself half-expecting to get up at the end of the service, turn, and see Alan himself leaning against the back wall of the church, grinning sardonically at the fuss being made over him. But when the service was over, and she stood at the door of the church with her daughter, her feeling of momentary nostalgia faded quickly away.

No one, she realized almost immediately, knew quite what to say. Should they offer condolences to the woman who had divorced the man they were honoring?

Nor did they know quite what to say to Beth, for the gossip had not yet died down, despite the statement Norm Adcock had issued the day after Alan died. So as Alan's friends filed slowly out of the church, they paused for only the briefest of moments to speak to Carolyn, and eye Beth with ill-concealed curiosity. Then they hurried on. As soon as was decently possible, Phillip shepherded her to the waiting car. Carolyn, as they drove toward Hilltop, had found herself relieved that in his will Alan had specified cremation for his remains. A service at the cemetery, she was sure, would have been too uncomfortable for anyone to have borne. She found herself wondering if Alan had arranged for there to be no graveside service just for that very reason. It would, she decided, have been very much like him.

The next afternoon they had gone back to the church for Abigail's funeral. Once again the church had been full, but for the most part it was a different group. For Abigail, people had come from as far away as Boston, and the streets around the church were lined with Cadillacs and Lincolns. The same minister conducted the service and the eulogy, but this time he spoke about someone he had barely known. The eulogy, rather than evoking memories of Abigail, was little more than a recounting of the accomplishments of the Sturgess family. As Carolyn listened, she quickly became acutely aware that the woman the minister described bore no relationship to the woman Carolyn herself had known.

This time, as she stood at the door next to her

husband and her stepdaughter, everyone lingered, offering her condolences on the loss of the mother-in-law they all knew perfectly well had hated her. Carolyn forced herself to play the expected role, her eyes cast down as she murmured the proper words.

In the late afternoon there had been the burial at the mausoleum. Abigail's place, next to her husband, was outside the ring of columns, and she was not, as her husband had been, presented to Samuel Pruett Sturgess. That, Carolyn privately reflected, was apparently an honor reserved only for blood relatives.

After the interment they had all returned to the house, and repeated the reception that had been held for Conrad only a few months earlier. And as with Conrad, the only mentions of the deceased were a few automatic phrases whispered in hushed tones of mourning, after which the men clustered together to catch up on business, and the women finalized plans for various committee meetings and social gatherings, none of which included Carolyn.

And then, at last, it was all over, and Carolyn and Phillip were alone in the library.

Both girls had gone quietly to their rooms as soon as they'd returned from the burial service. Upstairs, there was only silence. For that, Carolyn was grateful. She sat wearily in one of the big wing chairs and sipped the drink Phillip had poured for her, reflecting, with a shudder she could barely conceal, on the way everyone had stared at Beth at the funeral services, as if they were all wondering, still, what had really happened to Alan, though no one had dared speak the question aloud.

At Hilltop, too, the air had been heavy with silence and the weight of unspoken questions for the last three days. Even Tracy had been nothing but demure and polite, the perfect child, appropriately sad at the passing of her beloved grandmother.

Carolyn had observed her cautiously but had so far said nothing. Since the moment she'd brought Beth back from the hospital the morning after Alan died,

Tracy seemed to have changed. When she and Beth had come in, Tracy had been waiting for them. She'd told Beth how sorry she was that her father had died, then gone out to the car to bring in Carolyn's overnight case and Beth's suitcase. And when they'd gone upstairs, she'd even offered to help Beth unpack.

And so it had gone. Tracy, as far as Carolyn had been able to see, was finally doing her best to accept both of them.

Except that Carolyn had noticed almost immediately the fact that all the crystal in the library was gone, and that both the door and the floor were severely scarred. Though Phillip had said nothing about it, and she had so far refrained from asking him, she was certain that Tracy had been responsible for the damage. Now, she decided to face the issue.

"I have noticed," she said carefully, "how well Tracy has been behaving. And I've also noticed that something obviously happened in here. Do you want to tell me about it?"

Phillip hesitated, but knew he couldn't conceal the truth from his wife. As briefly as possible, he told Carolyn exactly what had happened the night Abigail had died. When he was finally done, Carolyn sat silent for a long time. Then she stood up and went to the window, gazing out into the fading light of the summer evening. And despite the warmth of the air outside the open French doors, she found herself shivering.

"You think I did the wrong thing, don't you?" Phillip asked when Carolyn's silence had gone on longer than he could bear.

"I hope not," Carolyn replied so softly he could hardly hear her. "But I'm afraid she must hate us now more than she ever did before." Then she turned to face her husband. "I'm afraid, Phillip. I'm so very afraid."

Tracy had the door of her room closed and locked, and now she sat at her desk going through the contents of her grandmother's jewelry box. The best things, she knew, were kept in the vault at the bank, and her grandmother had brought them home only once a year, for Christmas and New Year's. Those were the things Tracy really wanted—the diamond necklace with the big emerald drop, which had a bracelet and earrings to go with it. And there was a sapphire tiara. The stones had been specially chosen to match the color of her grandmother's eyes. Tracy knew they would match her own eyes as well.

But still, there were some nice things in the jewelry box, and she was having a hard time trying to decide which ones to take. She had to leave a lot of it so no one would notice that some of it was gone, and she had to leave some of the best stuff, too.

Except that maybe she didn't.

A lot of the stuff in the box that she really liked, she couldn't remember her grandmother ever even wearing, so there was a good chance that her father wouldn't remember it either.

And some of the things in the box had been her mother's. She'd leave those—surely her father would give her mother's jewelry to Carolyn.

She picked up a large jade pendant, carved so that it had a different pattern on each side, and held it up to her neck. The chain was a little too long, but that didn't matter. The jade itself, she decided, was a perfect color for her—a very pale pink, and, when she held it up to the light, so transparent that the two patterns on either face combined to form yet a third. She opened her own jewelry box, lifted out the tray, and slipped the pendant into the tiny hidden compartment under what looked like the bottom of the case.

Suddenly there was a soft tapping at her door—two knocks, followed by a short silence, and then a third. It was the code she'd given Beth, telling her it would be a secret between them. And Beth, as Tracy had hoped, was too stupid to realize that all it did was give Tracy a chance to hide things before she let Beth into her room.

The whole thing her father had demanded had, in fact, been a lot easier than Tracy had thought it would be. It was almost like a game, and the object was to find out just how stupid Beth and Carolyn really were.

And with Beth, to find out how crazy she really was, so her father would finally have to send her away.

So far, it looked like they were even dumber than Tracy had thought, though she still hadn't figured out how to get Beth talking about Amy again.

Beth, she'd decided, was really pathetic. When she'd opened the suitcase Beth had brought with her, it had been all she could do to keep from giggling out loud at the junk that was inside. It was nothing but faded jeans, and a bunch of blouses and dresses that had to have come from Penney's. But she'd oohed and aahed and begged Beth to loan her some of the junk sometime, and Beth had fallen for it.

And then, this morning, Tracy had dug around in her closet until she'd found a dress she hadn't worn for two years but hadn't bothered to throw away yet, and offered it to Beth to wear to the funerals. The dress had looked awful on her, as Tracy had known it would, but Beth hadn't noticed, and neither had her mother.

Instead, they'd both thanked her, as though she'd done something nice.

Now, as the knock at the door was repeated, Tracy shut her grandmother's jewelry box, and hurriedly shoved it up on the closet shelf before unlocking the door and opening it. Beth stood in the corridor, her eyes wide. Her face was the color of putty. The dress Tracy had loaned her was on a hanger that Beth held high enough so the hem wouldn't touch the floor.

"I . . . I got a spot on it," Beth whispered, looking to Tracy like a frightened rabbit. "I'm sorry—I don't know what happened."

Tracy composed her features into an expression of what she hoped was generous forgiveness. "It's all right," she said. "I'm sure it won't cost much to have it cleaned." She saw no point in telling Beth she was going to throw the dress away anyhow. "Come on in."

She opened the door wider, and Beth came into the room, and carefully laid the dress on the bed. Tracy could hardly wait to call Alison Babcock and tell her how Beth treated the old rag like it was a Halston gown.

"I . . . I'm really sorry about your grandmother," Beth said as she started backing toward the door.

"It's okay," Tracy replied. "She was so old it's a miracle she didn't die years ago. I mean, it's not like she was young, like your father." Tracy forced herself not to snicker when Beth's eyes flooded with tears. "I'm sorry," she said quickly. "I guess you don't want to talk about your father, do you?"

Beth quickly wiped the tears away, and managed a smile. "I just can't think about him very much yet. But Mom says I'll get over it." Then she frowned uncertainly. "But I don't know. It just hurts so much. Did you feel like that when your mom died?"

Tracy shrugged. "She died when I was born. I don't even remember her. My grandmother raised me."

Beth's frown deepened. "Then how come you don't miss your grandmother like I miss my father?"

"I told you. She was an old lady." She glanced at Beth out of the corner of her eye, then did her best to work up some tears. "Besides, she didn't love me anymore. She loved you more than she loved me."

Beth gasped. "That's not true—"

Now Tracy managed a little sob. "It is, too! She didn't ask to see me when she was in the hospital. At least not the first night. She only wanted to see you."

"But that was about—" And then Beth stopped short, afraid to speak the name that Tracy had used against her for so long.

"About Amy?" Tracy asked, her voice showing no hint of the mockery of the past.

Hesitantly, Beth nodded.

Tracy's heart beat a little faster. She had to be careful now, or she might scare Beth off. "Grandmother talked about her," she said, thinking as fast as she could. "She told me she wished you could come and live here again, because she wanted to know all about Amy."

"She . . . she did?" Beth stammered, wondering if it could possibly be true, and if maybe Tracy didn't think she was crazy anymore.

Tracy nodded solemnly, remembering her grandmother's last words. Maybe she could use them to get Beth talking. "And she said there was a fire." At the look in Beth's eyes, she knew she'd struck a bull's-eye.

"In the mill?" Beth breathed. "Did she really talk about the fire in the mill?"

Now Tracy hesitated. What if Beth was lying too, trying to trap her just as she herself was trying to trap Beth? But that was silly—Beth wasn't smart enough to do that. "I think so," she said. "When she was in the hospital, what did she tell you?"

"Nothing," Beth replied, and Tracy's heart sank. But then Beth spoke again. "Except that when she got home, she'd show me something that proved Amy's real."

A surge of excitement seized Tracy. *It's in the box*, she thought. *It's in the box Grandfather was always going through.*

But she said nothing.

# 24

It was a little past midnight. The house was silent, but from outside her open windows Tracy could hear the soft chirpings of crickets and the murmurs of tree frogs calling to their mates. Her feet bare, and only a light robe over her pajamas, she opened her closet and fished her grandmother's jewelry box off the top shelf. Then she turned off the lights in her room, and carefully opened the door.

The corridor outside was dark, but Tracy didn't even consider turning on the night-light on the commode. Her grandmother's door was only thirty feet away, and she could have walked it blindfolded if she'd had to.

She was halfway down the hall, moving carefully to avoid bumping into the commode that stood at the midpoint, when she realized that the corridor was not completely dark after all. At the far end, there seemed to be a faint glowing, as if a dim light were spilling from beneath a door.

Her grandmother's door.

She froze in the darkness, clutching the jewelry box tighter, her eyes fixed on the light. It seemed now to be flickering slightly. Why would there be light coming from her grandmother's room? It was empty, wasn't it?

Unless it wasn't empty.

But who could be in there? She'd been awake all night, listening.

Her father and stepmother had come in to say good night to her, and then she'd heard them going down the hall to the other end of the house. She'd even opened her door so she could listen, and been able to hear their voices until the closing of their door had cut off their words.

Twice, she'd crept down the hall to listen at Beth's door, and opened it just enough to hear the even rhythm of her stepsister's breathing as she slept.

The only other person in the house was Hannah.

So it had to be Hannah.

Hannah was in her grandmother's room, going through her belongings, looking for things to steal.

Her grandmother had told her about servants, and how they always stole things. "You have to expect it," her grandmother had explained to her. "Servants resent you for what you have, and they think they deserve it. So they simply take things, because they have no sense of right and wrong. You can't stop it—it's simply the price we pay for what we have."

And now, with her grandmother barely dead, Hannah was in her room, using a flashlight to go through her things, looking for things to steal.

Tracy smiled in the darkness, congratulating herself for having already removed the jewelry box from its place in her grandmother's vanity. She turned, and started back toward her own room.

But then she remembered how Hannah had always fawned over Beth, and how, for the last three days, she had refused to do even the simplest thing for Tracy herself. Slowly another idea came to her, and she knew exactly what she would do. She would catch Hannah in her grandmother's room, and then make her father fire her. Hannah could even be blamed for the pieces missing from the jewelry box. Maybe she could even fix it so the old housekeeper would go to jail.

She moved quickly on down the hall, stopping outside the closed door to her grandmother's room.

Pressing her ear close, she listened, then stooped down to peer through the keyhole.

The room was dark now, and she could hear nothing.

Maybe Hannah had heard her.

Gingerly, Tracy turned the knob, and pushed the door slightly open. Then she reached in, and flipped the switch just inside the door. The chandelier that hung from the center of the ceiling went on, and the room was flooded with bright light.

Tracy pushed the door open, and looked around.

The room was empty.

But there had been light under the door, she was certain of it. Her eyes scanned the room again, and fell on the door that led to her grandmother's dressing room, and the bathroom beyond.

The dressing room, too, was empty, as was the bathroom. She paused on her way back to the bedroom, and put the jewelry box back in its accustomed place in the top drawer on the right side.

Finally, she returned to the bedroom, and looked around once more. She couldn't have been wrong—she *couldn't*.

And yet, nowhere was there any sign that anyone else had been in these rooms. All was exactly as it had been earlier when she had stolen in to take the jewelry box in the first place. All the clutter—the things her grandmother prized so much, and that Tracy regarded as just so much junk—was exactly as it had always been. The lights, all of them except the chandelier, were off, so that wouldn't account for the strange light coming from beneath the door either.

She went to the window, and looked out into the darkness. In the village there were still a few lights on, and in the distance she could barely make out the shape of the mill. And then, as she watched, she saw the strange flickering light again.

This time, though, it was at the mill. It seemed to light up for just a moment, then disappear once more into the blackness of the night.

And then Tracy was sure she knew what it was. A

car, winding along the road, its headlights flashing briefly on the mill as it rounded a bend.

The same thing must have happened when she'd been in the hall—it had been no more than a car coming up the hill, its lights flashing into the room for a few seconds.

Tracy turned away from the window, and started toward the closet that had been her grandfather's.

Had she stayed at the window a few more seconds, she would have seen the strange light at the mill again. She would also have seen that there were no cars moving along River Road.

She found the box where it had sat for as long as she could remember, on the highest shelf of her grandfather's closet. She had seen it often there, but whenever she'd asked her grandfather what was in it, he'd told her only that when the time came, she would know.

Now she stared at it for several moments. There didn't seem to be anything special about it—it was simply a rectangular metal box, with a metal handle. She could tell just by looking at it that it was very old. She reached up and gently eased it off the shelf, then carried it gingerly back to the parlor, where she sat down in her grandmother's chair. When she pressed the button on its front panel, the latch stuck for a second, then popped open.

Inside, there was nothing but some sort of old book. She fingered it for a moment, wondering if she should read it here, then put the box back in her grandfather's closet. But then, as the beginnings of an idea began to form in her mind, she picked up the box and left the suite of rooms, pulling the door shut behind her.

Back in her own room, Tracy put the box on her desk, then took the strange-looking book out of it. Taking the book with her, she went to her bed, got under the covers, then opened the book to the first page.

It was a journal of some sort, written by hand in black ink, that was barely legible. The spiky handwriting looked very old-fashioned, and for a moment Tracy wasn't sure she would be able to read it at all. But then, remembering the book had something to do with Amy, she began studying the words more carefully. Slowly, deciphering the words one by one, she read through the old book.

By the time morning came, and she woke up from what had been a fitful sleep, she knew exactly what she was going to do.

She smiled, and hugged herself, luxuriating in the warmth of the summer morning, and the knowledge that by this time tomorrow, she would finally be rid of Beth Rogers.

I'm being ridiculous, Carolyn told herself as she sat at the breakfast table that morning. Everything is fine. Tracy is behaving like a perfectly ordinary child, and I have no reason to be suspicious.

And there was nothing going on at the table that should have made her suspicious, either. Beth and Tracy were talking together, and Tracy was suggesting that after breakfast, maybe she should give Beth a tennis lesson.

"But I've never even played," Beth said. "I'll just mess up."

"Everybody messes up," Tracy countered. "And besides, you can't go to the club unless you play tennis."

Carolyn felt herself stiffen, ready for the scornful comment that was sure to come. But instead, Tracy simply went on talking, nothing in her voice betraying the contempt for Beth she had always expressed before.

"Look. Everybody at the club plays tennis, right?"

Beth nodded.

"So if you don't play tennis, what are you going to do? Just sit there?"

"Maybe I won't go to the club at all," Beth suggested.

Now Tracy rolled her eyes, and again Carolyn felt a pang of apprehension.

"So what are you going to do? Sit up here all by yourself? What fun will that be? And you know you don't have any friends down in the village anymore—"

"Tracy—" Phillip interrupted, shooting his daughter a warning look. Instantly, Tracy looked apologetic.

"I'm sorry," she said to Beth. "I shouldn't have said that."

Beth shrugged, and stared at her half-eaten grapefruit. "Why not? It's true. They all think I'm crazy."

"Who cares what they think?" Tracy asked.

Beth eyed Tracy suspiciously. "You think I'm crazy too. You said so."

"That was before," Tracy replied. "I can change my mind, can't I?"

"But what about all your friends?"

"Stop worrying so much. Just let me teach you how to play tennis, and then next week I'll take you to the club. And I'll even let you wear some of my clothes. Or we'll make Daddy take us to Boston, and buy you some of your own."

"But what if I'm no good?" Beth asked, though her eyes were starting to betray her eagerness. "What if I'm terrible at it?"

"You can't be any worse than Alison Babcock," Tracy answered. "She can barely even hit the ball over the net. And when she serves, it's like getting free points."

"You won't laugh at me?"

"I won't laugh at you," Tracy promised, suddenly grinning. "Anyway, I won't laugh very much. Besides, who's going to see you?"

Ten minutes later the girls dutifully cleared the table of everything except their parents' coffee cups, and then were gone. A few minutes later, Carolyn saw them walking across the lawn toward the tennis court, Tracy already showing Beth how to hold a racket.

"Well?" Phillip asked, as if he'd been reading her

thoughts for the last half-hour. "You don't believe it, do you?"

Carolyn sighed. "I wish I could, but nobody changes as quickly as Tracy has. So, no, I don't believe it at all. I'm absolutely convinced that she's putting on some kind of performance, but I can't figure out what it's all about."

"Don't forget," Phillip replied. "I gave her a choice— she either behaves herself, or she goes away."

But Carolyn shook her head. "What she's doing goes beyond that, Phillip, and you know it as well as I do. I keep getting the feeling that she's up to something, and that she needs to get Beth's confidence." Then, at the hurt she saw in Phillip's eyes, she tried to apologize. "I'm sorry. I suppose I'm not being fair to her. But I just can't see her changing overnight."

"She probably hasn't," Phillip conceded. "But even if it's just an act, it's better than the way things were. And we have to give her a chance, don't we? You know as well as I do that if she gets to know Beth, she'll like her."

*I don't know that at all*, Carolyn thought to herself. *All I know is that I don't believe any of this. I feel like I'm living in a play, and I don't know what it's about.* But despite her private feelings, she made herself smile at her husband. "A couple of months ago that was certainly true enough. But after all that's happened—"

"It's all over now," Phillip declared.

Carolyn wished she thought he was right. "Is it?" she asked. "What about Beth's friend Amy?"

Phillip's eyes clouded, and Carolyn had the feeling he was keeping something from her. But he shook his head. "She'll forget about her. Beth was going through a rough period when she dreamed Amy up, but as things get better, she won't need Amy anymore." He looked at his wife pleadingly. "Honey, haven't we had enough problems this summer? Do we have to start looking for more? And besides," he added, "Beth hasn't mentioned Amy even once since she's been home, has she?"

"Can you blame her?" Carolyn replied more sharply than she'd intended. "Talking about Amy cost her every friend she had. If I'd been her, I'd have stopped talking about Amy long ago. But that wouldn't mean I'd stopped thinking about her."

Phillip frowned. "What are you getting at?"

"I don't know!" Carolyn rose from the table, and moved to the French doors. Beyond the terrace and across the lawn, she could see Beth and Tracy on the tennis. Had it been any two girls but these, the scene would have looked perfectly natural. But knowing all that had happened that summer, and remembering what Tracy had said in the restaurant the night Abigail had had her first heart attack, there was something frightening about watching Tracy show Beth how to hold the tennis racket. The scene looked so innocent, but Carolyn couldn't rid herself of the feeling that what she was watching was more than a simple tennis lesson. Tracy, she was increasingly certain, was up to something. But what? And then, as her gaze wandered past the tennis court and fell on the massive shape of the mill, it came to her.

Whatever Tracy was up to, it had to do with the mill. She turned back to face her husband. "What about the mill?" she asked. "Have you decided what you're going to do with it?"

Phillip felt dazed by her words. "What does that have to do with Beth and Tracy?" he asked.

"I'm not sure what it has to do with Tracy," Carolyn replied. "But it seems to me that it's obvious what it has to do with Beth. I want you to tear it down."

"Tear it down?" Phillip echoed. "Carolyn, what are you talking about? There's no way I can do that—"

Carolyn's heart beat faster, for even as she had spoken the words, she had known she was right.

"But you have to! Don't you see? It's not just Beth! It's everyone! Sooner or later, that mill destroys everyone in this family. Your brother—your father. Even Abigail and Alan. And I know who will be next! Phillip, if you don't do something, the mill will destroy Beth and Tracy, too!"

Phillip stared at her. It was like hearing his father again, rambling on about the evils and dangers that the old brick building harbored. But there was nothing to it—no more than superstition. "No! Carolyn, I won't have you talking like that. There's nothing in that mill—nothing at all!"

Carolyn heard his words, and desperately wanted to believe them. And yet, deep in her heart, she knew that he was wrong. There *was* something evil in the mill, and it was spreading out now, reaching out toward them. If they didn't do something, it would destroy them all.

But what could they do, short of destroying the mill?

Nothing.

She had to find a way to convince him she was right. And she had to find it soon.

"Did I really do all right?" Beth asked an hour later when Tracy finally called a halt to the tennis lesson.

"You did great," Tracy lied, wondering why she'd even bothered to suggest tennis lessons, when anything else would have done just as well. It had been so boring, standing there in the hot sun, throwing balls gently over the net for Beth to try to hit. And she'd hardly been able to keep from laughing as Beth kept chopping away at them, most of the time not even coming close to hitting one of them. Of course it had been kind of fun the last fifteen minutes, when she'd started throwing them all over the place, making Beth run back and forth as fast as she could.

"When are you going to teach me how to serve?"

"Tomorrow," Tracy promised. She jumped easily over the net and started gathering up the balls that were scattered all over the court. When they were finished, they started toward the house, but Tracy suddenly stopped, as if something had just caught her eye.

When Beth turned, Tracy was looking up the hill toward the mausoleum. When she could see Beth watching her out of the corner of her eye, she spoke. "I bet Amy's supposed to be buried up there," she said.

Beth's eyes widened. "A-Amy?" she stammered. "I thought you didn't believe there was any such person."

"I changed my mind," Tracy said. "I told you that this morning, didn't I? That I didn't think you were crazy anymore?"

Beth nodded hesitantly.

"So if I don't think you're crazy, and you think Amy's real, then I have to think she is too, don't I?"

"I . . . I guess so."

"Besides," Tracy went on, her voice dropping, "I snuck into my grandmother's room last night, and found something."

A thrill of anticipation ran through Beth, and her eyes widened. "About Amy?"

Tracy nodded.

"What?" Beth asked. "What did you find?"

"Promise you won't tell anyone?"

"I promise."

Tracy eyed the other girl narrowly. "Swear on your father's grave?"

"Th—that's not fair," Beth protested, struggling against the lump that had suddenly formed in her throat.

"If you don't swear, I won't tell you," Tracy said.

Beth hesitated, then nodded. "I . . . I swear."

"Okay, I found a book, and it tells all about Amy."

"What does it say?"

Tracy smiled mysteriously. "Want to read it?"

"You mean you still have it?"

"I hid it in my room. Come on."

They hurried into the house, and went upstairs. When they reached the landing, Tracy whispered into Beth's ear, "Go into your room and lock the door, and don't let anyone in until I give the secret code. And as soon as I come in, lock the door behind me. All right?"

Beth nodded, and scurried into her room, locking the door behind her. Giggling, Tracy went into her own

room, closed the door, then flopped down on the bed
and turned on her television. Half an hour later, when
she decided that if she waited any longer Beth would
decide she'd been joking, she pulled the metal box out
from under her bed, checked the upstairs hall, then ran
down and knocked twice on Beth's door, waited a second, then knocked again. Instantly the door opened,
and Beth let her in.

"What happened?" Beth whispered. "I thought you
weren't ever coming."

"I almost got caught," Tracy told her. "Every time
I tried to sneak out of my room, Hannah was snooping
around. And if she catches us with this, she'll tell my
father, and he'll whip us both."

Beth gasped. "Whip us? Really?"

Tracy nodded solemnly. "That's why we can't let
him know we have it." Then she took the box to Beth's
desk, and lifted the lid. Ceremoniously, she took the
book out, laid it on the desk, and carefully opened its
cover. "Read it," she said.

When Beth had finished deciphering the strange
handwriting that covered the pages of the little book,
she looked up at Tracy.

"What does it mean?" she asked. "What'll we do?"

"It means they buried her in the wrong place,"
Tracy replied. "Don't you see? She's supposed to be up
in the mausoleum, but she's not. That's what she wants."

Beth's eyes widened. "You mean we have to dig
her up?"

Tracy hesitated, then shook her head. "That wouldn't
be enough," she said. "What we have to do is get her
spirit out of the mill."

Beth swallowed. Her heart was suddenly pounding.
"How?" she whispered. "The mill's all locked up, isn't
it? How can we get in?"

"I know where Daddy hid the keys," Tracy replied. "So we'll do it tonight. All right? We'll go down
there together, and we'll let Amy out, and bring her up
to the mausoleum. Then she'll be where she belongs,

and she won't be angry anymore, and you can visit her anytime you want to. See?"

Beth nodded, but said nothing.

"Keep the book in here, okay? Hannah's always coming in to clean my room, and if she finds it, we're dead."

"But what if she finds it in here?"

"She won't. But even if she does, it won't be so bad, because you can say you didn't know you shouldn't have taken it out of Grandmother's room. Just stick the book in your desk, and hide the box in your closet."

"But what—?" she began again, but this time Tracy didn't let her finish her question.

"Just hide it, then come down to the stable. There's some stuff we've got to get ready for tonight." Then, before Beth could say anything else, Tracy slipped out of her room, closing the door behind her.

After Tracy was gone, Beth stared at the book for several long seconds, then slowly read it through once more.

Everything she read fit together with what she already knew about Amy.

So Amy was real after all, and even Tracy finally believed her.

Tracy, she decided as she hid the box in her closet and slipped the book into the top drawer of her desk, wasn't so bad. In fact, it was starting to look like they were going to be almost real sisters after all.

Tracy could hardly believe it.

She skipped down the path toward the stable, doing her best to keep from laughing out loud.

Beth had actually fallen for it. Just because of a name written in an old book, she'd actually been stupid enough to think it was proof that her dumb ghost was real.

She sauntered into the stable. Peter Russell was mucking out the stalls. He looked up at her and frowned.

"I thought you weren't supposed to come down here anymore," he said.

"There's some stuff I have to get," Tracy replied, her eyes narrowing angrily.

"What kind of stuff?" Peter challenged. "Your dad told me the stable was off limits."

"None of your business," Tracy replied, but when she tried to brush past Peter, he stepped out into the aisle and blocked her way.

"It is too my business. And until your father says different, you stay out of here."

Tracy hesitated, wondering if she should try to talk him out of it. And then she had an even better idea.

She'd just wait for Beth, and tell her what to get out of the tackroom. And Beth would do it, too. Now that she'd shown Beth that old book, she was sure Beth would do anything she asked her to do.

Anything at all.

# 25

A kind of somnolence hung over the house all that day, and more than once Carolyn had to resist an urge to go to her room, close the curtains, then lie down in the cool half-light and let sleep overtake her. But she hadn't done it, for all day long she found herself obsessed with the idea that hidden somewhere in the house was the key to whatever evil lay within the mill.

For a while, after breakfast, she tried to fight the growing obsession, telling herself that Phillip was right, and that there could not possibly be anything inherently evil about the old building. She reminded herself that Phillip's father, in his last years, had been senile, and that Abigail, in those last weeks of her life when she had changed her mind about the mill, had already been weakened by a heart attack.

And yet every argument she presented herself with fell to pieces in the face of her growing certainty that there was something in the mill that neither Conrad nor Abigail had quite understood, but had nevertheless finally been forced to accept.

Finally, after lunch, she started searching the house.

She began in Abigail's rooms, opening every drawer, searching through the stacks of correspondence the old woman had kept filed away, looking for anything that might refer, even indirectly, to the mill.

There was nothing.

She went to the basement, then, and spent two hours searching through the jumble of furniture that had been stored there. When she finally emerged, covered with the dust and grime that had collected through the years, it was only to climb the long flights of stairs to the attic, where she began the search once more.

Again she found nothing.

But it was strange, for she did find that the Sturgesses, apparently for generations long past, had been inveterate collectors. Aside from enough discarded furniture to fill the house half-again, she had found box after box of old albums, piles of scrapbooks, cartons of personal correspondence, and even yellowed school reports done by Sturgess children who had long since grown up, grown old, and passed away.

And yet, among the collected detritus of the family's life, there had been not one scrap of information about the mill upon which their fortune had been built.

In the end she decided there was a reason for it. The records, she was certain, would have too clearly reflected the realities of the mill—the theft of her own family's share in it, and the appalling conditions under which it had been run. The Sturgesses, she was sure, would not have wanted those records around as a constant reminder of the sins of the past.

Eventually giving up the search, she wandered into the dining room to sit among the portraits of the departed Sturgesses.

She dwelt for a long time on the picture of Samuel Pruett Sturgess, who today seemed to be mocking her as if he knew it was a descendant of Charles Cobb Deaver who was gazing at him, and was laughing at her efforts to discover the secrets he had long since destroyed.

At last, as the afternoon faded into the kind of hot and sticky evening that promised no relief from the humidity of the day, Phillip came home. He found his wife still in the dining room.

"Enjoying the pleasure of their company?" he asked. When Carolyn turned to face him, he regretted his bantering tone. Her hair, usually flowing in soft waves, hung limply around her shoulders, and her white blouse was smudged with dirt. Her face looked haggard, and her eyes almost frightened. Phillip's smile faded away. "Carolyn, what is it?"

"Nothing," Carolyn sighed. Then she managed a weak smile. "I guess I'm behaving like an hysteric. I've been turning the house upside down all day, trying to find the old records from the mill."

"They're probably in the attic," Phillip observed. "That's where practically everything is."

"They're not," Carolyn replied. She pulled herself to her feet, and started out of the room. "And if you ask me, old Samuel Pruett destroyed them all himself."

For a moment, Phillip thought she must be joking, but there was nothing good-humored in her tone. He followed her into the library, where he fixed himself a drink, then poured her a Coke. "What about the girls?" he asked. "Any problems?"

Carolyn sank into a chair, shaking her head. "None at all. They've been together all day, and I kept waiting for the explosion. But it hasn't come."

Phillip's brows arched hopefully. "Maybe," he suggested, "you were wrong this morning."

"I wish I could think so," Carolyn replied. "But I don't. I just have a feeling something's going to happen. And I wasn't wrong about the mill this morning, either," she added. "I really do want you to close it up again." She met his eyes. "I know it sounds crazy, and I can't explain it, but I've just gotten to the point where I believe your parents were right. There's something evil about the place, and I think your whole family knew it. I think that's why I can't find any records. And I mean, none at all!"

Phillip hesitated, then, to Carolyn's surprise, nodded. "You might be right," he said at last. "Anyway, I can't really say I think you're wrong anymore." His gaze shifted away from her for a moment, then came back. "I went down there again today, and something happened to me. And it's not the first time."

As clearly as he could, he told Carolyn about the strange experiences he'd had—the odor of smoke he'd noticed in the mill when he'd been there with Alan back when the restoration was just beginning, and the sense of panic he'd had the day Alan had died.

He even told her about the hallucination he'd had, as if he'd slipped back a century in time, and felt as if an angry mob had been reaching out to him, trying to lay their hands on him.

"I felt as though they were going to lynch me," he finished. "And I went back this morning."

"And?" Carolyn prompted him.

Phillip shook his head. "I don't know. I didn't like being in the place alone, but I kept telling myself it was nothing—that the place has so many bad associations for me that I couldn't feel any other way. But the longer I stayed, the worse it got. And I couldn't go into the basement at all. I tried, but I just couldn't do it. Every time I looked down those stairs, I had the feeling that if I went down them, I'd die." He fell silent, then drained his glass and set it aside.

"What did you do?" Carolyn finally pressed when it seemed as if Phillip wasn't going to go on.

"Went to see my accountant." He chuckled hollowly. "When I told him I was thinking about giving the project up, he told me what I told you—we can't. Only he had the numbers to back himself up with."

Carolyn frowned now. "The numbers? What numbers?"

"All the figures on the amount of money we've committed to the project. The loans, the contracts, the cash layouts—the whole ball of wax. And the bottom line is that we literally cannot afford to abandon it. There's just too much money invested." He smiled bitterly. "The best thing that could happen," he added, "would be if the place burned to the ground."

For the rest of the evening, Phillip's last words echoed in Carolyn's mind, and when she at last went to bed, she found it difficult to sleep.

The mill, for her, had become a trap, and she felt its jaws inexorably closing on all of them.

Tracy Sturgess awoke at midnight, just before the alarm on her night table went off. It wasn't a slow wakening, the slight stirring that grows into a stretch and is then followed by reluctantly opening eyes. It was the other kind, when sleep is suddenly snatched away, and the mind is fully alert. At the first sound of the alarm, she reached out and silenced it.

Tracy lay still in the bed, listening to the faint sounds of the night. She had not intended to fall asleep at all—indeed, she had not even bothered to undress that night, and when her father had come in to say good night to her, she had merely clutched the covers tight around her neck. But when he was gone, she'd set her alarm, just in case.

She slid out of her bed and went to the window. The moon, nearly full, hung high in the night sky, bathing the village below in its silvery light. Even from here, each of the houses of Westover was clearly visible, and when Tracy looked at the mill, the moonlight seemed to shimmer on its windows, making it look as if it were lit from within.

Tracy turned away from the window, put on her sneakers, then crossed to the door. Opening it a crack, she listened for several long seconds. From below, the slow regular ticking of the grandfather clock in the foyer seemed amplified by the silence of the house, and Tracy instinctively knew that everyone else was asleep.

She opened the door wider, and stepped out into the corridor, then moved silently toward Beth's room. When she came to the closed door, she paused, listening again before she tried the knob. It turned easily, and when she pushed the door open, there was no betraying squeak from its hinges. Then she was inside, and a moment later she stood by Beth's bed, gently shaking her stepsister.

"Wake up," she whispered as loudly as she dared.

Beth stirred, then woke up, blinking in the dim moonlight. She looked up at Tracy. "Is it time?"

Tracy nodded, then pulled the covers away from Beth. To her disgust, Beth was wearing pajamas. "I told you not to undress," she hissed. "Hurry up, will you?" Beth reached out to the light on her nightstand, but Tracy brushed her hand away. "Don't turn on the lights. What if someone sees? Will you just get dressed?"

Beth scrambled out of the bed, and scurried into her closet. In less than a minute she was back, wearing jeans and a gray sweatshirt. On her sockless feet she had a pair of sneakers almost identical to Tracy's. She sat down at her desk, and quickly tied the laces, then followed Tracy out into the hall. But at the top of the stairs, Tracy suddenly stopped.

"What's wrong?" Beth whispered.

"The bed. We forgot to fix it so it looks like you're still in it."

"But everyone's asleep," Beth protested.

"What if they wake up? Wait for me downstairs by the front door." Then, before Beth could protest, Tracy scurried back to Beth's room and disappeared inside.

But instead of arranging the pillows under the covers of Beth's bed, she went to the desk, opened the top drawer, and took the old book out. Opening the book, she laid it facedown on the desk, then hurried out of the room.

She left the door standing wide open.

Downstairs, she found Beth waiting nervously by the front door. She pulled the drawer of the commode out, fished around until she found the right set of keys, then closed the drawer. A moment later they were outside.

They darted across the lawn, and between the twin stone lions that guarded the path to the mausoleum, then paused to pick up the lantern that Beth had sneaked out of the tackroom that afternoon.

"But why can't we just turn on the lights?" Beth had protested when Tracy had told her what she wanted.

"Are you crazy?" Tracy had replied. "If we turn on

the lights, everyone in town will know someone's inside. But who's going to see a lantern?"

Now Tracy checked it once more. Its tank was full,
and the wick, which she had carefully trimmed, was
still undamaged. The knife she had used to trim the
wick—an old rusty jackknife that had also come from
the tackroom—was safe in her pocket, along with three
books of matches.

Carrying the lantern, Tracy started up the trail to
the mausoleum, Beth behind her.

The great marble structure seemed even larger at
night, and the moonlight shot black shadows from the
pillars across the floor. One of the shadows fell across
the chair in which the ashes of Samuel Pruett Sturgess
were interred, giving the girls the fleeting illusion that
the chair had disappeared entirely. Standing by the
broken pillar, they gazed out toward the mill.

"Look," Beth breathed. "It's burning."

Tracy felt a derisive laugh rise in her throat, but
choked it off. "It's Amy," she whispered. "She knows
we're coming." Out of the corner of her eye she saw
Beth hesitate, then nod. "Shall we stop at her grave?"
she asked.

This time, Beth shook her head. "She's not there,"
she whispered. "She's still in the mill. Come on."

Now, with Beth leading, they started down the
tangled path that would eventually stop at the river.

"Are you scared?" Tracy asked. They had come to
the end of the trestle over the river. On the other side,
across River Road, the mill gleamed in the moonlight.

"No," Beth replied with a bravery she didn't quite
feel. The wooden bridge stretched out before them,
seeming longer and higher at night than it did in the
daytime. "Are you?"

Tracy shook her head, and started out onto the
narrow span, placing her feet carefully on the ties,
keeping to the exact center of the space between the
twin rails. Behind her, Beth followed her movements
precisely, concentrating on staring at the ties, for when

she let her vision shift, focusing on the river below, a
wave of dizziness passed over her.

Then they were on the other side of the river, and
solid ground once more spread away on either side of
the tracks.

They paused at River Road, then darted across.

They came to the back of the mill, and Beth pointed
to the loading dock. "That's where she lives," she whispered. "There's a little room under there."

Tracy ignored her, starting up the path along the
side of the building. They were exposed now, the full
light of the moon shining down on them, and they
could easily be seen from any car that might pass by.

The third key Tracy tried fit the padlock on the
side door, and when she twisted it the lock popped
open. Then, as she pulled the door itself open, she felt
Beth freeze beside her. She turned to look, and saw
that Beth's eyes were wide, staring in through the open
door. Her whole body was trembling slightly, and in
the pale moonlight her skin was the color of death.

"What is it?" Tracy whispered. For a second she
didn't think Beth had heard her, but then the other girl
slowly turned, her fearful eyes meeting Tracy's.

"Daddy," she said softly. "Look. The moon's shining right down on the place where Daddy . . ." Her
voice trailed off, and once more her eyes shifted to the
interior of the mill.

Tracy followed Beth's gaze.

Inside the building, the moonlight was streaming
through the skylight. The colors of the dome itself were
faintly visible, but the moonlight had robbed them of
their vitality. Instead of sparkling brightly, they cast a
nightmare pall over the interior.

Across the floor lay the huge spider's web formed
by the shadows of the leaded glass above.

Near the center of the rotunda, a single beam of
clear moonlight shone down, illuminating the spot where
Alan Rogers had died.

Grasping Beth's hand, Tracy pulled her inside the
building, closing the door behind them.

The faint chirping sounds of the summer night disappeared, and silence closed around the two girls. It was as if they'd stepped into another world, a strange dead world that reached out to enclose them, drawing them to its cold bosom.

They started slowly across the floor, unconsciously avoiding the spiderweb shadow cast by the skylight, as if by touching it they could become entangled, to be held prisoner for whatever strange creature might lurk in the shadowy reaches, waiting for its prey.

In the distance, seemingly unreachable, lay the stairs to the basement, and Tracy wanted to run to them, wanted to be away from the strange light and terrifying shadows.

As in a nightmare, her feet seemed mired in mud, each step a terrible effort.

But finally they were there, staring down into the pitch blackness below.

Tracy knelt, set the lantern carefully on the floor, then lifted its chimney off. She struck a match, cupped it in her hands for a moment, then held it to the wick.

The wick sputtered, then caught, the flame spreading quickly along its length. When it was burning brightly, Tracy replaced the chimney, then adjusted the wick. The flame's intensity increased, but still the light was all but lost in the vastness of the building around them.

"Come on," Tracy whispered, getting to her feet once more and picking up the lantern.

But Beth hung back, staring fearfully into the darkness below. In her mind, she began to remember the hellish vision she'd seen last time she had been in the little room behind the stairs. "M-maybe we shouldn't—" she breathed.

But Tracy reached out with her free hand and grasped her wrist once more. "She's your friend, remember?" Tracy hissed, letting her anger begin to show for the first time since Beth had come back to live at Hilltop. "You can't chicken out now. I won't let you!"

She started down the stairs, holding the lantern

high. Beth resisted for only a moment, but as Tracy's grip tightened on her wrist, she gave in. Her heart beginning to pound, she reluctantly followed Tracy into the basement.

The yawning blackness seemed to open before them, welcoming them.

# 26

Carolyn rolled over in her sleep, then slowly began to wake up. At first she resisted it, rolling over once more, and keeping her eyes resolutely closed.

It did no good. In a moment she was fully awake, and she sat up, listening, trying to decide what had disturbed her sleep. But there was nothing. The sounds of the crickets and frogs were drifting through the window as they always did, and the faint creaking of the old mansion still complained softly in the background. She glanced at the clock.

One A.M.

She flopped back down on the bed, and felt Phillip stir beside her at the unexpected motion. Once more she tried to go back to sleep. Once more she failed.

Slowly, almost imperceptibly at first, a strange feeling began to grow in her. An uneasy feeling that something was wrong.

The house felt incomplete.

Abigail, she told herself. It's just that Abigail isn't here anymore.

But it was more than that, and she knew it.

She got out of bed, slipped into a robe, then stepped out into the corridor and turned on the lights.

Halfway down the long hall, Beth's door stood open.

Beth's door, she knew, was never open at night.

Frowning, she hurried down the hall, and switched the light on in Beth's room.

She saw the covers piled at the foot of the empty bed.

Even though all her instincts told her it, too, would be empty, Carolyn crossed the bedroom and checked the bathroom. There was no sign of Beth.

She felt the first flickerings of panic beginning to build inside her, and firmly put them down. Beth might only have gone down to the kitchen to raid the refrigerator. She left the room, and started toward the stairs, but instead of going down them, she went past them, stopping at Tracy's closed door. She hesitated, then turned the knob and pushed the door open just far enough to see inside.

Tracy's bed, too, was empty.

Now Carolyn hurried down the stairs, and searched the house, finally coming to Hannah's bedroom off the kitchen. She rapped softly on the door, then harder. At last there was a stirring from inside the room, the door opened a crack, and Hannah peered out at her, her eyes still red with sleepiness.

"Hannah, I need your help. Something's happened to the girls."

"Our girls?" the old servant asked, opening the door wider, and wrapping her robe tightly around herself. "What do you mean, something's happened to them?"

"They're not here," Carolyn replied. "They're not in their rooms, and they're not down here, either."

Hannah's head shook, and she made a soft clucking sound. "Well, I'm sure they're here somewhere," she said.

"They're not," Carolyn insisted. "I'd better get Phillip. Will you look downstairs?"

Hannah nodded, saying nothing as she started shuffling toward the basement stairs.

Less than a minute later, Carolyn was back in her bedroom, shaking Phillip awake.

*    *    *

Tracy stopped at the bottom of the stairs, and looked around. The lantern's faint glow was quickly swallowed up by the maze of pillars supporting the main floor, and her mind began to play tricks on her as she gazed into the darkness beyond the lantern's reach. There could be all manner of things lurking there in the darkness.

She could almost feel eyes on her, watching her.

Tendrils of fear reached out to her, brushing against her so that her skin began to crawl. When she heard Beth's voice, she turned quickly away from the threatening darkness.

It's back here," Beth was whispering. "Behind the stairs."

Tracy held the lantern up once more, and its orangish glow spread out in front of her. She saw a large metal door, hung from a rail, standing partly open. And beyond that was the room where Beth was so certain that a ghost dwelt.

To Tracy, the room looked perfectly ordinary. It was empty, and its walls were blackened as if there had been a fire here sometime long ago. In fact, she thought as she stepped inside, she could still almost smell it. There was something in the air, a faint smokiness, that made her wrinkle her nose.

"Where is she?" she asked, still whispering despite the fact that they were alone.

"She's here," Beth said. "I always just came down here and waited. And after a while, she sort of—well, she just sort of came to me."

Tracy set the lantern on the floor, then looked up at Beth.

In the light of the lantern, Beth could see Tracy smiling at her. The way the light struck her face, the smile looked mocking, and Tracy's eyes seemed to have the cruel glint in them that Beth hadn't seen for months.

But that was silly.

Tracy was her friend now.

And then Tracy spoke.

"You really *are* crazy, aren't you?" she asked, reaching into her pocket and fumbling with something.

Beth's breath caught in her throat. "Crazy?" she asked, her voice barely a whisper. "I thought—I thought—"

"You thought I believed you, didn't you? You thought I was dumb enough to think there was really a ghost down here."

Beth froze, her heart pounding. As she watched, Tracy pulled the rusty jackknife out of her pocket, and unfolded its blade. "Wh-what are you doing?" Beth whimpered. She started to back away, but then realized that Tracy was between her and the door.

"You killed him, didn't you?" Tracy asked, her eyes sparkling with hatred now. She moved slowly toward Beth, the knife clutched in her right hand, its blade flashing dully in the light of the lantern. "You killed him just so you could come back and take my father. But I'm not going to let you."

"No," Beth whispered. "I didn't do anything. Amy—it was Amy—"

"There isn't any Amy!" Suddenly moving with the speed of a cat, Tracy leaped at Beth, the knife flashing out.

A stinging pain shot through Beth's left arm, and she looked down to see blood oozing out of a long deep cut. She stared at it for a moment, almost unable to believe what she was seeing. And then she felt a movement close by, and looked up. The knife was arcing toward her, and behind it was Tracy's face, contorted with fury.

"I hate you!" Tracy was screaming. "You're crazy, and I hate you, and I'm going to kill you!"

Beth ducked, and the knife glanced off her shoulder, then ripped down through her right arm. She tried to twist away, but Tracy's left hand was tangled in her hair now.

"*No!*" she screamed, the word almost strangling in her throat. "Please, Tracy! *Nooooo!*"

But it was too late.

Tracy's right arm rose, and then the knife came down once more, plunging into Beth's chest. Tracy twisted at it, then yanked it free, only to plunge it in again.

"Noo . . ." Beth moaned. "Oh, please, no . . ."

Tracy suddenly let go of her hair, throwing her to the floor. Bleeding from both arms and her chest, Beth tried to scramble away, but Tracy's foot shot out, kicking her in the stomach.

As she doubled up, the knife came down again, ripping through her back. Tracy jerked it out, then dropped to her knees, grabbing Beth's hair once again.

Pulling Beth's head back, she tightened her grip on the knife, then pulled it with all the strength she had across Beth's exposed throat.

The knife cut deep, and suddenly there was nothing left of Beth's screams but a sickening gurgling sound as the blood, pumped from a severed artery, mixed with the air being exhaled from her lungs.

For a moment Tracy froze where she was, staring down into Beth's open eyes, etching in her mind every detail of the fear and pain that had twisted Beth's face in the last seconds of her life. Then she dropped the corpse, letting it roll away from her as she rocked back on her heels.

The bloody knife dropped from her hand.

And then, in the flickering light of the kerosene lantern, her clothes stained with her victim's blood, Tracy Sturgess began to laugh. . . .

Phillip came awake slowly, then stared up at his wife's worried face, shading his eyes against the brightness of the chandelier. "What is it?" he asked. "What time is it?"

"Early. It's a little after one-thirty. Phillip, the girls are gone."

Phillip came instantly wide-awake, and sat up. "Gone? What do you mean?"

"They're gone." Quickly she explained what had happened. "Hannah's looking in the basement, but I'm sure they're not there. When I woke up, I had a funny feeling that something was wrong, that something was missing. It's the girls. I haven't searched the whole house, but I'm almost certain they aren't here at all."

Phillip, already out of bed, was pulling on a pair of khaki pants and a golf shirt. With Carolyn at his heels, he strode down the hall, first to Tracy's room, then back to Beth's, where Carolyn was waiting for him.

"They've *got* to be here," he said.

"But they aren't!" Carolyn insisted.

"Did you look upstairs?"

Carolyn shook her head. "No, of course not. It's all closed up. There's nothing up there—"

"Well, they have to be somewhere. They wouldn't just take off. Not in the middle of the night." He started down the hall toward the back stairs that led to the long-empty third floor of the old house. Carolyn was about to follow him, when something caught her eye.

On Beth's desk, there was an old leather-bound book.

She stared at it. She'd never seen it before, and she was positive it didn't belong to Beth.

What was it, and why was it here?

She had no ready answer for either question, but suddenly, with the certain knowledge born of instinct, she knew that whatever the little book was, it was directly connected with the girls' absence.

She picked it up and began reading, desperately deciphering the crabbed handwriting that filled the pages. After reading only a few lines she was certain she knew where Beth and Tracy were.

She went to the door, calling out her husband's name. Then, as she was about to call him again, she saw him appear from the back stairs.

"They're not up—"

"Phillip, I know where they are! They went to the mill!"

Phillip stared at her. "The mill?" he echoed. "What on earth are you talking about? Why would they go down there?"

"Here," Carolyn said, holding the old journal out

to him. "I found this on Beth's desk. I don't know where they got it, but they must have read it."

Phillip reached out and took the book from her. "What is it?"

"A journal. It tells about the mill, Phillip, and I know that's where the girls have gone. I know it!"

Phillip stared at his wife for a moment, then made up his mind. "I'm calling Norm Adcock," he said at last. "And then I'm going down there."

"I'll go with you," Carolyn said.

"No. Stay here. I . . . I don't know what I'll find. I don't even know what to think right now—"

For a moment Carolyn was tempted to argue with him, but then she changed her mind. For already, in the back of her mind, she knew that something terrible had happened in the mill. Something out of the past had finally come forward, reaching out for an awful vengeance.

Tracy's laughter slowly subsided until it was little more than a manic giggle.

She glanced around the room once more, furtively now, like an animal that was being hunted.

Then, in the soft glow of the lantern light, she dragged Beth's body over near the far wall. High up, beyond her reach, there was a small window. Tracy placed Beth's body beneath the window, one arm leaning against the wall, stretched upward as if it were reaching for the window above.

She returned to the place where Beth's corpse had first fallen, and knelt down to dip her hand into the still-warm blood. When her hand was covered, she went back to the wall, and began smearing her bloodied hand over its blackened surface, leaving crudely formed marks wherever her fingers touched. Over and over she gathered more blood, until at last the message was complete.

Still giggling softly to herself, she went back to the lantern, and bent to pick it up.

And then, suddenly, the lantern light seemed to fade, and the darkness closed in around her.

She was no longer alone in the room. All around her, their faces looming out of the darkness, she saw the faces of children.

Thin faces, with cheeks sunken from hunger, the eyes wide and hollow as they stared at her.

Tracy gasped. These were the children her grand-mother had seen. And now she was seeing them, and she knew they could see her too, and knew who she was, and what she had done. They were circling her, closing in on her, reaching out to her.

She backed away from them, and her foot touched something.

She gasped, knowing immediately what it was. She bent down once more, but it was too late. The lantern had tipped over, its chimney shattering.

The cap of the fuel tank had been knocked loose and the kerosene had spilled out, running quickly in all directions. And then it ignited, and suddenly Tracy was surrounded by flames. She stared at the sudden blaze in horror, and then, dimly, heard the sounds of childish laughter. All around her the faces of the children—the children who couldn't possibly be there—were grinning now, their eyes sparkling with malicious pleasure. She turned to the door, and started toward it. And then, as she came close to it, she saw another child.

A girl, no more than twelve years old.

She was thin, and her clothes were charred and blackened, as if they'd once been burned. Her eyes glowed like coals as she stared at Tracy, and then, as the flames danced close about her feet, she backed away, through the door.

The flames, fed by the spreading kerosene, followed her.

As Tracy watched, the door slowly began to close

"No," Tracy gasped. She took a step forward, but it was too late.

The door slammed shut.

She hurled herself against it, trying to push it aside, but it was immovable. Then she began pounding

on it, screaming out for someone to help her, someone
to open the door.

But all she heard from beyond the door was the
mocking sound of the girl's laughter.

Behind her, she could feel the spirits of the other
children gathering around, waiting to welcome her.

The flaming kerosene spread rapidly across the
floor of the basement, oozing under a pile of lumber,
creeping around the pilings that had for so long supported the weight of the floor above.

The lumber caught first, and now the fire spread
quickly, tongues of flame reaching out to find new fuel.
Then the pilings began to catch. Tinder-dry after more
than a century, they burned with a fury that filled the
basement with a terrifying roar. Then the floor itself
began to ignite, the fire spreading through its hardwood
mass, turning into a living thing as it ranged ever wider.

The temperature rose, and cans of paint thinner
began to explode, bursting into new fires that quickly
joined the main blaze.

The heat reached the level of a blast furnace, pene-
trating even the metal door that sealed off the room
beneath the stairs.

Tracy was surrounded by blackness now, the kerosene having burned itself out.

But she could feel the fire, and hear it raging
beyond the metal door.

And then, as she watched, the door itself began to
glow a dull red.

She backed away from it, whimpering now as terror overwhelmed her. Then she tripped, and fell heavily to the floor. Dimly, she was aware of Beth's body
beneath her.

Then, as the brightening glow of the door began to
illuminate the room once more, she remembered the
window.

She stood up, and tried to reach it.

And the sound of that awful laughter—Amy's
laughter—mocked her efforts.

She began screaming then, screaming for her father to come and save her.

Each breath seared her lungs, and her screams
began to weaken.

She slumped to the floor, her mind beginning to
crumble as the heat built around her.

Her father wouldn't come for her—she knew that
now. Her father didn't love her. He'd never loved her.
It had always been the other child he'd loved.

With the remnants of her mind, Tracy tried to
remember the name of the other child, but it was gone.
But it didn't matter, because she knew she'd killed her,
and that was all that was important.

Her grandmother.

Her grandmother would save her. It didn't matter
what she'd done, because her grandmother was always
there.

But not this time. This time, there was nobody.

She was alone, and the heat was closing in on her,
and she could feel her skin searing, and smell her
singeing hair.

She writhed on the floor, trying to escape the
death that was coming ever closer, but there was nowhere to go—nowhere to hide.

The whole room was glowing around her now, and
she was afraid, deep in her heart, that she had already
died, and would be confined forever to the fires around
her—the fires of hell.

Once again she called out to her father, begging
him to save her.

But she died as Amy had died, knowing there
would be no salvation.

Her soul, like Amy's, would be trapped forever,
locked away in the burning inferno. . . .

# 27

By the time Phillip reached the mill, it was already clear that the building was doomed. Three fire trucks were lined up along the north wall, and two more stood in the middle of Prospect Street, their hoses snaking across the sidewalk and up the steps to the shattered remains of the plate-glass doors. But the water that poured from the hoses into the building seemed to evaporate as fast as it was pumped in.

The roar of the blaze was deafening, and when Phillip found Norm Adcock, he had to put his mouth to the police chief's ear in order to be heard at all.

"It's no good," he shouted. "There's no way to stop it."

Adcock nodded grimly. "If they can't get it under control in ten minutes, they're going to give up on the building and just try to keep the fire from spreading."

But they didn't have to wait ten minutes.

The main floor had burned through now, and the fire was raging through the new construction. The heat and flames rose upward, and suddenly, as Phillip watched, the great dome over the atrium seemed to wobble for a moment, then collapse into the firestorm below. The gaping hole in the roof combined with the shattered front doors to turn the entire structure into a vast chimney. Fresh air rushed into the vacuum, and

the blaze redoubled, lighting the sky over the town
with the red glow of hell. Over the roar of the inferno,
the wailing of sirens sounded a melancholy counter-
point, a strange dirge accompanying the pageant of
death the mill had become.

"The girls," Phillip shouted, straining to make himself heard over the deafening crescendo.

Again Adcock shook his head. "By the time I got
here, there was no way to get inside. And if they were
in there . . ." There was no need to finish the sentence.

The firemen had given up on the building now,
and the hoses were turned away, pouring water onto
the ground around the mill. And yet there was really
little need for this. Always, the mill had stood alone
between the railroad tracks and Prospect Street, the
land on either side of it vacant, as if no other building
wished to be associated with the foreboding structure
that had for so long been a brooding sentinel, guarding
the past.

Prospect Street itself was filling now as the people
of Westover, hastily dressed, began to gather to witness
the last dying gasps of the mill.

They stood silently for the most part, simply watching it burn. Now and then, as a window exploded from
the pressure of the heat within, a ripple of sound would
roll through the crowd, then disappear, to be replaced
once more by eerie silence.

It was a little after two in the morning when the
brick walls that had stood solid for well over a hundred
years finally buckled under the fury of the fire and the
weight of the roof, trembled for a moment, then
collapsed.

The entire building seemed to fall in on itself, and
almost immediately disappeared into the flames.

All that was left now was a vast expanse of flaming
rubble, and once more the fire fighters turned their
hoses toward the blaze. Clouds of steam mixed with
smoke, and the roar of the inferno suddenly dissolved
into a furious reptilian hissing, a dragon in the final
throes of death.

Now, at last, the crowd came to life. It stirred, murmuring softly to itself, drifting closer to the dying monster.

It eddied around Phillip Sturgess as if he were a rock dividing a current. He stood alone as the mass of humanity split, passed him by, then merged once more to flood into the street.

And then, finally, he was alone, standing silently in the night, facing the ruin that had once been the cornerstone of his family's entire life.

Carolyn stood on the terrace with Hannah, watching the flames slowly die back until all that was left was an angry glow. She could see the black silhouettes of people, looking from Hilltop like no more than tiny ants swarming around the remains of a ruined nest.

*It should have happened a hundred years ago.*

The thought came unbidden into her mind, where it lodged firmly, until she finally spoke it out loud. For a moment Hannah remained silent; then she nodded abruptly.

"I expect you're right," the old woman said softly. Then she took Carolyn's arm in her gnarled hand, and pulled her gently toward the house. "I won't have you standing out here in the night air, not when there's nothing you can see, and nothing you can do."

"I have to do *something*," Carolyn objected, but nevertheless let herself be guided inside. She followed Hannah into the living room, then sank into an overstuffed chair.

"You just stay there," Hannah said gently. "I'll put some tea on so it will be ready for Mr. Phillip when he comes back."

Carolyn nodded, though the words barely penetrated her mind.

Slowly, she relived the short time since Phillip had left the house.

She'd followed him downstairs, the strange book she'd found in Beth's room still clutched in her hand.

Only when he was gone had she taken it into the living room, and read it through carefully.

Just as she had finished, Hannah had appeared, to tell her the mill was burning.

Even before she'd gone out on the terrace to look, she'd come to the certain realization that both Beth and Tracy were dead. And in the numbness following the first overwhelming wave of grief for her daughter, she'd also come to understand that there was a certain unity in what had happened.

It was as if the tragedy that had occurred in the mill a century ago—a tragedy that had never been fully resolved—was finally seeking its own resolution, and exacting a terrible revenge on the descendants of those who had for so long avoided their responsibilities.

Except for Beth.

For the rest of her life, she knew, she would wonder why Beth had had to die that night.

Now she sat alone in the living room, waiting for Phillip to come home, trying to compose her thoughts, preparing herself to explain to her husband what had happened in the mill so many years ago.

At last, just before three, she heard the sound of his car pulling up in front of the house. A moment later the front door opened and closed, and she heard Phillip calling her. His voice sounded worn out, defeated.

"In here," she said quietly, and when he turned to her she could see the anguish in his eyes.

"The girls—" he began. "Tracy—Beth—"

"I know," Carolyn said. She rose from her chair, and stepped out of the dim pool of light from the single lamp she had allowed Hannah to turn on. She went to her husband, and put her arms around him, holding him tight for a moment. Then she released her grip, and drew him gently into the living room. "I know what happened," she said softly. "I don't understand it all, and I don't think I ever will, but I know the girls are gone. And I almost know why."

"Why?" Phillip echoed. His eyes looked haunted

now, and there was a hollowness to his voice that frightened Carolyn.

"It's in the book," she said softly. "It's all in the little book I found in Beth's room."

Phillip shook his head. "I don't understand."

"It's a diary, Phillip," Carolyn explained. She picked the small leather-bound volume up from the table next to Phillip's chair and put it into his hands. "It must have been your great-grandfather's. Hannah says she's seen it before. Your father used to read it, and Hannah thinks he kept it in a metal box in his closet."

Phillip nodded numbly. "A brown one—I never knew what was in it."

"That's the one," Carolyn replied. "Hannah found it in Beth's closet right after you left."

"But how did it—?"

"It doesn't matter how it got into Beth's room. What matters is what was in the diary. It . . . it tells what happened at the mill. There was a fire, Phillip."

Phillip's eyes widened slightly, but he said nothing.

"There was a fire in a workroom downstairs."

"The little room under the loading dock," Phillip muttered almost to himself. "The one behind the stairs."

Carolyn gasped. "You knew about the fire?"

"No," Phillip breathed. "No, I'm sure I didn't. But one day I was down in the basement with Alan. We were looking at the foundation. And right at the bottom of the stairs, I smelled something. It was strange. It was very faint, but it smelled smoky. As if something had burned there once."

"It did burn," Carolyn whispered. Now she took Phillip's hand in her own. "Phillip, children died down here."

Phillip's eyes fixed blankly on his wife. "Died?"

Carolyn nodded. "And one of the children who died there was your great-grandfather's daughter."

Phillip looked dazed, then slowly shook his head. "That . . . that isn't possible. Tracy is the first girl we've ever had in the family."

Carolyn squeezed his hand once more. "Phillip,

it's in the diary. There was a little girl—your great-grandfather's daughter by one of the women in the village. Her name—the child's name—was Amelia."

"Amelia?" Phillip echoed. "That . . . that doesn't make sense. I've never heard of such a story."

"He never acknowledged her," Carolyn told him. "Apparently he never told a soul, but he admitted it in his diary. And she was working in the mill the day of the fire."

Phillip's face was ashen now. "I . . . I can't believe it."

"But it's there," Carolyn insisted, her voice suddenly quiet. "Her name was Amelia, but everybody called her . . . Amy."

Phillip's face suddenly turned gray. "My God," he whispered. "There really was an Amy."

"And there's something else," Carolyn added. "According to the journal, Amy used her mother's last name. It—Phillip, her name was Deaver. Amy Deaver."

Phillip's eyes met hers. The only Deavers who had ever lived in Westover were Carolyn's family. "Did you know about this?" he asked now. "Did you know all this when you married me?"

Now it was Carolyn who shook her head. "I didn't know, Phillip. I knew how my family felt about yours; I knew that long ago they'd lost a child in the mill. But who the child's father was—no, I never heard that. I swear it."

"What happened?" Phillip asked after a long silence. His voice was dull now, as if he already knew what he was about to hear. "Why didn't the children get out?"

Carolyn hesitated, and when she finally spoke, her voice was so quiet Phillip had to strain to hear her. "He was there that day," she said. "Samuel Pruett Sturgess. And when the fire broke out, he closed the fire door."

"He did *what?*" Phillip demanded.

Carolyn nodded miserably. "Phillip, it's all in the diary, in his own handwriting. He closed the fire door and let all those children burn to death. Even his own daughter. He let them burn to death to save the mill!"

"My God," Phillip groaned. He was silent for a moment, trying to absorb what Carolyn had just told him. The story was almost impossible to believe—the cruelty of it too monumental for him to accept. And yet he knew it was true—knew it was the secret that had finally driven his father mad.

Even his mother, at the end of her life, had discovered the tale, and accepted its truth.

"I don't believe in ghosts," he said at last. "I never have. I never will."

"I don't either," Carolyn agreed. "But I keep thinking about it. The children, caught in a fire. Tonight, our children, caught in a fire. And the other people who have died in the mill. Your brother. And Jeff Bailey. The Baileys had an interest in the mill once, didn't they?"

Phillip nodded reluctantly. "But what about Alan?"

"The reconstruction," Carolyn whispered. "Don't you see? Your father was right. The project never should have started to begin with."

Phillip's head swung around, and his eyes met hers. "And what about Beth?" he asked. "What did she do to deserve what happened tonight?"

At last Carolyn's tears began to flow. "I don't know," she said through her sobs. "She was such a sweet child. I . . . I just don't know!"

Phillip put his arms around his wife, and tried to comfort her. "It was an accident, darling," he whispered softly. "I know how it all seems now, but whatever happened tonight, it couldn't have had anything to do with what happened a hundred years ago. It was just a terrible accident. We have to believe that."

*We have to,* he repeated to himself. *If we don't, we'll have to spend the rest of our lives waiting for it all to start again.*

And then, against his will, a picture of his daughter came into his mind.

He saw her once more as he'd seen her the day

Alan Rogers had died, and she'd gazed into the mill at the broken body of Beth's father.

Her eyes had glittered with malicious hatred, and her lips had been twisted into a satisfied smile.

He held his wife closer, and shut his eyes, but still the vision lingered.

Late the next afternoon, both Phillip and Carolyn stood with Norm Adcock as a pair of workmen pried away the metal plate that had covered one face of the loading-dock wall for the last hundred years.

Samuel Pruett Sturgess, in the last pages of his diary, wrote of the metal plate, and his hopes that it would seal the room from the outside, as the firmly bolted metal door sealed it from the inside. It was his intention, in the last days of his life, that no one ever enter the workroom behind the basement stairs again.

Grayish wisps of ash still drifted toward the sky from the smoking ruin, and its heat still caused a shimmering in the summer air.

The men, their shirts stripped off against the combined heat of the sun and the fire, worked quickly, using a cold chisel and a maul to break away the bolts that secured the metal to the concrete of the dock. At last it fell away, and the window, its glass long ago broken out of the frames, was exposed to the sunlight for the first time in a century. The workmen stepped back, and Norm Adcock, with Phillip at his side, moved forward.

Residual heat drifted from the room, but when Adcock reached out and gingerly touched the concrete itself, he realized that it was no longer too hot to go inside. He dropped to his knees, and shone a flashlight inside.

At first he thought the room was empty. Opposite the window, he could see the remains of the metal door, twisted and buckled by the intensity of the heat that had all but destroyed it, hanging grotesquely from its broken support rail.

He worked the light back and forth, examining the floor.

Everywhere he looked, there was nothing but blackness.

And then, at last, he shone the light straight down.

"Jesus," he whispered, and immediately felt Phillip Sturgess's grip tighten on his shoulder. "I'm not sure you're going to want to look at this, Phillip," he said quietly.

"They're inside?"

Adcock withdrew his head from the window, and faced Phillip. "They're there. But I really think you should let us take care of it. Take Carolyn home, Phillip. I'll let you know if we find anything."

Phillip hesitated, but finally shook his head. "I can't. I have to see it for myself." When Adcock seemed about to protest further, he spoke again. "Carolyn and I have talked about it," he said. "And we decided that whatever is in there, I have to see it."

Adcock's brows rose. "Have to?"

"I'd rather not explain it," Phillip said. "Frankly, I doubt that it would make much sense to you. But I do have to see what happened."

Adcock weighed the matter in his mind, then reluctantly nodded. "Okay. I'll have the men put the ladder in, then we can go down."

When the ladder had been lowered, Adcock disappeared through the window. Phillip followed him. He carefully avoided looking down until he was on the floor and had stepped carefully away from the ladder. Then, as his eyes became accustomed to the shadowy light of the little room, he let himself look at what Adcock had already seen.

The heat of the fire had all but destroyed the remains of the two girls.

Their clothes had burned, as had their hair. There were still fragments of skin clinging to the skulls, and the skeletons themselves were wrapped in the emaciated remains of the soft tissues of their bodies.

Phillip was reminded of photographs he'd seen of

the Nazi concentration camps after the war. He struggled against the nausea that rose in his gorge, then made himself kneel, and reach out to touch what was left of his daughter.

Tracy's body lay curled tightly, as if she'd died trying to protect herself against the heat.

Around her neck there was a chain, and attached to the chain, clutched in the bony remains of Tracy's right hand, was a jade pendant that he recognized as having been his mother's.

If it had not been for the pendant, he was sure he wouldn't have known which of the hideous, almost mummified bodies was Tracy's.

His gaze shifted to Beth's body. It was stretched prone on the floor, one hand up; its fleshless fingers seemed to be reaching toward the window.

Slowly, he became aware of the marks on the wall. At first they were only a blur, almost lost in the blackness on which they had been smeared. But as he stared at them, they gradually began to take shape, and he realized that before the girls had died, one of them—he couldn't be sure which one—had left a message. Now the message was clear.

It consisted of only one word: AMY.

"It looks like blood," he heard Norm Adcock say. "There's some more on the floor." Then his voice dropped. "Phillip?"

"I'm listening," Phillip replied.

"I can't be sure, but right now I'd say only Tracy died from the heat. I think Beth was already dead before the fire started. Look."

Reluctantly, Phillip made his eyes follow Adcock's pointing finger.

Despite the damage done by the fire, the seared skin and the shrunken flesh, the marks were clearly there.

Either before, or just after she'd died, Beth Rogers had been hacked nearly to pieces.

Phillip groaned as he realized what it must mean; then his mind rejected the knowledge, and his body finally rebelled. He could fight the nausea no longer. His stomach heaving, and his throat already filling with the sour taste of bile, he retreated to the far corner of the room.

Ten minutes later, pale and shaking, but once again in control of himself, he emerged from the little room into the daylight outside. Carolyn was still there, standing where he'd left her, waiting for him. She looked at him, her eyes asking him a silent question.

He took her in his arms, and held her close. "It's over," he said. "It's all over now."

Carolyn shuddered, and let her tears flow freely. She felt numb, empty, as if she'd lost everything that she had loved.

But that's not true, she insisted to herself.

I still have Phillip, and we still have our baby.

And then, for the first time, she felt their unborn child stir within her.

*We'll get through it,* she told herself. *We'll get through it all, and we'll survive. Whatever's happened, we'll survive.*

She took Phillip's hand and pressed it to her belly. "It's not over, darling," she whispered. "We just have to begin again. And we can. I know we can."

Once again, the tiny child within her moved, and this time Phillip felt it, too.

# Epilogue

Almost a year had passed.

On the morning of July 4, Carolyn Sturgess started across the lawn toward the two stone lions that flanked the path to the mausoleum. She walked at an easy pace, enjoying the warmth of the sun. The sky was a deep blue that morning, and nowhere was there even a trace of a cloud that might foreshadow an afternoon shower. The day, she knew, would be perfect.

She wished Beth were there to share it with her.

The pain of her loss had eased with the passage of time, and as she remembered her daughter today, there was only a dull ache to remind her of the terrible days of the previous summer. And even that ache, she was finally beginning to believe, would someday fade away.

She stepped into the shade of the path, and started up the gentle grade toward the top of the hill and the marble structure that guarded the remains of her husband's ancestors. The light was different here, filtered into a soft green by the leaves of the trees above her head. Here and there the sun shone through, its rays dancing on specks of dust that hung in the air. A squirrel paused in the path a few yards ahead of her, sat up, and examined her with bright inquisitive eyes before darting up a tree to chatter angrily at her from a perch twelve feet up. Carolyn stopped to chatter back at the squirrel, laughing softly at the indignant thrashings of its tail. When the squirrel finally gave up its tirade and disappeared into the treetops, she moved on, coming at last to the mausoleum itself.

There was a seventh chair at the table now, and the broken pillar had at last been repaired. The addition of the chair and the new pillar had changed the feel of the monument, as well as its looks. No longer did it have an air of mystery to it, as if it were filled with unanswered—and unanswerable—questions. There was a completeness to it, as if the addition of the chair for Amy Deaver Sturgess had closed the family circle around Samuel Pruett Sturgess. Now he sat with his wife at his side, and his four sons flanking them. But directly opposite him now, providing a kind of symmetry, was his only daughter's chair. And beyond her chair, the new pillar blocked the view of the place where the mill had stood for so many decades.

No longer would Samuel Pruett Sturgess spend eternity gazing at the source of both his wealth and his guilt. Now he would sit with his completed family, his long-denied daughter acknowledged at last. For Carolyn, the mausoleum had finally lost its feeling of the grotesque, and had become a place of peace.

She paused there that morning, then moved on down the trail that would eventually lead to the river. But that trail was no longer an overgrown tangle of weeds and fallen trees. It had been cleared and widened, and neat stone steps had been carefully installed to look as if they'd been there forever. So well had the work been executed that even the week after they had been laid the steps had blended perfectly into the hillside.

Carolyn came to an intersecting path, and turned left, following the well-worn trail she had once used nearly every day. Since spring, though, she had found herself coming here less frequently. Indeed, she realized as she came into the little meadow where both

Beth and Tracy were buried, it had been almost two weeks since she had been here last.

Now, as she slowly approached the graves that lay flanking the slight depression where Amy's bones had once been buried, she remembered the funeral that had taken place here last summer.

There had been no question of separate funerals for the two girls—they had been bound too closely together by their deaths.

Almost all of Westover had been there that day, and both Carolyn and Phillip had come to realize that their tragic loss had not been totally in vain. Though nothing had been spoken, there was a feeling that the funeral for the two young girls marked a turning point for the town, a final severing of its ties to the past, a laying to rest of the last vestiges of resentment toward the Sturgesses and the other old families who had once controlled the lives of the townspeople.

After the service there had been a reception on the front lawn, for even the mansion itself had not been large enough to hold the crowd. And as Carolyn and Phillip had moved through the throng of people, accepting the condolences that were that day genuinely offered, they began to sense the healing that was taking place.

It was that night that they had decided to build a park on the site of the mill, and donate it to the town. Then, during the weeks when the park was being built and the charred remnants of the mill were being obliterated, they had discussed the naming of the park.

It was Phillip who finally suggested they dedicate it to the memory of Alan Rogers, and Carolyn had immediately concurred. It seemed fitting that the Sturgess name would no longer be associated with that part of Westover.

Carolyn gathered a few wildflowers, and placed them as she always did between the two graves where Beth and Tracy lay. As always, she wondered fleetingly what had really transpired in the basement of the mill the night the girls had died, but she had never asked

Phillip what he'd seen in the little room beneath the loading dock, nor had he ever volunteered to tell her. Though she knew in her heart that it was a fiction, she liked to believe that they had simply gone out together on what was intended to be nothing more than an adolescent adventure, an adventure that had gone disastrously wrong.

The truth, she knew, was something too painful for her to bear.

She turned away from the graves, and started back to the house, putting the past behind her.

"We're only going on a picnic," Phillip observed wryly as he watched Carolyn pack the immense basket with more things than he could imagine her finding a use for. "It's not as though we're going to be gone for a week."

"Babies may be small, but they're great little consumers," Carolyn replied placidly, adding two more diapers, and a stuffed bear that was even bigger than their child to the contents of the already overfilled basket. "Besides," she added, "didn't I hear you telling Hannah to put two extra cases of beer in the car?"

"I don't want to run out, do I?"

"Heaven forbid. Of course some people might suspect you of trying to buy votes with beer, but I suppose it's better than just handing out money." She finished with the basket, and tried to close its lid, which seemed to be impossible. "Here," she said, hefting the basket and handing it to Phillip. "It'll be good for your image if you're seen dragging baby stuff around the park. Gives you the domestic look."

"That, I suppose, is as opposed to the idly arrogant look of the old aristocracy?" Phillip asked as he took the basket.

"Whatever. Take it down and put it in the car, and I'll bring the baby. And if you want to kiss her, do it now. I won't have you kissing every other baby in town, then bringing the germs back to your own daughter."

"Candidates for alderman don't kiss babies," Phillip sniffed good-naturedly. "That's strictly state and federal stuff. See you downstairs."

*Alderman*, Carolyn thought as she picked the baby up from the crib and began wrapping the blanket carefully around the little girl's robust body. *Who ever would have thought a Sturgess could run for alderman?* Yet it had happened, and not through any effort on Phillip's part. Rather, a delegation of merchants had come to him back in December, while Carolyn was still in the hospital after delivering their baby, and after a great deal of awkward hemming and hawing (which Phillip had delighted in detailing for her the next day) had finally informed him that they had met among themselves and decided that what Westover needed was an alderman who had the time to make tending to the town business a full-time job. And it had to be someone with some business sense, and strong ties to the town. After giving it due consideration, they had come to the conclusion that Phillip Sturgess was the man they wanted.

Phillip had been shocked. He'd noticed that since the funerals for his daughter and stepdaughter, the attitudes of the townspeople had changed. They spoke to him now whenever he went down to the village, stopping to pass the time of day with him as they did with each other.

Conversations no longer eased when he came near. Instead, circles widened to include him.

The same thing had happened to Carolyn.

It was as if the town, recognizing that even the Sturgesses were not immune to tragedy, had closed ranks around them.

And now they wanted Phillip to lead them.

When they arrived at the park twenty minutes later, they found that Phillip did not, after all, have to put on the great display of domesticity that Carolyn had threatened him with. Instead, Norm Adcock grabbed the basket of baby supplies, while four of his men unloaded the beer.

Eileen Russell appeared out of the crowd, and pulled open the front door of the Mercedes, reaching in to take the baby from Carolyn.

"I swear to God, Carolyn," she said as the other woman released the seat belt and got out, "if you don't start using that baby seat I gave you, something horrible is going to happen to Amy."

Then her face turned scarlet as she realized what she'd said, but Carolyn—as she always did at moments like this—ignored the gaffe, knowing it had been unintentional.

"When she gets older, she goes in the seat. For now, I just prefer to hold her." Then she took Amy back, cradling her gently in her arms.

Amy.

At first both she and Phillip had been reluctant to give the child the name that had come to both their minds even before she was born, but in the end, they realized, there was really no other choice.

But this time, there was no chance that Amelia Deaver Sturgess was going to have anything but a perfectly happy life.

There had been a few shocked looks when people first heard the baby's name, but after either Carolyn or Phillip had explained to them where the name had come from, and what had happened to the first Amy, people had quickly come to understand.

And Amy, too, had become a part of the healing of Westover.

Carolyn began threading her way through the crowd, doing her best to keep up with Phillip. Everywhere they went, people flocked around them, chatting with Phillip for a few moments, then clucking and cooing over the tiny dark-eyed baby nestled in Carolyn's arms.

And Amy, her big eyes serious, looked up at all of them almost as if she recognized them, even though she was only six months old.

At last they came to a spot near the back of the

park, where the wall separating the park from the railroad tracks lent some shade against the afternoon sun, and the babbling of the fountain in the wading pool made it seem cooler than it actually was. Phillip spread a blanket, and Carolyn gently laid their daughter in its center.

The moment she touched the ground, Amy Deaver Sturgess began screaming.

The spot Phillip had chosen for the picnic blanket was exactly where the little room behind the stairs in the basement of the mill had once been. Though Phillip and Carolyn were unaware of it, their child was not.

For even in her infancy, Amy Deaver Sturgess remembered perfectly everything that had ever happened in that room.

She remembered, and her fury still grew. . . .

## ABOUT THE AUTHOR

JOHN SAUL's first novel, SUFFER THE CHILDREN, was published in 1977 to instant bestsellerdom. PUNISH THE SINNERS, CRY FOR THE STRANGERS, COMES THE BLIND FURY, WHEN THE WIND BLOWS, THE GOD PROJECT, NATHANIEL and BRAINCHILD, each a national bestseller, followed. Now, John Saul's trademark setting, a sleepy, isolated town where suddenly no one is safe, forms the background for this master storyteller's most chilling novel yet. John Saul lives in Bellevue, Washington, where he is at work on his next novel.